SHADOWS OF LIGHT

E V A M A R I E E V E R S O N

BARBOUR
PUBLISHING

© 2003 by Eva Marie Everson

ISBN 1-59310-015-9

All rights reserved. No part of this publication may be reproduced or transmitted in any form or by any means without written permission of the publisher.

This book is a work of fiction. Names, characters, places, and incidents are either products of the author's imagination or used fictitiously. Any similarity to actual people, organizations, and/or events is purely coincidental.

Cover image © GettyOne

Scripture taken from the HOLY BIBLE, NEW INTERNATIONAL VERSION®. NIV®. Copyright © 1973, 1978, 1984 by International Bible Society. Used by permission of Zondervan Publishing House. All rights reserved.

Published by Barbour Publishing, Inc., P.O. Box 719, Uhrichsville, Ohio 44683, www.barbourbooks.com

 Member of the
Evangelical Christian
Publishers Association

Printed in the United States of America.
5 4 3 2 1

Dedication

To "Sir Francis" Chadwick,
my friend and the coauthor of
Shadow of Dreams and *Summon the Shadows*.
For encouraging a sparrow to soar with the eagles.
May God continue to bless you!
. . .and to my brother.

The people walking in darkness
have seen a great light;
on those living in the land of the
shadow of death
a light has dawned.

—Isaiah 9:2

PROLOGUE

Dark Asian eyes, set perfectly against a honey complexion, peered through the bare windows and onto the French countryside beyond. The woman behind them leaned against the window frame. Before her—through the glass panes—the gentle hills were covered in snow, glistening like white diamonds in the early morning sunlight. Behind her, the living room of the warm and inviting chalet—decorated heavily in floral and stripe chintz, winter floral arrangements, and worn quilts—was homey and bright. She sighed heavily, looking upward. From the looks of the sky, it would snow again today. Another day, unable to leave this place. Another day spent with the man she had lived with platonically for nearly two years. . .the man she loved. . .the man who she feared would never love her.

She closed her eyes and allowed herself to remember how they had come to be here, then shuddered, opened her eyes, and pushed herself away from the window. It was nearly time for breakfast, and he would be hungry and wanting her to sit with him at the table where they would sip the strong coffee she made and speak about what they would do with the day.

She left the brightness of the living room, walked through the dark stone and panel dining room and into the cozy and rustic simplicity of the kitchen. She had set the table the night before, using a faded, floral cotton tablecloth she purchased the first part of the week at a local flea market. She hoped it would make the day a bit cheerier. . .brighter. . .happier. It certainly enhanced the scarred, pine tabletop that had come with the rented chalet.

On her way to the counter, where coffee brewed atop the stove and a waffle iron stood hot and ready next to an old farm bowl half-filled with batter, she stopped briefly at the table to adjust one of the china teacups that hadn't set quite right on its saucer and to shift the centerpiece of dried flowers slightly to the right. Next, she poured the coffee, a cup for her. . .a cup for him. The intoxicating scent of it reached her nostrils on the cloud of steam rising from each cup. No sooner was that done than she heard him walking into the room behind her. He smelled of soap. She turned her pretty face slightly and smiled. "Good morning."

"Good morning." He inhaled deeply. "Coffee smells delicious. Did you sleep well?"

She returned the coffeepot to the stove and began to prepare their waffles. "Yes. And you?"

It was the same every morning. The same routine. . .the same questions. . .the same answers.

"Fairly well," he answered, sitting at the table.

"Did you wake at all?"

She heard him sip his coffee and return his cup to the saucer. "Once. Maybe twice." She turned to look at him, resting her slender hip against the counter as the waffles were cooking. He was buttoning the cuffs of the long-sleeved black shirt he wore under a gray and white sweater. "Do you think I'll ever know what these dreams mean?" He turned and looked up at her, thin and boyishly handsome.

She turned back to the waffle iron, opened it, and lifted the waffles from the griddle and onto a waiting plate. "I'm sure you will, one day." She brought the plate over to the table, sat across from him, and dropped a waffle onto his plate and then one onto hers. She smiled. "When your mind is ready to understand, you will."

He reached across the table and took her hand. "I can never thank you enough for being here for me. You've been like an angel who dropped from a cloud in the sky."

"No need to thank me." She slipped her hand away from his and reached for the small jar of syrup she'd placed on the table earlier. "Your friendship has been payment enough."

He didn't speak. He leaned back in his seat, crossed his arms over his abdomen, and looked out the window beside him, contemplating something. . .she could see that. . .but it was something she couldn't quite read in his eyes. She picked up her fork and knife and began to cut her waffle. "What are you thinking about so serious over there?"

He shook his head no.

"No? No, what? No, you don't know or no, you aren't telling?" She slipped a forkful of the warm waffle into her mouth. It was light and deliciously sweet. "Mmmm," she said, hoping to encourage him to eat as well. The man ate hardly enough to survive.

He turned his eyes back to hers. They seemed mysterious and yet, at the same time, bewildered. "If I ask you a question, will you be honest with me?"

Her eyebrows raised and she swallowed hard. "Haven't I always been?"

He nodded. "I think you have, yes."

"Then, of course, I will now." She felt her fingers gripping the utensils they held.

He leaned over, rested his forearms against the table, and looked intently into her eyes. "Do I know a woman named Katie?"

Andi Daniels took a deep breath, blinked twice, looked out the window once, then down to her waffle. When her eyes finally met his, she whispered, "Yes."

CHAPTER ONE
January 2002

Katharine Morgan Webster, known to her friends as Katie, sat curled like a kitten on the sofa in her living room. With one hand she gripped a cordless phone to her ear; with the fingertips of the other she played with the draperies at the windows behind her. Beyond was the gray skyline of the city she loved, her home: New York, New York. It was early January and bitterly cold outside. On the streets below the fifth floor apartment of The Hamilton Place, the hotel she both owned and was interim president of, she watched pedestrians scurry to and fro. Then, looking up, she noticed steam from the building's heating systems rising at various levels, forming thin veils of clouds over her little section of Midtown Manhattan.

Nestled in the comfort of her apartment, she wore warm leggings, an oversized quilted shirt, and thick socks. Maggie, her British housekeeper, had tucked a throw around her legs and backside before retiring for an afternoon nap. Feeling quite content, Katie smiled as she listened to her best friend in the whole world, Marcy Waters, on the other end of the line.

"So then what happened?" Katie asked, holding back a laugh.

"So then Mark says, '*Parlez vous French fries?*' You can imagine how angry that made Michael with his brother. Michael takes his French so seriously."

Michael, Marcy's son. A senior in high school with three years of French studies behind him and a desire to continue his education in college. Katie remembered the day she'd met him. She'd been gone from their hometown of Brooksboro, Georgia, for twenty-five years when she'd seen Marcy for the first time in as many years. When she went to Marcy's for coffee and a game of catch-up, Marcy filled Katie in on her life as a wife to Charlie and mother to Michael, Melissa, and Mark. Later, Michael and Katie had engaged in a fun conversation spoken entirely in French. Marcy had given her grief over it, but Katie didn't go into an explanation of how her husband had insisted she take lessons in cultural things like French, art, literature, and the like.

"Mark is a rascal," she commented on Michael's younger brother, the mischievous youngest of her childhood friend.

"So what's new up there in New York? Georgia is freezing cold, but I assume it's twice as cold up there."

"You know New Yorkers. We like to do everything bigger and better than the rest of the world."

"I hear you."

Katie breathed in and out her nose, then replied, "Nothing really. I'm just so happy that today is Sunday I could croak." She shifted back on the sofa, turning away from the window.

"You sound tired."

"I *am* tired. Being president of a large hotel during the holiday season is no easy task, you know. I'm surprised no one's called me, even today. We have three functions going on this afternoon." Katie kept a lilt of jest in her voice, knowing that still—even from a thousand miles away—Marcy could hear the seriousness of the words. "Alright, Marcy, stop frowning," she added knowingly.

"You're right there. I am frowning. I'm also remembering not to mention that you almost got yourself killed just before Christmas. *And* involved your very best friend in the whole wide world, I might add."

There was a pregnant pause. "I did do that, didn't I?"

"Any word on your twin friends?"

"Zane and Zandra? No." Zane and Zandra McKenzie were twins who had tried to kill Katie the month before. Their motive had been simple: revenge.

Katie had never met them before they became the managers of Jacqueline's, the troubled boutique in THP. Zandra had been the lover of David Franscella, a man who'd kept Katie "back in the day." Strange, she thought, how he continued to haunt her, even after her marriage to Ben. Even after his sudden demise at the hand of Maggie, who had killed him the night—nineteen months ago—when he'd attacked Katie in her home in the Hamptons.

"Nothing?"

"Other than that they're still sitting in Rikers, no."

"I've been subpoenaed for the trial; did you know that?"

Katie sighed. "When did that happen?"

"Friday. I didn't want to burden you with it. I figured you'd find out soon enough anyway."

"Let's talk about something else, shall we?"

"My friend, the control guru. Just like in the boardroom, she speaks and I obey," Marcy teased. When Katie remained silent, she added, "Okay. Okay. What do you want to talk about?"

Katie chuckled. "I love it when you submit to my power," she joked, then gave her best Bela Lugosi laugh. When she sobered, she said, "Let's talk about my new spa and resort."

"Sounds like a plan."

"It *is* a plan. And only a plan at this stage."

"Tell me something."

"What's that?"

"And just shoot me out of my chair if this is too personal, but. . ."

Katie giggled. Conversations with Marcy were like a tonic, and she thanked God for her renewed relationship with her old pal.

"How do you fund something like that? I mean, do you just have all that money sitting around in a coffee can or. . .well, how does that work exactly?"

Katie laughed again, then sobered. "You're so unbelievably funny. It's called stocks, Marce."

"Oh. Not an area I'm all that sharp in, I'll have to be honest with you."

"To be honest with you, me neither. And to be further honest, because I didn't have the total backing of my board on this project I've allowed some of the private stock in THP to go public in order to raise the funds."

"Private stock?"

"THP is family owned. And only family owned. Make sense?"

"If you say so."

"Well, anyway, the parent company—or holding company—is THP. THP itself has vested interest in other companies, which are publicly owned, but THP is privately owned. Unless you're family, you don't get a share. For the most part, the shares have been given as gifts throughout the family. A little here and a little there. Naturally, Ben and his parents own the majority of the stock."

"Can you see my eyes from up there?" Marcy teased. "I think they just glazed over."

"Just listen," Katie admonished. "If I repeat this enough, it might just make good sense to me, as well."

"Yes, ma'am."

"When I first approached the board with the spa idea—something totally different from what they were used to, I might add—they balked. Old stuffies." She heard Marcy giggle. "Then my comptroller suggested I offer up 20 percent of my portion of the THP stock to go into a cash position. With the downfall of the industry—and the stock—since 9-11, there's been more than a little threat of a downturn in the economy."

"How will that affect you?"

"Hopefully, it won't. But, if necessary—according to my comptroller, Byron Spooner—I can always up the cash position to 31 percent."

"So when do you start? Officially, I mean?"

"Ashley and I have a meeting tomorrow with the developer and one of his architects from Montana to talk about it."

"You're flying out there or are they flying in?"

"They're flying in." Katie glanced down to her wristwatch. "Actually should be flying in any minute. I'm having Simon pick them up at the airport and bring them to the hotel."

"And how is my favorite chauffeur?"

"Fine. He asks about you all the time. Mrs. Waters this and Mrs. Waters that."

Marcy laughed. "Like an overgrown teddy bear, that one is. Nice guy, too. Hasn't he found anyone special yet?"

Katie moaned a bit before answering. "I have some suspicions."

"About?"

"Believe it or not, Ashley."

"No!"

"Yep."

"Well, I'll be dogged. They'd make a cute couple, you know that?"

"I think so."

"When did all this start?"

Katie filled her in on one of the protégées she'd taken from a gentleman's club known as Mist Goddess several months earlier. The three young women, Ashley, Brittany, and Candy (disdainfully called the ABCs of THP by The Hamilton Place General Manager, James Harrington) had been given a second chance when Katie took them out of the dance circuit, giving them jobs in the hotel and a hope for the future. Candy had gone back to dancing and eventually was killed by a maniacal client. Katie had been filled with tremendous grief but had turned that grief into something positive by continuing to focus on Ashley and Brittany, as well as a young woman named Misty, who had fled the manager of the club for the opportunity Katie offered.

Though the women were given jobs initially in housekeeping, Ashley had shown great ability in research and development and had become an apprentice to Katie, helping her in the groundwork for The Hamilton Place Resort and Spa, which was to be built in Wyoming. The land had been purchased before the end of the year and now the difficult phase of getting started was finally under way. Katie was ready to have it done and over with, and she said so to Marcy.

"I know you are," Marcy agreed. "But the work will keep your mind off things."

The work did keep her mind off things, and Katie knew specifically what "things" Marcy was talking about—what everybody was talking about. Her having almost died at the hands of Zane and Zandra. The ever-present concern as to the whereabouts of Bucky Caballero and his sister, Mattie Franscella, ironically the wife of David. The fact that they were now in a new year and another season of not knowing where her husband, William Benjamin Webster, was. It had been in June 2000 that he and Katie had discovered an illegal escort service operating out of Jacqueline's, the hotel's boutique. A very long nineteen months ago.

Now, off the telephone and sitting at the desk in her home office, Katie looked at a photo of Ben, held in a silver frame and sitting to the left side of the phone. "Ben," she called him, though everyone else called him William, or if were they hotel employees, Sir. Ben's employees held him in the highest regard, and his contemporaries had profound respect for him. Katie only hoped that one day they would all feel the same way about her.

Not that most of them didn't. They did. With the exception of James Harrington, a man she'd worked so hard to please.

There were times when she thought perhaps she'd won the war but discovered later her victories had only been small battles. She still had work to do to prove herself with him, and she hoped the spa would help.

She picked up the photograph and brought it closer to her heart. "If I can put that spa up like you would," she said to the image of her husband, "then perhaps he will take me seriously in my role here." She paused, frowning at the thought of talking with an inanimate object. "Oh, Ben," she sighed. "Where are you?"

CHAPTER TWO

"Katie. . ."

The words came to her as though through a tunnel. Feathery soft. Beguiling. Beckoning her to follow the sound and find the one who called her name.

"Katie. . ."

"Ben?"

She was dressed in a formal red gown, standing in a large hallway, decorated with ornate paintings and Oriental rugs. On either side were closed doors with beveled panels and brass scrolled handles. She wasn't sure how she knew that each door was locked to her, but she knew.

At the end of the hallway was an oversized floor-to-ceiling window, covered with white sheers that billowed toward her. "Katie. . ." The voice seemed to come from there, from beyond the curtains and the opened window, to the grounds below. She took a step toward it, a difficult step. It felt as though she were moving through a dense fog.

"Ben?"

She'd no sooner said the name than the curtains flew away from the window and enveloped her. She raised her arms and began to fight them. How is it they had come so far from the window? She couldn't breathe. . .couldn't breathe. . . .

"Where are you?" She heard the voice again, clearly the voice of her husband.

"I'm here. . .I can't. . .I can't. . ." She grabbed hold of a piece of the fabric with both hands and fisted them, jerked them toward her. A grunt escaped her as she tumbled to the floor, enmeshed in shimmering fabric. She worked furiously to tear herself away from the imprisonment and, when she could finally stand freely again, pushed the yards of cloth away from her. She ran to the bare window—easily this time—and braced her hands on the facing.

She realized she was on the second floor of a large struc-ture, possibly a house, though she wasn't quite sure, with Corinthian columns and a long row of balconies. Below was a lawn of shadows cast from the full moon as its light danced along the silhouettes of low shrubs and fat trees.

"Where am I?" she whispered, her eyes skimming the perimeter of the foreign property. "Ben!"

She thought she saw something—someone—darting from shrub to shrub below. Thought she saw his face look up at her in silent invitation to join him.

"Ben," she said, turning from the window, stepping over the torn curtains and running down the hallway to the place where she knew she'd find a long and curving staircase toward the foyer of the first floor.

And then she was outside, though she wasn't sure how she got there. She shuddered, feeling the chill of the night air, then looked down and found herself dressed in white linen nightclothes. "How did I. . . ?"

Her words were interrupted by the fleeting sound of laughter from just beyond a vine-covered wall. "Ben?"

"Katie, come quickly," she heard him say. "Come quickly."

She began to step in the direction of his voice. "I'm coming. I'm coming, Ben."

She ran along the length of the wall, looking for an opening. She'd stop only long enough to catch her breath, periodically glancing back toward the house, finding it to be farther away than she'd anticipated. "How do I get around this thing?"

She'd no sooner said the words than she heard a rumble behind her. Turning, she found the wall had fallen away, reveal-ing a well-lit garden. Her eyes immediately fell to the figure of a man who stood near a glorious fountain, his back to her.

"Ben?" she asked, moving toward him.

The man didn't move.

"Ben?" She was no more than two feet from him. She stopped, pressing her lips together. This was it. This was the moment she'd been living for. He was here. He was right in front of her, and he was her husband.

She reached and lightly touched his shoulder. "Ben."

He turned toward her smiling face, and when he had fully done so, her face fell. "Oh, no. . .no. . . ."

"Hello, Mrs. Webster." Bucky Caballero stood before her, peering at her through narrow, dark eyes.

"I thought—"

"You thought I was your husband, did you not? No. So sorry. Your husband's not here, Mrs. Webster. Where, oh, where, could he be?" The man's voice was menacing.

Katie set her jaw. "You don't scare me."

"Don't I now?"

"No."

He leaned closer to her. "Then go," he whispered. "Go find your husband. He's waiting for you, Mrs. Webster. He's wait-ing. . ." He turned toward the house. ". . .just over there. Right where you came from."

CHAPTER THREE

Welcomed or not, the clock alarm at Katie's bedside went off as usual the following morning. She moaned, rolling over on her right side and reaching for the snooze button with her fingertips. Unable to find it by habit, she opened one eye and focused until the face of the clock came into view. 5:30 A.M.

She located the snooze bar and pushed, smiling contentedly as the blaring ceased in its quest to wake her. "Don't you know I'm just not a morning person?" she mumbled, rolling back to her preferred left side, pulling the body pillow she wrapped herself around each night closer to her. She snuggled her face into it, inhaling the scent of Kouros Fraicheur, Ben's favorite cologne, that she'd sprayed on the slipcover. Again she moaned, this time in delight. "Ben," she whispered, then furrowed her brow at the memory of the night's dream.

Just then her bedroom door opened. Katie didn't look around her shoulder. She didn't have to. She knew exactly who it was. "Good morning, Maggie." Her voice was low and groggy.

"Miss Katie," the housekeeper returned. "I see you hit the snooze button again."

Katie moved to her back. "Why do I even bother? I know you'll be in here within minutes anyway."

The plump, aging woman, who had served the Webster household first as Ben's nanny and then as his housekeeper, stood next to Katie's bed, bending to pick up the house slippers kept in the hidden compartment of the bed stool. "There's a good girl, now. Sit up and let's get started, shall we?"

Katie sat up and pushed the heavy covers from her slender frame. She pulled her knees up to her chest and wiggled her toes at Maggie, who slid the slippers over her feet. "What would my toes and me do without you, Maggie?"

"You'll know soon enough, love, when the Lord calls me home." Maggie walked toward the bath. "Come now, let's get you ready for the day."

Katie leapt out of bed, fully awake now, and followed her beloved housekeeper and friend to where she was turning on the water in the shower, adjusting the temperature to Katie's preference. "What do you mean, Maggie? Are you feeling all right?"

Maggie turned to her, shaking the water from her hand as she stepped toward the vanity. "Oh, I'm fine, dear. But this old soul is getting closer to Glory. When you get to be my age, you know the time is getting shorter and shorter still."

Katie smiled, but her eyes held grief. "Oh, Maggie." She shivered. In her haste to follow the housekeeper, she'd left her robe on the end of the bed.

"You'll catch *your* death," Maggie huffed. "Now into that hot shower with you, and I'll make you breakfast as always."

"Good morning, Vickey," Katie greeted her assistant as soon as she walked through the door leading to their offices.

"Good morning. Your nine o'clock is already here." Vickey widened her eyes and gave a toss of her blonde hair.

Katie gave a quick look to her wristwatch. "It's only 8:15."

"I know. They were here when I got here at eight. I made sure they were comfortable in the sitting area and served coffee already."

Katie sighed. She'd hoped to get a few things out of the way before the meeting with the developer and architect. "Okay. Good. Thank you. Would you call Ashley and Byron Spooner and have them join us as soon as possible?"

Vickey reached for the phone. "Will do."

Katie entered her office with an air of excellence and competency. "Gentlemen," she greeted them as they stood; then she glided across the room and shook their hands.

"Mrs. Webster," they returned in greeting.

"Please be seated. I see you have coffee. Can I order anything else for you? Pastries?"

David Roberts, the middle-aged, slightly balding resort developer she'd hired from Montana, was dressed in dark slacks, black long-sleeved shirt, and silvery gray tie. The last time Katie had seen him, in Montana, he'd worn jeans and a workman's shirt. She liked the professionalism with which he presented himself, and she smiled in approval. First-rate and award-winning architect, Bart Bartlett, had been Katie's obvious choice from the architects Mr. Roberts had suggested from the Northwest. Like Roberts, he wore dark slacks but was more casual in a white oxford with a navy tie.

Katie joined them on the opposite white leather sofa from which they sat. "You two certainly got an early start," she commented with a smile. "Trying to be real New Yorkers?"

"I'd have to say we're a little disoriented from the flight," Bart commented, resting his elbows on his knees. "You have a beautiful hotel, Mrs. Webster. I can't help but admire the work."

"It's over a hundred years old, Mr. Bartlett. It has been in my husband's family from day one. At one time it had fallen into a bit of disrepair, but when Ben—my husband—took over the flagship, he turned it into the style and sophistication one would expect to find in a Midtown hotel."

There was a tap at the door, and Ashley and Byron entered. Ashley had changed drastically in her appearance from just a few months before, working diligently to appear the carbon copy of her new employer. Her hair, streaked blonde by nature rather than a bottle, was pulled back and clamped into a chignon, with bits of wispy hair spilling over like water in a fountain. She was tall, slender, and extremely attractive. Beautiful, in fact. When Katie took her out, she was very much aware of the young men's heads that turned and looked at the peaches and cream sophistication Ashley portrayed. These days, however, Ashley only had eyes for Simon, Katie's chauffeur.

Byron Spooner was a young and distinguishingly handsome man with an uncanny gift for numbers, which was why, when Ben's comptroller had died suddenly just months into Katie's presidency, she'd moved the elder gentleman's assistant, Byron, up to the position. He was young but brilliant.

The men in the room stood, as did Katie. "Gentlemen, may I introduce Ms. Ashley Johannsen. Ms. Johannsen, this is Mr. David Roberts, who will serve as the developer of our Montana project, and Mr. Bart Bartlett, who is our chief architect. Gentlemen, Ms. Johannsen has been key in the research and development of this project." The three shook hands and Katie continued. "May I also introduce my comptroller, Mr. Byron Spooner?" Again, everyone shook hands. "If everyone will follow me, we'll meet in the conference room just through this door." She motioned to a door in the corner of the opposite side of the room.

The following hour was spent mainly discussing the building site, topography, and earthwork. To Katie's delight, when she brought up the subject of environmental and historical issues, Ashley brought out four folders with her research on the area. "Early settlers called it the 'Land of Shining Mountains.' Mrs. Webster, you may want to think about using this as a sort of theme. It also is rich in American Frontier history, another possible theme." Ashley continued, bringing up climate, water supply, and governmental policies.

David Roberts smiled with approval. "You seem to have done your homework on our great state," he said.

Ashley returned the smile, genuine and bright. "You may also find it interesting that the Gideons placed their first Bibles in a hotel in Montana."

Katie tilted her head ever so slightly. "Really?"

"And that there are more gem sapphires there than any other state. Again, we can look to this as a theme."

Katie leaned forward slightly, lowered her lashes in thought, then looked back at the men. "Something to do with sapphires. . . the mountains. . . ."

Ashley had obviously waited for this moment. "The true gem of the Land of Shining Mountains: The Hamilton Place Sapphire Resort and Mountain Spa." She spoke as though she were reading ad for a commercial.

Bart Bartlett spoke. "I can do a lot with this, Mrs. Webster."

"I hope you brought something with you, Mr. Bartlett?"

Bartlett pulled several blueprints from a cylinder sitting at his feet. The three men and two women stood and leaned over the table. The meeting continued for the next half hour, with Byron commenting occasionally about cost efficiency and taking notes to the effects of what was said.

At one point, Katie crossed her arms as she spoke. "A few years ago, my husband and I took a trip to Israel, to a resort/spa called *Mizpe Hayamim*. It was a botanical masterpiece, as well as one of the most serene places I've ever visited. While I'm not trying to duplicate it, there are certain things I'd like to see for certain."

"Such as?" Bart asked.

"Individual cottages, Mr. Bartlett, for those willing to pay a little more. The cottages will be connected to the main building by winding interior walkways with a feel for the outdoors. Do you know what I'm asking?"

"I know exactly what you're asking," Bartlett answered.

"Good. I want the indoor pool to have the same feel. If they didn't know better, they'd think they were outside. As they are being pampered poolside, they should have perfect views of the snow-covered mountains and lakes."

"That's not a problem."

Katie nodded her head once. "Good." She picked up a nearby phone and paged Vickey. When her assistant answered, she said, "Vickey, our meeting is almost over. Would you prepare to walk our guests down to the concierge and make certain they are taken care of for the rest of the day? . . . Thank you." When she hung up the phone, she turned back to the others. "Gentlemen, I hope you don't mind."

Bartlett and Roberts smiled at one another. "I'd have to say no," David Roberts answered. "That's very kind of you, actually."

"Nonsense," Katie replied, moving toward the door of her office. "It's the least I can do."

As everyone was preparing to leave and making verbal arrangements for their next meeting, James Harrington tapped on the door and stepped inside.

"Mr. Harrington?" Katie greeted him.

Harrington cleared his throat discreetly. "Mrs. Webster, Vickey said you were about to dismiss in your meeting. If I might have a moment?"

Katie squared her shoulders. "Of course." She took a deep breath, then exhaled slowly. "Just let me see these people out." She turned back to her guests. "I will leave you now to do what you do best. I would say we should meet again in about a month. How does that sound?"

"A month should do it," Bart said. "By then we'll have everything you've asked for today."

"Wonderful." Katie began the process of escorting everyone from her office. "I'll have my assistant contact you within seven business days concerning a date. In the meantime, Mr. Bartlett,

Mr. Roberts, I understand you will be spending another day in our city. Please allow our concierge to assist you in any plans you might make."

The men thanked her, followed by appropriate handshakes. When their backs were turned, she gave Ashley a wink and then closed the door. Katie took another deep breath and turned to her GM. "You needed to speak to me about something in particular, James?"

James had seated himself in one of the chairs across from Katie's desk. He shifted, bracing his elbows against the arms and crossing one leg over the other. "Yes." His eyes narrowed as he watched Katie return to her seat behind the desk before him.

Katie jerked slightly. The man made her so nervous. She hated to admit that, but it was true. "What is it?" she asked, tucking a wayward strand of hair behind her ear, and managing to keep eye contact with the hazel eyes of the slightly middle-aged, noticeably handsome man before her.

"Forgive me if I'm being presumptuous. . . ." James ran a hand over his silver hair, then returned it.

"Yes?"

"Something is wrong."

Katie looked down at her desk and back up to him in one fluid movement. "What do you mean?"

"With you. Particularly." He uncrossed his legs then and leaned forward. "I don't mean to get personal, but I feel I owe William that much—to see to it that you take care of yourself."

Katie's shoulders slumped. "Oh."

"You've had a difficult time of it, Katie. Last month's. . .*situation*. The holiday season is enough to exhaust anyone in this industry, but you had the added circumstance of the McKenzies trying to kill you."

Katie only nodded and James went on, this time standing and pulling a trifolded piece of paper from his inside coat pocket. "My wife and I own a little house in Vermont not too far from here. Five- or six-hour drive, according to how hard you press the accelerator." He dropped the paper on to the desk in front to her. "Actually it belonged to someone in Julia's family, and as they got older and found themselves unable to take care of it, they put it on the market."

Katie opened the paper slowly, glancing from it to the man in front of her and back down again. Before her was a realtor's sheet with information and a photograph about a two-story cottage nestled in a cluster of trees and thick shrubbery. "It's lovely," she commented.

"And empty most of the time. We use it for a holiday getaway, and during the summer months, when the children were younger, Julia would take them up there. I'd join them on weekends, that sort of thing. Now, just Julia and I go up there, of course. It's a wonderful place."

Katie looked back at the paper. "Are you thinking of selling it?" She glanced back up at James, who looked back to the paper.

"Oh, no. No, no. This is actually a copy from the realtor's book when we bought it. Julia framed the original and placed it on the wall of my home study. That's how much we love it." He moved back to the chair and sat.

Katie lifted her hands palm up. "Then why are you showing this to me, Mr. Harrington?"

Harrington crossed his legs again. "Now why did you do that? Why suddenly change to the formal use to my name? I told you this was personal and not professional."

Katie sighed. "I'm sorry, I just. . .I'm afraid I'm a bit in the dark here."

"I spoke with Julia last night, and we agreed. You're overworked and overwrought. In fact, she commented that she'd seen you last week in the boutique, talking to the new owners."

"Yes. She and I were both looking over the new merchandise."

"She also said your girl Brittany is doing a fine job as a sales-clerk there."

Katie nodded, allowing the paper to slip from her hands as she leaned back in her seat. "Yes, she is."

"But Julia also said you looked exhausted."

Katie sighed heavily. "Is it that obvious?"

"I'm afraid so. Which is why she insisted I encourage you to take some time off and go to Vermont, to our home, and get some rest."

"But I have my home in the Hamptons. I could always go there."

"I'd be willing to bet you do work while you're there."

Frowning, Katie responded, "That much is true."

"What I'm proposing is a whole new view, Katie." James leaned forward. "My house is in the township of Sanford, Vermont. Population about fifteen hundred. Seriously. And no one there cares who you are. It's a great place to get away, to *not* be the president of THP. To just relax. There are trails behind the house for hiking, and the house is fully stocked. This is a perfect season. New England in the winter." He stood, pulling a single key from his pants' pocket. "Here's the key. Think about it. There's nothing going on here that the rest of the staff can't handle." He slid the key across the desk pad, then tapped it twice with his finger. "Think about it and let me know."

Katie stared at the key. "Mr. Harrington," she said, standing as well. "May I be honest with you?"

"Please do."

She crossed her arms. "You baffle me, Mr. Harrington. You really do. I don't know anyone who fought harder against me than you—"

"That was in the beginning, Katie."

She let out a sarcastic laugh. "Mr. Harrington, just within the last few months you've fought me on every single thing I've tried to do here."

She watched his brow furrow and his cheeks flush with anger. "For example?"

"For example, my Christmas tea, which was, by the way, an absolute success."

Harrington crossed the room, making his way toward the wet bar where he poured himself a glass of water. "I'll admit that much. It just seems to me that you jump into these ideas you have without thinking things through."

"Isn't that my prerogative? After all, I *am* the president here. Not just of THP-New York. I am the *president*, Mr. Harrington, of the entire chain. Which I suppose brings us to another point. You fought tooth and nail to see to it that I didn't take this role. And now. . .now you offer me a place of respite? Do you see where I'm coming from here?"

James finished his water, setting the glass firmly down. "You know, I asked Julia the other night when we were discussing this why I'd even want to bother doing this. I've told you before that this is nothing personal. I've tried to do what I thought William would want me to do. And yes, I think that perhaps I could have helped a little rather than. . ."

"Hindering?" Katie stepped to the side of her desk and leaned against it, gripping the edge with her fists.

She watched his face fall. "Look," he said, pointing to the desk where the key still lay, "it's there if you want it. Think what you will; I don't care. But I really am trying to do the right thing here." He started walking toward the door, then paused to look at her. "I may not agree with everything you've done—right down to taking the role of president in the first place—but I can't deny you've done an exceptional job."

Katie straightened and took a deep breath. "Thank you, Mr.—" She smiled briefly. "Thank you, James," she said with a slight nod of her head.

"Like I said, it's there if you need it. Just let me know."

He turned, and Katie watched him leave her office. She looked from the door to the key to the paper and back to the door again. She blinked once and raked her teeth over her lower lip. *What are you up to, James Harrington?* she wondered. *What are you up to?*

From the observer's position, sitting curbside on Fifty-seventh, there was a perfect view of the front door of The Hamilton Place hotel. Miguel, the old doorman, stood soldier straight inside his booth, looking pristine and professional in his light gray, brass-buttoned uniform. As guests of the hotel approached its entrance, whether from the elegant inside or frigid outside, he hopped to his duties as he had done for years on end.

Sitting there watching was no easy task, but it was one that had to be done. Katie Webster was sure to exit the building at some point today, and the one who patiently waited knew the woman well enough to know she always used the front exit. Never pretentious, never too proud. Always perfect, Katie Webster.

The onlooker began to hum a faint tune. *Hmmmmm.* "*Come out, come out, wherever you are. . . .*"

Time passed like the ticking of a clock. Rhythmically. The city ran in its typical workday cycle. Yellow cabs whizzed by, weaving in and out and around the other automobiles. Buses screeched to their predestined stops just across the street, a few yards from the hotel. Pedestrians, having returned home from their jobs, began the task of walking their little four-legged, furry pets, dog leash in one hand, pooper-scooper in the other. Some of the animals were large, panting happily at being outdoors, even if the earth beneath their paws *was* cement. Others had eyes that looked toward the park. A daily ritual that must have felt like a holiday. A few, tiny and nearly furless, wore sweaters like a sign of their owner's social status. "See me? My master can afford such luxuries. Can yours? Mine comes with a diamond collar. Does yours?"

"It's all about status, isn't it?" the voice said to no one.

There was a quick lifting of the chin. The white limo, the one the Websters always used, pulled into the covered semi-circular driveway in front of the grand hotel. The chauffeur, a hulk of a man, stepped out, blowing smoke from his nostrils as his warm breath met the cold air. Within moments the poised figure of Katharine Webster slipped from the door Miguel held open for her. There was an exchange of words between them. "Thank you," or something close to it. A tipping of the cap from Miguel. A warm smile from his employer.

Well, wasn't that just perfect.

An eyebrow arched. The grande dame of THP looked picture-perfect as always. Her chestnut hair fell in soft waves to her shoulders, and she wore what appeared to be a wool, cream-colored pantsuit with matching coat. *How is it that you never seem to age? What a life you have, Katie Webster. What a life you've always had.*

The quiet voice spoke in the warmth of the automobile. "I may or may not be your friend when all this is over, you know. You may wish you'd never met me. . . ." A tongue moved unhurriedly over a bottom lip, as though to languish in the viewing of the beautiful woman. Though she stood nearly six feet tall, in a fluid movement she slipped into the backseat of the limousine, adjusting herself and her coat as the door closed behind her.

The voyeur slipped the gearshift from park to drive. "*Now where are you taking me, Katie Webster? Where to today?*"

CHAPTER FOUR

"Katie. Good to see you again."

Katie stepped across the threshold of the Silver household. "Gail, thank you for asking me to dinner." She pressed her chilled cheek to the warmth of Gail's. "Sorry, it's a bit cold out there."

Gail peered around the front doorway before closing it. "Your chauffeur, where is he going?"

"I told him I'd call him later." Katie began to unbutton her coat, then stopped as the man of the household—her husband's childhood best friend—appeared on the landing of the stairway before her. "Phil."

Phil Silver, ex-FBI agent and now professor at John Jay College of Criminal Justice, sometime private investigator and all-the-time protective friend. Like Katie's husband, he was good-looking with a slight hint of gray scattered through his dark hair. And, like Ben, those who knew him best could read his thoughts by looking at his eyes.

"Right on time as usual," Phil said, walking down the stairs. "Then again, you wouldn't have it any other way." He reached the woman he'd felt such responsibility for over the past two years, since her husband's disappearance, and kissed her cheek. "Let me take your coat," he added.

Katie continued to unbutton the wrap and allowed Phil to slip it from her shoulders as she shifted her clutch purse from one hand to the other. "Thank you." She looked back at Gail. "Something smells wonderful."

Gail smiled. "I hope you're hungry."

"I'm always hungry. I just can't always find time to eat."

The two women made their way through the living room and toward the kitchen, Katie following the woman who was an unusual mix of Jewish/American Indian ancestry and who continued to look a decade younger than she really was. "Katie, you're almost too thin. You can eat more than you realize."

Katie laughed as they entered the kitchen. "Look who's talking. Gail, you could model, I swear you could."

Gail walked over to the stove where several covered pots sat atop the heated eyes and lifted one of the lids. Steam rose upward, and in a quick and familiar movement, Gail flipped the switch of the vent-a-hood. She replaced the lid as she looked over her shoulder. "No, thank you."

Katie walked over to the nearby breakfast nook and sat in one of the chairs at the table, laying her purse on the tabletop beside her. "I can't say that I blame you. Look what happened to me the last time I said I'd model." She raised her eyebrows in jest, though the last thing she felt was humor.

Phil entered the kitchen then, watching his wife as she joined Katie at the table. "Something to drink, ladies? A glass of Chardonnay?"

Katie nodded. "That would be lovely."

Gail gave a loving glance to her husband. "Me, too."

Phil turned back toward the living room. "I'll be right back."

Gail placed her hands on the tabletop. "Would you be more comfortable in the living room?"

"No, this is fine. This is. . .familial, you know? There's something endearing about sitting around a kitchen table talking.

Where are the kids?"

Gail leaned back in her chair. "With friends in study groups. That's why we thought tonight a perfect time to have you come over."

"But I love your children! They're so much fun to be around."

Phil appeared again, carrying a tray with three glasses of wine. "Like their old dad," he interjected into the conversation. He reached the table and placed the tray atop it.

"Not that I had anything to do with it," Gail commented as Phil handed a glass first to their guest and then to his wife.

He took the third glass and held it before him in a toast. "To good friends and quiet evenings," he said with a wink.

The three friends touched the rims of their glasses together, then sipped at the chilled white wine. Phil pulled out a chair and joined the women. "So what are we talking about?"

Gail set her glass down. "Let's see. Absent nearly adult children, the joy of sitting around a kitchen table, and fashion shows."

Phil frowned. "Let's *not* talk about fashion shows. You know what happened the last time you got involved with one of those," he said, looking at Katie.

Katie reached toward him and patted his arm. "That's what I said."

It had been just one month previous that Katie had agreed to be in a fashion show that involved Zane and Zandra McKenzie. Of course, it had all been a ruse. There was to be no fashion show, only a ploy to get Katie to their apartment where they intended to kill her. Discovering a framed photograph of David Franscella in Zandra's bedroom catapulted Katie into one of the most fearful hours of her life. She had valiantly fought the McKenzies, causing Zandra to fall unconscious to the bathroom floor and repeatedly stabbing—though not mortally wounding— Zane before she could escape through the front door. "The trial is in six weeks," Katie added as an afterthought.

"I know," Phil said. "I've been called as a witness."

Katie gave a wry smile. "So has Marcy." Both she and Gail laughed as Phil's shoulders slumped.

Gail took another sip of her wine. "Marcy Waters is the only woman in the whole wide world that can get his dander up."

Katie couldn't help but be amused. "I just don't understand it," she said to Gail, keeping her voice low, as though they were sharing a secret between the two of them. "I mean, Marcy is the nicest person you'd ever want to meet. She's kind, considerate, smart—"

"Intrusive," Phil added. "Sneaky, apt to take matters into her own hands. . .matters, by the way, that don't belong in her hands, near her hands, or around her hands."

Katie and Gail laughed out loud. "Okay, Phil," Gail said. "We understand." She stood and walked toward the stove, aware that two pairs of eyes followed her there. "Ten minutes and we'll be ready to eat."

Katie turned back to Phil. "Phil?"

He looked at her, his gaze soft and caring. "Mmm?"

Katie reached for her purse, opened it, and pulled out the folded piece of paper James Harrington had left with her earlier in the day. "Take a look at this." She slid the paper a few inches across the table.

Phil picked the paper up, studying it for a moment. "What's this? Are you thinking of buying this?"

"Oh, no. It belongs to—someone offered to let me go there for a little R & R."

Gail rejoined them, looking over her husband's shoulder at the realtor's sheet. "How charming. Four bedrooms, two and a half baths, living room, dining room, kitchen, *three-season room.* Wow. Library/study, small balcony, and two fireplaces. Can I go?"

Katie sat up straight. "What do you think? Phil? Two weeks in Vermont? Me. Alone. Nothing to do but rest and take nature walks and, I don't know, listen to old Frank Sinatra albums."

Phil dropped the paper. "Why ask me? You know your schedule. God knows you could use some rest. You won't be needed for anything to do with the case for another month or so."

Gail placed her hands on her husband's shoulders, almost intuitively. "Who owns the house, Katie?"

"James Harrington." She shot a quick glance to Phil.

"Oh, I see," he commented. "Do you think that's a good idea? After all, this man has fought you vehemently from day one."

"I honestly don't know. The man has very few kind things to say to me, has been a thorn in my flesh pretty much since I took over at the helm at THP, and. . .I just don't know what to think about this offer. He says he's trying to do the right thing. . . always was. I don't know, Phil. He almost seems apologetic about the past and wants to make the future right."

Phil shook his head. "I wouldn't go."

"Why not? Because it's not good for me to be away or because it's Harrington's house?"

"The latter. You could certainly afford a vacation. You've worked harder to make the hotel a success than most male executives ever dreamed of working."

"He's right there, Katie." Gail returned to her seat.

"What did he say, exactly, when he made this grand gesture?"

Katie shrugged. "That I had been working hard, the situation with the McKenzies, the holiday season. . .he said his wife mentioned she'd seen me in Jacqueline's recently and that I looked a little worse for the wear, so to speak. He said that Julia, his wife, was concerned and so was he. Owed it to Ben. . ."

Phil looked back at the paper. "Why not just go to the Hamptons? You have an estate there that makes this place look like a tinker's cottage."

Katie sighed. "I mentioned that, but he said I'd just take up work like I always do, and he's right. The house in the Hamptons is also my home. I need to get away." She placed her hands flat on the table. "I have to tell you. Since I laid eyes on this place, all I can think about is sitting by a boisterous fire, curled in an oversized chair, reading a good book. Taking nature walks. Spending more time with God. Quiet conversations are sometimes hard to have with Him in my world, you know. I could really use this retreat."

She looked from Phil to Gail and back to Phil again. "I don't trust Harrington any more than you, but I really felt he was being genuine. I guess I just need some reassurance that I'm doing the right thing, but at the same time it feels like something I am *supposed* to do."

"Two weeks. A man could take over a corporation in two weeks."

"Yes, he could. And maybe even more so since I've let some of our stocks go public. However," she said, pointing a finger heavenward, "I happen to know what the man makes annually and believe me, while I pay him well, I don't pay him well enough to buy me into a corner." She watched Phil's eyes narrow in thought. "And you know Vickey wouldn't dare let anything happen that I didn't know about, and I'd put Cynthia on full alert." Vickey, her assistant, had at one time been Ben's assistant as well. She'd proven loyal, not only on a professional level, but on a personal one as well. Cynthia Ferguson was Ben's cousin, Katie's ex-employer, and one of the best corporate attorneys in the city.

"I still say I'm wary. But. . ."

"But?"

"Something tells me I couldn't stop you if I wanted to. You'd take Maggie?"

"Of course."

He nodded. "Well, at least I know one of you knows how to use a gun."

Life in Canada over the past nearly two years had afforded Bucky Caballero more than he'd ever expected. Rather than falling into debt due to not being able to run his Madison Avenue real estate firm, he had flourished financially by buying and selling stocks and fine works of art, using an old friend from New York City as his "front," or middleman.

He and his sister Mattie had managed to blend in with the residents of the Canadian city where they'd settled. Though there were very few of Italian descent, there were a high number of Catholics. Therefore, what small bit of a social life they had came from their religious rather than their ethnic background. It certainly did not come from their economic status, which they kept to themselves.

Keeping to themselves altogether wasn't so difficult for Bucky. He wasn't a man who enjoyed the company of others . . .unless, of course, it profited him in some way. But Mattie had had a more difficult time with it. Living in an adequate apartment, passing themselves off as husband and wife—Tony and Ana, to be exact—rather than the siblings they really were, had kept her from pursuing a life with the "stronger sex." The very thought made Bucky chuckle. There would never be a man—save himself—who was stronger or more powerful than Mattie. Even her husband, David, had not managed to tame her before his untimely death.

David. Bucky shook his head at the very thought of him. The man originally hired as an escort for their international business. . .the man who came from nothing but had somehow managed to convince Mattie to marry him. Or perhaps it had been the other way around. Mattie had hardly discussed such issues with her brother.

Money had changed David. . .as it did everyone who'd ever found themselves suddenly surrounded by it. He'd bought fancy cars, expensive clothes, and jewelry. . .and not only for himself or his wife. He'd lived life on a dangerous curve and had met and "kept" a young dancer from Hell's Kitchen.

A young dancer who eventually married William Benjamin Webster and became a woman of power and influence.

A woman named Katie.

David's death had been an unfortunate one, but it only proved his inadequacies where the family business was concerned. He'd been killed by an old woman, for the love of Mike, leaving Mattie a widow before her time, though Bucky suspected she really didn't care all that much. She never even so much as shed one tear over it, though she did manage to wear black for a few days.

He chuckled now, thinking about it. How like David it had been to leave a woman a widow and to die in the home of his ex-mistress, all the while leaving another mistress behind.

Zandra McKenzie. Bucky hadn't known the woman, of course, but her sudden appearance a few months ago had done a world of good for his chronic dark moods. She and her brother Zane had nearly killed the fine Mrs. Webster, but like David, had failed. Not that Bucky regretted it. He was actually rather glad. He didn't want Mrs. Webster to die. Yet. He wanted her to lose everything first, and deciding how that would take place filled his days with much planning and thought.

Mattie filled most of her days reading, dining out, visiting galleries, or shopping, while Bucky preferred sitting in his home office, reading international periodicals, studying the market, and keeping himself apprised of the latest in art. Though he missed his beloved New York City, he was content. That is to say, he was content financially.

Personally he still had one axe to grind, one mission to complete. Somewhere out there, William Benjamin Webster was watching him, and he knew it. Or, at the very least, watching *for* him. He had to be. There was no other excuse for the man's obliteration from the world as they knew it, especially when it came to Webster's wife, Katie.

It gave him more than a little to think on. To ponder. To question.

Bucky's typical daily routine was to rise early, walk two miles, return home, and shower. Having done this, he would make coffee, eat a healthy breakfast, watch the morning news, and then go to his office where he "worked," which meant managing his stocks, buying and selling art, and the like. He often ate lunch out with Mattie, stopping on the way home to purchase the daily newspapers from around the world. Home again, he would return to his office and begin to read them, carefully devouring each and every line.

He was eternally grateful his father had insisted on their learning several languages as children. *Oh, the power of knowledge,* Bucky often thought.

Today, he and Mattie had dined in her favorite bistro, a narrow restaurant not far from their apartment, which was decorated in gold tones and frequented by upscale clientele. Because Mattie had taken their only car earlier in the day for the purpose of shopping, Bucky walked the four blocks, ate *paella* and sipped on white wine, while Mattie talked incessantly about a church function that was to be held at the home of a friend later in the month. Mattie had, according to the descriptions of her day so far, spent hours looking for the perfect dress and had come up empty-handed.

"If we were only back in New York," she said firmly, shaking her head in such a manner as was hardly detectable. She had been afforded the good grace of looking like their mother: slender in build, deep-set, dark eyes that belonged somewhere between the boardroom and the boudoir, a narrow, distinguished face that leaned more toward handsome than glamorous. Most days she wore her hair, which was thick and kept professionally dark, in a tight chignon, giving her the air of superiority she'd always worked so diligently for. "There would be none of this nonsense," she continued. "I would merely call my shopper, and she would find *the* dress for me." She took a sip of her wine, looking away. Bucky knew his sister. She was attempting to gain composure.

He had finished his meal and was sitting back in his chair—his legs crossed—with an aura of complete control. He attempted to pacify her. "Now, now. Let's not be so melodramatic, pet. Besides, if we were back in New York, I dare say you would not be attending a church function."

Her lips pursed and her eyes narrowed. "I am so sick of this life I could scream. In fact, I just may scream."

"What would you have me do? Take us back to the city? Allow us to walk into some trap whereby all your fashion needs are obliterated?" He leaned forward just enough to drive his point. "My dear, you won't look good in stripes." Then he smiled faintly to soften his next words. "And you know gray is not your best color."

Mattie dabbed at her lips with the napkin she'd draped over her lap. "Bucky," she hissed. "I am *not* going to stay here the rest of my life."

"And just where would you like to go?" He frowned. "Do not say New York. If you say New York, I'm going to stand up and walk out."

She stared at him for a moment before answering. "Why not Paris? Or Rome?" She paused again. "Or Paris?" She laughed lightly, laying a hand against the bodice of the Oscar de la Renta linen dress she'd chosen for the day.

He smiled, relieved that her moment of pouting was done. So far she'd managed to stay connected to reality—at least in public. There had been moments at home, moments when he was forced to lock her in her room until she promised to be a good girl.

Being the "big brother" wasn't always what it was cracked up to be, especially when the "little sister" was Mattie Franscella.

"You know," he said now, "that leaving is out of the question until I finish my business."

Mattie leaned toward her brother. "Bucky, this obsession you have with Webster is driving me insane. You and I both know you didn't set that bomb, which means he's playing us. The only way you can allow him to win is to continue to play the game with him. Let's throw in the towel, move to Paris, and get on with our lives. We can blend in there. We can start over." She grinned. "Think of all that French art," she whispered, then nodded her head. "Come on."

"Mattie, in Canada, this close to the border, I can slip into the country easily should Webster ever make an appearance. You know that. Now, if you would like to move to Paris, fine. I can arrange it. But I will not move with you. Not yet." He took a final sip of his wine. "Besides, something new has happened that's about to change things for us."

"What do you mean?"

A server approached carrying a bottle of the wine Bucky was drinking. "Sir?" he asked.

Bucky placed his hand over the rim of his glass. "No, thank you."

The server turned Mattie, saw that her glass was half-full, but asked, "Madame?" anyway.

"Please," she said.

When the server was done and had stepped away, Bucky remarked, "You drink too much these days, pet."

"A glass and a half of wine at lunch? Who are you now? The pope of moral conduct?"

Bucky stood abruptly, leaned over his sister, and spoke to her through clenched teeth. "You forget yourself, Mattie. Do *not* speak to me in that manner. I will return home now. When you grow up, why not join me there?"

And with that he left the bistro.

CHAPTER FIVE

"We're almost there, Maggie. What do you think so far?" Katie had leased a 2002 SUV with snow tires for the trip to Vermont. Having accepted James Harrington's proposal, she had spent the rest of the week getting business in order.

Katie and her housekeeper had risen early on Saturday morning and, having packed the night before, were ready to leave by eight o'clock. The sky was clear, the air was crisp and wintry, the city streets were coming—once again—to life, and it seemed that even New York was bidding them farewell.

Katie couldn't remember when she had looked forward to anything with such enthusiasm. She saluted Miguel on her way to the SUV, which Simon had brought around for her. "Sure you don't want me to drive you?" he'd asked.

She'd patted his back. "Time off for you, too, Simon. I'm a big girl now; I've been driving since I was fifteen, so no need to worry. Maggie and I are going for some R & R, and I suggest you do the same."

He'd frowned, like everyone else had, but Katie didn't let it stop her from grinning as she pulled the gearshift into drive and eased away from the semicircular drive.

And now they were almost there. She'd played Maggie's

favorite big band CDs on the way up and had entertained her by singing off-key and dropping little bits of information she'd gathered about Vermont since she'd made her decision to go.

Maggie had been a bit resistant at first, but the closer they came to Sanford, the more she seemed to relish the thought of change.

"Look at the mountains, Maggie," Katie commented. "God's in His heaven, and all's right with the world."

"He is that, all right." Maggie peered out the passenger's window. "Now there's a scene you don't see every day in the city."

"I've been doing some reading about the architecture in Vermont." Katie bobbed her head a bit. "Actually, it started off to just be research about Vermont but quickly became one of architectural design. There are so many different styles we'll see, Maggie. Federal, Queen Anne, Bungalow, Colonial Revival. . ." Katie turned her head. To their right was a farmhouse nestled in a valley, blanketed in a thick coat of snow. The main house, clapboard painted white, blended with the landscape. The red barn offered a taste of Americana. Next to it, a silo that glinted in the noon sunlight rose proudly against the royal blue sky. A row of trees with bare branches ran along one side and, as they passed it, the farmhouse slipped quietly from view.

"If my time calculations are correct, we're getting close, Maggs. Just over this hill and into the valley. James told me that most of the villages—they're called villages, Maggie. *Villages!*—most of the villages were built in valleys." Katie looked over to the woman who, even in the warmth of the car, still wore a thick sweater. *Poor soul,* Katie thought, *she's getting older. . .more frail.*

Maggie jutted her head forward. "Reminds me of that book. . . ."

Katie looked ahead. They were coming over a bend, heading toward a covered bridge, painted in a deep terra cotta. "Oh, Maggie!" Katie slowed the SUV, wanting to relish the experience. As they drove through, she breathed as though to take the excitement into her lungs and therefore into herself. When they'd come through to the other side, Katie asked, "What book?"

"What was it? Something about covered bridges."

Katie thought for a moment, then chuckled. *Bridges of Madison County?*"

"That was it."

Within minutes they saw the beginnings of Sanford, a dotting of farms beckoning them into the township and on into the village. "Would you dial a number for me on my cell phone, Maggs?" Katie asked. She pulled a small piece of paper from a cubbyhole in the dashboard and handed it to her. "It's the phone number of the real estate office there. I'm supposed to speak to a Kristy Hallman."

With her peripheral vision Katie watched Maggie awkwardly dialing the number. She smiled. *Some parts of new technology will be forever lost on the old generation,* she thought. "Hello," she heard Maggie say. "Miss Kristy Hallman, please." There was a pause. "Hold for Mrs. Webster, if you will."

Maggie handed the phone over to Katie, who nodded in appreciation. "Thanks, Maggie. Hello, Miss Hallman? This is Katharine Webster." She frowned at the use of her formal name. "Katie Webster," she corrected.

"Hello, Katie. And please call me Kristy. You're calling at just the time I expected you."

"I can see Sanford just down the hill. What should I do next?"

The voice was deep and sensual. "I imagine you're driving up Bailey's Farm Road."

Katie looked left and right. "I really don't know," she admitted with a bit of a laugh. "There's really nothing out here but snow-covered hills and a few farms along the way."

"Did you drive through a sort of orange-colored bridge?"

"Yes."

"Then you're on Bailey's Farm Road. It will end as you get closer to town; the road that crosses it is Old Montpelier Road."

"Old Montpelier. Okay."

"It Y's off. Veer to the left."

"To the left." Katie consciously slowed the SUV as the winding road they'd been traveling began to straighten and ribbon over gently rolling hills.

"Come to the crossroads of the village. Take note because there aren't any stop signs around here or traffic signals."

"Seriously?"

"Ayup. You'll be dead center on Main Street. Turn right. My office is the second building on the left. It's a large two-story structure with a cupola on top."

Italianate, Katie thought. "I'm at Old Montpelier." Katie came to a near stop at the intersection and looked left and right. There were no cars coming either way.

"Then I'll see you in about five minutes."

Five minutes was just about right. Katie had found the real estate office easily enough. As Kristy had described it, it was a large brick building sitting behind the post office and just up a slight incline. Katie drove the SUV around the building by turning left on Fox Run Road and pulling into the back parking lot of the building. She and Maggie looked at one another and smiled.

"Well, Maggs, what do you think of Sanford?"

"Quaint."

Katie laughed. "It is that, isn't it? But for the next two weeks, this is our little piece of America. Our hometown, as it were. Grab your coat, Maggie."

"You won't have to tell me that. Frigid cold out there; that much is for sure."

The women reached into the backseat for their coats and slipped them on before opening the doors and climbing out. They made their way toward the back door of the imposing and looming building, the snow crunching under their booted feet. Before Katie could knock, it opened wide and a strikingly beautiful olive-skinned woman with long dark hair and almond-shaped eyes met them. "Hello! I saw you driving around." They stepped past her as she added, "I have some coffee, perfect for warming you. Just head straight up this hallway."

It was not much warmer in the hallway than it was outside. Katie wrapped her wool coat more tightly around her and stepped aside to allow Kristy, who seemed perfectly content in no coat, to lead them up to the front office, which was a room to the left of the staircase with large floor-to-ceiling unadorned windows and a French door entryway, where a space heater gave extra warmth to the already centrally heated room. As they entered the sparsely decorated room, Kristy added, "We don't heat the back rooms unless something is going on. This is a realty office, but the back can be rented out for meetings and things like that." She smiled a perfectly even smile. "Not that they often are. Town meetings are apt to be held in the town hall, but sometimes the church holds special things here. Upstairs is our historical society, which you may find of interest while you're here. It's open Tuesdays, Thursdays, and Saturdays from noon to six." Kristy Hallman looked from Katie to Maggie and back to Katie again, then extended her hand with a jump toward her. "I'm sorry. I'm a bit of a talker when there's actually a human being in here. I'm Kristy Hallman."

Katie shook her hand. "I hope so! I'm Katie Webster. This is my housekeeper and companion, Maggie."

Kristy shook Maggie's hand next. "Maggie. Nice to meet you. Coffee?"

Katie shook her head no.

"Are you sure? Well, then. Are you ready to see your home away from home for the next two weeks?"

Katie glowed at the thought. "I'm more than ready. I'm

keeping the cell phone turned off and have dared my staff to try to reach me," she teased.

Vermont. The follower wondered what Katie Webster was doing there in the New England countryside village of Sanford, Vermont.

It had been a long trip and keeping a safe distance hadn't been easy. In fact, by not knowing where Katie was headed with her trusty housekeeper, the most difficult part had been wondering where they would end up. A quick glance at the dashboard clock confirmed that an immediate trip back to the city was necessary to arrive before dark. And a trip back to the city was imperative.

Tomorrow. Tomorrow new decisions would have to be made. But not until tomorrow.

CHAPTER SIX

James and Julia Harrington's Vermont home sat just off Main Street as serene and inviting as a Christmas postcard. While snow clung to the shingles of the house, it had been recently shoveled from the brick walkway and steps leading to the small, rectangular front porch that extended from the front door to the left side of the house.

Katie slowed her SUV to a stop in front, followed by Kristy's small economy car. The three women exited their vehicles together with Katie commenting, "It's exactly as I pictured it."

"Mr. Hatcher takes care of the sidewalk here on Main Street," Kristy called out as she rounded the front of her car, slipping between the two automobiles. "As you can see," she continued, smoke puffing from between her lips as she turned back toward the village, "my office is just down the road on the other side. So." She reached Katie and Maggie. "If you need anything or want to just walk down for a cup of coffee, I'm always up for company."

The three women turned toward the front door, and Kristy pulled a key out of her coat pocket. "I came by earlier and turned the heat on for you." She looked up at Katie and stopped. "Geesh. I didn't realize how tall you were before."

Katie smiled. "Almost six foot."

"Geesh," Kristy continued, making her way up the six small steps leading to the porch. "Anyway, Mr. Harrington called early this morning and asked me to make certain the house was nice and toasty for you when you got here. I've also made a grocery run. There's food enough for dinner tonight and tomorrow. Have you had lunch?" She put the key in the keyhole, twisted, and opened the door.

Katie looked at the door as she walked across the threshold. "Not yet. No dead bolt?"

Kristy stepped behind her and into the warmth of the foyer. "For what?" She shut the door, slipped out of her coat, and hung it on the antique coat tree that dominated one wall of the foyer. "Welcome to Sanford, Katie Webster. This isn't New York City. No one here is going to hurt you."

Katie was taken aback. *Just what did she mean by that?* Instead of commenting, however, she turned to survey the interior of the house as she began to unbutton her coat. "Oh, Maggie, look. It's perfect."

Maggie and Katie hung their coats next to Kristy's and began their official first tour of the house. It was everything Katie had hoped it would be. The rooms were decorated in a blend of traditional New England and Victorian. Katie found the combination to be charming and welcoming. "Just perfect," she repeated.

"To the right here," Kristy said, her feet clomping across the polished hardwood floor, "is the living room." She led them through an arched doorway and into a room that extended farther to a three-season room, shut off by French doors. "As you can see, the three-season room is closed off right now. It's just too cold." She walked over to the fireplace. "Would you like for me to start a fire?" The fireplace had been prepared earlier.

"That would be nice," Katie answered.

Kristy reached to the hearth for a cylinder box of fireplace matches, struck one, and then lit the fire. "This room is the most wonderful place for reading. Do you like to read?"

"I love it when I have time."

"Good, because Mr. and Mrs. Harrington have a classic assortment in the study, which is right beyond this wall."

"Classics? James Harrington? My goodness."

Kristy laughed. "I always say you can really get to know a person by perusing his home."

"I suppose you're right."

"It's probably not so easy to really know a person when you just see them nine to five. I understand you and Mr. Harrington work together?" It was said as though she weren't really sure.

Katie grimaced. "Something like that."

The tour lasted close to an hour with Maggie lagging behind in the kitchen to assimilate herself to it and Kristy and Katie chatting over pieces of furniture or New England folklore paintings. The staircase wall was cluttered with old photographs of Harrington family ancestors. Kristy knew who each one was and commented on them individually.

"I'm impressed," Katie commented as they continued their way upstairs.

Kristy smiled back at her. "I have a photographic memory," she said. "Apparently it extends not only to what I see but to what I hear as well."

Katie nodded. "I believe they call that audiographic."

"Really?"

Katie paused. "I think so."

Before Kristy left them, she suggested lunch at the one café in town. "Just head straight back up Main Street. When you cross Old Montpelier you'll see what used to be our general store on the left but is now our video store and café. It's called Darlene's, and you absolutely can't miss it. It's a white building with little white frilly curtains in the window. She serves marvelous homemade soups if you'd like that for a nice hot lunch."

"It sounds perfect," Katie responded, walking Kristy to the door. "Thank you again, Kristy. This means more to me than you can possibly know."

Kristy lifted her coat from the coat tree hook and slipped her arms into the sleeves. "Mr. Harrington told me you'd had a difficult month last month. No specifics, of course, but just to make sure you were well taken care of."

Katie looked around her. "I think we have everything we'll need. I imagine we're in for two weeks of winter quiet, don't you?"

Darlene's was easy to find. Then again, from the trek down Main Street, it appeared that everything in Sanford would be easy to find. After lunch Katie and Maggie decided to drive around and become better acquainted with life in Sanford, but after only a short time, they decided they were ready to return to the house and rest awhile.

Maggie, especially, was ready.

"You're tired, aren't you, Maggie?" Katie asked from the driver's seat.

"That I am, child. That I am. One would think just sitting in this seat all day wouldn't do that to me, but I suppose this old soul is getting on up there. Frightening sometimes."

Katie slowed the SUV to a stop in front of the house. She reached across and placed her gloved hand on Maggie's. "Why do you say that, Maggie?"

Maggie turned to look at her. Her eyes were watering just enough to show she was fighting tears. "I don't mind leaving this earth to be with my Lord," she said matter-of-factly. "But every night I pray that the Man upstairs will let me see my William one last time before I go."

Katie felt her own hot tears surfacing. "Oh, Maggie." Her hand rose and cupped the dear woman's soft, pale cheek, then ran along the silvery hair kept short and close to her head. "I miss him, too."

"Like my own son, he was."

"He'll come home, Maggs. I know he will."

Maggie inhaled deeply, turned her head, and looked straight ahead. "Then where is he now, child? It's been a long time since I held his hand in mine. A very long time."

Katie straightened. "I know, Maggs. Nineteen months. I don't want to give up, but sometimes. . ."

Maggie nodded. "I know. I know."

The two women remained silent, sitting with slumped shoulders and downcast eyes as the SUV hummed around them, enveloped in a cloud of smoke from the exhaust. Finally Katie said, "Let's go in, Maggie. We'll take a nap and dream about the moment we see him again. Dark and handsome. Your William. My Ben."

Katie stood along the side of a highway dominated by covered bridges. The road ribboned itself between hills and valleys until it finally disappeared between two snow-covered mountains that whispered her name.

She was cold, chilled to the bone, and she sought cover. Looking from the right to the left and back to the right again, she sprinted toward the first covered bridge. The sound of her heartbeat reverberated within her, keeping time with the thump-thump *of her feet against the pavement. When she'd finally reached the bridge, she slipped under the shelter of it, pressing her back against the wooden walls. She shoved her hands into the pockets of her jacket, hunching over to catch her breath.*

"Whooo," she said, letting out a deep breath.

She saw movement out of the corner of her eye, something at the far side of the bridge, and she jerked upright, turning to face it. Standing just under the archway, feet braced apart, hands at his side, was her husband.

"Ben!" she screamed, heading out in a dead run toward him.

But just as soon as she did, he was gone.

Katie slowed to a stop, then picked up the pace when her husband came into view in the archway of the next bridge up the road.

"Ben! Wait!"

"Come for me!" he shouted back at her, then disappeared again.

Katie ran toward where he had stood, stopping only when she'd reached the middle of the covered bridge. She gasped for breath, placing her hands on her thighs and again bending slightly forward.

The noise that began to surround her sounded like the creaking of a door. She cut her eyes first one way and then another, straightening. As the seconds passed, the creaking changed to a howl. She felt the boards begin to rumble beneath her, shaking violently as she tried to stumble to the safety of the road just beyond the light at the end of the bridge.

Instead, she fell to her knees. "Help me." The words were choked back in the farthest place of her throat. "Dear God, help me!"

It was her last moment of cognizance; a millisecond later, the bridge gave way, and she plummeted to the very pit of the earth.

CHAPTER SEVEN

The next two days were like heaven on earth for Katie. In the early mornings she dressed warmly, then stepped outside for a long walk. The air was clean, clear, crisp, and scented with wood-smoke from neighboring fireplaces. Her first morning there she headed toward the north end of town, past homes in every conceivable form of New England architecture and, for the sake of modern times, a convenience store where men driving pickup trucks had come for a morning cup of coffee. She shoved mittened hands deeper into her down jacket and marveled at how they were dressed—short-sleeved shirts without coats of any sort. Kristy had told her about this the day before. People in Vermont were acclimated to the frigid weather and dressed almost in rebellion. To go from the heated truck to the heated stores, they'd wear no coats. Once in their fields, they would, of course. But not until then.

From where she walked, she could see them gathering inside, standing in small clusters, a Styrofoam cup of steaming brew in one hand, the other tucked loosely into the pocket of their jeans.

She continued on past the store, deep in thought and prayer, walking steadily up a hill until she came to an old cemetery. She'd always enjoyed the antiquity of old gravestones and easily made her way past the wrought-iron gate that looked as though it hadn't been closed in years. For several moments she wandered around the old headstones and markers, reading aloud the names of the souls from Sanford who'd lived and worked there in another time. Some, another century.

It made her vastly aware of her own mortality. And of Maggie's. "Lord," she whispered, "don't take her anytime soon. Please. At least let her be here when Ben comes home."

As she turned to head back, she looked through the bare branches of the trees, down the hill, and to the still village below. Other than a lone SUV that had just driven past her, life was barely stirring. *How different from New York,* she thought. By this time the streets and sidewalks were crowded with people rushing from one place to another. Her eyes caught a picture of the columns of smoke rising from chimneys and illuminated by the bright sunlight. Eventually the smoke leveled off, caught and trapped by the warmer air holding the colder to the ground.

"Sometimes," she prayed in a whisper, "that's the way I feel, Lord. Leveled off, but trapped." She smiled weakly. "But You, Lord. You hold me to the ground. You keep me focused." Katie took a few breaths, thinking back to words from the Psalms she had read earlier. "As with David, You are my refuge and my fortress. You are the One I trust." Katie closed her eyes, then opened them again. "Thank You for this picture. Thank You for these next few days. I believe You will do something awesome here for me."

On her second morning Katie left the house a bit later and walked toward the center of the village.

"Maggie," she'd said the night before as they made their way up the staircase for bed, "I want you to promise me you'll sleep in. I'm going to the village for breakfast."

"You'll do no such thing."

Katie stood firm. "Oh, yes, I will. I want to. I want to experience life here and that includes breakfast at the café. Don't argue with me now." She grinned. "Remember who signs your paycheck."

Maggie humphed, then turned and walked into her bedroom.

Now Katie sat in the warm and intoxicating café, eating a full breakfast of two scrambled eggs, three to four slices of crispy bacon, four silver-dollar pancakes, and a small plate full of hash browns, which Katie hadn't eaten in so long she couldn't even remember when she'd had them last. She slathered them in ketchup and ate with her eyes closed more than open. This was like die-of-high-cholesterol heaven, and she wanted to savor every minute of it.

After paying her bill she slipped into her jacket, adjusted her fuzzy earmuffs, and headed back up Main Street toward the house. The sun was shining brightly against the freshly plowed snow; it glistened like splinters of undiscovered diamonds. Katie slipped her gloved fists into the pockets of her jacket, inhaled deeply, then exhaled in absolute exhilaration. She couldn't remember a time within the past year and a half when she'd felt more at peace.

She hurried across Old Montpelier, not because of traffic but more out of habit, then continued on down the sidewalk. A glance over to the real estate office revealed opened office window blinds. On a whim she crossed over, waving at Kristy, whom she could see sitting at her desk sipping on a cup of coffee. The Realtor nearly leapt from her desk, moving around it and toward the plank front door.

"Hello!" she called out, opening it wide. Katie immediately noticed the carefree way Kristy dressed—black slacks with an oversized red, black, and cream sweater—something Katie would have never seen in one of her offices back in the city. Kristy's curly dark hair was pulled back into a ponytail, caught with a red and black scrunchie. "Coffee?"

Katie stepped into the chilly office, pulled the earmuffs from her head, and smiled as Kristy shut the door behind her. "I was going to say 'no, I've had my fill,' but it's cold in here!"

Kristy laughed lightly. "I know. First-thing-in-the-morning blues. Would you like cream and sugar?"

"Please," Katie answered, sitting on the love seat, unzipping her jacket, and removing her gloves.

"Powdered cream okay?" Kristy asked with something that resembled a wince and a smile all together.

"Sure."

Kristy poured the coffee in a dark green mug and continued her conversation. "So where've you been this morning?"

"Darlene's. I overindulged on her house special breakfast and will probably berate myself the rest of the day, but it was worth it."

"Ayup. That Darlene can cook. Her husband George is known for his meat pies. Next time you're in there, ask for one of them." Kristy added the desired ingredients into Katie's coffee.

"I'll do that. I overheard one of the patrons saying they'd be back for pizza later. Pizza's good, I take it."

"Pizza is the best," Kristy confirmed as she handed the coffee mug to Katie, who took a sip while Kristy stepped back over to her desk to retrieve hers. It was then that Katie spotted a framed photograph of a young, impish-looking child of about seven or eight. "Your little girl?" she asked, nodding toward the image of bright eyes and long, curly brunette hair flecked with gold.

Kristy glanced over her shoulder as she made her way back to the sofa. "Mmm-hmm. Hailey. Miss Hailey Irene Hallman, if you ask her. Don't die over that middle name; it was my mother-in-law's, and Jonathan, my husband. . .my late husband. . .insisted on throwing it on the birth certificate."

Katie's eyes enlarged. In one brief moment she'd learned more about the woman than she knew about most of the people on her staff.

Kristy read the look on her face. "I'm sorry. I know I talk a lot, but I really don't have anyone here I'm close to, and sometimes I just tend to yak away." She smiled an endearing smile, and Katie felt the warmth of it.

"It's okay. I'm sorry about your husband."

"Yeah, me, too. It's lonely, you know?"

"Oh, yeah. I know. What. . .happened; if you don't mind my asking?"

Kristy shook her head no and took another sip of coffee. "Geesh, cold already." She stood and walked over to the small table and coffeemaker, topped off her cup, and continued. "Car accident. Actually, he and his mother were both killed. Jon's dad had jumped ship and run off before he was even born, and my family is out West so. . . It was almost six years ago. Hailey hardly remembers him." She gave a light shrug of her shoulder. "Actually, she doesn't remember him at all. She only remembers what she's heard and thinks she remembers it."

Katie placed her mug on the nearby end table and slipped out of her jacket, then retrieved the coffee with a shake of her head. "I'm so sorry."

"It's hard, you know? Raising a child on your own."

"But what about your family? Why not go to where they are? I mean, so you wouldn't have to go it alone?"

Kristy crossed one slender leg over the other. "Long story. We never really got along—my parents and I—and when I married the 'hick,' they disowned me."

Katie was stunned. "Come again? The 'hick?' "

Kristy laughed then. "My parents are well-to-do southern Californians. Dad is a plastic surgeon and Mother is a socialite. I hated every minute of my life out there and decided to go to school in Boston, which was fine by them. That's where I met Jon. He was the cousin of my roommate, and we fell head over heels in love the minute we saw one another." She paused for a moment. "Honestly, it was the fact that he was from a middle-class Vermont family that intrigued me most. How could I resist? A real slap in the face, huh? Well, I guess God paid me back big-time."

Katie frowned, knowing the story all too well. In her high school years she'd been in love with the guy from the wrong side of the tracks and had hated her upper-class lifestyle as much as anyone. But in the end, it wasn't about her family's social status; she had made her own poor choices. "I don't know, Kristy. God? Or are you punishing yourself?"

Kristy looked Katie directly in the eyes. "Good point. My pastor says the same thing. I guess I'd just rather believe that God is against me rather than that I am against me. God's wrath I may be able to survive, but I'm not sure about my own."

Katie leaned into the sofa. "Sometimes it's just life, you know? Sometimes it's not so much a matter of punishment as it is the natural progression of day after day, week after week, month after month, and year after year. Life."

The two women looked at each other for a moment, then simultaneously took sips out of their cups. "So who takes care of your daughter after school?"

Kristy seemed to glow. "Sweet Aunt Mitzi! A little darling if ever there was one. She's an older woman from the church. . .lives on a pension from her husband's 'days-o'-war,' as she calls it and seems to enjoy the little ones. The bus takes Hailey to her house, and then at the end of the day I come over and cook dinner for the three of us. That's all she charges me, too. Good thing, because it's all I can afford." She paused again. "So what about you? You married, Katie?"

"Where are we going?" the deep voice asked from the passenger's seat.

"Vermont."

He turned and looked at the driver. "Because?"

"You're going to have to trust me on this one. I know what I'm doing. I've never failed you before, and I'm not about to start now."

He turned to look out at flurries of snow dancing in the city air beyond the windshield. "Are we meeting someone there?"

The driver didn't answer.

"I said—"

"I heard you!" Then a more passive, "I heard you. Sorry, okay?"

"Okay."

"It's just that I don't know how to answer this right now. You've got to give me time; you've got to allow me to think. Okay?"

"Okay, then. Let's go."

CHAPTER EIGHT

Katie nodded almost imperceptibly. "Yes, I am."

"Your husband? He obviously isn't with you. Is he on business somewhere?"

Katie paused, almost unsure how to answer. "No," was all she said.

Realization crossed Kristy's face, albeit incorrect. "Oh."

Katie responded quickly. "Oh, no. No. My husband disappeared almost two years ago after a car bombing."

Kristy blinked. "How tragic. Oh. . .oh! The hotel guy?"

Katie looked down briefly, then back up at Kristy. "Yes." The coffee was leaving a bitter taste in her mouth, and she set the cup down.

"I don't know why this didn't connect sooner," Kristy said with a shake of her head. "I knew Mr. Harrington worked for a hotel, and I remember him telling me something about Mr. Webster some time ago. But I just didn't put the pieces of the puzzle together. Oh, Katie. I'm so sorry." She slapped her forehead. "Oh, geesh. No wonder you looked at me so funny when I asked you if you worked with Mr. H."

"It's okay. Technically I guess we do work together. It's just that my name appears on his paycheck. . .so to speak."

"Funny, he never mentioned that."

Katie didn't answer. She just breathed in and out, conscious of her own heartbeat.

"Can I get you some more coffee?" Kristy's voice was softer than before.

"No, no, thank you." Katie cleared her throat a bit. "So you see, I understand completely about being lonely."

"And about having to go to work."

Katie's brows knit together. The last thing she'd had to do was go to work. "Well, not exactly *had to*."

"But now you run the hotel? Have to or not."

"As best I can."

Kristy paused. "I remember reading in the paper. . .you believe your husband is in hiding."

"I do. I won't give up hope that he's coming back someday."

"Then I won't give up hope either."

Katie gave a faint smile. "Thank you."

"I can see it now. He'll come home, you'll run into his arms and hand over the keys to the executive washroom all in one swoop."

Katie cleared her throat again. "Something like that."

"You don't think?" Kristy leaned toward Katie ever so slightly.

"I rather like my job." She bit her lower lip and grinned. "But I'll certainly make a copy of that key and share the washroom with him."

Kristy laughed. "Ayup! The new American woman. I like you, Katie. Something tells me we have more in common than just being lonely at night."

Katie and Kristy chatted no more than another fifteen minutes before Katie stood and said, "I should let you get to work."

Kristy stood also and began to walk Katie to the door. "As you can see, the phone hasn't rung once. Most of what I do is take care of some of the rental property around here. . .businesses, farmland, etc. It's boring, but it's a job." She peered out the window. "Here comes the snow again."

Katie turned a bit to look over her shoulder. "My goodness. It's really starting to fall out there."

"Welcome to Vermont. You'd better get on back to the house. When it starts out this hard, it's really about to come down."

Katie nodded, reached for her jacket, and slipped into it, zipping it up to her throat. She then adjusted the earmuffs over her ears. "Thank you for the coffee."

Unexpectedly, Kristy reached over and hugged her. "Thank you for the visit." Kristy opened the door, and Katie stepped back into the gray blue day of severe snow flurries. She looked back at Kristy. "Wow," she mouthed, then grinned and began to cross the street.

She was barely out of eye-range of the realty office when she felt the pressure of the snowfall increase. She stopped just long enough to look up and ascertain the distance she would need to walk in order to make it back to the house where she imagined Maggie would be fretting. She frowned—it was farther than she wanted to admit—then began to walk again, unable to go at much of a pace. From somewhere below she could hear muffled crunching and squeaking of snow under her feet. A couple of times she slipped but didn't fall. She thought she heard something behind her and instinctively turned her head toward the village. Headlights in the distance attempted to cut through the white sheet of precipitation slicing across the village that had almost become a blur of occasional color. The mountains in the distance were no longer visible and attempting to find them only resulted in snowflakes against her eyes, making it even more impossible to see. She pushed her hands deeper into the jacket's pockets and turned back toward home. She was met full force with a gust of wind that knocked her backward and, this time, onto the sidewalk.

"Aaaaow!" she squealed as she went down, though no one could have heard her. Katie immediately pulled herself back up, aware the headlights were getting closer. She began the trek homeward again, brushing the snow from her backside in the process. From the corner of her eye, she could see the headlights as they met the part of the street where she walked. She cut a glance sideways. The car was a dark SUV, windows tinted and up. She stopped long enough to watch the window slide down, but she still had no clear picture of the driver.

Katie turned and kept going, in spite of the fact that she had little feeling in her feet and legs, aware that the SUV was edging ever so close to the sidewalk. She looked over again, narrowing her eyes against the whipping of the snow against her face. It stung.

A sound came from the vehicle, and she reached up and pulled the earmuffs off. "What?"

"I said, 'Do you need a lift?'" The voice belonged to a man.

Katie stepped closer to the passenger's side; the entire car seemed to be engulfed in white exhaust. "No, I'm almost there, thank you." She peered in. A handsome man of about thirty-five to forty sat in the driver's seat—the steering wheel in one hand and a steaming cup of coffee in the other—for all the world grinning at her.

"You sure? I saw you take that fall. Thought you might could use a ride, 'cause I know you're not from around here."

Katie gripped the upper portion of the windowsill exposed above the window shaft. "No. No, I'm not." She glanced up the street again. The house was no longer visible, and she wasn't sure if her phantom feet could make it. "Um. . ."

"I don't bite, I promise," the man said with a chuckle. "But if I do, I know a good doctor who can stitch you up."

Katie opened the door, sliding a bit as she lifted herself into the heated car. The window automatically rose upward. "Hi," she said, extending her hand. "I'm Katharine Webster."

The man grinned all the more, wrapping his warm hand around the wet glove that covered hers. "Katie, from the way I hear it."

Katie was taken aback, then remembered where she was. "Small towns."

"Gotta love 'em," the man added. "I'm Harrison Bynum. Mayor Harrison Bynum, if that helps to impress you any. And I believe you're staying at the Harrington house."

Katie nodded and the SUV proceeded north. "It's really just right there," she pointed.

"Yeah, I know." Harrison had an impish look on his face. His voice bordered on nasal, but it wasn't unattractive or annoying.

Katie adjusted herself a bit and looked forward. "I appreciate this. I really do. The snow started up so quickly."

"It'll do it. I'm glad I happened by."

Katie smiled. "Me, too. There. Right there. There it is."

Harrison slowed his SUV, edging it toward the curb. "Do I frighten you, Katie Webster?"

Katie turned to look at him as her hand reached out to grip the door handle. "*What?* No."

He chuckled again, looking back out the windshield.

"Thank you for the ride. Really. I appreciate it."

"Thank you for the entertainment," he said back at her. "Really. I appreciate it."

Katie paused. The man was mocking her but in a charming way. "Bye." She opened the door.

"Careful on the way up the steps. They get slippery fast."

"I will." She shut the door behind her and began a slow ascent to the front door of the house where Maggie waited with a stern look and an anxious heart.

CHAPTER NINE

"A hot bath for you." Maggie bustled ahead of Katie, up the staircase to the second floor landing. "What in God's good name were you thinking, going out there in the early morning, walking about like you know where you are?"

Katie knew a good scolding when she got one. "Oh, Maggie," she said with a laugh, forcing her numb feet upward.

Maggie stopped near the top of the stairs. "Don't you 'Oh, Maggie' me, my dear." She continued on until she reached the top floor and turned toward the bath where a claw-footed tub would be filled with a hot-water-and-milk bath. Katie was right behind her, already stripping out of her clothes.

"Yes, ma'am," Katie said with a lilt in her voice.

Maggie began the process of preparing the bath. "And looks to me from the telltale signs on your backside there that you took a bit of a fall."

Katie angled herself toward the mirror over the vanity. Sure enough, there was a large wet area against the dark color of her jeans. She unzipped and stepped out of them. "It's nice and warm in here." Clad only in her bra and panties, she stepped over to the basin and began to brush her teeth. "Food was good at the diner, Maggs, but not nearly as good as yours. Still, I enjoyed it."

"I don't want to hear about it."

Katie brushed a moment longer, spit, rinsed her mouth, and wiped it on a towel. When she turned, Maggie was twisting the faucets to the off position. Steam rose above the milky surface of the bathwater.

"You slip yourself under the comfort of this water, and I'll go fetch your robe. It's nearly time for lunch. Hope you're hungry."

Katie wasn't, but she wasn't going to push the issue. She was already in enough "trouble" with Maggie. She finished undressing and slipped into the water; it was pleasant and warming. "Mmm," she moaned, bending her knees and dipping herself up to her neck. Within minutes Maggie returned with a thick terrycloth robe, which she draped over the closed lid of the toilet.

"And just who was that you took a ride from?"

Katie rubbed her arms, allowing the milk bath to soften her skin. "Harrison Bynum. Nice guy. I really appreciate him coming along when he did."

Maggie frowned. "Could have been a mass murderer."

Katie giggled. "Oh, Maggs. Why would a murderer come to Sanford, Vermont?"

Katie had dressed, eaten lunch, and ordered Maggie upstairs for a nap while she read by the fireplace when a gentle knock sounded on to the front door. She put the current best-selling novel she'd sent Vickey out to buy for her before leaving the city on the sofa cushion beside her, uncurled herself, and walked to the front door, her stocking feet sliding against the hardwood floor.

She opened the door to find Harrison there, donned in a denim jacket and a warm smile. His blond hair was flecked with snowflakes and, peering around him, she saw that the weather had cleared a bit. "Hi," she said, taking a step back. "Come on in."

Harrison stepped in but not before wiping his boots on the front mat a few more times for good measure. "Hi, yourself. I hope you don't mind my stopping by like this."

"No." Katie closed the door behind him. "I was just reading by the fire. It's a good deal warmer there than outside on the sidewalk."

Harrison pulled off his denim jacket and hung it on the coat tree as though he'd done it a hundred times or more. He then turned and looked around, peering into the hominess of the living room. "This is a great house, isn't it? I grew up here; did you know that?"

"Here? In this house?" She began to walk toward the living room with him beside her.

"Well, sort of. My best friend's grandmother lived here, and every day after school we'd come here and eat her food. Great cook, that woman. So I *feel* as though I grew up in this place." He paused, looking over at her. "Mind if I ask you a question?"

"How tall am I?" She presented the forever-inquiry with a bright smile. "Just under six feet."

He nodded. "I was going to say that. I'm just a tad over six, and I can honestly say I've never looked a woman in the eye without looking down." He looked down then. "And in your stocking feet, no less."

Katie's toes curled a bit, and she blushed. "Would you like something to drink? Hot tea? Coffee?"

Harrison tilted his head in disappointed thought. "Um, no. That's not hitting the mark."

Katie raised her right index finger. "I brought some Ghirardelli Double Chocolate hot chocolate from New York. Does that hit the mark?"

"Whipped cream?"

Katie grinned as she turned toward the kitchen. "But of course. With chocolate shavings."

Harrison was right behind her. "I like chocolate shavings."

Katie and Harrison made their way into the kitchen, and Katie began the process of preparing hot milk on the kitchen's gas stove. "So to what do I owe this honor? Of your visit, I mean."

Harrison sat at the breakfast nook table as if, like he said, he'd been doing it all his life. "Just thought I'd make sure you got in okay. . .that you thawed out."

"Needed any extra medical attention? Like a healing to my pride?" Katie rubbed the upper half of her backside. "I'm going to be sore from the fall, I know."

"Poor thing." Harrison made a pouty face.

Katie gave a tiny smirk. "Very rude attitude for the mayor. Is that a full-time job?"

Harrison shook his head no. "Oh, no. I don't really get paid, if you want to know the truth of it. My full-time job is that I own the local hardware store."

"Really? A hardware-store-owning mayor?" Katie said with a giggle as she poured the hot chocolate into oversized mugs, dolloped whipped cream on one, and topped it off with some chocolate she'd shaved from a cocoa bar while waiting for the milk to heat. She brought the mugs over to the table where she handed one to Harrison, who said, "Thank you," as he stood.

"Would you like to go back to the living room?" Katie asked him.

"Sounds good."

They were quiet as they walked back into the living room. Katie glanced up the staircase ever so briefly, which caught Harrison's attention. "Someone here with you?"

Katie nodded, returned to her seat on the sofa, leaving the book on the cushion beside her as a gentle way of indicating she'd prefer Harrison not sit next to her.

He took the hint and sat in a nearby chair, stretching his legs out in front of him and crossing them at the ankles. "Who? A child?"

Katie shook her head no. "No. My housekeeper. She's getting on up in years, poor dear, and I'm forcing the afternoon nap issue. . .much to her British chagrin."

He nodded. "Well, then, tell me about Katie Webster."

Katie curled her feet up under her. "I wouldn't know where to start." She attempted to take a sip of her chocolate, but it was too hot so she blew gently against it, causing a small ripple across the frothy top.

"Let's start with the obvious. Is there a *Mister* Webster?"

She nodded. "Yes."

"He didn't come with you, though."

Katie looked into her mug. "No. My husband disappeared about a year and a half ago." She explained brief details of Ben's disappearance.

"Tell me more about him," Harrison requested in a kind voice.

Katie grinned. "Well, he's very tall."

"He'd have to be." There was a twinkle in Harrison's eyes.

Katie looked down, then back up. "And I believe he's alive."

"Why's that? Why continue to hope when you haven't heard anything. . .when you can't seem to even find a trace of him?"

"I. . .I have these dreams sometimes. Dreams about his return. . .dreams about him asking me to find him. . .dreams."

Harrison sat forward, leaned his elbows on his knees, and wrapped his tanned hands around the mug of half-consumed hot chocolate. "Well, I won't say that I'm not disappointed."

Katie's eyes widened. "Excuse me?"

Harrison laughed. "Pretty woman. . .alone on vacation. . .well, with the exception of a housekeeper. Okay. So maybe I got my hopes up. . .as a man and all. But let's backtrack. Nothing saying we can't be friends. . .at least while you're here."

"I should say not."

"So, then. Employed?"

"Yes."

"Specifics please." Harrison took another gulp of his drink.

"I'm the president and CEO of The Hamilton Place chain of hotels. My office is located in New York City. Midtown."

"Oh, I see. I'm impressed." Katie gave him a doubtful look, and he laughed. "No, no. I really am impressed. It's not as good as being the mayor of Sanford, but then, hey—what is?"

"What about you? Obviously not married or you wouldn't have been here trying to pick up a virtual stranger."

Harrison pounded at his chest. "Oh, that hurts. That really wounds me," he said in jest, then sobered and stood, walking over to the fireplace where he picked up the poker and stabbed at the logs a few times. He placed the mug of hot chocolate on the mantel, squatted down, and added another piece of wood from a nearby basket to the fire, then rested there for a moment before looking back at Katie. "No, not married. But I have been. . .to a wonderful woman. . .the love of my life. She was diagnosed with inoperable cancer not too long after our son was born."

"Oh, Harrison. I'm so sorry."

"Yeah, me, too. But I have a great little boy."

"What's his name?"

"Matthew."

"Age?"

"Six."

"Good age."

"Great age. Wants to grow up and be the mayor like his old pop." Harrison grimaced. "Well, that or postman or a football player or a fireman. One day he came home and said he wanted to grow up to be tourist. I said, 'A tourist?' and he said, 'Yeah, like I want to be paid to go to Disney. And Dad,' he said, 'have you ever noticed that tourists always have money?'" Harrison ended with a laugh, and Katie laughed with him, then he sobered as he sighed deeply. "But he's a great kid. His mother would be so proud."

"I'm sure you've done a marvelous job."

Harrison looked down at his watch. "Well, I gotta be going." He slapped his hands on his knees and stood. "Matthew will be home from school shortly."

Katie stood. "They didn't close the school on a day like today?"

"Oh, no. This kind of thing happens all the time, and if they closed the school every time it snowed, it'd just about never be open."

Katie chuckled. "I see." She led Harrison to the door and watched him slide into his jacket. "Thank you for the hot chocolate," he said quietly.

"Thank you for the company. Meeting new people is always nice."

Harrison reached for the doorknob, turned it, and opened the door just a bit before turning back to Katie. "Would you like to meet him?"

"Who?"

"My son. Matthew. You two would really hit it off, and I'm sure we could throw something together and make it look like dinner. Would you like to come over for dinner? Tonight?"

Katie opened her mouth to say no, but something caught in her heart. *The man is lonely. . .face it, so are you. Just say yes. He knows you're married. He doesn't seem like the type to take advantage of the situation. . . .*

"Say yes. Come on. Say yes."

Katie nodded, lips folded together in a smile. "Yes. I'd love to have dinner with you and Matthew. What time?"

"Pick you up at seven?"

"Seven is good."

Harrison grinned like a young man who'd finally gotten the nerve to ask the high school yearbook queen out to the prom and had been accepted. "See you at seven," he said, then opened the door and stepped out onto the bitter cold of the front porch before turning back. "Take care."

Parked just down the street from the house, the driver found the departing guest to be an interesting one.

He was a handsome enough man. And he'd stayed long enough for. . .a lover perhaps?

Katie Webster had come to Vermont to meet her lover. Was that it? Was that why she seemed so eager to leave the city?

What other schemes was she up to? Perhaps she was planning to do more than be interim president of THP. Perhaps she was planning to have her husband declared legally dead.

Perhaps, perhaps, perhaps. . .

The driver drummed fingers along the center console of the car. Too many questions; not enough answers. More work was needed. Perhaps.

"Perhaps, perhaps, perhaps. . ."

CHAPTER TEN

To say that Maggie was upset at Katie's dinner invitation was putting it mildly, but she somehow managed to keep her emotions to a silent stew.

Katie sat at the vanity of one of the guest rooms she'd chosen for herself. In spite of James's insistence, she'd been unable to use the master bedroom. It was sacred, in a way. A place where James and Julia were husband and wife and to even think about sleeping in their bed made her all the more lonely for Ben. "Maggie," she said, turning from the mirror and facing the woman who stood behind her, adjusting the clothing she'd laid on the bed for her evening out. "I know where this attitude of yours is coming from. But look. . .Maggie, I told Harrison about Ben. We're just two adults having dinner with a six year old. Now how much harm can that be?"

Maggie huffed in disapproval. "Well, Miss Katie, if you don't know, it wouldn't do me any good to tell you."

She started for the door until Katie's words halted her. "Maggie." Maggie turned. "You know, I've talked to two people today who lost their spouses at an early age. This isn't such a big place that this much sadness should be told to me twice in one day."

"Is there a point?"

Katie shook her head no. If Maggie didn't understand what she was thinking, then it didn't do any good to go there. Maggie's allegiance was with Ben, and in her mind Katie was stepping away from her vows and commitments. Katie watched Maggie walk out, and she looked down to her knees and folded her hands, speaking in a whisper to God who she knew was just a breath away. "Am I wrong, Lord? Am I breaking a vow?" She paused. "I'm so lonely. Is it wrong to be so lonely?" She remembered her pastor saying that during his earthly ministry, Jesus had also experienced every emotion man ever felt. "Did You feel lonely, too?" Again she paused, waiting for the still, small voice to resonate within her. *Like you wouldn't believe. . .thousands of people all around do not fill every gap. I longed for My Father. . .and the day we'd be together again.*

Katie nodded. "I know," she whispered back. "I know."

Katie chose a turtleneck dress with boots for her dinner. Harrison arrived promptly at seven. Rather than have him come in and meet Maggie, who in turn might hurt his feelings in some way, she stepped out onto the front porch as soon as his SUV pulled up next to the curb. She knotted the belt of her full-length wool coat and stepped to the end of the porch just as he reached the steps.

"Wow, don't you look nice?" he complimented, reaching a hand toward her to help guide her down the steps.

"I'm hoping to impress Matthew," she said, slipping her ungloved hand in his gloved one.

They walked toward the SUV, no longer holding hands, and Katie grinned at the cherub straining at the neck to see her from the backseat. "I take it that's Matthew."

Harrison paused briefly, cocking his head to look to the back of his car. "Um. . .no. No, that's not Matthew. That's just some kid I saw on the side of the road. He's cute, huh?"

Katie slapped him on the back of his shoulder. "I can see

right now I'm going to have a problem with you."

Harrison laughed, reaching the passenger door and opening it for her. Katie leaned in, peeked her head around the back of the seat, and smiled at the towheaded child, who was an exact replica of his father and who sat on his hands, tucked just under his jeaned thighs. "You must be Matthew."

"Yeah. You must be Mrs. Webster."

Katie stretched her arm for a handshake. "Nice to meet you, Matthew."

A tiny hand in a maroon mitten came out from under one of his legs for the handshake. "Nice to meet you, Mrs. Webster."

As soon as the trio walked through the front door of Harrison's restored nineteenth-century farmhouse, they were met by two golden retrievers, who greeted them as though they'd been away a lifetime. They welcomed Katie with warm breath and tails that zigged while the rest of their bodies zagged.

The whole scene made Matthew giggle. While his father removed first his own coat and then Matthew's, Katie knelt down to play with the pups, all the while looking Matthew in the eye. "Who do we have here, Matthew?"

Matthew pointed first to one dog and then to the other. "This is Sam and this is Dixie."

"Oh, I see. Are they husband and wife?"

Matthew nearly doubled over with laughter as Harrison began to pull his coat off his shoulders and down his arms. "Um, Katie," Harrison said, clearing his throat. "Sam and Dixie are both girls."

Katie pressed her lips together and wiggled her eyebrows at Matthew, then stood. "Oops," she mumbled, then placed her hands firmly on her hips. "Wait a minute. A girl named Sam?"

"It's short for Samantha," Matthew informed her.

"I understand," she said, now coming out of her own coat. "You see, my name is Katharine, but my friends call me Katie."

Matthew took her by the hand and began to drag her down the center hallway. "Come on, Katie," he said. "I'm going to show you my trucks."

Dinner was hamburgers, oven-baked French fries, dill slices, steamed broccoli, and for dessert, chocolate cake. The three dinner companions sat around the oak pedestal kitchen table, eating and chatting as though they'd known one another for years. Sam and Dixie sat curled at the base of the table, content just to be in the presence of the warm kitchen.

"Who's your best friend at school, Matthew?" Katie asked, picking up a dill slice and bringing it to her mouth.

"Yeah, tell Mrs. Webster about your best friend," Harrison urged.

Matthew blushed, then rubbed his hands over his face. "Oh, Daaaaaad."

Katie looked from son to father and back to son again, who now beamed his face upward toward the brass lantern lamp that hung over the table, shedding what little light the dark kitchen afforded. "I'm curious now, Matthew. Who is your best friend?"

Again, Matthew rolled his eyes. "Tell you what, Matthew," Katie coaxed. "I'll tell you about my best friend if you tell me about yours."

"Okay," the child said, straightening in his seat, looking only minutely taller than he had the moment before.

"You go first."

"Her name is Nichole."

Katie's eyes widened with her smile as she glanced over to the boy's obviously proud father. "That's my boy," he said, pointing a speared stem of broccoli toward his son.

"I'll bet she's pretty. Is she pretty?"

More giggling. "Yeah."

Harrison interrupted, speaking to his son about cleaning his plate before there would be any dessert.

For Katie their voices seemed to fade down a dark tunnel. *I should have had children of my own,* she thought. *But you stole that from me, David Franscella. You took that from me the night you beat me senseless. And for what? Because I was carrying your child, that's for what.* Katie pressed her lips together and tried to smile at the conversation she could see but not hear across from her. *Ben always said we could adopt. Why didn't I listen to him? If he ever. . .when he. . .returns. . .I swear, I'll talk to him about it, God. I swear. If You'll just bring him home to me. . .*

"Katie?"

Katie started. "Oh! Sorry, I was just. . .well, I was deep in thought here. What were you saying?"

"Matthew said it was your turn to tell us about your best friend."

"Oh. Well. Hold on to your hats because this girl is for the records. . . ."

"And then I told them about you." Katie spoke low into the telephone. As soon as she'd slipped into the warm quiet of her temporary home, she'd slid her boots off and tiptoed up the stairs. She moved without a sound down the hardwood floor of the long hallway and into her bedroom, closing the door softly behind her. She padded over to the bed where she sat curled in the middle between the collection of pillows with her back resting against them and then dialed Marcy's home in Georgia from her cell phone.

Marcy had been sleeping, but it didn't take her long to shake the sleep from her brain and take the cordless phone from the bedroom she shared with her husband Charlie into the upstairs office where she wrote a weekly column for the *Savannah Morning News.* "I cannot believe you actually went out on a date," she spoke in hushed tones into the phone, wrapping a little more snuggly in the small quilt she'd pulled from the end of her bed on her way out.

"It wasn't a date."

"Uh-huh. Who are you talking to here?"

"Marcy." Katie ducked her chin. "It really wasn't a date/date."

"Wasn't it just the other day that you told me you were lonely?"

Katie picked at a loose thread on the jacquard comforter. "I don't remember saying anything like that."

"You didn't have to. I could read it in your voice."

Katie paused. "I am lonely, Marce."

"I know." The words came soft and sweet.

"I'm ready for Ben to come home. . .if he's coming."

"Are you beginning to doubt?" Marcy rubbed her eyes just a bit, then looked over at the digital clock on one of the bookshelves. Nearby rested a dusty photograph of Katie and her, taken when they were children. It was now nearly midnight.

"Maybe. I don't know. Maybe it's time I quit looking in the past and start looking to the present. Never mind the future. I've got to catch up, if you know what I mean. Do you know what I mean? Crazy. I don't even know what I mean. I don't know. I don't know. I don't know." Katie all but moaned.

"Katie, tell me what you're thinking right now. Exactly. Don't hold back."

Katie took a deep breath and sighed as she squirmed around to pull the comforter from under her and then wiggle herself up under it. She laid her head back against the coolness of the pillows. "I'm thinking that he's a nice man."

"Who are we talking about here?"

"Harrison."

"Oh."

"And he has a sweetheart of a son. And if I were not married, I could see myself getting totally involved here. But I am married. Married and lonely because I don't know where my husband is or even if he's. . ." Katie trailed off toward the obvious.

"Alive."

"Yes."

"How did the date end?"

"It wasn't a date, Marcy. It was just dinner. Two adults and one child having hamburgers and chocolate cake."

"Oh. Okay. So how did the evening end?"

Katie turned her face into the pillow, then back out. "It still sounds like a date the way you say it."

"Katie. You're stalling."

"Okay, okay. It just ended. He put Matthew to bed, we talked for awhile longer in the kitchen while we. . .uh. . ." Another deep sigh. ". . .cleaned up."

"How very domestic."

"Stop it."

"Go on."

"And then we talked for awhile longer in the living room. . . different chairs. . .and he talked about how good I was with Matthew and asked why I didn't have any children of my own."

"What'd you tell him?"

"I didn't tell him the truth. I didn't tell him that when I was a dancer, I'd had an affair with a man who beat me senseless when he learned I was carrying his child, thereby eliminating any chance I'd ever have for conception."

"Of course not." Silence. "So what did you tell him?"

"Just that Ben and I hadn't been married that long when he disappeared."

"Good answer. And then what happened?"

"And then his neighbor came over to watch Matthew while he brought me home." She exhaled. "The end."

"Nah-ah. Then what?"

"Then he walked me to the door, said, 'Thank you for a lovely evening,' shook my hand, and that really, really is the end."

"No kiss?"

Katie sat up straight. "Marcy, of course not! Even if I weren't married, I'm not into kissing on the first date. Where is your sense of morality?"

Marcy didn't answer for a few moments, then asked, "So what do *you* think *he's* thinking right now?"

Katie had to be honest. She couldn't be anything but honest with Marcy; if she weren't, Marcy would know anyway. "That he wishes I weren't married."

"Bingo."

"It's just that he's so lonely and he's a really nice man and. . . you know, Marcy? He's the second single parent I talked with today. Kristy Hallman, the Realtor, is a young widow with a little girl, and she and I talked about the loneliness, then not a few hours later I'm having nearly the same conversation with Harrison." There was no return on the other end of the phone. "Now what are *you* thinking?"

"I'm singing the words to 'Eleanor Rigby' in my head."

Katie giggled. "I'm tired; I'm not sleeping all that well."

"How come?"

"I've been having a lot of those dreams again."

"The ones about Ben?"

"Yeah. The last one was horrible. I. . .I don't really want to talk about it. . .I just had to talk to you. . .had to share all this with someone. I know I was walking a thin line tonight, but please don't judge me, Marcy."

"I won't." Another pause. "What are you doing tomorrow?"

"I don't know. Rest some more. There's a video store here, and I thought I might go rent some movies, pop some popcorn, and just watch movies all day."

"Just take my advice and don't go renting anything mushy like *Sleepless in Seattle*. You don't need that kind of pressure."

Katie giggled again. "*Sleepless* is out. Hey."

"Yeah?"

"On that note, you get some sleep, and I'll call you soon."

"Sounds like a plan."

CHAPTER ELEVEN

"Where are you, Mrs. Webster?"

The dream was beginning again. . .the one she'd had a month or so ago. The one that began with a moment she and Ben had actually shared.

Her sleeping form twisted under the mounds of covers.

> *"Hmmm?"*
> *"I asked you where you were. . .walking along all starry-eyed and dreamy."*

Katie attempted to subconsciously remind herself that this was a dream. . .*déjà vu*. . . and asked herself why she was dreaming it again.

> *"Somewhere between reality and the place where dreams are made."*

Everything remained the same. . .the path they walked, the sunlight spilling through the trees, the way Ben kissed her. . .gently at first, then more amorously. The same burst of sunlight winked at her from beyond the tree branches.

"Where did you learn to kiss like that, Mr. Webster?" she asked.

"What was her name?" he teased, as he had done before.

They laughed, then Ben told her about the chalet in France. "As it turns out, a friend of mine has the most charming little chalet near the Lötschen Valley. . . ."

"Where is that?"

"It's part of the Swiss Alps."

Katie again felt as though she were about to burst. "Are you serious? You're taking me to the Swiss Alps for Christmas?"

"Don't forget about the little chalet."

Katie stopped in their walk again and turned to face her husband. "Ben, I know you. When you say 'little,' it's big. But I don't care about that. I've never seen the Alps." She clapped her hands for effect. "I'm going to the Alps! I'm going to the Alps!"

Ben laughed again. "Okay, hold my hand and walk with me. I'll tell you the truth."

Katie frowned. "The truth? You aren't taking me to the Alps?"

"Yes, sweetheart, I'm taking you to the Alps. I want to tell you the truth about the little chalet."

"Oh."

They began to walk—just as they had done before—and Katie listened to her husband as he described the place he would be taking her. "You'll be so impressed. It truly is perfect. Perfect for healing from emotional bruises and things like that."

"And Christmas holidays?"

"Most especially Christmas holidays. It's very French Country. Stone fireplaces and hearths and polished stone floors with scattered rugs. Louis Philippe furniture. Fantas-

tic tapestries and a kitchen filled with lots of baskets hanging from the ceiling."

"I love it already."

"You will love it more when you see it. The countryside is breathtaking, Katie. In the morning, if we wake up early enough, we can sit outside and sip on hot French coffee and watch the sun rising over the lake behind my friend's place."

"A lake?"

"A fantastic lake. Mist on the water. . ."

"It sounds magical."

"It is. In the distance, you can hear the cowbells echoing up through the valley."

Katie stopped walking and turned to her husband. "Take me there, Ben. Take me there now."

She closed her eyes. Cupping her face in his hands, Ben kissed her again. Again and again and again until she was breathless from the sheer pleasure of it. His lips traced a line from her mouth to her eyes and finally to her ear where he whispered something to her in French. . . something she couldn't quite make out in the feathery softness of it.

She kept her eyes closed as she asked, "What?" Her voice was nearly inaudible and—this time—her heart pounded, desperate to understand what she was being told.

He said it again.

"I don't understand," she whispered back, tears spilling down her cheeks.

"Yes, you do." He spoke into her ear, nibbling here and there as he made love to her with his words.

"No. No, I don't understand."

"Listen. Listen with your heart, not your ears."

He released her face, took a step back from her, said the words a third time.

"Cherche-moi toujours."

This time Katie heard him clearly, something she'd never done before. Katie's breathing was slow and steady as she deciphered the words. "I won't stop looking for you, Ben," she whispered, then became aware of the stillness and silence around her. She opened her eyes.

He was gone. He was gone, and she stood alone on a small country lane leading nowhere.

CHAPTER TWELVE

The following morning Katie ate her breakfast at home.

"I'm going to the village in a little bit, Maggs."

"Whatever for this time?" Maggie sat on the other side of the small square table, sipping at a cup of tea and poking at a bowl of cinnamon oatmeal.

"I thought I'd pick up some videos for us today. Let's just have a day of movies, okay? Just the two of us? Pop popcorn? We can rent some classics."

"Whatever you say."

Katie dropped her spoon into her bowl of oatmeal. "Maggie, please don't act like this."

Maggie stood and walked resolutely toward the sink, taking her untouched bowl of hot cereal with her. "I don't know what you're talking about."

Katie stood as well, then made her way over to the woman who was more than just an employee and wrapped her arms around her from behind. "Maggie. I'm sorry. Please don't be angry with me." Katie felt a fallen tear from Maggie's cheek plop against her forearm. "Oh, Maggie," she whispered.

"I just don't want you to forget my William." The voice was strained.

"I haven't forgotten Ben, Maggie. How could I?" She nuzzled Maggie's neck.

"By having dinner with other men, that's how."

Katie smiled. The strength had returned to Maggie's voice within a flash. She released her grip and turned Maggie to face her. "I have to make these decisions on my own, Maggs. I even have to be the one to make some mistakes along the way. I'm not a baby, you know. I'm a grown woman with wants and needs, and I think I've earned the right to make my own choices. Don't you?"

Maggie turned to look out the side window. "No," she said firmly, but then she smiled.

Katie put her arm around Maggie again, tugging at her to leave the kitchen. "Come on, Maggie. Go sit in the living room and read the paper while I clean up a bit in here."

"You'll do no such thing."

"I will, too. And then," she added as she and Maggie stepped through the doorway, "I will get dressed and go to the video store and bring back something classic and wonderful in black and white."

"I'm not sure we've any popcorn," Maggie said as they walked down the hallway.

They turned into the living room. "Then I'll go to the store and buy some."

Maggie stopped and looked at her charge. "Independence is certainly becoming on you, you know," she commented with a light touch of her finger to Katie's nose.

Katie leaned down and brushed her nose against Maggie's. "You don't say. . ."

When Katie stepped out the front door she was surprised to see Harrison's SUV parked and running idle a few feet from the front of the house and against the curb on the opposite side of the road. She paused at the top of the front porch steps, waved, then took the snow-shoveled steps one at a time. The tinted driver's window was up, and Harrison's silhouette was difficult to make out, but she was certain he had his face turned toward her.

"Hi!" she called out; a puff of condensation blew back into her face as she continued across the lawn.

Just then the SUV seemed to jerk to life and drove toward the village, leaving Katie to stand in the middle of the shoveled sidewalk, her arms outstretched to half-mast, wondering what she might have done wrong.

"Stupid, stupid, stupid," Katie muttered to herself as she strolled toward the village. "You've obviously offended him. You came here to relax and in the process you have upset Maggie *and* a nice man who didn't deserve this kind of open-heart surgery in any form or fashion." She breathed heavily, realized she was stomping more than walking, and changed her pace. "Oh, Lord, why did I ever get in that SUV? Why didn't I just crawl back to the house?" Katie stopped for a moment, crossed her arms over her abdomen, and squeezed. If she weren't so strong, she'd cry, and she knew it.

"But I am strong. I'm strong and I'm the president of THP, for heaven's sake. Ughhh!" She continued in her walk, keenly aware of the light traffic, even around the center of the village. She looked at her watch. It was nearing ten o'clock.

The village's video store was located on the back half of Darlene's café. As Katie walked up the three steps leading to the front door and entered, she could smell the leftover aromas of this morning's breakfast. Scattered about the tables were a few older patrons, who were lingering over cups of coffee and fresh pastries. Katie inhaled deeply, wishing she'd spent a little more time with the bowl of oatmeal Maggie had served at home. Her stomach rumbled, and she stopped midway through the restaurant, wrestling with her physical needs and common sense to grab two or three videos and vamoose. Still, she convinced herself, what would one cup of coffee and a piece of toast hurt? She took the seat at the table nearest her, facing the door, and was immediately met by Darlene, who today wore jeans, a long-sleeved flannel shirt, and a rectangular white apron around her waist.

"Good morning, Darlene." Ben had taught Katie long ago that the most proper way to treat those who wait on you is the way you'd want to be treated were you in the same station in life. It wasn't too much of a stretch of the imagination for Katie. She'd been in supposedly lower stations than waiting tables and slinging hash browns for a living.

"Morning." Darlene was just as chipper and friendly as she'd been the day before. "What can I get you this morning?"

"Just a cup of coffee."

"That's it?" Darlene looked over the rims of her glasses. "Are you going to sit there and tell me you didn't enjoy your breakfast yesterday?"

Katie laughed. "No, I'm just trying not to overdo on the calories."

"Little thing like yourself? How about some eggs and hash browns?"

Katie wrestled a bit more with her conscience. "Mmm, no. But I will settle for an English muffin with some jelly."

Darlene smiled. "You got it. Be right back with the coffee."

Katie passed the minute and a half by adjusting the napkin holder on the table and then looking around the room, noticing it more this morning than she had during her visit from the day before. Before she'd only been interested in the food, a delicacy she would not allow herself to indulge in today. No matter how disappointed Darlene appeared to be.

Darlene's was a comfortable place decorated in country blue-and-rose-striped wallpaper. A strip of wainscoting, painted white like the trim of the large, single-paned windows, was topped with a coordinating wide border. Crisp white valances that hung in thick pleats and dropped low on either side flanked the windows. There were approximately twenty dark wood, four-person tables, draped in white linen and set off with Colonial bent-arm chairs. They were hard for sitting but perfect for resting one's elbows while waiting.

"Katie?"

Katie turned to look over her right shoulder. "Hello."

"I thought that was you. Mind if I join you?" Before Katie could say yes or no, Harrison Bynum sat in the chair opposite her. When he was comfortable, he looked over at Darlene who was already approaching with an empty mug and a pot of freshly brewed coffee. "Ah, my favorite gal," Harrison flirted innocently.

Darlene smiled at him, setting the mug on the table and filling it with dark, steaming liquid. "How is our little Matthew, Mayor Bynum?" she asked casually.

"Great. He's great, Darlene. Ask Katie here. She came over and had dinner with us last night."

Darlene looked from Harrison to Katie and back to Harrison again. "Is that right?"

Katie sat motionless, lips pressed together and eyes locked on Harrison's face.

"Ayup. We had a great time, but don't go reading anything into it, now. Mrs. Webster and I are friends and only friends. But Matthew really enjoyed meeting her."

At that Katie finally looked up at Darlene, who was now looking back at her, and smiled, though only with her eyes.

"More coffee, Mrs. Webster?"

"No. No, thank you." She looked back at Harrison, who was

grinning. When Darlene left the table, Katie spoke firmly. "What was that about?"

"What?" The dimples in Harrison's cheeks deepened.

Katie shook her head lightly. "I'm confused."

He took a sip of his coffee. "About what?"

"You. This morning. . ." Katie trailed off, waiting for an explanation. When she got none, she reiterated, *This morning? When I was walking toward you?*"

Harrison clearly was taken aback. "When was this? I've been out at the Bakers' farm since about six o'clock. Mr. Baker needed some extra plywood for his new barn, and I told him I'd take it out to him," he said by way of explanation.

Katie reached for her cup of coffee, then set it back down. "You weren't in front of the house a half hour ago?"

"No."

"You're sure?"

"Katie, come on. A man knows when he's parked outside a woman's house. Besides, I haven't done that kind of thing since high school. Now just what are you talking about?"

Katie looked around for a bit and then shook her head for good measure. "Forgive me. I'm sorry; I just assumed it was you. When I walked out of the house to come down here, I saw a car that, I swear, was just like yours. I thought it was you, and when I walked toward it, the driver suddenly sped away. I mean. . .as fast as one can speed on these icy roads."

"Probably just someone who had parked long enough to look at a road map. The driver probably never saw you."

Katie drained the last of her coffee and stood. "I've got to get moving here." Harrison stood with her. "I promised Maggie a day of old movies and popcorn."

Harrison nodded. "Well," he said. It was all he said. Then, "Maybe I'll call you later."

Katie smiled. "Do that." She took a step toward the back of the store. "And tell Matthew I said hello, okay?"

Armed with *Casablanca, Bringing Up Baby, Random Harvest,* and a box of microwave popcorn, Katie began her walk back up Main Street toward the house. Passing in front of the realty office, she looked over for signs of Kristy in the front office. Apparently she was not in, so Katie pointed herself northbound with her arms by her side, one hand carrying a small plastic bag from Darlene's. The snow from the day before had been plowed from the sidewalk and made little glistening, slushy mountains that peaked and rolled on either side of her. Beneath her feet, the cement squeaked under her snow boots. The air was clean and crisp, and she breathed deeply. . .happy that this day would be a good day. . . a relaxed day. . .a day of old videos and popcorn and Maggie, whom she seemed to pray for constantly.

"Lord," she whispered aloud, closing her eyes but continuing to walk, "if not for me, for Maggie. Bring Ben home, Lord."

When her eyes opened, she was near enough to the house to see the SUV she'd seen earlier, again parked outside her home, this time to the curb closest to it. The veil of smoke emitting from its tailpipe indicated it was sitting idle. Katie stopped, her breath catching in her chest. The last time she'd approached the vehicle, it had sped off. This time. . .

No sooner had Katie tried to ascertain her plan then the car jerked into gear and, once again, drove northward.

The SUV slowed considerably after passing the old cemetery on the right side of the road. The driver hadn't even bothered to look back, to see whether or not Katie Webster had noticed the car.

Katie Webster. What an enigma. Why had she walked over earlier this morning, waving and almost displaying a sense of welcome? Was she clueless? Or had she mistaken the car for someone else's?

Yes, that was it. That had to be it. She was not a stupid woman, not by a long shot. So clueless wasn't the issue.

Then again, what was about to happen to her would escape even *her* wildest dreams.

CHAPTER THIRTEEN

Katie and Maggie watched a movie, had lunch, then both decided to take naps followed by more movies. Katie walked into her bedroom, an adequately sized room tastefully decorated in a soft floral print that extended from the comforter of the bed to the wallpaper and draperies, which hung royally from two windows against the street-side wall. She shut the bedroom door behind her, walked over to the closer of the two windows, slipped her hand behind the sheer lace curtain and twisted the blinds shut. She then moved almost methodically to the other to do the same, this time peering outside before shutting off the outside world.

Everything was calm. The snow had stopped falling the day before and now blanketed everything in a shimmering white. The branches of the trees strained under the weight of it, lending themselves to a picture of yielding to the power of nature. The very thought made Katie sad in one respect and empathetic in another. They bent, but they did not break. She sighed, then twisted the rod of the blinds.

There was a small radio/CD player in one corner of the room, atop a small round table. Next to the player were several CDs, and while she hadn't bothered to look at them yet, she did so now. Going through the selection of ten or so, she found a collection of instrumental classics such as "Clair de Lune" and "Jesu, Joy of Man's Desiring." Katie opened the case, extracted the CD, and placed it into the player. Within seconds the sweet sound of ethereal music filled the room.

Katie pulled off her sweatshirt and jeans, laying them across the padded bed bench, then snuggled herself into a long zippered robe and climbed into the bed, burrowing herself under the covers. She closed her eyes and allowed the dark and the music to wash over her. . .helping her drift into a world of dreams.

"Katie?"

"Mmm?"

"Are you awake?"

Katie opened her eyes slowly, allowing the room to come into view. The flowers on the wallpaper seemed to pirouette like music box dancers. She squinted her eyes for a moment, watched them curtsey, then stand still. The room slipped from light to dark and back to something in between. She felt more than heard a movement at the window, and she jerked her head toward it. "Who's there?"

"Sweetheart. . ."

Katie sat erect. "Ben?" She faced the window in front of her; saw his masculine frame silhouetted against it. "Ben." She held out her arms, but he didn't walk toward her.

"Did you look for me?" he asked.

Her arms dropped. "Yes. Ben, please come to me." She extended her arms again. "I want to see your face. . .to hold you. . . ."

"I can't just yet."

"Why not?"

"Soon."

"When?"

"Soon. When everything is right."

"Everything is right. Everything is perfect. And, Ben, I'm worried about Maggie."

"Maggie will be fine." He turned his head ever so slightly, and she realized then that his back was to her. "I love you."

"Oh, Ben. I love you, too."

"Then look. . ."

"I don't know what else to do." Katie scrambled to her knees; the covers pooled at her knees.

"Look."

"Where?" She edged a bit forward. Perhaps if she could just touch him. . .

"Je suis ici. I am here."

It seemed then that he stepped through the window and into the world beyond. Katie jumped to reach for him but fell to the floor instead.

"Oomph!" Katie hit the floor with a thud, her breath momentarily knocked from her chest. She struggled, pushing herself up by her forearms, gasping for air until it came in short, hard waves. As it steadied, she began to cry, though she wasn't sure if it was because of the dream or the pain of falling out of bed. She sat back against the end of the mattress, her knees up around her chest and her elbows resting on them, and wiped her face with her fingertips. She sniffled once. . .twice for good measure. . .then stood and walked over to the bedside table for a tissue.

She blew her nose, daintily at first then with more force, almost in anger. She tossed the tissue in the nearby wastebasket and rested her hands on her hips. The digital clock told her it was just a little after three in the afternoon. She should get Maggie up. They would watch another movie, eat some popcorn, and she'd forget about the dream.

"Je suis ici."

The words hung in the air as Katie turned slowly toward the window where, in the dream, her husband had stood. Her eyes were hooded as she took it in. "Where?" she whispered, then walked over to the window and separated one blind from the others.

Her breath caught in her throat.

There it was.

The SUV.

Katie's bare feet dashed down the stairs, her hand dragging alongside her on the banister. She had to hurry. . .it didn't matter if she became a solid mass of ice from frostbite; this was Ben and she knew it.

She jerked the front door open, running out on the front porch. The SUV was sitting idle again, against the opposite curb, facing the village. "Ben!" Katie shrieked. She darted down the steps, oblivious to the cold air that sliced through the thickness of her robe, piercing her feet and knifing its way up her legs. "Ben!"

She saw the silhouette of the driver turn toward her. She wouldn't let him get away. Not this time. She didn't bother to glance up and down the street. There was never any traffic anyway. She ran straight across the road, grabbing for the door handle as the car, again, shuddered to life and pulled away.

Katie wasn't giving up. She ran alongside the car, beating on the dark tinted window. "Ben!" she cried out once, then slipped on a patch of ice in the road and struggled to right herself.

It was the distraction the driver needed. The SUV drove away just as Harrison Bynum's car appeared from a side street on the other side of the road.

Bucky Caballero couldn't believe his luck. . .the way things were falling into place for him.

" 'The time has come, the Walrus said,' " Bucky began to quote Lewis Carroll.

" 'To talk of many things: Of shoes and ships and sealing wax. Of cabbages and kings. . .' "

Bucky chuckled.

"Of cabbages and *queens*. . .' " He chuckled again. " 'And why the sea is boiling hot. . .and whether *pigs* have *wings*.' "

And then he laughed and quoted the last three words one final time.

CHAPTER FOURTEEN

"Good gosh, Katie!" Harrison swung out of the driver's side of his car, reaching for the woman who panted in the middle of Main Street, her arms wrapped around her middle.

"What are you doing?"

"What?" She felt herself being led to the passenger's side of Harrison's car.

"Get in. Get in. You'll freeze out here. Where are your shoes?"

Katie slid into the automobile, and Harrison closed the door behind her, walked around the front of the car, and entered the SUV from the driver's side. He shut the door and looked at her. "You okay?"

She looked straight ahead and continued to pant. "Yeah."

"Let me get you in the house." He put the car in gear and drove the few yards to the front of the Harrington's house, shut the car down, and proceeded to get out. "Don't move," he ordered.

Katie looked toward the house and saw Maggie standing at the front door. She closed her eyes. *How am I going to explain this?*

Harrison opened her door and scooped her into his arms.

"What are you doing?"

"You're not going to walk in this snow; I can tell you that."

Katie allowed herself to relax as he took her to the door. "You must be Maggie," he said by way of introduction.

"Dear child," Maggie said, reaching to touch Katie. "Put her in the living room," she said.

Katie scrambled to be released from Harrison's arms. "I can walk," she said, but he held on tighter until he got her to the sofa where he deposited her. Maggie was right behind him with a throw, which she wrapped around Katie's tender feet and legs.

"I'll make a fire." Harrison moved to the fireplace authoritatively. "Maggie, do you have any coffee here? Tea?"

"Of course I do, young man," she bristled, leaving the room.

Katie rolled her eyes, leaned her head back against a large pillow, and wrestled with her thoughts. *What is going on here?*

Harrison remained quiet until the fire started up, then pulled an ottoman up to the sofa and sat next to Katie, studying her. "Was that the SUV you told me about earlier?"

"I think so."

"What in the world were you doing out there chasing it?"

Katie didn't answer quickly. She had to think. She had to reason. It would be one thing to try to figure out why Ben would be sitting in an SUV—if it were Ben at all—in front of this house in Vermont. The events of the previous month told her that Bucky Caballero could easily slip in and out of the country. His joy at making her squirm had been painfully clear. The concept of James Harrington playing a game flickered into her thoughts but only long enough for her to dismiss it. And what about the dream?

"Katie?"

Katie started. "I had a nightmare. . .and I really have no explanation. . . ."

Maggie reentered the room with a tray of steaming teacups, which she placed on the coffee table near Katie and Harrison, who had stood. "Have a seat, young man," she said. "Good thing you happened along when you did." She handed him a cup of tea, and he returned to the ottoman. "Drink this to warm you, and then we won't keep you. I can take care of Miss Katie."

Katie fought the urge to smile by pressing her lips together as Maggie handed her a cup as well, then took one for herself and plopped at the end of the sofa nearest Katie's feet. Katie looked from the elderly dear to Harrison and winked. "Truly. Drink up and don't worry. I'm fine. I'm prone to vivid dreams, aren't I, Maggie?" She looked at Maggie again, who responded with a nod as she took a sip of tea.

"Beats all I've ever seen, this one does."

Harrison returned his untouched teacup and saucer back to the tray. "Obviously this is none of my business. I don't mean to pry, I just. . .well. . .nothing." He stood again. "Katie, I'll leave you in the very capable hands of your housekeeper." Katie moved to get up. "No, no. Stay right there; I can see myself out."

Maggie stood. "I'll be happy to see you out, sir." She nearly marched to the front door.

Katie looked up at Harrison with a glimmer in her eye. "I'll talk to you later," she whispered.

He replied by touching her shoulder, then walked out of the room. "It was nice to meet you, Maggie," she heard him say, followed by, "Thank you again, sir," and the shutting of the front door.

Maggie walked unhurriedly into the living room.

"I suppose you did your best to be nice," Katie said.

"Would you like more tea?"

"Avoiding the issue, are we?"

Maggie returned to her seat. "Never mind me. Would you care to explain yourself?"

Katie scooted a little taller in her place on the sofa. "Maggie." She took a deep breath and exhaled slowly. "Maggie, this morning on my way to the video store, I noticed an SUV extremely similar to Harrison's. I thought it was his, and so I waved and walked toward it. But just as I got to the road, it took off toward town."

"Was it him in the driver's seat?"

Katie shook her head. "That's just it. The windows are tinted very dark, and I couldn't really make out the person, just the silhouette."

Maggie nodded. "I see."

"On the way home, I noticed it was in front of the house again and then, this afternoon, when we were napping, I dreamed about Ben. I dreamed he told me he was here and then he. . .sort of. . .walked out the window of my bedroom. I literally fell out of the bed, Maggie. When I got up, I looked out the window, and there was the SUV again." A giggle escaped her.

"What's so funny?"

"I just got a picture of me running out in my bare feet."

Maggie smiled but only briefly. "And you thought it might be my William in the car?"

"Yes, but obviously that's not the case. Ben wouldn't drive off like that, nearly dragging me down the road with him."

Maggie stood and began to walk out of the room.

"Where are you going, Maggie?"

"To get the phone. I think it's time to call Mr. Silver."

CHAPTER FIFTEEN

Phil Silver sat at his office desk at John Jay College of Criminal Justice on Tenth Avenue in Midtown. He had just been given an assignment to head a new workshop on workplace securities and was navigating through the Internet for recent stats. He kept his desk in fair order. In one corner was a framed photograph of his wife and two children; next to it sat a large crystal bowl filled with sticks of gum, which had been a Christmas gift from Katie Webster. Katie knew how much he loved chewing gum.

He had just swung around from his computer desk to reach for a piece of the foiled delight when his cell phone rang.

"Silver."

"Phil?"

"Katie? How's Vermont? I hear you had quite the snowfall yesterday, no?"

"You can say that again. It's beautiful here, truly. But I—"

Phil rested his forearms against the edge of his desk. "What's going on? Don't tell me you're ready to come home this soon."

Katie laughed lightly on the other end of the phone. "I think I could move here sometimes, but no. Listen, Phil. There's been a situation."

"I knew it." Phil's voice was low.

"What do you mean?"

"I just had a feeling. An intuition that something would happen. Talk to me."

Curled on one end of the living room's sofa, Katie filled him in on what had occurred in the last two days, waited for a response, but received only silence. "Phil?"

"I'm thinking."

"Would you care to share with me?" A log in the fire shifted slightly, sending crackling sparks of embers upward.

"Okay. . ." Phil paused again. "Okay. I'm just trying to fit all the pieces into place."

"I understand."

"Before I go any further, you haven't called your friend in Georgia about this, have you?"

Katie's shoulders sagged, and her mouth formed a momentary frown. "Phil—"

"Because if she's on the next plane—"

"No, I haven't called Marcy about this." It was disheartening to Katie, this animosity between her best friend and Phil, a man she held such respect for. She understood that, in his eyes, Marcy had interfered with his job—not once but twice—even though the results had been quite positive. "However, I'd like to remind you that it was Marcy who figured out that Zane and Zandra were behind the events of last month. If it hadn't been for her, I might be six feet under right now."

"If I remember correctly, you were holding your own in that apartment. Zandra McKenzie spent nearly a week in the hospital from the injuries she sustained from your scuffle, and Zane was hospitalized for—what was it?—nine days?"

"Eight, but who's counting?"

"Apparently you are. Okay, back to the situation at hand. I want you to keep all this as quiet as possible, you hear me?"

"Yes, sir," she said in mock salute.

"Katie, this is not funny. You have to take it seriously. That's your problem, you know. You aren't taking this seriously. I should have put you somewhere two years ago under some sort of witness protection program."

"Oh, Phil, really! I can't just crawl into a corner and die."

"It would have been for your own good."

"Besides, someone has to run that empire."

"Back to what I was saying."

"Yes."

"I'm going to wrap things up here and head out as quickly as possible. I'll call you from my car to get exact directions to Harrington's. Speaking of whom—"

"My next call is going to be to him. I've already figured you'd be suspicious of him, and a quick call to the city will fix that. My daily phone reports from Vickey haven't revealed anything I should be apprehensive about; then again, I don't want you stressing over it."

"Let me know if he's not in."

"I'm sure he will be."

"My next thought is, of course, Caballero."

"Naturally. He's at the top of my list. I'm afraid the man won't rest until he's made me pay on a regular basis. Sometimes I think he'll enjoy watching me squirm the rest of my life. It'll beat killing me any day of the week."

"Don't even joke about that."

"I'm not joking." Katie paused for a brief moment. "Phil," she said, her voice dropping a notch, "there's someone at the front door."

"Where's Maggie?" He leaned his elbows on the desk and rubbed his eyes and thought how desperately he wanted this saga to end. Somewhere out there. . .somewhere out there were two men he needed to find. One a friend. The other an enemy.

"I sent her upstairs to rest a little longer. She's not doing well,

Phil, and I— The person at my front door is knocking again. What should I do?"

"Is there a peephole?"

"No."

"If you look out the front window, can you see the front porch?"

"Not well enough. But I'll be able to see the street."

Phil listened from too many miles away to the muffled sound of Katie's footsteps across the floor.

"It's an SUV," she finally said. "But it could be Harrison's."

"Go to the door, then, but stay on the phone."

"Who is it?" Phil heard her as she called out. There was a pause. "Who's there?" she asked again.

"Katie, please open the door." Phil heard the distant voice of a woman.

"Who is it?" Phil asked, aware for the first time that he'd stood up at some point.

"I don't know," Katie whispered, "but obviously a woman who knows me." Phil could hear the squeaking of the front door from the other end of the line. "Katie, wait!"

"Hello, Katie," the woman said.

"Who is it?" Phil asked with a voice filled with anxiety.

"May I come in?" the woman asked.

"Phil," he heard Katie answer. "You won't believe this."

"What?" Every nerve in his body had come to attention.

"Andi Daniels is standing at my front door."

Phil could hardly believe what he was hearing. "Come again?" He sank to his chair.

"I said 'Andi Daniels is standing at my front door.' "

"For crying out loud, Katie, it's cold out here," he heard the woman say whose whereabouts he'd somehow managed to lose nearly two years ago.

"Let her in, Katie."

"Yes, I'm sorry. Come in."

Phil stood again, scrambled in the pockets of his pants for his keys, extracted them, and said, "Try to keep her there. Don't let her out of your sight. I'll be there as soon as I can get there."

He could hear the front door of Katie's Vermont vacation home closing, the shuffling of footsteps and Katie's muffled, "Please, come in. You can hang your coat here."

"Katie, did you hear me?" he asked.

"Yes. Yes, Phil. You have the number here?"

"Yes. It registered on my cell. You'll hear from me soon."

Katie escorted the Asian/African-American woman she'd once called her friend into the living room where the fire had begun to die down. "Please have a seat," she said.

Andi took the seat on the sofa in the exact spot where Katie had earlier curled like a kitten while speaking to Phil. She, in turn, walked over to the fireplace, stooping down to add another log to the fire. She grabbed the poker and stoked the fire, then returned it to its stand. Turning, she looked directly at Andi, who sat erect, one slender leg crossed over the other. She hadn't changed in the nearly two years since Katie had seen her. She was still exotic and elegant. Her long black hair lay like silk over one shoulder. Her eyes were large and accentuated by perfectly applied makeup, her nails manicured and painted bloodred. Her lips shimmered seductively under red-tinted frosted lip gloss.

"What are you doing here?" Katie finally managed to say.

"We need to talk."

Katie walked to the other end of the sofa and sat, willing herself to remember that for the past nineteen months she'd successfully run one of the best-known hotel chains in the world. This was *her* home, however temporary. She would be in charge. "I would assume so. I would also assume that was you earlier today."

"Yes. I'm sorry about what happened," Andi said with a toss of her head, though to Katie she didn't seem sorry one bit. "I just didn't know what to do when you came running at me like you did."

Katie nodded. "How did you find me? And for that matter why—after all this time—"

Andi licked her lips and sighed. "I've been watching the hotel for awhile. We. . .I followed you here."

"You followed me? I don't understand. Why on earth would you be following me?"

"That's what I need to speak with you about." Andi paused. "I'm assuming that was Phil Silver on the phone just now."

"Yes."

"He knows I'm here then."

"Yes!" Katie felt exasperated. "Andi, what are you doing here?"

Andi looked down for a moment, then to the fireplace and back to her hands, which she used to press the top of her navy blue slacks. "I have your husband with me."

For a moment, though only a moment, time was suspended. Katie was aware that she'd stopped breathing, stopped hearing even. Her eyes misted over with hot tears that quickly receded on her orders. When the beating of her heart became like a drum, pounding violently in her ears, she forced herself to breathe again. "I don't believe I heard you correctly."

Andi gave her a look of indignation. "You heard me correctly. I have your husband with me. William? Remember him?"

A noise at the open doorway to the foyer caused both women to turn from their places. Maggie stood, one hand clasping a portion of the doorframe. She looked so old, so fragile, so worn-out by life. "My William?"

Katie stood. "Maggie—" She moved quickly from around the sofa, attempting to reach the elderly woman in time, but it was too late. Maggie teetered, then collapsed onto the hardwood floor.

CHAPTER SIXTEEN

"Maggie. Maggie." Katie spoke firmly to her housekeeper—her friend—slapping her gently across the face. "Maggie, open your eyes and look at me." Maggie's watery blue eyes batted, then opened fully and looked directly at Katie. "Maggie," Katie whispered. She looked at Andi, who stood nearby, appearing to be somewhere between hopeless and helpless. "Help me get her to the sofa."

Andi attempted to assist, but with her diminutive size, she wasn't much good. It was a struggle, but somehow they managed to get Maggie situated. "Stay here with her," Katie ordered, heading for the doorway.

She moved quickly down the hall and into the kitchen where she grabbed the teakettle, set it firmly on an eye of the stove, and flipped the heat to high. *Ben. Ben.* She reached for the canister of tea bags—Earl Grey—and laid one on the counter nearby. *Why have you been with her? What does this mean?* She paused long enough to grasp the counter's edge, to take in a deep breath and then another and another, and finally to breathe normally again. She turned toward the right counter and cabinets where the cups and saucers were kept, took one out of the cupboard, and returned with it to the tea bag.

The teakettle hissed and she jumped, then turned the stove off and clasped the handle, pouring the water slowly into the china cup. *Has he been with her this whole time? He has to have been. But why?*

"She's asking for you."

Katie jumped again, startled to see Andi standing at the kitchen doorway. "I asked you to stay with her." Her voice was sharp, but she couldn't seem to help it.

"Look, Katie, I didn't come here to fight with you." Andi threw her arms up, then let them fall back to her side.

Katie laid the tea bag into the cup, dunking it over and over until the clear water turned dark brown. "I'm sorry. It's just that I'm very confused right now. I would think you could understand that."

Andi glanced over to the table, saw a small tray sitting atop it, and walked it over to Katie. "Of course I can."

Katie stood over Andi, breathing as though she'd just run a short race. "Has he. . .has he been with you all this time?" She couldn't look at Andi when she answered; she laid the tray on the counter and the cup and saucer on the tray.

"Yes."

Katie whirled around. "Where? Exactly."

"France."

Katie stared for a moment, then reached for a napkin, folded it, and nestled it near the saucer. "France."

"Yes. Look, Katie, if you'd just let me explain."

Katie picked up the tray. "I need to take this to Maggie while it's hot. But yes. You have a lot of explaining to do, and I have a lot of questions to ask." She made her way toward the door.

"What do you want me to do now?"

Katie paused, looking over her shoulder. "Come with me. Maggie has been my rock through all this. She has every right to hear the truth."

Andi followed Katie down the hall and into the living room.

When Katie had served Maggie, she sat next to her and indicated with a wave of her hand that Andi should sit in a nearby chair. "Maggie," Katie began softly, "do you remember Andi?"

Maggie took a tentative sip of her tea. "I remember her, yes."

"Andi tells me that Ben has been with her in France since. . . well, since all this began."

Maggie jerked her head toward Andi, who sat ramrod straight in her seat. "I don't believe it. Master William would never do such a thing, leaving you here to fight that monster Caballero, leaving you here alone to try to exist without him. Not my William."

"If you would allow me to explain."

Katie nodded. "Please do so."

Andi took a deep breath, letting it out ever so slowly. "Back when all this began, I met William in Central Park to give him some information in a manila envelope."

Katie knew the envelope. She had nearly gotten killed trying to find the place where Ben had hidden it. "I know about the envelope. We found it."

"Yes. I read in the papers that you had."

"In the papers?"

"Yes. I was in Paris at the time. William and I flew to Atlanta and from there he put me on a plane to Paris. He'd arranged for a fake passport, everything I needed, actually. He told me to go to *L'Endroit de Hamilton*, his hotel there in Paris, and he would have someone waiting there for me who would give me a job and help me begin a whole new life until it was safe to come back into the country. He was convinced that with the information I'd given him about Bucky, he could have him arrested and put away."

Katie touched her brow with her fingertip and pressed gently. "Because of what you were doing at Jacqueline's." It wasn't a question, really.

"Not only that. The services we supplied as an escort service were the tip of the iceberg. Do you remember the gala benefit we went to. . .the night you and William found out about Bucky's operation? About. . .me?"

"Like it was yesterday," Katie replied.

"Those benefits made Bucky a lot of money. Bucky was on the take for everything he could possibly get his hands on. He's corrupt through and through; make no mistake about it. William knew one thing for sure; he was dealing with a very dangerous man in Bucky Caballero. Then, of course, there was his sister Mattie." Andi looked over for a moment. "I swear, if it weren't for her, Bucky would. . .wouldn't. . ." She paused. "Anyway, then we heard about the bombing. I swear to you, I thought it was true. I cried for days."

Katie's eyes narrowed. "I've cried for nearly two years." She saw that Maggie was not drinking her tea. "Drink up, Maggs. You'll need this."

Maggie obeyed and Andi went on. "Then, one day while I'm in my hotel room, I get a phone call. It's William—"

The women were startled when, as though on cue, the phone rang. Katie looked over, saw that the cordless was propped on a nearby table, and answered it. "Hello?"

"Katie? Phil."

"Phil." She watched Andi stiffen. "Where are you? The noise is deafening."

"I've managed to get a friend of mine who is a pilot to fly me in his private plane to Vermont. There's a small airstrip near Sanford, used for agricultural reasons. My friend is having someone meet me there and bring me to you. I'd say I'm not more a half hour from landing. . .another half hour to the house."

"I see."

"Are you okay?"

Katie looked over at Andi. "Phil, Andi is here and. . .according to what she's saying, she has Ben with her."

Phil didn't respond right away. "Where?"

Katie responded by asking Andi. "Where is my husband, Andi?"

Andi shook her head no. "I'm not saying."

"Excuse me?"

"Not until you know the whole story. I'm not saying. And there's nothing you can do to make me."

CHAPTER SEVENTEEN

Phil nearly barked an order to Katie. "Listen to me. Do you hear me?"

"Yes, I hear you."

"Keep her there at all costs. Got it?"

"I've got it, Phil." Phil couldn't help but hear the "I'm a woman in control" tone in her voice. "That's my girl. I'll be there as soon as possible."

Katie hung up the phone and returned her attention to Andi. "I want to hear what else happened, and then I want you to take me to my husband."

Andi licked her lips, then shifted a bit in her seat. "Where was I?"

Maggie answered. "You had gotten a phone call from my William."

Andi pondered a moment, then continued. "It was William. I was. . .stunned. I cried all the more. And then he instructed me to meet him in a small town outside of Paris. He said he was staying at an inn and would meet me at this restaurant nearby. . . I don't remember the name of it now." She took a breath and went on. "I did exactly as he said. I packed my bags and took a cab to the restaurant where, as he said he would be, William sat at the very back of the restaurant."

"Unharmed?" Katie asked.

Andi's eyes widened. "Oh, yes. Completely unharmed. He was fine. The bombing was a setup. He told me his plan was to get me and return to the States. He said that Phil Silver was out of town, and he hadn't been able to confer with him, but that by the time we returned, he'd be back. He said it was imperative that we play every step of the game to precision. We talked for awhile, set his plan in motion, and then left the restaurant." Andi paused, casting her eyes toward the floor, then back to Katie. "It had begun to rain. William told me to stand by the door, and he would bring his car around to pick me up. I. . .I don't really know how it all happened then. A car came by, spraying us with water. William stumbled a bit. . .his arms went. . .up. . . and then he fell. . .onto the street."

Katie's eyes misted with tears, but even through the veil she could see Andi's eyes doing the same. Katie blinked, allowing the droplets to slip down her cheeks. "What are you telling me, Andi?"

"William hit his head pretty hard, Katie. There was blood everywhere. I was terrified. Not only at the prospect of William's injury, but also at the international exposure it might bring. An ambulance came and whisked us away to a nearby hospital, ironically in the next town, even farther away from Paris and the hotel there where everyone would have recognized him." She paused again. "I could use something to drink."

Maggie shifted to stand.

"No, Maggie," Katie said, reaching out to place a gentle hand on the woman's arm. "Sit right here. I'll be right back."

Katie darted out of the room and down the hall. She didn't allow herself to think any further than what Andi had already told her. She simply filled a glass with ice water and returned to the living room, where Andi and Maggie sat silently looking at one another.

"Here," Katie said, offering Andi the glass.

Andi took it. "Thank you," she said, then took a tentative sip. She cupped the glass in her hand as though life depended on it.

Katie returned to her place on the sofa, this time sitting closer to Maggie. "Go on."

Another sip. "The hospital personnel assumed we were married. When they brought me his personal effects, I saw that he'd used a fake passport. In fact, everything in his wallet was fake. Jean Luc Louisnard was the name he used."

Katie slumped against the back of the sofa. "I don't believe this," she whispered.

"It's the truth."

Katie returned her eyes to Andi. "Oh, I don't think you are making this up. I'm saying I just can't believe Ben would. . .do. . . something like. . . What happened then?"

"He was in the hospital for several days, in and out of consciousness. I told the doctor that I was American born, but that William—Jean Luc—had been born of French parents and had lived most of his life in America." Andi smiled. "I said we were from Omaha."

"Omaha?"

"I know." She took another sip of water. "I wanted there to be no connection between us and New York."

"I see."

"William had a lot of money in his wallet. He'd apparently already converted it, and I told the doctors we were looking into buying a place there. By the time William fully recovered, I'd found a chalet out in the country. It was for rent. I took care of everything."

"And then what?" Katie sat erect again. "You took my husband to the country and played house?"

"Dear Father in heaven," Maggie prayed aloud.

Andi reached out a hand. "Please allow me to explain. William wasn't well enough. . .hasn't been well enough. . . ."

"For nearly two years?" Katie stood. "You're going to sit there and tell me that for nearly two years my husband has been. . .what? Weak? *What?* A broken leg? A cracked rib?"

Maggie stood and placed her arm around Katie's waist. "Miss Katie, sit down now."

Katie sat just as Andi stood. She straightened herself, swallowed a few times, then walked over to the bay window and gazed out. "My gosh, I'm so sick of snow."

Katie closed her eyes and exhaled. "We're going to talk about the weather now? Please tell me what's going on with my husband."

Andi turned back to Katie and Maggie. "Katie, William has had no memory of anything that happened before the accident in France. He doesn't remember you, he doesn't remember New York, and he doesn't remember Bucky or the hotel or anything."

"No!" Maggie began to cry.

"Maggie, shhh," Katie soothed. She stood and walked over to the window so she could get a better look at a woman she just simply couldn't read. "My husband doesn't know who I am?"

"No."

"Nothing?"

"Not really."

"What do you mean, not really?"

Andi tucked a strand of hair behind her ear. "Just recently he's begun to have dreams. The doctors in France said it would come slowly if it came at all. We've been living in that chalet, working as storeowners in Bar-sur-Aube, but William knew I wasn't his wife. I told him that he and I were just friends, but that I didn't want to air any laundry with the doctors. He seemed to go along with that."

"You said he'd been having dreams."

"Yes. Just recently he asked me if he knew a woman named Katie. I told him he did. I decided that afternoon that it was time to return home. I had become. . .good friends. . .with a man in government there and. . .he was able to take care of our passports, etc." Andi moved back to her chair. "The rest you know."

"You lay in wait, watching me in New York, following me here, nearly dragging me down the road earlier today?"

Andi looked back at Katie. "Yes."

Katie crossed her arms over her abdomen. "Why not just call me and tell me, Andi?"

"I've been taking care of William for two years, Katie. I feel as though I'm somewhat responsible here. I don't know where you stand with anything. You don't understand how fragile. . .I have to make sure that—"

The slamming of an automobile door from outside caused Katie to turn back toward the window. She could see Phil staring up at the house, then looking back at a small piece of paper. "That's Phil," she said, then turned and walked toward the front door to allow him entrance.

CHAPTER EIGHTEEN

Katie and Phil agreed—having spoken to Andi for another hour after Phil's arrival—that the best plan of action was to have Ben immediately taken back to a hospital in the city, but it was a decision not easily reached.

Phil had observed the two women from a living room chair as Katie had stood her ground, literally. "I want you to take me to him right now," she demanded of Andi. "I'm his wife. I have every right—"

"Look, Katie," Andi interrupted, clearly ready to hold on to her position in the reunion. "I've worked hard for nearly two years to help this man. I'm not about to just give in to your whims because you think you have some legal right—"

"Some legal right? What are you, nuts? I'm his *wife*." Katie jabbed at her chest with her index finger. "His wife, Andi. I'm not some woman who spent the better part of her life doing God knows what—" Katie stopped short. "Oh, dear God," she whispered, dropping her head into her hand.

Phil braced his elbows on his knees and cracked the knuckles on both hands before speaking. He was well aware of what Katie was thinking. The fact of the matter was, she *had* spent the better part of her life doing God knows what; she was simply forgetting that she now served a God of forgiveness. He looked Andi directly in the eye. "Exactly what does William know about his whereabouts?"

Andi shook her head. "Very little. But he trusts me. . . ." She looked over to Katie. "And only me. He knows I wouldn't hurt him. Haven't hurt him. I haven't even lied to him." She squared her shoulders. "When he asked if he knew a woman named Katie I could have lied, but I didn't. I brought him back home as quickly as I could. The doctor in France felt. . .that perhaps this could be the breakthrough we'd been waiting for."

Katie returned to the sofa, staring at the dying embers of the fire. Maggie had gone upstairs to pack. Ben's childhood nanny and then housekeeper was nearly beside herself in anticipation of seeing "her William" again. "I'm going to call the best doctor in the city. . .in the country, if I have to."

"Dr. Ron Robinson," Phil supplied. "Phil Jr. hit his head once while diving in competition. Dr. Robinson was the doctor we saw."

"Where is he located?"

"New York Hospital."

Katie nodded. New York Presbyterian Hospital, affiliated with Weill Cornell Medical College and Columbia University, was considered one of the most comprehensive hospitals in the world. "With it being at Sixty-eighth, it will also be close by."

"Top doctors in the nation," Phil reaffirmed.

Katie and Phil looked at one another and then to Andi, who sat silent. She spoke first. "Remember me? The one who actually *has* William?"

Phil focused on the exotic beauty again, wondering what her game was. One moment she seemed willing to help, the next almost hostile. Phil attempted to keep the situation in control. "Let's go back to my question. Just what does William know?"

"When we flew into the city, there seemed to be a flicker of recognition of the skyline. He even said. . ." Andi frowned. "He said it looked as though something were missing."

Katie and Phil nodded, and Andi went on. "I took him to a hotel in Jersey—a nice one—thinking that seeing the activities of hotel management might trigger something. But. . .there was. . .nothing."

"What has he been doing since you've been here? Have you taken him to any sites or anything to try to jump-start his memory?"

"He's been doing little to nothing. I would tell him to stay in the room, and he'd do it." Andi shrugged her shoulders almost imperceptibly.

Katie buried her face in the cup of her hands. It was hard—no, impossible—to believe that the strong man who had brought so much into her life was being commanded to "sit," or "stay," and like an obedient dog, he was doing so. She raised her head again, looking directly at Andi. "Take me to him. Right now. I mean it, Andi."

Phil stood, walked over to Katie, and put a hand on her shoulder. "Wait a minute. Katie, we have to be logical here. We've waited a long time, and you certainly don't want to upset the applecart or do anything that might endanger William."

Katie pushed his hand away, standing. "I don't care—"

"Yes, you do, Katie." Phil watched her as she moved to the window. He knew she had begun to cry. "Here's what we'll do," he said, his voice gentle but commanding. "Katie, I want you to go back to the city with Maggie. Andi and I will go to where William is now. We'll pick him up and head back home. First thing in the morning, I want you to call Dr. Ron Robinson. Tell him you know me. He's head of neurology."

"Okay." He watched her head bob slightly between her shoulders.

"Tell him I'm bringing William directly to him. Ask him where he'd like to meet me, etc. Got it?"

"Yes." She turned then to look at him, brushing the tears from her cheeks. "Where will you stay the night?"

"We'll go back to the hotel in Jersey."

"He's not in Jersey," Andi interrupted.

Both Katie and Phil turned their attention to her. "What? Where is he?" Phil asked.

"He's here. Not too far from here. In Vermont. We've been staying in an inn just a bit down the road."

Katie made a move toward Andi, but Phil caught her. "Don't, Katie." He took a breath. "Okay, then. Andi and I will go to the inn. Tomorrow we'll head for the city. Let's just remember that we don't want to do anything that might disturb William's ability to process what's happening to him. I know very little about this kind of thing, but it makes good sense to take it nice and easy."

Andi stood, placing her hands on her hips and keeping her eyes on Phil. "That's what the doctors in France said. We can't rush him. If we do, everything I've worked for these past two years will be for nothing."

Anger flashed across Katie's face as she spoke. "I'm sick of hearing about what you've been through—"

"Katie," Phil said, raising his hand to stop her. "Let's just get through today, okay? I'll call you as soon as I can."

Katie looked at her watch. Outside it was growing darker by the minute. She and Maggie would not get home until the earliest hours of the morning, but she didn't care. This time tomorrow, she would be seeing her husband again for the first time in nineteen months. Whatever she had to do would be worth it.

The time had finally come.

CHAPTER NINETEEN

Phil ran his fingers through his dark hair, looking down at his watch, as Andi pushed the inn's key card into the guest room door.

"He may be asleep," Andi whispered, turning the knob and opening the door. "William?" she called out, though not too loudly.

"Yeah."

Phil recognized the voice immediately, and his heart quickened. All the imagined scenarios had not prepared him for this moment. In front of him, Andi stepped across the threshold, tilting her head a bit to the side. The television's volume was set on low, the sound of CNN reaching his ears before he was able to see the man sitting in a chair across the room, who had turned his head to see the two of them come in.

He stood, and Phil was taken aback. He was much thinner than Phil had anticipated, in spite of Andi's warnings to the effect. William's cheekbones were prominent, high above the hollowed area beneath them, and his eyes appeared even darker against his pale complexion. This was definitely not the man Phil had last seen nineteen months ago.

"Hi, there," William said to Andi. Phil noted how pleasantly he greeted her. William's attention went from her to him. "Who's this?"

Andi stepped to one side. "William, this is Phil Silver."

The two men met in the middle of the room and shook hands. "Do I know you?" William asked. "Are you someone I knew?"

"I'm Phil, William," Phil responded. "You and I grew up together. At one time we were best friends."

William seemed to study him, though nothing registered within his eyes. "I see," he finally said, then turned to Andi. "Did you go get him? Is that where you went today?"

Andi only nodded. She'd pulled her scarf and coat off and laid them on the nearest of the room's two beds, then pointed to the connecting door on the opposite wall. "That's my room," she said. "And I'm exhausted." But she turned to William anyway and said, "I've asked Mr. Silver to stay with you tonight. I hope that's okay."

William seemed confused. "I guess so."

"I think the two of you have a lot to talk about." She smiled weakly. "Tomorrow, we're going back to New York."

"For what?"

Andi moved past Phil and placed a hand on William's upper arm, giving it a gentle squeeze. "It's okay, William. Really. It's just that it's time to go back and see a new doctor."

William exhaled, closing his eyes and shaking his head. "Another one?"

"Yes. I promise it won't be too bad. We're moving on, you and I," she said, raising her voice a bit as she moved toward the connecting door. "Now. If you boys will excuse me, I'm going to bed."

"Good night," William said, resting his hands on his hips and looking down at his feet.

"Good night, Andi," Phil replied as well. "We'll see you early in the morning."

When Andi had closed the door behind her, Phil turned back to William. "Sit down, William. I know you must have a lot of questions for me, and I'm here to answer them."

William returned to his chair. Since there were two chairs in the room, Phil took the unoccupied one. They didn't speak for a few minutes. William stared at him as though he weren't sure what to do or say, then began with, "So you and I were childhood friends." It wasn't really a question.

"Yes."

He nodded. "Can you tell me something about myself, then?" His face broke with a wary smile. "Because as you must know, I don't know anything."

"I know." Phil patted his knees once with the palms of his hands. "So, where do we begin?"

"My parents, I guess."

"Donald and Lois Webster. Good people."

"Are they still alive?"

"Oh, yes."

William leaned forward and rested his elbows on his knees for a moment before straightening again and asking, "Have they worried. . .about me?"

"Of course. Your mother especially, but that's what mothers do."

William shook his head. "We lived in New York?"

"Oh, yeah. Both of us. . .you and I. Our parents were good friends."

"Where did I go to school?"

"After high school?"

"Yeah. Sure."

"Cornell. You graduated in hotel management."

"Do I—did I manage a hotel?"

Phil had to laugh. "Yeah, you could say that."

"I did say that."

"Yeah. You did."

"What about you? Did you go to Cornell, too?"

Phil shook his head. "No. I went Harvard. . .originally." Phil decided to change the subject. "Do you have any memory at all of the two of us going to Vegas? It's where I met my wife."

William thought for a moment. "No. Sorry."

"That's okay." Phil wanted to bring the subject to Katie but thought better of it. *Better to let the doctors do what they know how to do,* he decided, and stick with what he knew best as well. He pointed to the beds. "Which one is yours?"

William pointed to the nearest bed. "This one. Why?"

"I'll take the other one. Hey, do you remember camping out when we were kids? Our mothers hated it. . . ."

Katie barely slept once she and Maggie arrived home. By six o'clock she was awake and had showered and was putting on her makeup. Maggie, who'd slept off and on during the trip home, was stressing over what Katie should wear to the hospital.

"Something simple, Maggie," Katie said, peering into her closet. "That." She pointed toward a simple black suit. "With my pearls. Simple."

Katie fussed for a half hour with her hair; pulling it up, back, and just letting it fall to her shoulders. She finally settled on the latter, tucking one side behind an ear. She was especially careful with her makeup; she wanted to look her absolute best for Ben, even if he didn't know who she was. One day in the future he might recall this day, and she wanted his memory of their first meeting to be good.

By seven-thirty she'd called Kristy Hallman in Vermont, leaving a message on the realty office's answering machine. "I'm sorry, Kristy. An emergency has brought me back to the city. But I want you to know how much I enjoyed the few days I was there and that I certainly intend to come back soon." She hung up, took several breaths, and then dialed the New York Presbyterian Hospital's main phone line.

"Dr. Ron Robinson," she said when the operator answered.

"Is this a physician?" the woman asked.

"No. This is Katharine Webster. I was told to contact him first thing this morning."

"I can connect you to his office," she said quickly, disconnecting Katie from the switchboard and entertaining her with a few measures of Muzak.

"Neurology. Dr. Robinson's office."

"Is this Dr. Robinson?"

"No. This is his PA."

"I see. My name is Katharine Webster and I was told. . ." Katie began her explanation, trying to fit in as much pertinent information as she could in a short period of time. When she was done, the man on the other end said, "I'll have Dr. Robinson call you as soon as he comes back from rounds, Mrs. Webster."

Katie released a pent-up breath she hadn't even realized she was holding. "Thank you. I'll stay by the phone."

She and Maggie sat at the kitchen table sipping tepid tea for the next forty-five minutes. When the phone rang, both women—dressed and ready to go—jumped toward it.

"Hello?"

"Mrs. Webster?"

"Yes." Katie gripped the cord of the kitchen wall phone.

"This is Dr. Robinson. My PA has relayed your information to me."

For long minutes, doctor and patient's wife spoke at length until he concluded with, "When Mr. Silver calls, have him bring your husband directly to my office at the hospital. Someone on my staff will bring me in immediately. And tell him to be sure to bring all his meds with him. . .any medical records from France, should he have them."

"What about me, Dr. Robinson? Should I be there?"

He paused, and Katie bit her lower lip. *Dear Lord, don't let him say no.* "Yes. I don't know if—by what you are telling me—he's going to be ready to see you, but I won't know until I examine him. Oh, and one other thing. Being he is who he is, we will want to admit your husband under another name."

"I suppose that makes sense."

"Believe me. It does."

"Thank you, Dr. Robinson."

"See you later, then, Mrs. Webster."

Phil called not five minutes later. By this time Katie had moved back to her bedroom to finish unpacking her luggage before Maggie could. The woman's health was another concern resting on Katie's plate at the moment, and she didn't want to add to it by tiring Maggie. "How is he, Phil?" Katie asked.

"Katie, I'm not going to lie to you. He's very thin."

"Did he. . .did he recognize you?"

"No."

Katie could hear cars passing in the distance from the other end of the phone. "Where are you?"

"Outside of the hotel room. On the patio. Freezing myself to death."

Katie sat on her unmade bed. "Where is he?"

"Inside. Getting ready. He and I stayed in the same room last night. It was. . .strange. He's asking a lot of questions; I'll give him that much. And I answered him as honestly as I could."

"Questions about?"

"Our growing up together mostly. I told him of the many nights we'd camped out or spent the night in each other's homes. I told him about his going with me to Las Vegas where I met Gail. But nothing brought about any signs of recognition."

"Did he ask about me?"

Phil was silent.

"He didn't ask about me? But Andi said he asked about a woman named Katie."

"He did, Katie," Phil answered in as kind a voice as he could.

"But that was in France. He hasn't asked since, according to Andi."

Katie fought tears. "All right. I can live with that. Dr. Robinson wants you to bring Ben directly to his office in the hospital. He also said I could be there, but he wasn't sure if I could see him. Oh, and he said to bring all his medications."

"Andi has everything. Every medical record, everything."

"Well, I suppose I should thank her for that. When will you leave?"

"Within the hour. When we get to the hospital, I'll call you."

"You won't have to. I can't just sit here passively waiting. Call me on my cell phone."

Katie and Maggie went to New York Presbyterian Hospital about a half hour later. After talking with someone at Information, they took the elevator to the neurological unit, taking seats in a small waiting area near Dr. Robinson's office. Katie attempted to read a magazine but couldn't concentrate on the words on the page, though she wasn't sure if it were due to the fact that her husband would soon be there or pure fatigue. Maggie entertained herself by watching a show on the television bracketed in the far upper corner of the room. At one point, Katie reached over, took Maggie's hand, and squeezed. The women looked at one another and smiled.

"I'm trying to imagine what it's going to be like," Katie spoke softly so as to not bother the three or four others in the room. "Seeing him again." She was aware that though both of her feet were on the floor, one was bobbing up and down.

"I know, child."

Katie smiled. "Your color's back, Maggs."

"I'm going to see my William," was all she said in reply.

"Maggie, later today I'm going to go out to Ben's parents' home. This isn't the kind of thing I can tell them on the phone. Especially with his father's health being like it—" Katie stopped.

Beyond the glass walls of the waiting area, Katie saw Andi walking ahead of Phil, who was nearest the glass, and her husband. *Ben*. She started, forcing herself not to jump and run to him. "Oh, heavenly Father," she breathed out at last, knowing Maggie's attention was on him, too. "He's so thin." She felt Maggie's fingernails digging into her own flesh, but she was unaware of the pain. Nothing mattered anymore. She had just seen her husband. . .alive. . .after all these months.

CHAPTER TWENTY

"Where are you?"

It was Phil, calling from somewhere just down the hall. For Katie, the location teetered between half a world and a breath away. Ben was right down the hall, and yet she couldn't freely go to him.

"I'm in the waiting room. I saw you walk by just a few minutes ago."

"Then you saw—"

"Yes. I saw him, Phil. I. . .I'm truly shocked at his appearance." Katie stared out the glass walls between the waiting area and the hallway. Maggie, next to her, sat seemingly transfixed to the television, though Katie was sure she wasn't paying attention to a minute of it.

"He's lost probably thirty pounds or more."

"I can believe that. What are you doing now?"

"Waiting for Dr. Robinson. He should be here any minute. Andi is in the exam room with William now; I'm right outside the door."

Katie could feel her shoulders slumping. "She's where I should be. I have to tell you; I've gotten up no less than a half dozen times, determined to head right down there."

"Don't do this to yourself, Katie."

Katie answered with momentary silence. "I'm his wife. This isn't right. It isn't even fair. Phil, I'm his wife."

"Just hold on. We're only talking a short period of time here. You need to prepare yourself for the possibility of the doctor saying you shouldn't see him yet."

"I can't do that."

"Yes, you can. You're Katharine Morgan Webster. You've been running an empire for the last two years. You can do anything."

Katie smiled in spite of her anxiousness. "Phil, please let the doctor know I'm here. . .and I'm waiting."

"I will. Talk to you shortly."

Katie sighed. It wouldn't be shortly enough.

It was nearly an hour later when a man, somewhat short in stature with thick salt-and-pepper hair and flashing blue eyes, walked into the waiting area. He wore a lab coat over a gray shirt and black slacks. His shoes were of fine Italian leather—Katie recognized the quality immediately—and he wore a stethoscope slung around his neck. He paused about midway into the room to scan the small groups gathered there, then approached Katie and Maggie.

"Mrs. Webster?"

Katie stood, causing the man to tilt his neck back. "Yes." Maggie stood beside her.

"I'm Dr. Robinson." He introduced himself with a quick handshake.

"I'm Katharine Webster, and this is our housekeeper, Maggie. Maggie has been with Ben since he was a baby."

"Even before," Maggie reiterated.

Dr. Robinson smiled kindly. "Would you like to go into my office with me so we can talk?" he asked Katie. "You and Maggie?"

Katie reached for the small clutch purse she'd brought in

with her, then straightened and followed the doctor down a short hallway to the left that led to a set of secured double doors. With a swipe of a security card, the doors swung open, allowing them entrance.

The hallways were white and sterile. Their footsteps echoed in the corridors, past closed doorways until they came to another set of double doors that Dr. Robinson pushed and held open for the two women. "Just here to the left," he said, indicating a small conference-style room.

Katie entered first, followed by Maggie and finally Dr. Robinson. "Why don't you have a seat at the table, Mrs. Webster, Maggie?"

They sat, tentatively at first, anticipating what Dr. Robinson would have to say to them. When they were settled, he cleared his throat and began. "I've examined your husband."

"Yes?"

"Let me begin by explaining trauma and what we know about amnesia in as simple of terms as I can."

"I appreciate that."

"The definition of a trauma is a memory that controls you. A traumatized patient will remain in the grips of his or her illness until he or she controls the memory. Amnesia affects the long-term memory of a person rather than the short-term memory. In other words, your husband will remember what he had for breakfast this morning but not his elementary school years or memories of Christmas or of your wedding day. Things like that."

"I understand."

"There are different types of amnesia. It's not important that I go into all of them or tell you their names—" He smiled warmly. "There won't be a test at the end of this meeting or anything like that."

Katie smiled in return. "I appreciate that, too."

"There's amnesia that's caused by drugs or alcohol abuse, but that's clearly not what we're dealing with here. We have amnesia caused by age, by hypnosis, by traumatic psychological events, known as fugue states. Again, I don't believe this is what we're dealing with in your husband's case. What I believe your husband has is called retrograde amnesia, meaning that he is unable to remember anything from before his injury up to the moment of the trauma."

Katie nodded.

Dr. Robinson pressed his hands against the black lacquer of the table. "I haven't had a chance to fully study the records sent from France and—unfortunately—they're written in French, which means I will need to have them translated."

"I can do that. Or at least, in part. I'm fluent in the French language."

Dr. Robinson smiled at Katie as though he were consoling a child. "I understand, Mrs. Webster, but that would mean your husband's medical records would no longer be confidential, and I—"

"Oh, I see." She looked down to her hands, folded together in her lap, clasping each other.

"I know you just want to help. . .to see your husband get well."

Katie's tear-filled eyes met the doctor's. "Of course."

"Let's move on. The brain of a human being is both complicated and fascinating. I want you to picture it as a large room with floor-to-ceiling shelf space. . .like a library. Shelves everywhere. Every day of his life, before the accident, Mr. Webster went out and purchased treasure, brought the treasure to the room, and placed it on a shelf. One day, he came back to the room and found that it had been swept clean, robbed of all content. This is essentially what your husband is experiencing now. He knows that he had a life before the accident—which I don't believe he'll ever remember the events of—but he can't find the treasure that used to dwell there."

"What do you think will help to bring that about?" Maggie spoke for the first time. "That boy and I go back, you know. I could tell him about his childhood. . . ."

"Time is what he needs, Maggie. His friend who's been with him in France informed me that he asked about a woman named Katie."

"That's me."

"I assumed so. While he may remember you when he sees you, Mrs. Webster, he also may not. Then again, he may remember you but none of the shared memories you have. Are you willing to take that chance?"

Katie didn't even have to ponder the question. "Yes. Absolutely, yes. I can't just sit back and wait. I've been doing that for nearly two years, and I'm over it."

Dr. Robinson stood. "Then let me take you to see your husband, Mrs. Webster."

CHAPTER TWENTY-ONE

William Benjamin Webster waited in a comfortably furnished room that had been decorated with small matching sofas lining all but one wall and separated by ornate side tables. Above each table were oil paintings, rich in subject matter. In the center of the room was a small rectangular table, flanked by four Louis XVI reproduction chairs.

It was in one of these chairs that Ben sat, facing a wall dominated by a mirror he somehow knew was a two-way glass. He wasn't quite sure how he knew it. He just knew it.

He wondered who might be on the other side. Was Andi there? Or the man who'd stayed with him the night before? Phil Silver, he'd said his name was. A longtime friend. A childhood friend. He closed his eyes and tried to remember, tried to force the memories from behind the tattered veil, thick and dark, that seemed to separate him from his past.

The doctor he'd seen this morning, Dr. Robinson, had asked him a lot of questions. Some were simple. "Count backward from one hundred in groups of three." *One hundred. . .ninety-seven. . . ninety-four. . .ninety-one.* Others were more difficult. "Do you remember your mother? Your father?" No. Even if he tried to relax, the memories of them wouldn't come. "Are they still alive?" he'd asked, though he'd asked the same thing of his old friend the night before and had been told they were.

The questions about the woman named Katie were the ones, however, that had him on edge. Who was this woman? His sister, perhaps? A girlfriend? A wife? And, if she were a wife. . .oh, what she must have gone through. Moreover, was the woman named Katie the same tall woman he often dreamed of. . .the one who whispered his name. . .but it wasn't his name? *What was it?*

He'd asked Andi about Katie—repeatedly asked—but she kept telling him the same thing. "I'd rather not answer that, Jean Luc. I think it's best we get you back to the United States and let you speak to a doctor there first."

Jean Luc. She never referred to him by his real name, which she'd told him on the way back to the States was William Benjamin Webster.

William Benjamin Webster. It didn't even ring a bell.

He studied himself for a moment in the reflection of the mirror. He didn't look like a William. Maybe he was called Will. Or Willie.

Will. Or Willie.

What was it. . .what was it. . .what was it that was trying to force its way through the tears in the curtain?

The door opened and William stood. Dr. Robinson walked in, closing the door quietly behind him. "Sit down, Mr. Webster. You're fine where you are."

He returned to his seat, but Dr. Robinson remained standing. "I have someone outside the door who wants to meet you."

"Someone from my past." William's amber brown eyes narrowed a bit.

"Yes. Do you feel that you are ready?"

"I think so, *oui.*"

Dr. Robinson smiled at him. "Good. Let me get her for you."

He turned toward the door.

"Are you—?"

Dr. Robinson stopped, turned back to his patient. "Yes?"

"Are you going to tell me who it is? Who *she* is?"

"I'd rather see if you can bring that memory up for yourself. But I want you to feel free to ask her any questions you feel you are ready to know the answers to."

William answered with a nod.

"All right then?" Dr. Robinson asked.

"*Oui.* All right. I'm ready."

Dr. Robinson turned once more, walked over to the door, opened it and stepped back, allowing the most beautiful woman William thought he'd ever seen to enter. She was tall and slender, had chestnut hair and cool blue eyes. He stood again, transfixed by her image. She was definitely the woman he'd dreamed about. But was she Katie?

She walked across the room slowly, her hands clasped in front of her. When she'd finally reached the other side of the table, he noticed the tears filling her eyes, spilling over and down her cheeks, running along her jawbone and disappearing down her slender throat.

"Hello," she said.

"Are you Katie?"

She smiled then, like a child with a new and expensive present. "Yes."

Dr. Robinson stepped over just then. "Do you remember her, Mr. Webster, or are you assuming?"

William tried to take his eyes away from the woman, but he couldn't. He continued to stare at her as he answered, "I'm assuming." He watched the radiant smile fade and a willowy hand reach up and touch the strand of pearls at her throat.

"Why don't the two of you sit," Dr. Robinson suggested. "I'll just be right over here on one of the sofas, but I want you to speak freely to one another, as though I'm not in the room."

They sat and when they had done so, the woman nodded. "Yes, I'm Katie."

William looked down to the table where her hands rested, noticed the wedding set on her left hand, then raised his eyes back to hers. "Are you my wife?"

"Yes, I am."

There lay between them a silence, which she patiently waited through. "I must have put you through such misery."

Her hand automatically reached for his, but by instinct he recoiled. "I'm sorry—" she began.

"Je suis dé solé."

They both laughed, though only a light chuckle.

"No," she said. "You haven't put me through misery. Your time away has been difficult, but I don't blame *you* per se."

"Do you mind if I ask you some questions?"

"Of course not."

"How long have we been married?" He hated to ask it, but Dr. Robinson had told him to ask questions if he wanted answers.

"We were married five years before you disappeared. Almost two years since then. So, seven years."

"Do we have children?"

She shook her head. "No."

He pondered this. "Were we planning to?"

He thought he saw her blush. "No. You. . .you wanted to adopt. But I. . .I wanted to wait."

"To see if we might have children of our own?"

"No. I'm unable to have children." She looked away for a moment, then back to him.

"Je suis—I'm sorry."

"It's okay. It's nothing to do with you. And. . .it's okay if you speak to me in French. I'll understand."

"Parlez-vous français?"

"*Oui*. You insisted on my learning."

"Good for me," he said; his voice held approval.

They fell silent. The woman named Katie—his wife—reached up and tucked a strand of hair behind her ear in a movement he found both somehow familiar and endearing. "What's your full name?" he then asked.

"Katharine." She smiled. "Katharine Elizabeth Morgan Web—"

"Webster," he said, finishing with her. He smiled back. He liked her smile.

"Yes." She breathed in and out. "Do you. . .do you remember your full name?"

William looked over to the doctor, who sat flat against the sofa, arms outstretched against the back, and one leg crossed over the other. "Don't look to me," he said. "You are talking to your wife only right now." William turned back to Katie.

"William Benjamin Webster, I was told."

"Yes."

He laughed then.

"What is it?"

"I don't think. . ."

Katie's smile was crooked. "What?"

He turned to the mirror again. "I don't think I look like a William, do you?"

She gasped. William was aware of the doctor straightening slowly in his seat as he turned back to her. "What did I say?"

"You just said something very similar to a remark I made on our first date." Katie sat straight and tall in the chair.

"Oh, did I?"

She looked to the doctor and then quickly back to him, leaned over and rested her chin on the fists of her hands. "Hmm. . .you don't look like a William to me. Anyone ever call you Bill?"

He could feel the blood drain out of his face. He was getting uncomfortable, but for the life of him he couldn't understand why. "What? *Je ne sais pais.* . . .I don't know. I'm sorry."

She closed her eyes in disappointment, then opened them. The blue had changed from cool to determined. "You don't look like a William to me." Her voice was firm. "Anyone ever call you Bill?"

He knew then that these must have been the words she'd said on their first date. He might have said yes. He might have said no. He didn't want to get it wrong; he felt that it was imperative that he get it right and not lose the grip on this little ghost of reality he'd managed to grasp ahold of. "No?"

"Will?"

He stopped breathing; he was certain he did. "Will or Willie? Was there something about Will or Willie?"

Her shoulders fell a bit, then came back up with her smile. "Yes, that's it. I'll bet someone called you Willie once, but—"

"I had to kill him. . . ." He looked at Dr. Robinson again. "I don't know where that came from."

"Go with it, Mr. Webster."

He looked back at the woman who said she was his wife. "Did I say that before?"

The tears were back in her eyes. "Yes. Yes, you did."

"And then what happened?"

"We talked for a moment. I was self-conscious because I felt that people were staring at me, but you said they were just jealous. And then you said something wonderful—" Katie couldn't help it; she bit her bottom lip as she blushed.

"What did I say?" he asked, his grin boyish and endearing.

"You said—let me see if I can remember this correctly—"

"You, too?" he bantered.

She smiled again. "No. Not me, too. You said, 'It's you they are compelled to stare at. Every woman in this room is wishing she looked like you, and every man regrets that he is not sitting where I am sitting at this moment.'"

William shook his head. "I don't remember that, but I can certainly believe it."

"Thank you." She pinked again. "You were always very romantic."

"And then what happened? On our date, I mean."

Katie pressed her lips together. "And then I called you—"

He held up a hand as though to stop her. "Wait. Don't tell me." He paused, took a deep breath, and then another and another, the whole time pressing his lips together in thought. When he finally looked up at her, his dark eyes met hers with intensity and surety. He nodded. Once. Twice. "And then you called me *Ben*."

CHAPTER TWENTY-TWO

Andi Daniels brushed a final stroke of powdered blush across her high honey-colored cheekbones, then gently set the brush back into the cosmetic tray. She stared into the vanity mirror of the hotel room she'd been occupying for over a week and pressed her full red lips together as she leaned forward, checking for any slips in cosmetic application. She blinked. Looked a little longer. As always, she was perfect.

Standing erect, she reached for the hairbrush she could see reflected in the mirror, brought it up to the silky black hair that fell just beyond her shoulders, and ran it through a few times. Laying the brush back on the marble countertop, she scooped her hair up, twisted it, and set it stylishly into place with a set of amethyst-colored banana clips.

She turned from the mirror, walked over to the bed, and picked up the dark lavender jacket that matched the formfitting slacks and light lavender turtleneck sweater she planned to wear for the meeting she'd been summoned to earlier that day. She sighed deeply. "This is all so futile," she said to no one as she slipped her arms into the jacket and headed for the door.

Phil Silver was waiting for her in THP's lounge—Robespierre's—

just as he said he would be. When he saw her enter, he stood, motioned her toward him, and smiled. She supposed it was his way of trying to keep her calm, to appease her, to get her to open up, even. "Futile," she whispered, then half-hoped he'd been able to read her lips.

She turned to the hostess that approached to lead her to a table. With a raise of her hand, she said, "That's okay. I see the party I'm meeting."

The hostess turned toward the interior of the restaurant, saw Phil standing, and nodded. "Very good, madame."

Andi made her way toward the table, weaving through the sparsely populated lounge, moving almost in time to the pop instrumental music that played overhead. She kept her head held high, her chin firm. "Good afternoon, Miss Daniels," he said when she'd reached him. He extended a hand for a handshake, and she obliged him.

"Andi, please," she corrected. Phil pulled a chair out for her and she sat, then, with his aid, slid toward the table.

As soon as he returned to his seat a waiter came to the table. "Good afternoon, madame. Sir."

Phil looked at the young, brown-skinned man who, if Phil was any judge of people, was working his way through college. Andi stared straight ahead. "Good afternoon," Phil returned.

"What can I get you from our bar this afternoon?"

Phil looked at Andi, who turned her head slightly to look at him. "Martini, please."

Phil returned his attention to the waiter. "Martini for the lady, and I'll have the same."

"Thank you, sir. I'll be right back with your drinks."

Phil watched him walk away, then turned back to Andi, who had tilted her head ever so slightly. "An old-fashioned kind of guy?" she asked.

"Pardon me?"

"Martini? You don't hear a lot of people ordering them anymore."

Phil nodded and smiled good-naturedly. "I will admit it's been awhile." He folded his arms and rested them atop the round table decorated only by a royal blue linen tablecloth and small lantern with a lit, blue votive candle in the center. "So," he said. "How have you been?"

"This has been one long week."

He nodded. "I can imagine."

"Can you?"

Phil paused long enough to allow their server to set their drinks before them. "Let me know if you need anything else," he said.

"Thank you," Phil said. He took a sip of his drink, watching Andi do the same. "Not bad," he commented. "Not bad at all."

Andi set her glass on the table and leaned back in her chair. "To what do I owe the honor of this drink?"

Phil leaned back as well, crossing one leg over the other. "I thought it was time we talked a little more. To find out how you're doing. If I know William—and I do—he would want me to make sure the woman who cared for him these past months was okay."

Andi wrapped her arms across her narrow middle. "Make sure I'm not going to cause any problems for Katie?"

Phil shifted a bit. "Andi, why would you say that?"

Phil thought he saw her smirk. "I know how I would feel if I were in Katie's shoes."

"And how might that be?"

Andi took another sip of her drink. "If she's concerned about—" she paused, then took another drink. "If she's concerned about whether or not I was intimate with her husband. . ."

Phil pressed the fingertips of his hand along the thigh of his right pants' leg and brushed away an imaginary piece of lint. "Would you blame her for wondering?"

Andi finished off her martini. "I suppose not."

Phil looked at the empty glass. "Another one?"

Andi rested her elbows against the arms of her chair and chuckled. "Why not? I've got nothing else to do but lose myself in this glass."

Phil turned toward the bar, raised his hand for their server's attention, all the while saying, "I don't think there will be any need for that, but I don't think one more will hurt you." Andi watched him stretch his index finger. "One more for the lady," he said to the server, who had made it halfway to their table before turning back toward the bar.

"What were we saying?" Phil asked, his attention back to Andi.

"*We* weren't saying anything, really. You were wondering what kind of a relationship I had with William."

Phil nodded but didn't say anything.

"The answer is, we had a platonic relationship and only a platonic relationship. My job was to take care of him while he—though he didn't know it—kept me safe from the likes of Bucky Cabarello."

The server returned with Andi's drink, which he placed on the table before whisking the empty glass away. "Anything else for you, sir?" he asked Phil.

"No. No, thank you."

"All right then, sir." He walked away.

"A win-win situation for you both, I suppose."

Andi took a healthy sip of her drink. "I suppose."

Phil pushed the based of his glass along the tabletop before speaking again. "I sense anger from you, Andi."

Andi raised her brow. "Do you blame me? I've spent nearly two years of my life spinning in a wheel like a hamster, taking care of a man who didn't know so much as—" She broke off, looked away, then turned her concentration back to her drink.

Phil cleared his throat as he watched Andi fight back tears.

"You told Katie the two of you managed a store in France."

She smiled then. "We managed a little antiquities shop in town. Made fairly good money. The chalet we rented wasn't badly priced. We did okay and basically stayed to ourselves with the exception of doctor visits. I think that, maybe, I'd like to go back when all this is over. Pick up where I left off."

"What about now? What are you doing to keep yourself busy? To occupy your time?"

Andi laughed sardonically. "As you may know, the FBI has been interviewing me on a daily basis. Going over all those old files. I'm doing that and going over to the hospital to spend time with William until he. . .doesn't need me anymore." She took a deep breath. "The doctor—Dr. Robinson—has asked that I spend a little less time with him every day so he can begin to grasp hold of the here and now and not try to hold on to what he felt was safe in France."

"I suppose that makes sense."

"And, of course, the basics in my life are taken care of. Katie has been kind enough to see to it that I have a roof over my head, but I know the truth. She just wants to keep an eye on me. I'd be willing to wager money that when I walk out of the hotel's front door, someone is on the phone, calling her. Alerting her. She doesn't trust me." She sipped her drink again. "I don't care. I go to the hospital once a day, when I know she's not there, and spend time with William. I'm still the one he trusts, whether he remembers anything or everything."

"Katie tells me he's remembering more with each passing day."

Andi froze momentarily, then shook her head. "Good. I'm glad. Now they can get on with their lives, and I can get on with mine."

Phil leaned forward again. "Andi?"

"What?"

"By any chance have you heard from Caballero?"

Andi's lips parted. "Of course not." She squinted, aware that Phil was studying her. "Why would he contact me anyway? To kill me? To finish what he should have finished a long time ago?"

"No. I would hope not. But with the news being in the papers recently. . .about William's return. . ."

Andi snorted lightly. "Shocked beyond words that Mrs. Webster let that out."

"I don't think Katie had anything to do with it. Some news just can't be kept quiet."

"I suppose."

Phil finished his drink. "Well, then."

"Yes. Well, then."

"Is there anything I can do for you? To help you until you know what you want to do?"

Andi blinked, slow and easy. "Yeah. You can give back me the last two years of my life."

A vital part of Bucky Caballero's day was walking to a nearby periodical stand and buying the daily papers. It had rained the day before—stormed really—and he'd not attempted to get out. He didn't worry—didn't concern himself—with the thought that he might miss anything, however, because he knew the operator well, and had prearranged that the young man would always hold his daily order for him.

"Mr. Martino," the thirty-something, balding, and slight-of-build man greeted him as he approached. As he spoke, he reached under the front counter without taking his eyes off Bucky. "I've got yesterday's papers here for you, sir," he said, pulling a small stack from beneath.

Bucky returned the greeting with his best smile. "I can always count on you, Thad." He slipped his hand into the front pocket of his slacks, retrieved a money clip, and pulled a few bills from it. "This should cover yesterday's, today's, and a little something extra for your trouble."

There was an exchange of money and daily publications. "Thank you, sir," Thad said. "I knew with the weather like it was, you wouldn't be out."

"I detest rain," Bucky replied. "It's one thing to be inside working. It's another to be forced to stay there."

"You're a man who won't be dictated to, huh, Mr. Martino? I said that the first time I met you. Said so to my wife, in fact. 'Now there's a gentleman,' I said to her. 'A real class gentleman.' It's a pleasure doing business with you, too." Thad snatched a plastic bag from behind him and handed it over to Bucky.

"Thank you, Thad." Bucky folded the papers and slipped them into the plastic bag Thad was extending to him. As he took a step away, Thad continued, "Ever been to New York, Mr. Martino?"

Bucky stopped short, turned, and looked Thad directly in the eyes. "Once or twice. Why?"

"Interesting story in the *Post* yesterday," he answered. "Some man thought for dead back from the grave."

Bucky's brow furrowed. "You don't say?"

"Yes, sir. Interesting." Thad's eyes widened as another patron approached his stand. "Have a good day, Mr. Martino."

"You, too, Thad."

CHAPTER TWENTY-THREE

When Katie walked into her office the following morning, Vickey was two steps behind her, carrying a cup of coffee in one hand and Katie's appointment calendar in the other. A pencil was wedged between her teeth, making her speech slightly impaired.

"We godda tulk," she said.

Katie turned to look at her, dipping her chin slightly. "Come again?"

"Eere," she said, extending the Noritake cup and saucer filled with a perfect mix of coffee, cream, and sugar. Everything Vickey did for Katie was beyond perfect. Katie had increased Vickey's salary twice since she'd taken the presidential position and had even teased Vickey that if she raised it again, their paychecks would match. Vickey had only smirked at her. Besides being loyal in the office as her executive assistant, Vickey was also a good friend.

Katie took the cup and saucer. "Thank you," she said with a smile, then turned back toward her desk. "Now, take that pencil out of your mouth like a good girl and talk to me." Once seated she saw that Vickey had taken her place across from the desk, sitting in one of the two chairs facing Katie. The pencil was now situated between her slender fingers, and she was opening her appointment calendar.

"I said, 'We need to talk.' And we do."

Katie had worn an ice blue suit to work that day. As she slid back in the oversized executive's chair, she unbuttoned the elongated jacket and crossed one long leg over the other. The knee-length skirt rose discreetly up her leg, and she smoothed it with her left hand, watching the diamond of her engagement ring wink at her in the early morning sunlight that streamed in from the window behind her. "About?"

"You have no idea how many calls we've gotten between yesterday afternoon and this morning. I swear, ever since yesterday's article came out in the *Post*. . ."

"Phone calls from whom?"

"*Newsweek. Time. People.* Even the *Atlanta Constitution* and the *Chicago Sun.* Periodicals and newspapers from France, England, Switzerland, Italy. . .everywhere that THP has a location. Everyone wants an interview with you, Katie. Not only are you the wife of the back-from-the-grave William Benjamin Webster, it's suddenly at the forefront of everyone's mind that you have managed to hold down the fort—so to speak—in his absence. Oh, and *Fortune* wants an interview *yesterday*. If I don't call them back in a half hour, they'll be in my office. I'm not kidding, either. That's what the man said."

Katie sighed. "Ugh." Then she laughed. "How's that for a high-powered president and CEO? Tell them, 'Mrs. Webster said, "Ugh." ' "

Vickey laughed, too, but quickly sobered. "Then, of course, there are people like James Harrington. He's called numerous times. Katie. You're going to have to talk to these people. The press, the staff. You certainly don't want either of them calling every hospital in the city, trying to find William. . .trying to see him or get an interview with him."

Katie nodded. "This is why we had Ben admitted under a false name. Dr. Robinson seemed to almost anticipate this kind of thing happening. What I don't understand is how the *Post* even knew he was in a hospital."

"My guess is that some money-strapped hospital employee is now sitting on about twenty-five-thousand dollars."

"You're probably right. Maybe I should have issued a statement right away. But I really thought remaining private was the best thing."

"You've managed to stay out of the spotlight to a degree until now. I suppose we can be happy for that. Unfortunately, my dear, those days are over."

Katie narrowed her eyes, then turned to look toward the part of her office dominated by white leather sofas, an entertainment center, and a different, albeit similar, view of Manhattan than the one behind her. "Something just dawned on me."

Vickey rose higher in her seat. "What is it?"

"If I start doing interviews, how long will it take before Bucky Caballero finds out Ben is back in the city? Let's face it. He would then know that I realize that he didn't kill my husband. He also would know that the FBI would be aware of that as well."

"This is not good."

Katie raised an eyebrow and an index finger. "But it could be." She turned back to look at Vickey. "I need to talk with Phil before I do any interviews. Perhaps he can talk to whoever is handling this case now at the Bureau. We could use the articles to our advantage."

Vickey frowned. "You mean, like a sting operation?"

Katie only nodded.

"I don't like it, Katie. I think you've been dancing on the dark side of danger enough. I think you both have."

Katie leaned over, took a dainty sip of her coffee, then returned the cup to the saucer. "Shadow dancing," was all she said. She leaned back again.

"Shadow dancing?"

"Mmm."

"Like the old Andy Gibb song?"

Katie smiled. "No. As in, it seems that my whole life I've been dancing in the shadows. Sometimes closest to the edge of darkness and other times closer to this thin veil of light. The problem has always been that just as I determined to do one more pirouette toward the light, I'd stumble or trip back into the darker recesses." She leaned forward again, rested her elbows on the desktop, and looked Vickey dead in the eye. "I'm ready to dance in the light, Vickey. I'm ready to do what Ben said so long ago. . .to fight the demons of both my past and present so that I can actually *have* a future."

"I think I understand what you're saying. I don't necessarily like it, but I understand it." Vickey stood. "I'll get Mr. Silver on the phone for you."

"I want to talk to him about something else anyway. He was supposed to meet with Andi yesterday afternoon. I want to know how it went with her."

Vickey frowned. "I don't know whether to slap that girl or hug her for what she's done."

Katie looked from the desk, then back to Vickey. "Welcome to my world."

It was a little after noon when Katie paged Vickey.

Rather than picking up the phone, Vickey hurried into Katie's office. "What can I do for you?"

Katie gave Vickey a warm smile. "You don't have to run in here every time, you know."

"I know."

Katie extended her hands over the top of her desk, which was fairly well covered with files and paperwork. "Look at all this. There's no way I can finish this and get to the hospital later this afternoon if I take a lunch, but I forgot breakfast, and I'm so hungry I've hit famished."

Vickey crossed her arms over her slender middle. "Maggie let you out of the apartment without breakfast? Since when?"

Katie raised one eyebrow. "Since she was still asleep when I left. She's probably beside herself right now, thinking she let me down in some way. But, honestly, she's just worn out lately, Vickey, and I didn't have the heart to wake her."

"What a sweetheart she is."

"So, would you mind ordering something from Bonaparte's for me? You know what I like."

Vickey turned back toward her office. "No problem."

"Vickey?"

Vickey looked back from the doorway. "No, I haven't heard from Mr. Silver yet. His associate said he was in classes all morning and he'd call a little after noon."

"How do you do that? How do you know what I'm going to ask before I ask it?"

Vickey smiled. "Comes with the job. Let me order a grilled chicken salad for you, and I promise I'll patch Mr. Silver through as soon as he calls."

"Thank you."

Phil arrived at Katie's office just as Vickey was rolling in her chicken salad, nicely arranged on a linen-covered cart along with a single rosebud in a small bud vase, a stemmed crystal glass, and silver utensils. Katie had motioned for Vickey to put the cart near the window of the sitting area. "Phil, can we order anything for you?" Katie asked.

Phil kissed Katie's cheek, then pulled himself out of his outer coat and laid it over the back of one of the sofas. "No, thank you. I stopped at a deli on the way over."

"Are you sure?" Katie asked, pulling a small chair over to the cart.

"Maybe some hot tea."

"Got it," Vickey said before Katie could say anything else.

Phil walked around the sofa and sat just as Katie lowered herself into the chair. "Go ahead and eat, Katie."

"Thank you. I have to tell you, I'm nearly starved to death."

As Phil sat on the sofa he asked, "Are you eating well these last few days?"

Katie began to pour the salad dressing from a silver serving dish and looked up at Phil simultaneously. "When I remember." Her shoulders sagged. "Oh, Phil. This has been so difficult. All so difficult. Every day I go down to the hospital and spend time with a man who is slowly remembering me but doesn't seem to connect to me. His mother and father—God bless them—have been there every day, bringing photo albums and mementos."

"I know. I talked to his mother yesterday. They're caught between exhilarated and exhausted."

Katie stabbed at her salad and took in a small mouthful, chewed thoughtfully, and then swallowed as she nodded.

"How's Maggie holding up?"

Katie shook her head. "Maggie's tired, Phil. She's doing less and less, though I'm not so sure she's aware of it. I'd hire more help if I didn't think she would be hurt. . .or hurt me." She chuckled. "You know what I mean."

"I know."

Vickey came in then and set a tray with Phil's tea on the coffee table before him. "Anything else?" she asked.

"No, thank you," Phil answered with a smile.

Vickey turned to Katie. "Call me if you need anything."

Katie nodded, then stabbed at the salad again. "Phil?" she asked, watching Vickey exit through the office door.

"You want to know about Andi?"

Katie dropped her fork and dabbed at the corners of her lips with the napkin that had been in her lap. "Yes. For one thing."

"We talked, but I'm not really sure I got anywhere. She's angry, Katie. At what or who I don't really know. Well, maybe I do." Phil leaned over and rested his elbows on his knees and began to prepare his tea. "I think she expects more from you than she's getting."

"More from me? What does she want from me?" Katie stood, dropped her napkin next to her plate, and slipped her hand around the crystal glass, bringing it up to her mouth. She took a sip, then moved toward the opposite sofa from where Phil sat.

"Perhaps some appreciation for what she did these past nineteen months or so."

"You mean like keeping my husband's whereabouts secret from me? Oh, Phil, really. She could have called." Katie sat, crossing one leg over the other in a fluid move.

"Maybe she was thinking that her silence was keeping him safe."

"Maybe she was thinking that her silence was keeping *her* safe."

Phil leaned back against the sofa, bringing his tea with him. "You're probably right there."

They were silent for a moment until Phil spoke again. "You're finished with your salad?" He took a sip of his tea.

Katie shook her head. "I can't eat. Not really. I'll finish it later." She looked to the cart and back again. "I want to talk to you about something else anyway."

"All right."

"I'm getting a lot of requests for interviews since the news release by the *Post*. And I'm thinking that if I do them, this will let Caballero know—if he doesn't already. It might just bring him out of the woodwork." Katie pressed her lips together before continuing. "Like a sting operation."

Phil held up a hand. "No, no, no. And don't call Marcy

Waters to start planning something either. You haven't called her, have you?"

"Only every night; but not about this, no." Katie leaned forward, placed the glass on the coffee table that separated them, and said, "Phil. If I don't do these interviews, they'll either make a story up or try to find Ben. After all, what do you suppose happened here? I'll tell you: Some employee of the hospital called the *Post*. I'd ask you to try to find out who, but there's always reporter privileges."

"True."

"I'm sorry, but I'm not willing to just sit back and let Caballero get by with this. And now would be the best time. Ben is well-protected and will continue to be. That agent who worked the case with you a couple of years ago called a few days ago, telling me that when Ben is released, they want to talk to him extensively. They're already staking out the hospital and this hotel. Did you know that?"

Phil shook his head no. "I'm not privy to that anymore. Though I'm sure if I called Agent Richards—Sabrina—she'd be willing to talk with me."

"Good. I trust you, Phil. I trust *you*. The other thing I wanted to tell you is that I've had Vickey schedule a meeting of the higher staff at THP. Poor Vickey, she's been screening calls—not only from this hotel but from the others, as well."

"When is your meeting?"

"First thing tomorrow morning. Eight o'clock. I'd like for you to be here, if you can."

Phil took another sip of tea, then returned the cup and saucer to the tray and stood. "I appreciate that, and I'm sure I can make it. Now, walk me to the door."

Katie stood. "What about the press interviews?"

Phil turned. "Let me call Sabrina and see what she thinks. This is no longer my case, Katie. And now. . .with William back. . .we have to play it right down the line. You understand what I'm saying?"

Katie narrowed her eyes, though they danced playfully. "No calls to Marcy."

"No phone calls to Marcy."

Katie walked Phil to the door, gave his cheek a quick kiss, then closed the door behind him. Leaning against it, she smiled. "But who's to say she can't call me?"

CHAPTER TWENTY-FOUR

Ben sat in an oversized chair, which was set at an angle in one corner of his large hospital room. Unable to sleep late, he'd gotten up earlier than usual, dressed, and had begun to look through the photo albums his parents had brought to him, and which his mother had lovingly divided into three groups: childhood, adulthood, and Katie.

Katie.

Though he wanted to start his study of the photographs from the beginning of his life to the present, he couldn't help but allow his gaze to linger over the albums of "post-Katie" photographs. With each flip of the page, new scenes—memories—would come to the surface of his mind, though typically in only a flash. Sometimes he could hear words spoken, other times he just had the sense that he'd actually been in the places revealed in the photographs.

He studied their wedding photographs in great detail. Apparently they'd married in a small stone chapel in the country. He and Katie had found it—he remembered—while driving about one weekend.

"Oh, Ben, look," she had said, gazing up at the unlit oil sconces that hung on the walls next to each pew. "I don't even think this place has electricity."

No more than fifty people could have fit in that little sanctuary. He remembered his mother's concern over the guest list. "William, darling, you are a Webster. If we invited our family alone, it would fill that chapel three times over."

Ben stopped in his thoughts. *What happened next? How did we resolve it?*

He reached for a pen and pad of paper kept next to his bedside. Adjusting it on his lap he wrote: *Ask about the wedding.*

The photos indicated he and Katie had married in the chapel, but the reception—which, according to the photographs, was packed with people—had been held in some sort of banquet hall. He narrowed his eyes and considered the photo a bit harder. The room looked so familiar. . .so very familiar. . . .

"Good morning, Mr. Webster."

Ben looked up as one of the floor nurses walked into his room.

"Good morning."

"I see you're looking at your photo albums."

The nurse, a young blonde who couldn't have been more than twenty-three or twenty-four, held a stethoscope in her small hands.

"Yes. I see you're packing a stethoscope."

She laughed lightly, taking the necessary steps to reach him. "That's right. I need to take your pressure."

By habit Ben extended his arm for the necessary procedure. As the young woman pulled the blood pressure cuff from a small wire basket adhered to the wall just above the bedside table, she leaned over slightly and looked down at the photographs. " 'Sat you, Mr. Webster?" She pointed to a photo of him, Katie, and a few other people, casually chatting and laughing in a semicircle in the room he couldn't quite remember.

"Yes."

"You looked very handsome there in your top hat."

"Thank you."

She pointed again, this time to Katie. "Your wife, I presume."

"You presume correctly."

"She's beautiful. Honestly, she looks like a princess."

She did look like a princess. She had chosen a cream-colored, strapless dress for her wedding gown. The skirt was quite full and dotted with an occasional embroidered pink rosebud. She hadn't worn a veil but rather a small tiara that held her long chestnut hair away from her face. As the nurse pumped air into the blood pressure cuff, he studied the face just a bit longer.

Dear heavens, she was so beautiful.

He closed his eyes and struggled to remember how they had met.

Nothing. Not even a glimmer of memory. He ground his teeth together. *Surely we had to meet,* he thought. Surely they had been introduced by someone. . .perhaps someone in his family—

"Blood pressure's good," the nurse said, interrupting his thoughts.

Ben nodded. "Good. Good."

She folded up the cuff and stuck it back into the basket. "Well, enjoy your albums."

He looked up at the young woman. "Thank you."

She smiled, then turned on her heel and walked out of the room, closing the door behind her.

He returned to the photos, moving on from the wedding. There was a postcard from Maui. He pulled it from its protective sleeve and flipped it over.

Dear Mother and Dad:

    Katie and I arrived and are having a wonderful time. I would say that I wish you were here, but I don't.

                    All our love,
                    William and Katie.

Apparently, he now thought, *I had a sense of humor.* "I wonder where it went," he said to the empty room.

He hadn't always found a lot to laugh about since the accident, but he wasn't sure why. Still, he and Andi had had good times in France, though Andi tended to be somewhat serious most of the time. Too serious, actually. But they'd shared a lot of secrets. . .and jokes. . .and days on end together, trying to help him get well.

The door opened again, and he looked up to see Andi standing there. He smiled, happy to have her company. "Hey," he said.

She walked in, allowing the door to close behind her as she pulled off her long wool coat. *"Bonjour, mon amie. Comment allez vous?"*

"Frustré."

Andi threw the coat over the foot of the bed, walked over to Ben, and leaned over to kiss his cheek. "What's got you so frustrated?" she asked, furrowing her brow and then turning to sit on a nearby love seat.

"Right now? My life. I'm remembering just enough to provoke me but not enough to give me any relief. I want. . ." He balled his hand into a fist. "I want to remember it all." He slammed the album shut and threw it on the floor.

"Oh, William. I'm so sorry."

Ben leaned over, pressed his face into the palms of his hands, and took in several breaths. "No, I'm sorry. I had no right to. . ." He leaned over to retrieve the album. "To act like that in front of you."

Andi laughed. "Please. You've acted a lot worse. Remember the time—"

Ben held up a hand. "If we're going to start playing 'remember the time,' you'll be here all day." He paused. "And I don't think. . ." This time he stopped.

"You don't think what?" she asked, cocking her head to one side.

"I don't think you have that kind of time." He gave her a

warm smile. "I know what they're doing—shortening the amount of time you visit every day."

Andi looked down at her hands, then back up. "Yeah," she whispered. "But it's really for the best, William. It is."

"I know."

They were silent for a moment before he added, "I also know you've been good to me. And I'll never forget *that*, I promise you." He waited for her to catch his play on words. When she did, she laughed openly, and he smiled, too.

"I needed that," she said.

He nodded. "Me, too. I needed that, too."

CHAPTER TWENTY-FIVE

Katie took a few minutes after Phil left her office to run upstairs and check on Maggie. As soon as she opened the front door of her hotel apartment, Maggie came bustling from the kitchen into the dining room, which was straight ahead from the foyer.

"Miss Katie?" she called out. "Is that you?"

"Well, good morning, Maggs." Katie kept her voice at a good-natured tempo.

Maggie stopped just shy of the table, placed her fists on her hips, and said, "Morning, my great-aunt Harriet. Afternoon is what 'tis."

Katie smiled, walked over to her housekeeper, and planted a kiss on her powdery and wrinkled cheeks. "I let you sleep in a bit," she whispered into her ear.

Maggie turned and headed back toward the kitchen. "I'll get you some lunch."

Katie was right behind her, pushing the swinging door open for the two of them. "Don't bother, Maggs. I had a salad brought up from Bonaparte's."

Maggie turned just inside the kitchen to look at Katie, who held the door open with her hand and forearm. "You haven't eaten enough to keep a sparrow alive these past few days. I'd say you had no more than two mouthfuls of that salad."

Katie grimaced. "One, but who's counting."

"I am, that's who," Maggie continued, moving toward the refrigerator. "I'll make you a sandwich, if nothing else."

Katie shook her head, stepping into the kitchen and allowing the door to swing shut. "No, Maggie. I only have a few minutes, and I'm only here to check on you. I'm going back down to the office and will leave sometime this afternoon for the hospital. Do you want to come with me?"

Maggie shook her head. "Love that boy like my own, I do. But not today. I don't think it's wise I go out in this cold every day. Besides, I want to get things ready for when we bring him home." She raised an index finger. "That's what I'm thinking."

Katie wrapped her in a warm embrace. "Good thinking, Maggs. I'll see you later this afternoon then." She stepped away. "Don't plan dinner. We'll go down to Bonaparte's, you and I."

Maggie spun Katie around and gave her a slight push toward the door, patting her back. "You've begun to take care of me more than I take care of you is what I'm thinking. But you're a dear for it. Still, this old woman hasn't taken her last breath yet, you know."

Katie made it to the door and turned. "I know. Indulge me, though. Okay, Maggie?"

Maggie looked up at her employer. . . .her *Katie*, as she thought of her. She reached up and stroked Katie's cheek, knowing her own was now streaked with a lone escaped tear. "I may not have raised you like I raised my sweet William, but I love you, Miss Katie. Like my own, you are. If you want to pamper me every so often. . . .well, I shan't stop you, but don't put this old mare out to pasture yet."

"Oh, Maggie," Katie whispered. "I love you, too."

Dr. Robinson called with an update after Katie returned to her office. "Mr. Webster just left my office," he said. "We had an interesting appointment, to say the least. He's keenly aware that we're shortening his visits with Miss Daniels, which is good. He's reasoning, and I'm happy to make a note of it."

"Ben has always been extremely observant. Very keen senses," Katie reported.

"Good." Dr. Robinson paused. "Mr. Webster brought in a photo album your mother-in-law had given to him."

"I know she's brought in quite a few."

"This is the one of your wedding."

Katie's heart quickened. "He brought that one in?"

"Yes. He's puzzled about the location of your reception. He knows it's familiar, but he's not sure as to the exact location. I uh. . . well, I recognized the room as being one of the banquet rooms at your hotel, having had medical conferences there from time to time. Banquets and the like. . ."

"Oh, yes, of course."

"I took him to the THP website on the Internet."

"Oh?" Katie sat up straight in her chair.

"He became very interested. He kept saying, 'This is my hotel? My hotel?' "

Katie felt her heart drop. His hotel. Her hotel. She shook her head, forcing the conflict of interest away. "Does he remember anything specific?"

"A little. He recognized the photographs taken of the lobby. There's a photo of the front entrance. . . ."

"Yes. . ."

"He pointed to the doorman and said, 'Miguel.' Is that correct?"

Katie's breath caught in her throat. "Yes. Miguel has been here since my husband's father ran the business. Did he remember anything more about Miguel? About his loyalty to the company. . .or about. . . Does he remember anything about running the company?"

"No. In fact, what I wanted to talk to you about is his emotional detachment from what he sees and remembers."

"I know. I've noticed. But I don't understand."

"Let me give you an example. Think of a special time you had with your mother or father. Or both of them." He paused. Katie stared ahead, waiting for him to continue. "Go ahead."

"Oh. You want me to tell you about it."

"Please," he said from the other end of the line.

"Hmmm. Okay. Well. One time. . .I remember—and this is just the first thing that comes to mind—one time my father took me to his office in Savannah on a teacher's workday. You know, those days when the teachers have to go in, but the kids get a free day from school?"

"I know."

"Well." Katie reached up to scratch lightly at her throat. "I was about eleven, I think. Eleven or twelve. I was old enough to dress for the occasion; I know that. And all the way there—it was about an hour's drive—my father spoke to me as though I were a young adult. We stopped and got coffee and a Danish in a little café before walking the rest of the way to his office. The rest of the day I stayed with him, meeting the people he worked with." She paused and laughed lightly. "Sometimes he would ask me questions as if my opinion would actually sway his decisions."

"And how did it make you feel?"

"Proud. Very proud and very grown-up. I remember thinking on the way home how much I loved my father and how I wanted to grow up to be just like him one day." Katie looked around the office where she presided as president of THP. The wide windows overlooking Manhattan, the leather sofas, the expensive works of art. *My father,* she thought, *would be so proud of me.* Her father would say, "Kitten, I always knew you had it in you."

Dr. Robinson's next words brought her back to the reality at hand. "Now, imagine having that memory, but without the pride or the love. No emotion tied to the memory at all."

Katie's shoulders sank. "Oh."

"That's what your husband is going through."

"Oh, I see."

There was another pause from the other end of the line.

"I have a suggestion," Dr. Robinson continued. "Would you like to hear it?"

Katie rested her elbows on the top of her desk, hung her head a bit, and worked the tension from the muscles in her neck with her free hand. It had been a difficult week. . .a difficult few months, actually, relieved only by those few precious days in Vermont. "I would love to hear it."

"Mr. Webster remembers a place that the two of you own in the Hamptons."

Katie's head came up. "Yes."

"Good memories there?"

"Very good memories. Except. . ." She cocked her head to the right just a bit. "That's where he came up with the idea of the car bombing."

"I see."

"What is it you suggest, then?"

"Time away. Take two weeks. A month, if necessary. Go to your home and get to know one another again. He's remembering you as his wife, Mrs. Webster, but he doesn't remember meeting you or falling in love with you. He has to make that connection all over again."

"I see."

"Allow him to get to know his friends and family. He needs more than just the time they spend here at the hospital, which can only be an hour here and an hour there. But I have to warn you, Mrs. Webster. Your husband's moods may swing during this process. The man you thought you knew will not necessarily be the man you take with you to your home. In time, we'll be able to fix this, I believe."

Katie turned to her computer and opened up her business calendar, which she had access to but Vickey kept track of. "I'm willing to deal with that. When are we talking about? How soon?"

"I know this could be a problem for you. You do have a company to run."

"Yes." She scanned the dates for meetings that might need to be attended. . .or pushed forward. . . . She noted that in two days she had an interview with *Newsweek*, highlighted in blue, which was Vickey's code for *not set in stone*.

"And I would need you to bring him to the city at least twice a week. But I think it's important for Mr. Webster's recuperation."

Katie looked up. "Then there's no doubt that we'll do it. I can do most of my work from our home. I may have to come in for a meeting or two, but that's not a problem."

"Good."

"When are we talking about?"

"The sooner the better. In fact, if you think you can be ready by tomorrow. . ."

"Tomorrow it is." Katie paused and bit her lower lip for a moment. "Have you told Ben?"

"No. Not yet."

"I'll be there this afternoon. I'd like to be the one to tell him, if you don't mind."

"I think that's an excellent idea."

Katie typed HAMPTONS in the lined box representing the following day in the calendar, then saved the entry and sent a reminder to Vickey via E-mail. "I'll see you around five o'clock, then."

"See you then." Katie disconnected the line, then connected again. "Vickey? Can you ask James Harrington to come to my office, please? . . . Yes, now. . .thank you."

CHAPTER TWENTY-SIX

Mattie was awake when Bucky returned from the newsstand. As soon as he walked in the door, he could see her sitting in the brushed gold chair near the French doors in the living room, reading her favorite *Town & Country* magazine. At least, he assumed that was her reading selection of choice; it tended to be the only magazine she ever read.

She'd lit a fire in the fireplace—obviously to try to appease him upon his arrival, for they had argued again the previous evening—and from the scents emanating from the kitchen, she'd begun to brew a fresh pot of coffee. Seeing him, she stood, folding her magazine and setting it on the oversized, low coffee table, which held a vase of fresh flowers nestled between his stacks of reading books. "Bucky," she whispered. He noticed immediately that she'd dressed in a pair of white slacks and one of his gray, pin-striped shirts.

Bucky stepped in slowly, determined not to give her even so much as an inch of hope that he was pacified. A light blue floral chair was before him. He carefully laid the plastic bag from Thad's onto its seat and began to peel off his outer coat. "Pet," he said, then lifted his coat to her with the extension of his arm. "Put this up for me, will you?"

He watched her shoulders fall, then rise again as her jaw set and she moved toward him, taking the coat. "Coffee?" she asked. She was barely audible.

Bucky leaned over the chair to retrieve the bag and to hide his smile. He sobered, straightened, and gave her a nod. As she began to step from the room, he added, "I hope you made it strong. . .like I like it."

She stopped and looked back over her shoulder. "Of course," she said, then continued on.

Bucky took a seat on the chair's matching sofa, which faced the fireplace. Sitting, he crossed his legs and began to pull the periodicals from the bag, aiming his attention on locating yesterday's *Post*. He pulled it from the stack just as Mattie reentered the room, carrying a tray of steaming cups of coffee served in his favorite stoneware mugs. Without looking up at her, he said, "Just put it on the coffee table, pet."

She obeyed, then knelt before him, wrapping her arms around his legs and peering up at him. "Bucky, don't be angry. I'm sorry about last night. I know you're tired of my incessant nagging about Paris, but you're my brother. You're all I have left in this world."

Bucky set the *Post* next to him, atop the other periodicals, and cupped her face with the palm of one hand. "My dear, if you don't learn to discern what you can and cannot say to me, you won't even have *me* left to call your own." He squeezed her jaw. *"Capisi?"*

"Capisi." She rose up on her knees and hugged him briefly, kissing him on both cheeks. "Friends?"

He smiled at her, this time genuinely. "Oh, Mattie. More than friends. You are my sister. I would die for you." He shook his head. "But you cannot forget who I am. . . ."

She leaned over and rested her head on his broad chest. The rich darkness of her hair tumbled across the starch white of his shirt. He dug the fingers of his right hand through the strands and tossed it playfully. "Up now," he said. "We need to talk about something."

She complied with his command, then reached for her mug of coffee and moved to sit in the chair where she'd been when he first came in. She sat, cross-legged, bringing the mug up slowly to meet her thin lips. "What is it?"

He picked up the *Post*, again turning his attention to it. She watched, silently and patiently, as he opened first one page and then another until his eyes rested on something that seemed to captivate him. His face changed repeatedly throughout the course of his reading; one moment he seemed amused and the next contemplative.

Mattie leaned forward. "Bucky?"

Bucky folded the paper until the only part showing was the section in which he had been reading, then reached across the space that separated them to give the paper to her. She leaned over to receive it, never taking her eyes off his until she had settled back into her chair. She then read the article about William Webster, laughing lightly as she read silently. When she was done, she looked up. "This is priceless."

Bucky stood and walked over to a corner desk near the windows and next to the fireplace where a gold case of his favorite imported cigars lay atop a small wooden box. He opened it, retrieved a thin smoke, and placed it between his teeth, looking back at his sister. "It gets better," he said.

Mattie turned to get a better look at him. "Do tell."

Bucky remained quiet as he prepared his cigar, snipping the end and lighting it, puffing the aromatic smoke toward the fire. "My sources tell me," he began, flipping the gold case back to the box and then moving to his place on the sofa, "that Katharine Webster has made certain stocks public at THP. According to what I am told, she is about to break ground on a spa in Montana."

"Are you thinking what I think you're thinking?" She turned her body again to face him.

Bucky grinned at her, an almost malicious expression settling on his handsome face. "Of course, pet. Time to diversify a bit. Time to own a part of Webster's empire."

"And in doing so—" she began.

"And in doing so," he interrupted, "to own a part of Webster himself."

Katie arrived at the hospital in time to have dinner with her husband. At her request and by special permission from Dr. Robinson, they dined at a small restaurant just down the street from the hospital, to which they could walk with an agent close behind them. She instinctively felt that it was best for Ben to again learn to associate with the outside world of the city and that the two of them should be seen publicly, especially as a couple.

The restaurant, intimate and Greek in theme, was fairly crowded for so early in the evening. As soon as they entered, she turned to Ben and said, "Are you comfortable here? Would you prefer to dine somewhere else?"

He shook his head. "This is fine." She noted that his voice was somewhat monotone, something it had never been in the past. At least, not to her. She could read his moods by the sound of his voice. But not now. . .not anymore.

She turned back. As the host approached them, she reminded herself not to take charge but to allow Ben to do so, which he seemed to do comfortably enough. When they had been seated and had ordered their drinks, Katie took a deep breath and sighed.

"Tired?" he asked her.

She nodded almost imperceptibly. "A little."

He smiled. "What is it you do all day?"

Katie placed her hands in her lap and pressed down. Her usual activities were enough of exhaust her, but today she'd had to meet with James Harrington as well. . .to tell him of her planned long-term absence and to answer his probing questions. He was quietly pleased at knowing Ben was back, unquietly displeased at learning he was not his old self, and then kind enough to tell Katie that he would not let her down in her absence.

"Ben," she began, looking down at her lap. "Ben," she said again, looking into his eyes, "do you remember The Hamilton Place?"

"I looked at a Web site with Dr. Robinson."

"But do you remember working there?"

He looked down. "Not really. No."

Their waitress returned with their drinks, setting them on the table and looked at the ignored menus. "Need another minute?"

Katie smiled at a woman who was probably not much older than herself but who appeared to be ancient. Lines crossed her face, and her faded green eyes were sad and tired. "Please. Actually," she continued as the waitress stepped away, "if you could just give us a few minutes to nurse our drinks and talk, then we'll order."

The woman nodded and retreated back to the bar area while Katie returned her attention to Ben, who had turned just enough to watch the waitress leave. When he turned back to her, he said, "You handled that well."

Katie took a sip of her drink. "I've had to learn to do a lot of things, Ben. Handling things well is just the tip of the iceberg."

He reached for his glass and brought it to his lips. "Tell me. Tell me what you mean."

Katie returned her glass to the table. "You don't remember being the president and CEO of The Hamilton Place?"

Ben looked sad but only for a moment. "Not really, no. I have. . ." He breathed heavily. "I have little glimpses. . . ." He placed the glass on the cocktail napkin it had come with.

"Now you tell me." She leaned forward, wanting him to gain a sense of trust and intimacy with her.

He studied the votive candle and lantern between them. "Large office windows."

"Mmm-hmm."

"I sometimes see myself at a desk. . .a rather large desk. . .and to the left of me are sofas." He stopped, looked down at his drink on the tabletop, and chuckled.

She smiled. "What is it?"

"Am I remembering correctly?" he asked, looking deeply into her eyes.

"Yes." She wanted to say, "That's your office," but then struggled with to whom the office actually now belonged.

"My office?"

"Yes."

His chocolate brown eyes danced. "I had a dream once. You were sitting on one of the sofas, dressed in a long sea green dress with little pink stones on it."

"I own a dress like that, yes."

"Then maybe it wasn't just a dream." He paused. "Did I buy it for you?"

She laughed. "Technically."

He smiled at her gaiety. "What does that mean?"

"It means you didn't necessarily go out and purchase it, but I suppose your checking account did."

"I see."

Katie leaned in closer. "Ben, how does it make you feel when you remember me sitting on the sofa in the sea green dress?"

He paled. "I'm sorry."

She reached over the small table and touched his right hand with her left one, which he turned palm up as he wrapped his fingers around hers. Bringing her hand up, he remarked, "I gave you this engagement ring, I suppose." He ran his thumb over it as she nodded yes, pushing it to one side to get a better look at the sapphire band encircled with crisscross diamonds she wore beneath it. "Hmmm."

"What?" she asked, tilting her head to one side.

"There's a bracelet to match."

Katie's eyes narrowed a bit. "No. No, I don't think so."

He looked up at her, clearly sure of himself. "Yes, there is. It's in my safe deposit box."

"Oh, Ben. I'm sorry. I. . ." She was aware that he was now clasping her hand.

"No. No, why are you sorry?"

She paused in contemplation before moving on in the conversation. "Ben, I checked your safety deposit box after you. . .afterwards. There was no bracelet."

But he continued to smile. "You're talking about the one at the bank."

"Of course."

He ran his free hand through his dark hair. "No. There's another one, in my office. Hidden. No one knew about it, not even—" He stopped and stared at Katie. "Vickey, right?"

"That's right."

"It's in there, Katie. I can tell you how to get it, if you'd like."

Katie shook her head no. "I have a better idea. Why don't I take you there?"

CHAPTER TWENTY-SEVEN

Katie insisted that Ben and she stay at the restaurant long enough to eat.

"You need to eat," she told her husband. "And so do I."

When Ben had excused himself for a few minutes, she called James Harrington on her cell phone. After explaining the situation to him, she asked, "Can you meet us in the private back entrance? I don't want a stir."

"I'll have everything cleared out."

"Thank you, James. I really appreciate this." She pushed her plate a fraction of an inch away from where it sat.

She then hung up and called Dr. Robinson, who agreed with her desire to take Ben back to the hotel's offices. "I'm very pleased," he added. "This is real progress. When we see Mr. Webster fully connecting to the world around him, I'd like to begin to take him step-by-step toward the events that occurred before the accident."

"But won't that just upset things?"

"Do you remember me telling you that trauma is the memory controlling the patient?"

"Yes."

"The only way to heal completely is to have the patient control the memory."

"Will you begin to work on that soon?"

"Yes."

Katie looked up to see Ben approaching her from the other side of the restaurant. She smiled at him, but he didn't return the smile. "Dr. Robinson, Ben is returning to the table, and we'll be leaving shortly for the hotel. Do you feel you should be there?"

Ben arrived at the table and sat in his chair. "Who are you talking to?" he asked.

Katie held up a finger.

"Not tonight," Dr. Robinson said. "But if you think—at any time—that you need me, I'm a phone call away."

"Who are you talking to?" Ben asked again.

"Thank you, Dr. Robinson. I'll let you know."

"Oh," Ben said.

Katie shut her cell phone off and slipped it back into the small purse she'd brought with her. "Dr. Robinson," she now answered.

"I know. I heard."

Katie attempted to get a read on her husband's face. "Are you okay?"

"Yes, of course." He smiled then. "Are you ready to go?"

"Yes."

Simon drove them to the hospital in Katie's private limousine. The agent assigned to Ben followed close behind.

"I don't remember him," Ben told Katie from his place next to her, nodding toward Simon.

Katie turned her head and smiled across her shoulder. "I hired him after you were gone."

"*You* hired?" Katie heard a hint of agitation in his voice.

She shifted a bit so she could get a better look at her husband. "Ben, I've been running this company for nearly two years. I thought you understood that. I've hired people. I've even fired a few. I've made executive decisions. I've had to." She watched his features harden and in an effort to gain control, she took his hand in hers. "Listen," she said softly. "I don't know what's happened in the last few minutes, but I'd like to see it get better."

Ben squeezed his eyes shut for a moment. Katie felt his warm breath on her face. The familiarity of it caused a rush up her spine, and she shuddered.

Ben's eyes opened. "I'm sorry. I'm okay." He smiled. "Are you okay?"

Katie nodded, tightening her hold on his hand. She wanted him to kiss her—to wrap her in his arms and tell her that everything would be all right. That they would be all right. To draw that part of her into that part of him that was intimate and precious. But one look at the emotional pain that seemed etched across his face told her it was too soon for such dreams. She relaxed her hand as she said, "I'm just a little anxious about the bracelet."

"You like jewelry?"

"Not nearly as much as you always liked giving it to me," she returned with a laugh.

Simon drove past the front of The Hamilton Place slowly, keeping time with traffic. Ben looked past Katie, leaning over slightly to peer out the window. "THP," he said.

"Yes."

"My hotel." He turned to gaze out the back window.

Katie looked down at her hands. "Yes. Your hotel."

Moments later, after asking a disgruntled agent to stay at the back door with Simon, they met James and slipped into the back entrance. Ben recognized his general manager immediately, and they shook hands. "Thank you for your help," Ben said.

James seemed taken aback. "Pardon me, sir?"

Ben flushed. "Your help. I'm sure you've been a big help to my wife. She tells me she's been running the business, but I'm sure she couldn't have done it without you."

Katie's back straightened and her shoulders squared. She held her breath and looked at James, who looked from his old employer to his present one and then back again. "She's done a remarkable job, sir. With or without my help."

Katie exhaled. "Thank you, Mr. Harrington." *One of these days*, she thought, *I might actually get a solid read on the man.*

James Harrington nodded. "Follow me," he said then. "I've made sure no one will intersect with us."

Katie and Ben followed James through back corridors and up a service elevator until they reached the floor where their office was located. When the elevator doors had opened, James held them in place and said, "If you don't think you'll need me, I'll wait here for you."

Katie and Ben walked past him. "Thank you again," Katie said. She took her husband's hand, guiding him down the semi-darkened hallway to their office. When they reached the door, she pulled the key from her purse and opened it.

A shaft of muted light cut through Vickey's outer office, giving ample illumination to their office door. "Do you remember any of this?" Katie asked him as they moved toward it.

"Yes," was all he said.

Katie unlocked the inner door and pushed it open, reaching in to flip the light switch. "I've got it," Ben said, turning the light on for them.

"Thank you," Katie replied, then watched her husband's expression change as he scanned his office. She stood in place, allowing him to walk over to the front of the desk, where his fingers lightly touched the grain of the wood, and then around to the chair behind it.

He grabbed the sides of the high back firmly in his hands, looking down at the neat stacks of files atop the desk. Katie could see his eyes rushing over them, trying to ascertain what they were, what they stood for, and just how much control he had lost in the time he'd been gone. Even with as much of him as she'd been confused by in the past week, she could still read his thoughts. "Quite a lot has happened," she said, the words bringing his head up to look at her.

"I'm not sure I'm even ready to know about it yet," he replied.

Katie extended her hand to him, and he moved back toward her. "Can I get you something to drink?" she asked, nodding over toward the wet bar.

He took her hand in his, squeezed, and then released it. "No. No, thank you." He paused. "You?"

"No."

He looked over to the sitting area then. "The flowers on the coffee table. That's new."

Katie looked over to the crystal vase filled with long-stemmed roses. "Yes."

They were silent until Ben finally said, "Well, then." He turned to her and smiled. "About that bracelet."

Katie smiled, too. "Yes."

Ben walked over to the entertainment center that stood against the right-hand wall between the two leather sofas and the heavy coffee table. He bent down, resting on his haunches, and pulled open the bottom drawer, filled with various trade magazines and old newspapers that Katie had not touched or even bothered to look through since she had taken over. "I'm surprised," Ben said, "that you didn't go through here and toss these."

Katie moved closer to where her husband was, peering over his shoulder. "I wanted to leave most things alone. I thought perhaps you might be saving those for a reason."

He shook his head no. "I don't think so. I think they were just magazines and such with articles I wanted to go back over but hadn't had the time." He raised an index finger. "Now watch this." He removed the magazines from the drawer, placing them on the floor next to his feet. Katie moved closer, watching him then twist the ornate brass drawer handle. The bottom of the drawer popped up, exposing a concealed underside. "This drawer isn't really as deep as it appears," he said.

"So I see." Katie watched her husband pull the bottom drawer away to reveal a slender metal box, just large enough to hold a few papers or jeweled treasures meant to later be given as gifts.

"Now then," he said standing with the box in his hands. "To open the box. . ." Ben walked over to the desk again. "Do you have the key to the desk?" he turned to her and asked.

"What? Oh, yes." Katie opened the clutch purse still in her hand and removed her key chain that held the tiny key.

"I'll take that," Ben said.

She laid the keys in the palm of his outstretched hand, then set her purse on the top of the desk and leaned over just enough to watch him set the box on the desk and then open the middle drawer. His fingertips ran along the top until he said, "Here it is," as he removed a small key that had been kept in place by a piece of tape.

"Oh, my gosh—"

Ben grinned at her. "What's more remarkable to you? That you never found this or that I can remember it?"

Her eyes met his. "I think a little of both."

He opened the box then, revealing a slender gift-wrapped box from Tiffany's.

"Oh, Ben," she said with a whisper, moving closer to him still.

"For you," he said, taking her hand and turning it palm up, then resting the box there. "Happy anniversary." He raised his brow. "At least I think it was for our anniversary."

Katie could only nod. She looked down at the box as a knot formed in her throat and tears began to cascade down her cheeks. "There now," her husband hushed her, stepping close enough that she could press the top of her head against his chest. She felt the strength of his arms go around her as she felt herself go limp and then heard the choked sobs escape from somewhere deep inside. Ben's hand came up and stroked her hair, gently at first, and then his fingers wove themselves through the thick strands, lightly tugging them. For the second time that evening, she shuddered, then stepped away and out from his embrace.

"I'm sorry." She walked over to a shelf where she kept a box of tissues, sliding one from its top position and discreetly blowing her nose. Then she laughed as she looked over to Ben, who still stood where she'd left him. "Why don't I open this?"

Ben took a few steps over and then stopped. "Are you sure you're okay?"

"Yes." She nodded again. "I'm fine." She began to pull the white ribbon away from the box wrapped in signature Tiffany paper.

He took another step toward her. "I didn't offend you, did I?" he asked.

Katie couldn't bring herself to look at him. The ribbon fell to the floor, and she popped the tape holding the paper in place with a fingernail. "No. Of course not." She pulled the paper away, aware that he'd taken another step toward her. And then another and another. She looked up at him, attempted a smile, then turned her attention back to the box. She removed the lid and then retrieved the inner box, narrow and square.

"I hope you like it," Ben said. He had now reached her and stood over her. Katie could feel his anticipation that matched her own nervousness.

"I'm sure I will," she whispered, then opened the box. "Oh, Ben!" Her fingertips trembled as she lifted the sapphire and diamond bangle from where it had stayed hidden for nearly two years. It was the perfect match to her wedding band. "It's exquisite."

Ben took the bracelet from her fingers. "Allow me," he said, opening it as he'd always done when he'd given her jewelry, and slipping it over her slender hand, clasping it in place around her wrist.

She looked up at him. "Thank you." It was all she knew to say.

"You're welcome."

They stared at one another for long seconds until Ben finally took a step back. "Well, then." He looked over to the emptied drawer and scattered magazines nearby. "I suppose we should put this back together and get back to the hospital."

Katie started slightly. "Yes. I suppose so." She followed her husband over to the entertainment center. "Allow me to help," she said.

He'd already dropped down to the floor, then looked back up at her. "No. Why don't you take care of the desk area? I'll take care of this."

She nodded in answer, then dutifully did as he'd suggested.

CHAPTER TWENTY-EIGHT

Three phone calls were made later that night, all of which affected Katie Webster.

The first one was from Katie to her best friend, Marcy, telling her of the day's events and the gift of the bracelet.

"I don't understand," Marcy said. "Why did you step away from him?"

Katie lay curled in the security of her bed—the one she had at one time shared with her husband—facing the empty pillow next to her. She had taken off the bracelet and laid it in the center of it; the stones winked at her in the glow of the bedside sconces. It gave her the sense that somehow Ben occupied their bed once again, and she closed her eyes at the wonder of it.

"Because. Because I thought it was getting a little too intense, and I don't think he's truly ready for that yet."

"Katie, really. If I'd waited for Charlie to be *truly ready*, we'd still be single."

Katie giggled. "Charlie and Ben are two different animals. Believe me."

"I practically had to hog-tie him so he'd propose."

"Marcy—"

"I'm sure Mr. Romantic had quite the evening planned for the two of you, though."

Katie thought for a moment, remembering Ben's proposal, the poetic nature of his words, the tenderness of his touch, and the sweetness of the kisses that followed. "Mmm. We were on a cruise in the Mediterranean."

"You shameless, wanton woman, you."

Katie rolled over on her back and closed her eyes. They burned with fatigue. "That was before I rediscovered my faith. So you can't judge me there," she half-teased.

"I wouldn't judge you anyway, my friend. I love you."

"I love you, too."

They paused in their conversation, and then Marcy asked, "Does he know yet?"

Katie opened her eyes. "Know what?"

"About your conversion?"

Katie brought the palm of her hand up to cup her forehead. "No. He hardly knows me as a person or his wife, let alone my religious beliefs."

"How do you think he will respond?"

Katie hadn't thought about it, and she said so. "I'll cross that bridge when we get to it."

"What if he doesn't like it?"

"What's not to like?"

Marcy chuckled from the other end of the line. "You'll see."

"Marcy—"

"I won't say another word."

"Thank you."

"What else is on your mind?"

Katie frowned. "Stop reading my mind, will you? Okay. There is something else on my mind. Marcy? Tell me what to do. . . ."

"About what?"

"Ben. And his presidency."

There was a moment of silence. "Katie, legally, he's the president, you know."

"Yeah, I know. But—"

"But, it's gonna be hard, huh? Letting go?"

"Yes. If I call you from time to time to cry on your shoulder, promise me you won't get too preachy."

"Promise."

"Thanks. How are the kids?"

"Good. Michael is under a little stress right now, of course. . . getting ready for his senior year to be over at good ole BHS. Due to the lack of rain we had last summer, our crops are failing and money is a little tighter than we expected it to be. Thank God for scholarships and college funds."

"Marcy, I want to give him something very special for his graduation, but I would want you and Charlie to talk about it first."

"Sure. What's that?"

"I'd like to take him to France for a very special time of learning more about their culture. . .something he couldn't get from schoolbooks or from a class trip."

"Katie, that's too—"

"No, no. I mean it. You guys talk about it and let me know. Now, I've got to get some sleep. Tomorrow I have an early meeting with some members of my staff, and then I have to get to the hospital to sign the release forms. We'll leave from there for the Hamptons."

"My regards to the cottage."

Katie laughed lightly. "Oh, Marcy. G'night, my friend."

"G'night."

The second call was between Phil and Sabrina Richards, Phil's old FBI partner.

"She wants to do the interviews," he was telling her. "She wants to try to provide some type of sting operation. Something to bring Caballero out of the woodwork."

"May work," Sabrina said. "I'll need to talk to Briggs on this." Briggs was Sabrina's supervising officer.

"Do that. I'll tell Katie to hold tight, but I think there may be an interview tentatively scheduled with *Newsweek* in a couple of days. She alluded to it in a conversation we had earlier today when she was on her way to the hospital."

"I understand from our on-duty agent that she and Mr. Webster left the hospital."

"Really? I hadn't heard."

"They dined at a Greek restaurant, then went to the hotel for about an hour."

"I didn't know that either."

"According to the agent, Mr. Webster remembered something he'd hidden in his office and wanted to get it."

"Anything you need to know about?"

"No. Something personal between the two of them."

Phil frowned. Sometimes, when Katie was silent, it meant trouble. He made a mental note to call her early in the morning. "Oh. Did William stay?" As a man who loved his own wife, Phil was hoping so.

"No. The agent said they returned to the hospital. All safe and sound."

"I see. Well, call me as soon as you have something about the interviews."

"I'm sure Katie will want you to be there," Sabrina commented.

"If so, then I will be. Otherwise, I won't."

"Talk to you tomorrow, then."

"Good night."

The final call was placed long distance, Canada to the United States. When the owner of the home answered, he was met with, "Good evening."

"Mr. Caballero."

"Bad timing?"

"Of course not, sir. I take it you've read the news."

"Indeed I have. You can't imagine how upset I am that I haven't heard from you on this matter. I would think the return of Webster would be of the utmost importance to you."

"Things. . .things here have been. . .a little hectic."

"That's not my concern."

"No, sir."

Bucky allowed a pause for the sake of control. "We have to make a plan, and we have to make it soon."

"Of course, sir."

"You'll hear from me again soon," Bucky said, then disconnected the line without so much as a good-bye.

The owner of the home replaced the receiver of his phone, looked around the room as though someone might have been listening, then wiped the sweat from his brow.

CHAPTER TWENTY-NINE

The next morning Katie met with her senior staff and board members, explaining the situation and answering questions as best she could, and then finalized some things at her desk that would need her attention before she could allow herself to leave the city for an undetermined amount of time.

She gave detailed instructions to Ashley concerning items that needed to be completed on the Montana project. She stopped by housekeeping long enough to check in on Misty, the ex-dancer whom she'd hired just a little over a month earlier.

"Are you doing okay?" Katie asked the young redhead.

"Yeah, sure," Misty answered from where she stood in the supply room, organizing cleaners.

Katie frowned a bit. Misty wasn't going to be an easy convert to reach in a short period of time. "I wanted to let you know that I'll be gone for a little while."

"Yeah, I heard."

"You did?"

"Yeah. Brittany and Ashley told me. Didn't want me to freak out or anything, you know?"

Katie smiled. "You have my cell phone number. If you need anything, call me, okay?"

"Yeah. Sure. Thanks."

"You're welcome. When I return, I want to talk to you a little further about what you'd like to do with the rest of your life. I apologize I haven't been able to spend more time with you since you came here."

"No problem. But, yeah, I'd like that. Sure."

Katie nodded. "See you soon, then."

As Katie and Maggie were leaving the hotel, they stopped by Jacqueline's where another one of Katie's protégées, Brittany, worked. The willowy, young black woman greeted them with her wide smile, showing white and even teeth. "Heeeeeey," she said. "I hear you're off to take care of your man for awhile."

Katie smiled. "I am. Just wanted to stop by and say you can call me on my cell if you need me."

"Sure thing." Brittany wrapped her in a quick good-bye hug.

Katie started for the door and then stopped to look back at Brittany. They exchanged final smiles, then Katie turned back toward the door, looping Maggie's hand into her arm and guiding her toward the lobby.

They arrived at the hospital shortly before eleven, where Sabrina Richards—a tall, thin, handsomely pretty woman in her thirties—waited for them. She and Katie discussed a plan of action, mainly that she and another agent would follow the limo to the Hamptons and take up temporary residence in Ben and Katie's home. Katie was not completely pleased, but she understood their reasoning.

"Phil Silver called me last night," Sabrina went on to say, running a hand over her glossy dark hair she'd pulled into a tight chignon. "He tells me you want to do an interview with *Newsweek*."

"More to the point, they want to do an interview with me."

"I've talked to my supervisor, and he agrees with your thinking. If Caballero isn't crawling out of the woodwork yet, he will be as soon as these interviews are published."

"Do you think he could already know?"

Sabrina shook her head. "Depends on where he's been keeping himself." She paused for a moment. "I also understand you and Mr. Webster went to the hotel last night."

Katie extended her wrist, displaying the bracelet. "He remembered hiding this in a secret compartment of my. . .his office."

Sabrina reached up and cupped Katie's wrist in the palm of her hand. "Nice."

Katie smiled, flipping her wrist over to show her ring. "It matches my band."

Sabrina's green eyes met Katie's blue ones. "Not a bad set, Katie. Not bad at all. So, are you ready to take your husband to the Hamptons?"

Katie nodded. "As ready as I'm going to be."

She had Ben checked out, in the back of the limo, and on their way to the Hamptons by noon with Sabrina Richards and another agent following close behind them.

"Hungry?" Katie asked Ben, who sat across from her and with Maggie, who patted his hand regularly.

Ben shook his head no. "Not really."

She had brought a briefcase full of work to do but decided against opening it during the ride to the Hamptons. Instead she pulled the nearly untouched novel she'd taken to Vermont out of an oversized shoulder purse. As she did so, her fingers brushed along another book she'd sent Vickey to a bookstore to purchase for her. This one was on amnesiac patients and their recovery.

She chose not to read this one in front of Ben either. She didn't want to make him uneasy in any way. She was, after all, uncomfortable enough for both of them.

There was so much to think about, to plan for, and though she somehow managed to read the words on the pages before her, she comprehended none of them. Instead her mind was racing with thoughts and ideas on how she and Ben would interact with one another once they reached their home. . .what they would do with their time. . .where they would sleep.

She didn't think Ben was ready for any kind of romantic involvement, even with his wife, the woman he'd pledged to love forever. She closed her eyes, remembering the night before, the way it had felt to be in his arms, to feel his breath so close to her face, to have his fingertips woven through the thick strands of her hair.

Opening her eyes again, she saw the bracelet he'd given her, encircling her left wrist. She flattened her hand against the pages of the open book, taking in the sight of the bracelet and wedding ring together, topped by the impressive diamond of her engagement ring.

She had lived the fairy tale.

She had survived the nightmare.

What, she wondered, would the rest of her life bring?

When they'd arrived at their Hamptons' home, Sabrina introduced the other agent as Dylan O'Neal. Agent O'Neal appeared to also be in his thirties. His complexion was pale and freckled and his hair caught somewhere between blond and red.

"We're going to scout the grounds," Sabrina told them. "We'll be back in the house in about a half hour."

Once inside, Katie sent Simon to a nearby deli for lunch. "You can bring in the luggage when you return," she said. After he'd gone, she then insisted Maggie go to her bedroom for a nap.

An exhausted Maggie did not protest. Rather, she turned to Ben, patted him lovingly on the arm, and said, "I'll see you when I wake, Master William."

Ben seemed ill at ease as to what to do. His body was unsteady as he leaned over and kissed the cheek of the woman who had been his lifelong nanny and housekeeper. "Have a good rest," he said.

Katie crossed her arms across her abdomen as Maggie shuffled out of the foyer and into a hallway leading to the downstairs bed-rooms. She waited for her husband to turn to her, to say something, but when he didn't, she spoke. "Do you remember anything?"

Ben turned to look at her. "Yeah. Yes, I do."

"Do you think you could walk through the house unescorted?"

Ben crossed his arms as his wife had. "I could find my way around, yes. I can't say that I know the house's blueprint in my mind right now, but I think that as each room came into view, the memory of it would, too."

Katie sighed. "I want you to be comfortable while we are here. There haven't been any changes from the last time you were here, so you should find everything okay."

Ben nodded, then turned and walked into the formal living room. Katie followed him, quietly watching him study their sur-roundings. After a moment or two, he moved toward an oil painting of an ornate goblet and a loaf of bread that he had pur-chased during their first trip to Paris together. "*The Bread and the Wine,*" he said, now standing directly in front of it.

Katie stood at the back of a chair, her hands clutching its top. "Yes. Do you remember anything specifically about it?"

He turned his head enough to look over his shoulder at her. His face wore a smile. "I remember that there's a wall safe behind it."

She smiled, too. "True."

"If you know that," he continued, turning fully to look at her, "then you know that's where I hid the file of information from Bucky Caballero's escort service."

Katie nodded. "And what an evening that was."

"Can you tell me about it?"

Katie motioned to a nearby chair as she moved to sit in the one before her. "Why don't we sit? Simon should be back soon with our lunch."

"Good. I'm starving," he said, sitting in the chair.

Katie raised her brow. "Do you want me to see if I can find

something in the kitchen?"

He shook his head. "I'll wait."

Katie pressed herself against the back of the chair. "My best friend from childhood is a woman named Marcy Waters. Do you remember sending me back to Georgia?"

"Yes."

"Well, she and I reconnected there. She's. . .she's quite a character. I can't wait for you to meet her, really. Marcy has a streak of adventure in her, but I've always felt safe when I was with her. When Phil and Sabrina came to Georgia to tell me you had. . . died. . .I asked Marcy to come back to New York with me."

Ben looked down at his hands, then back to Katie. "I'm so sorry about that. More sorry now, of course. I only meant for you to think I was dead for a week. No more than that."

"I know."

"So, then what happened?"

"Do you remember sending the book *Volpone* to me?"

Ben seemed to think about it for a moment, then nodded. "Yes. I had hidden the clues to where the file was within the text."

"I didn't really get that at first, but on the flight up here, Marcy did. *Drink to me only with thine eyes, and I will pledge with mine. . . .*"

"*. . .Or leave a kiss but the cup, and I'll not look for wine,*" Ben finished for her.

"As soon as she saw the painting, she knew the files had to be hidden behind it. We pieced together the other clues, found the keys, and then the file."

"I'm impressed."

Katie couldn't help but laugh. "Phil wasn't. I'm surprised we're still friends."

"Did you bring him in on it?"

Katie looked away for a moment, then back to her husband.

"No." There was a hint of mischief in her voice. "You'd have to know Marcy. Oh, and Marcy is a very sore subject with Phil, by the way, which I'll explain later. Marcy and I waited until everyone had gone to bed, slipped downstairs, and began to search for the keys. We found the first key with your set of cuff links, the second in the book *Playing the Rook,* and the third stuck to the bottom of the tennis racquet."

"I remember all that. And you and your friend—"

"Marcy."

"Marcy. You and your friend found all this by yourselves. Good."

Katie frowned. "What did you expect me to do, Ben? Didn't you expect me to find it?"

He didn't answer at first, then said, "I guess I expected you to show the clues to Phil and allow him to take it from there."

Katie smiled. "I think Phil would have preferred the same, but you two weren't counting on Marcy."

Simon stepped around the double doors of the living room. "Mrs. Webster." He glanced over to Ben. "Mr. Webster. I've brought lunch."

Katie stood. "Let's go get something to eat. I'll tell you what happened next later."

CHAPTER THIRTY

Katie chose to sleep in a guest bedroom that night. She hadn't really thought things through, and as the day wore on, the tension between Ben and her seemed to mount. Perhaps, she thought later as she lay alone in the room just down the hall from the master suite, her husband had been as anxious as she as to where they would spend their first night alone together as husband and wife after nearly two years. Or, even still, perhaps as he was getting to know her again, he was finding that he didn't like her very much. . .or love her, for that matter.

She slept very little, wrestling with these thoughts and others: Could he have been with Andi during their time together in France? Phil had told her that Andi insisted their relationship was purely platonic—that of the helpless and the helper—but she wasn't sure she believed it entirely. After all, Ben was a man, wasn't he? Full of desire and passion. Katie knew this firsthand. And Andi was a woman, wasn't she? A beautiful woman. . .also full of desire. . .and need. . . And if Katie knew anything about the human psyche, it was more a need to be loved than to love, especially by someone as powerful as William Benjamin Webster.

Several times during the night she went to the door of her bedroom, thinking that she would boldly approach the master suite. . .just to see. . .to discover. . .if Ben was struggling with the same thoughts as she. But as soon as her hand reached the brass scroll-shaped doorknob of her room, she would pull back. "He's not ready, Katie," she whispered aloud. "You would know if he were. . .and he's simply not." At one point she turned and pressed her back against the door, then allowed herself to slide down it. The hem of her ivory satin gown formed a puddle about her feet as she pulled her knees to her chest and wrapped her arms around them. Pressing her face into the space that formed a valley between her knees, she prayed for God's wisdom. "I know You ordained the marriage bed, Lord," she prayed aloud. "I just don't know if the man I married is really the man lying in the bed down the hall." She nodded. "Oh, yes, I know he's the actual person. But I'm not sure I know him anymore. One minute I feel as though I do and the next as though I am looking at a stranger." She remembered again the moment they'd shared the night before. . .the feeling of being in his arms. . .and she squeezed her legs harder still, pressing her lips together. "I want. . . ," she went on. "I want so much for him to love me again like he did before all this happened. Help us, Father. Help us."

Katie woke a little over a half hour later. She had closed her eyes and, resting her head on the tops of her bent knees, had fallen asleep. When her eyes blinked open, she was both stiff and cold. Pulling herself out of the position, she stood, walked over to the bed, and slipped into her nightgown's matching robe and slippers.

She left the guest bedroom, opening the door slowly in anticipation of it squeaking and possibly disturbing either Ben or the two agents who were taking up residency with them while they were in the Hamptons. When she had stepped out into the hallway, she drew the door toward her, allowing it to click shut, then turned and looked to her left—toward the master bedroom suite—where a sliver of light peeked out from the bottom of the closed door. *Ben is awake,* she thought, *or he fell asleep with a light on.* Either way, he was there and she was here, standing in her matching nightgown, robe, and slippers, and shivering in the chill of the house. She took a tentative step toward the closed door, then turned back and headed up the hall and toward the staircase. She raised the hem of her gown just slightly as she took the stairs, step by step, until she had reached the nearly pitch-black foyer. With the aid of the winter's moon shining in through the pedimented windows, she was able to feel her way through the room and to the doorway leading to the back of the house.

Katie stopped short as she reached the hallway closest to the kitchen; a faint light seemed to creep from around the doorframe, becoming less attenuated as it narrowed its way toward her. She listened intently, wondering if Maggie had possibly left the stove's overhead light on, or if someone might possibly be in the kitchen.

When she didn't hear anything, she took a step and then another, stopping again. What was that? An unusual noise. . .a sound like something being set down onto something else. Katie's breathing grew heavier. She looked back toward the foyer, questioning whether she should go back upstairs and get Sabrina. After all, she reasoned, the last time Sabrina was in the house, David Franscella had broken in and tried to kill her.

Katie frowned as her stomach lurched. The very thought of David Franscella did that to her. She had met him when she was a dancer—so many years ago, a lifetime ago when her naïveté and learned street smarts wrestled against one another. *This is,* she thought now, *what happens when you're eighteen and a runaway. You end up with men like David Franscella. . .married men. . . specifically, a man married to the sister of a man who would one day be your biggest nemesis, Bucky Caballero.*

Katie's heart quickened. After Ben's disappearance, when David had broken into the house to steal the file about Bucky that Ben had so carefully hidden. . .and kill Katie in the process. . .

Maggie had awoken, heard the scuffle, grabbed for the small pistol she kept at her bedside table, and had shot and killed David. If someone were in the house now—more specifically, in the kitchen—then they were in the room right next to Maggie's. Since Maggie had become more frail over the past nineteen months, Katie wondered if she would hear an intruder should he manage to get past the alarm system—a feat David had proven possible. Worse, if someone had broken in, would he have hurt Maggie? Could she be lying in a pool of her own blood, struggling for life?

Katie started to turn. She'd made up her mind to get Sabrina . . .to allow someone trained to investigate her own sense that someone was in the kitchen.

As she did so, a shadow moved across the open doorway. Katie's hand flew to her throat in an attempt to muffle her own fear. Her eyes widened as she stared at the form of a man who peered around the doorframe.

"Hi," her husband whispered.

"Oh, my gosh. You nearly scared me to death," she whispered back.

"What are you doing out here?"

Katie's shoulders sagged. "I came. . .what are *you* doing down here? Could you hear me out here in the hallway?"

A devilish grin spread across his face, the kind that had—in part—caused her to fall in the love with him eight years ago. "I heard you when you were coming down the stairs. Quiet as a church mouse but not so quiet I couldn't hear you." He crooked a finger at her. "Come on," he invited her. "I'm just having a glass of juice. Want some?"

He turned to step back into the kitchen, and Katie followed him, quickly running her fingers through her hair, all the while mentally kicking herself for not having brushed her hair before she came downstairs.

When they were both inside the kitchen, he whispered over his shoulder, "Juice?"

Katie nodded. "I'll get it. You go ahead and have a seat." She kept her voice low.

"Two years ago," she said as she sat at the table a moment later with a glass of cranberry-apple juice in her hand, "Maggie would have heard everything." She looked down as she placed the glass on the table.

"I'm having some problems with Maggie."

Katie's head popped up. "What do you mean?"

Ben looked toward the closed bedroom door just off from the kitchen, then back to Katie. "I remember her. . .I do. . .but not like this. I remember a woman full of spunk and sass."

Katie smiled. "That would be our Maggie. But, Ben. . .she's getting so old now. I've been struggling with whether or not to hire someone to replace her, but I know she'd be hurt and. . ."

"Or she'd hurt you," he added with a smile.

Katie pointed a playful finger at him. "That's what I said to Phil just the other day. Great minds—"

"Think alike," he finished for her.

They smiled at each other; then both took a sip of their juice. "I'm glad you came down," he said.

She looked up, allowing her eyes to study his. "You are?"

"I was thinking about all this." He looked around the room as though he were looking around the entire house. "This afternoon you asked me if I remembered the house. . .and I do. . . . I told you I thought I would remember the rooms as I came to them."

"Did you? Remember them, I mean?"

"Yes. I remember them." He stopped then and gazed at her. Katie could feel his eyes running down the form of her body, and she nervously reached for the glass of juice again, bringing it to her lips with a hand that betrayed her by its trembling. When she caught that he was smiling at her, she returned the glass to the table untouched. "You don't have to be afraid of me, you know." His voice was low and sweet.

"I'm not," she returned quickly, though her eyes darted to another part of the room.

Ben leaned over the table, resting his forearms along the edge. "Katharine Elizabeth—"

Katie's eyes cut back over to him. "What did you just call me?"

He smiled. "Oh, I remember your name. And I remember calling you that every time you tried to get around a subject, too."

"Ben."

"Want to know what else I remember?"

She answered with a nod.

"I remember that great big bedroom at the end of the hallway."

"You do." It wasn't a question.

"Yes. But you want to know what I don't remember?"

Katie ran her tongue over her lips. "What?"

"I don't ever remember a night since we married that you stayed in the guest room while I slept in our bedroom."

Katie felt her cheeks grow hot. "I didn't think. . ."

"Didn't think what?"

"I didn't think you were ready. I'm. . .I'm not even sure I am. What I mean to say is: Dr. Robinson said you had the memories but not the emotions tied to the memories."

"That's true," Ben admitted. "In part."

"In part?"

He sat back then, crossing his arms across his abdomen, seemingly to study her with the darkness of his eyes.

"What?" she asked. "What are you thinking?"

"I remember you, Katie," he said. "I remember holding you and kissing you and loving you." His eyes never left hers.

She was almost too afraid to allow hers to leave his. "But do you remember being *in love* with me?"

He didn't answer at first. He just stared at her, breathing in and out almost mechanically. . .deliberately. Finally, he shook his head. "No."

Katie brought her fingertips up to rub her temples, then returned her hands to her lap. "That's what I thought." She stood, and he grabbed for her wrist.

"But I want to remember. . . ."

She pulled her wrist from the light hold he had on her, keeping her eyes on his. "And I want you to remember. I do. I want you to know me and know the kind of love we had for each other." She reached down, kissed his cheek, and said, "Until then."

She turned and began to walk toward the door. "Katie," he said.

She looked back over her shoulder, knowing instinctively that she made quite a picture—standing in the shadows, dressed in flowing ivory and satin, chestnut hair spilling across her shoulders. "Yes?"

"Tomorrow."

"What about tomorrow?"

"Let's spend the day together. Just you and me. We'll go shopping and. . .oh, I remember. You always liked to go sledding. We'll do that, followed by dinner in town. And a sleigh ride."

"It's freezing out there." Her voice was barely above a whisper.

He stood, walked over to her and, taking her by the shoulders, turned her to look at him. "Oh, come on. What do you say? Make me fall in love with you again," he whispered.

He tipped her chin with his index finger, forcing her to look into his eyes, then brought his lips down on hers, barely touching them at first, and then deepening the kiss. When he broke away, he winked at her. "Until then," he said, then turned her by the shoulders again and gave her a gentle push toward the door.

CHAPTER THIRTY-ONE

"Word is," the confidant began, "Andi Daniels is back."

Bucky sighed on the other end of the phone. "Dear me. So she's the undisclosed woman I read about in the papers. Who would have thought?" He knew the level of sarcasm in his voice was just enough to throw off the man on the other end of the line. He reached for a cigarette from a dispenser kept atop his desk.

"There's more."

"I'm sure." He lit the cigarette using a gold and crystal Piezo table lighter.

"She's here."

"Where?" Bucky reached for the table lighter's matching ashtray.

"Here in the hotel. Katie is keeping her here."

"And Webster? Is it true he's in a hospital?"

"He *was* in a hospital for awhile. No one here knew anything about it until just before they left."

Bucky's brow rose. "Who left?"

"The Websters."

"What to you mean, they left?"

"They're in the Hamptons."

"And Andi?" Bucky asked, again drawing deep on the cigarette.
"Like I said, she's still here."

Bucky blew a stream of smoke from his lips. "Could this be any more perfect?"

"What do you plan to do?"

Bucky took a final draw from the cigarette. "That's none of your business. At least not now." He stabbed the cigarette out in the ashtray. "I pay you very well for what you do at the hotel." He reached for another cigarette and lit it, drawing deeply on it and, tilting his head back, sent the smoke from between his lips. "I want you to see the importance of this."

"I think I'm very well aware of the importance. By the way, Miss Daniels is staying here under an assumed name, but I can get her room number easily enough."

"Katie Webster. Is she still holding down the presidency, or is Webster himself?"

"She is. He's. . .I suppose you read that he suffered a head injury."

"Yes."

"So it'll be awhile. I'm guessing anyway."

Another draw of the cigarette and again, Bucky pressed the glowing embers of its end into the ashtray. "Then I'm guessing we don't have a lot of time. Thank you for the information. I'm sure you'll be hearing from me again today."

"I look forward to it."

"I'm sure you do."

CHAPTER THIRTY-TWO

It was a little after nine when Katie slipped undetected into the carriage house behind their home. Closing the door of the small and cozy living room, she turned and peered out of the nearest window, back toward the main house, hoping she'd not been seen.

She pinched the bridge of her nose with one hand, clutched the Day-Timer she refused to give up for a palm pilot in the other, then slowly mounted the stairs to the second floor where she'd recently transformed one of the three bedrooms into an efficiency office.

Even Ben didn't know about this room, about how she'd altered it, and she felt somewhat content knowing that he didn't. For now, it was hers and hers alone. She could come up here anytime, work for a couple of hours, and never be missed. Or, like this morning, she could make her phone calls to the city to touch base with Vickey, James, and particularly with Byron Spooner, who was supposed to have some new numbers for her on her Montana spa.

Once in the room, she stripped herself of her heavy winter coat and draped it over the small love seat pushed against one of the large windows overlooking the covered pool and tennis courts. When she'd made herself comfortable in the office chair, she placed the first call to Vickey, who reminded her of the telephone interview with *Newsweek*.

"I told the reporter *you'd* call *him*, okay?" Vickey said from across the miles.

"Good. I certainly don't want people calling here all day."

"Of course not."

Katie pulled at a drawer handle of the antique banker's desk she'd found at one of East Hampton's many antique shops and retrieved a pen. Poising it over that day's box in her opened Day-Timer, she said, "Go ahead."

Vickey gave her the number. Twice. "Got it?"

"Got it. Anything else I need to know?"

"Everything's fine here. What about there?"

Katie sighed. "Everything will be okay soon enough, I'm sure."

"Meaning?"

Katie returned the pen to the drawer, pushed it shut, and then sat back in the chair. "There's just the getting-to-know-each other thing. You know. As if you'd married a perfect stranger but were expected to be madly in love on your first night together."

"And how was that first night together?"

"Hmmm. Spent in separate rooms." Katie straightened herself in the chair, glanced over her shoulder, and through a front window. She had a clear view of the back of their house and could see Ben, coffee cup in hand, standing in front of the French doors of their living room. "Gotta go. Can you transfer me to James, please?"

"You've got it."

Katie's conversation with James was benign enough, though he did mention that Valentine's Day was right around the corner and the hotel staff was gearing up for the lover's specials Katie had implemented after the holiday of the previous year.

"Good," Katie said. "I approved ads for *WHERE New York,* the *New Yorker,* and *Town and Country.* Attention to detail, Mr.

Harrington. Attention to detail. We've got champagne, roses, and Broadway specials for lovers of all ages. We want to be known for this. We want people to pout, even, when they learn our rooms are filled during Valentine's weekend."

She thought she heard James chuckle from the other end, but she knew better. "I will see to everything in your absence. I will have to say that Julia thinks this is by far your most innovative idea for THP-New York."

"Just wait 'til she sees my spa," Katie noted aloud, though she couldn't help but think the man was "kissing up" to her. After all, Ben was back and, in Harrington's mind, this would mean a new change of guard. The last thing James Harrington wanted was for William Webster to think he had been anything but helpful to the president's wife. "But if this goes well, we'll begin the implementation in our other hotels. Especially in Paris. I've got great ideas for *L'Endroit de Hamilton*." She paused, knowing they were both thinking the same thing—Paris. . .Ben. . .Andi—and she quickly changed the subject. "Until then we must stay on task. Would you connect me to Byron Spooner, please?"

"Call if you need anything."

"Thank you. I will."

Waiting for Byron, Katie doodled on her Day-Timer, pondering her often-stormy relationship with the GM. For so long he'd fought her every move and idea. These days, especially since she'd almost been killed by the McKenzies, he was much more supportive, almost protective. His offer for the house in Vermont proved that.

Vermont.

Long walks in snow-covered lanes. The hills. . .the valleys. . . the old cemetery where she'd prayed for Maggie. The little shops. Darlene's. New friends like Kristy Hallman and Harrison Bynum. She closed her eyes. . .*what if,* she allowed herself to wonder. *What if. . .a man like Harrison. . .a child like Matthew?* In her heart, she so wanted a child. More so, she wanted what pleasures a simple life with a good man and an adorable child could offer her. As much as she loved Ben, she couldn't help but think, *What if he hadn't returned?* Would the relationship with Harrison have continued?

Is it wrong to wonder, Lord? Even in times like these?

Katie opened her eyes, then glanced over her shoulder again to find that Ben had moved away from the window. She wondered where he might have gone. Was he exploring? Talking to Maggie or perhaps to Sabrina Richards or Dylan O'Neal?

"Mrs. Webster?" The voice of Byron Spooner cut into her thoughts.

"Mr. Spooner, thank you for taking my call."

"Thank you for holding. I was. . .had stepped out for a moment."

"Not a problem. I'm hoping you have those numbers for me."

"Today's your day, Mrs. Webster. I understand you're in the Hamptons, so I can fax them to you or attach them in an E-mail. Which would you prefer?"

Katie thought for a moment. "E-mail them to me, please."

"You'll have them within the next five minutes."

Standing, Katie thanked her comptroller and then hung up. On her way out of the room she reached for her coat, slipping her arms into it as she bounded back down the stairs. She peered out the front window of the living room once more before opening the door and heading back to the main house, where she would see her husband and talk about what they'd do the rest of the day.

She ducked her chin to her chest, watching her booted feet as they crunched across the snow-covered stone path to the house. *"Make me fall in the love with you again,"* he'd said. The thought of it made her quiver inside, and she looked up again, wondering if she were really blushing or just imagining that she was. It was then that she saw Ben standing at the French doors again, arms folded across his chest, head tilted just a bit to the right.

She slowed in her walk, paused for a moment, then smiled and continued forward.

Ben opened one of the doors. "Good morning," he called to her.

"Good morning," she called back, suddenly aware that she'd left her Day-Timer on the desk in the carriage house.

"I thought perhaps you'd gone down to the shore for a walk," he said just as she reached him.

She stopped, turned her head toward the place where the shoreline ran behind their estate, and felt her hair as the wind whipped it across her cheeks. Ben reached up, gently pulling the strands away and tucking them behind her ear. She looked back up to him.

He smiled. "Good morning," he said again, then dipped his head and kissed her briefly on her lips.

She narrowed her eyes as her tongue darted out to touch her bottom lip and then retreated. "Good morning," she whispered back, taking a moment to just look at his handsome features. "No. No walk along the shoreline."

"I know. I saw you coming out of the carriage house."

She nodded. "Yes." She wrapped her arms around herself. "Brrr. Are you going to let me inside, or am I to become a frozen lawn ornament?" Ben stepped aside, allowing her entrance into the warmth of the living room, where a fire crackled in the fireplace. "Oh, good. A fire. Please tell me you did this and not Maggie."

"I did."

Katie hurried over to it, rubbing her hands together and watching as Ben shut the door and then joined her. "Good. She doesn't need to try to do that anymore."

"I agree."

Katie stopped rubbing her palms together, turned her backside to the fire, and began to slip out of her coat when Ben reached over to help. "Allow me," he said.

"Thank you, kind sir."

Ben threw the coat over to the sofa where it landed in a heap. "Now tell me," he began, but before he could go any further, she interrupted with, "I have an idea for today."

He turned to look at her. "Oh?"

"Let's head into East Hampton. Do you remember how much fun we used to have there? Antique shopping? C & V Wine Cellars?"

Ben smiled. "I remember a place called Barefoot Contessa. I remember that you liked to go there and buy coffee."

Katie moved to the sofa and retrieved her coat. "The best coffee anywhere. I can't imagine going to East Hampton—"

"—and not going to Barefoot Contessa."

Katie raised her eyebrows in a mock salute. "You remember."

"I remember."

She wrapped her coat around one arm, clutching the neck of it with the other hand. "So what do you say?"

Ben walked over to her and tapped her nose lightly with a fingertip. "You've got a date."

Katie sighed. The mere touch of his finger could melt her, still. "Ben," she whispered, taking a step forward and into his arms, where she allowed him to draw her close to him. She pressed her forehead into his chest and closed her eyes, breathing in the scent of him, until he whispered, "Hey."

She looked up. "Hey."

And then he kissed her, kissed her as deeply as he'd done the night before. As she dropped the coat wedged between them and slipped her arms around his neck, she thought, *I'll make you fall in love with me again, Ben Webster. I'll do it or die trying*.

CHAPTER THIRTY-THREE

Looking back on it later, Katie realized that things would have gone so well for her and Ben had she only thought everything through. But she hadn't. Hadn't anticipated the obvious. Hadn't realized that it was the little things in their relationship that had changed as much as the big things.

She drove them in her Jag to East Hampton, which he'd insisted upon. "I haven't driven here in awhile. . .everything is different, you know?" he said with a smile. A few wrinkles creased the area around his eyes, which only added to his handsome features.

"You're sure?" she asked, extending her car keys to him in the palm of her hand.

"I'm positive."

"Let's go then," she said, looping her arm around his and steering them toward the back door and beyond to their garage, which was a separate building behind the house.

Sabrina, Dylan, and Maggie waited for them there, Maggie smiling, happy and warm. "There you go, lambs. You have a good day."

Katie reached down and gave Maggie a kiss on her cheek.

"I'll bring you back some of that body lotion you're so crazy about, okay?"

"Ah, there's a love," Maggie said, kissing her back.

Ben hesitated a bit but also kissed the housekeeper/companion on her cheek. "Good-bye, Maggie," he said. "Stay warm."

"That I shall," she said with a nod.

"And rest," he added.

"That I shall also do. Spend a little quiet time with the good Lord, have a little lunch, and then take a nap."

Katie turned to Sabrina. "You'll follow us, then?"

"Always at a safe distance," she said. "Pretend we aren't even here."

Katie smiled. "You can count on it."

When they left, Maggie stood at the back door, waving her good-byes to them all. As Katie drove the car away, she waved back and chuckled inside. "That Maggie," she said. "I love her so."

"She's a dear," Ben commented. "Loyal, I'll give her that."

"You have no idea," Katie said, turning to look at him, albeit briefly. "Her devotion to you and her belief in you is what often-times kept us going. That and faith, of course."

"Maggie does have her faith."

Katie pulled onto the main road and away from the property of their estate. "Maggie's not the only one, Ben."

With her peripheral vision she saw him turn to look at her. "What do you mean?"

She pressed her lips together before answering, keeping her eyes on the road. "I mean, I also have faith. . .in God. Maggie's God."

"Well, of course you do."

Katie shook her head a bit. "I don't think you understand."

"I understand."

Slowing to a stop at a crossroad, she turned to look at him. "Do you?"

He shrugged his shoulders. "What's not to understand, Katie?"

He turned to look to his right. "The coast is clear. You can go."

Katie sighed, rolled her eyes a bit as she looked in the rearview mirror and spotted Sabrina and Dylan, then turned her attention back to the road. "I grew up in the church, you know. Granted, I made a few wrong turns when I came to New York, but. . . before. . .when I was younger, God was a natural part of my life."

"I would figure as much. Small southern town. Buckle of the Bible Belt, as they say."

Katie let out a tense laugh. "I think that's Oklahoma."

"What's Oklahoma?"

"The buckle of the Bible Belt. I'm from Georgia."

Ben was quiet before adding, "You know what I mean."

Without taking her eyes off the road, Katie reached over and laid her hand atop his. "I know what you mean," she said softly. She felt his hand turn, cradling her hand as he laced his fingers with her fingers. She smiled, slowed the car again—though this time there was no crossroad—and came to a stop. Turning to him, she lowered her lashes a bit as she said, "I love you, Ben Webster."

He squeezed her hand, leaned over, and kissed her lightly on the tip of her nose, then hovered close by.

She raised her eyes to meet his. "That the best you can do?" she asked.

His lips moved to hers. "That doesn't even come close to the best I can do," he teased. Moments later, when he had broken the kiss, he whispered, "Are they still back there?"

Katie dipped her gaze over her shoulder, across the back of the car, and to the Crown Victoria stopped behind them. "Oh, yeah."

Ben smirked. "Figures."

In *Bonnie Nuit,* a shop that specialized in lacy ladies' items and children's clothes, Ben pretended to browse through a sampling of children's clothing while Katie made a purchase of what she called "unmentionables."

"Don't mention it," Ben said with a grin, then turned away as she stepped toward the counter and, pulling her credit card from her wallet, made her purchase. From then on, for the most part, they just strolled arm in arm in and out of shops, with Sabrina and Dylan close behind, until finally Katie said, "I don't know about you, but I'm starved."

"What would you like to eat?"

Katie raised her face to meet his. "Red Horse to Go?"

Ben paused as Katie read his face. He struggled momentarily to remember the restaurant, then nodded. "I remember," was all he said.

It was during lunch that Katie noticed his growing silence and watched him seemingly stiffen as the meal went on. Questions asked of him were answered in monotone one-word answers. Finally, she said, "What's wrong, Ben? And don't say, 'Nothing.'" He looked down, and Katie watched as his jaw flexed. She could see his hands, poised above the table as he rested his forearms on either side of his plate, squeeze into fists. "Ben?" she asked again.

"I can't pay for this," he said.

"What?"

His eyes met hers, and she jumped a bit. They were cold. Hard. The amber flecks had turned to steel. "I—can't—pay—for—this," he said again, this time between clenched teeth.

Katie allowed her eyes to sweep the room. "Ben, don't."

"Don't?"

"It's okay," she said quickly, keeping her voice low. "Yes, you can pay for this. You're a millionaire, Ben. Don't you know that?"

"I may be a millionaire," he countered, raising his voice an octave. "But I *have no money!*" He slammed his hands down on the table. As plates and glassware rattled, Katie's attention went to Sabrina and Dylan, who sat just a few feet away, and whose interest was suddenly the two of them.

Katie turned back to Ben again. "Ben, please," she pleaded.

Ben dropped his head into his left hand and began massaging his forehead. "I'm getting a headache. Can we go, please?"

Katie reached across the table to touch his free hand. "Ben," she whispered, "I want to help you. Tell me what to do. I don't know what to do."

He swore then and, still gritting his teeth, said, "Just pay the bill and let's go."

Katie looked to Sabrina and Dylan again, then back to Ben. "Okay, Ben. Give me five minutes, and I'll have us out of here."

But he didn't answer her. He continued to rub his forehead until she stood and left him sitting alone as she sought out their server.

CHAPTER THIRTY-FOUR

It had been more than a week since the Websters had left for the Hamptons, and Andi Daniels was growing restless. To fill the hours, she'd done everything she could think of to do. She'd made a few calls to her parents—as she'd often done from France. They'd retired in California—a place where they felt their biracial marriage would be more readily accepted. They encouraged her to fly out, to spend time with them, to escape the possible danger she might be in.

She told them she'd think about it. And she had. Los Angeles offered some of the same nuances as New York. She knew this because she'd taken a trip out there with Bucky once. . .a trip she'd hoped would cause him to fall in love with her. But it hadn't. If anything, it had affirmed their roles to her. He was her powerful employer, a man who spoke in firm monotones that sent a shiver of fear through her spine.

Or was it desire?

With Bucky, she couldn't tell.

She wondered now where he was. If she knew Bucky Caballero—and she did—he wasn't far away. Especially now that the *Newsweek* article had come out. Bucky would be prowling the streets like a lion in winter, while she was now forced to spend most of her time in the suite Katie had seen that she be provided with. Though the suite was lovely and spacious, it closed in on her like the rooms of the chalet had begun to do.

Perhaps now was the time to place a call to California and take her parents up on their offer.

Instead, she plopped onto the settee in the master bedroom of the two-bedroom suite, snatched up a *Vogue* magazine lying next to her, and began to flip through the glossy, perfume-scented pages. When an ad for Saks Fifth Avenue came up, she paused. This was where it had all began for her. . . .

When Andi was growing up, her father had provided well enough for her and her mother with the salary he earned as a truck driver, but it had never been enough for Andi. She'd grown up wanting more. . .especially more than life had to offer a child of mixed blood. . .even if the combination of her mother's Oriental heritage and her father's African-American lineage had blessed her with an exotic aura and rare beauty.

She couldn't complain that she'd been ostracized. Rather than getting "the look" she'd seen other biracial children receive, she'd been showered with, "My goodness, aren't you the most gorgeous child I've ever seen?" Or something close to it.

She was also a gifted classical pianist. Her talents had garnished a scholarship to NYU, which, in turn, had brought her to the city. . .and all its trappings. She hadn't been able to shop at stores like Saks, but she could window-shop with the best of them.

And then, she'd met Bucky Caballero. In one night he'd taken a girl dressed in a clearance-rack dress from Saks from a promising career as a classical pianist to working behind a counter in a ladies' boutique, which was, in reality, a front for an international escort service.

Andi blinked back the tears that seemed to all but sear her eyes. She'd wanted it all. . .and she'd wanted it now. She closed the magazine, tossed it to the floor, and then stood and made her way into the sitting room where a wet bar beckoned her.

Since her arrival in New York, she'd been hitting the bottle too much, and she knew it. Not that she cared. The alcohol numbed the pain of loss and loneliness; she was actually able to tell herself that she was falling out of love with William Webster and in love with the almost ethereal feeling the honey liquid blanketed her in.

Just as she took the first angry sip, the telephone rang, and she jumped just a bit.

"Hello," she answered after the third ring.

"Andi. Phil Silver."

Andi downed the rest of her drink. "Mr. Silver. What brings you to telephone me on this absolutely dreary day?" She walked back to the bar and poured herself another drink.

"I thought I might take you to dinner. Something tells me you've been cooped up in that room about five minutes too long."

Andi guffawed. "Make that five *days* and you'll be on track. And, yes. Dinner would be perfect. But, please. Anywhere but here. One more meal at Bonaparte's and I'll puke."

"That bad, huh?"

"I refuse to discuss it. What time are we talking about?"

"I'll meet you in the lobby at seven."

Andi took another sip of her drink before continuing. "What shall the lady wear?"

"The lady should dress casually."

Andi frowned, remembering that Phil Silver—handsome as he was—was also a devoted married man who was, no doubt, taking care of her for William's sake. "I can do that," she said. "I'll see you at seven."

Phil hung up his office phone, then leaned back in his chair, resting his elbows on the armrests and clasping his hands together. He brought his index fingers up to his lips as he thought about the ever-complex Andi Daniels.

He'd never gotten the chance to meet her nearly two years ago when William had called him to tell him of the escort service being operated out of THP. . .and that Andi was the madam, of sorts. The only information he'd had was that Andi had flown to Atlanta with William after handing over the records to the escort service, including the names of high-profile officials. Immediately thereafter, Bucky Caballero and his sister Mattie Franscella had disappeared. By the time William's car had exploded—in what Phil now knew was a ruse—Andi Daniels, Caballero, and Mrs. Franscella were like phantom ghosts in the story—one moment here, the next gone.

Phil's first job had been to find Katie, to bring her back to New York safely, and to find the file he assumed William had hidden. He'd been successful, of course, but not so victorious when it came to finding the missing links. Now, Andi was back with William, and something told him Caballero and his sister would not be far behind. Especially now that Katie had begun to do press interviews. If he knew Caballero—and he did—the thrill of the catch would lure him back into the waters.

Every detail of this story had been an amusing sport or like *Clue*, a game he often used to help him solve his cases. Somewhere in the envelope were the name, the place, and the type of weapon used. In this case, the name was Caballero. . .the place was the city of New York. . .and the weapon was wit. Pure, unadulterated smarts.

Phil shook his head, clearing it of past thoughts. He reached for the phone again, this time dialing his home number.

"Hello?"

"Hey, sweetheart."

"Hey, good-looking," Gail answered back.

Phil smiled. Even after all these years, she knew how to say the right things to melt away the pressures of the world. "Look who's talking, there. No one better looking than the lady I married."

"You flatter me so. . .and, if I know my husband, you're calling to tell me you'll be late tonight."

Phil sighed. "Caught in the act."

"What now?" Gail was straightforward, but Phil didn't hear anger in her voice. He was grateful. Many a law enforcer's marriage had fallen apart because of time away from home. He didn't want to be a statistic, but he still had a job to do.

"I'm taking Andi Daniels out to dinner."

There was a pause before, "Should I bring my claws back in now or wait a few minutes?"

"Now, if you don't mind."

"Phil. Phil, you aren't working this case anymore. Do I need to remind you of that?"

"I'm not taking her out officially. I'm doing this as a favor to William."

"When did you talk with him last?"

Phil reached into the middle desk drawer in search of a piece of gum. "This morning."

"How is he? How is Katie?"

Finding an unopened pack, he began to tear into it. "He's still struggling. Katie seems a bit frustrated herself. She's trying to maintain her work from the Hamptons and help Ben to become fully connected again. I don't know how she's doing it."

"Maggie's there, right?"

He popped the gum into his mouth and began chewing. "Mmm. But Katie said her health is failing, and she's worried. Though, in typical Maggie style, Maggie is insisting she's just fine."

"What a dear."

"Mmm."

"Now, let's get back to you and that vixen."

Phil laughed. "I think we have to watch her, Gail. She's Caballero's link. Maybe no one else has figured that out yet, but I have."

"Again, my dear, sweet husband, this is not your case anymore."

Phil didn't answer.

"Are you hearing me?"

"I hear you. And you're right. But. . .I've got to finish this, Gail. I feel as though I failed two years ago and—"

"You're not a failure, Phil Silver."

"I didn't say that. I said I feel as though I failed."

"I see."

"Do you?"

"Yes. And I concede to your having dinner with Andi. Just behave yourself."

Phil sat up straight in his chair. "Yes, dear," he answered with a chuckle. "You're the bomb, you know that?"

"Oh, Phil." Gail laughed. "That's so past-tense. Get with the times, boy."

"What should I have said?"

"If you really want to compliment me, then say I'm off the chain."

"You're what?"

She laughed again. "See you later tonight."

CHAPTER THIRTY-FIVE

Katie sat in the living room of the carriage house, her most recent place of refuge. She'd been here for nearly two hours and had brought her afternoon tea in along with her Bible. The soft leather cover was now draped across her lap as she sat in what she called "the squooshy chair," a floral, overstuffed number left over from the days when Ben's mother had decorated the main house. The antiquity of it was soothing to her, reminding her of her own mother. . .and her mother's gardens and tea roses.

When she'd left the main house, Ben had been going over some files in his office while Maggie napped. She'd peeked in on her husband, asking what he was doing and if he wanted or needed anything.

"No," he'd said, looking up from his desk. "Just looking at some old records from the hotel." He dropped his attention back to the opened files spread out before him.

She'd nodded. "I see." Then, after pausing for a moment, she added, "I'm going to have some tea. Would you—?"

"No," he'd answered, bringing his eyes back up to her. "No, thank you. If I could just have a few minutes here. . ."

She hadn't answered him, simply turned and left, heading straight to her little piece of the world where silence and peace welcomed her, no one bothered her, and she could be queen of the castle. She thought several times about calling Marcy but found herself enthralled in the story of Esther instead, mesmerized by the fourteenth verse of chapter four.

"And who knows but that you have come to royal position for such a time as this?"

Katie sighed, curling her feet up under her, reading the passage again and again. Esther had become the queen by a series of events Marcy would call "God-cidence," rather than coincidence. Now, with the Jewish people—Esther's people—being threatened with death, she had the chance to save them. One wrong move, however, and she, too, would die. One wrong move. . .

Katie wept in prayer. "Oh, God. Please help me to do this right. Like Esther, go with me. Prepare me. As Esther sought the favor of the king, help me to somehow find favor with Ben again."

The afternoon shadows fell away as the gray of winter's sunset filtered into the room and Katie was forced to switch on the antique milk glass lamp next to her. Having done so, she turned her attention back to the Scripture before her. *"Find favor with the king,"* she heard a voice from deep inside her heart whisper. *"And Haman will be brought to justice."*

Haman. The king's prime minister, who sought to be better than the one he served and who sought to eradicate the Jewish people of Persia. To take away everything the king and queen held dear. Haman. A man not so unlike Bucky Caballero.

"Find favor with the king," the voice said again just as the front door of the carriage house creaked open.

Katie looked up.

"Hi," Ben said, bringing his head into the room and leaning against the doorframe.

"Hi," she said back, closing the Book in her lap.

Stepping in and closing the door, he looked around the room, as though seeing it for the first time. "You seem to spend a lot of time in here." Ben entered by a few steps. "I can see why. This room is suited to your taste."

Katie smiled. "How's that?"

"Southern things," he answered, stepping farther into the room. He shoved his hands in the pockets of his pants and shivered. "It's cold in here. Do you have the heat on?"

"You've just come in from the frigid outdoors. Where's your coat?" Katie placed the Bible on the small table next to the chair and brought her feet out from under her at the same time.

Ben's gaze went to the Bible. "What are you reading?"

"It's my Bible."

He walked over and picked it up, as though weighing it with a single hand, then replaced it next to the teacup and saucer. He looked at her and smiled. "And you're reading it?"

"Of course. I told you—"

"I know. . .I know. Let's not take things too far, though, shall we?"

Katie opened her mouth to protest, then closed it just as quickly. *Find favor with the king.* She took a few steps toward Ben and slipped into his arms, tilting her head backward and kissing his chin. "Let's do something fun this evening. Something better than sitting in the house reading or watching TV."

His arms encircled her, dropping to the curve of the base of her spine. "What do you have in mind?" His voice was low and seductive.

Katie thought for a moment before answering. "You said something about a sleigh ride last week. We never did do that."

Ben's dark eyes became smoky, and he pulled her closer to him. "There's a lot of things we haven't done," he coaxed.

Katie dropped her head, stepping away from her husband. "I know. But until—"

"Until I fall in love with you again."

She nodded in answer.

His hands went back into his pockets. "And what have you done to ensure that I do fall in love with you again?"

Katie crossed her arms. "I'm trying, Ben. I don't know what to do to *make* someone fall in love with me. I didn't do anything the first time. We just fell in love. . .in time. . .being with one another."

Ben stepped toward the narrow stairwell to Katie's right. She turned her body to follow him. "Is this where you spend so much of your time every day? In here? Up there?"

Katie closed her eyes and tried to follow the change of conversation. "What makes you ask that?"

"I've seen you," he said, turning back to her, leaning against the wall and placing one foot on the bottom stair. "You dart out here one or two times a day. Is this where you work? Because I know you're working. You can't run an empire without constant contact. Do you think I don't remember that?"

Katie took a step toward her husband. "No, I didn't think—"

"I remember. I remember running THP. It's *my* hotel, Katie. Mine. Thank you very much for your help while I was away, but I'm back now and—"

"And," Katie interjected, finding her strength at the very thought of losing what she'd earned, "I don't think you're ready to take over again. When you are. . ."

"Who's to decide when I am? *You?* Me? Who, Katie? Who decides?"

Katie walked to the back of the squooshy chair and gripped the top of it, as though it would anchor her in some way. She caught a glimpse of her Bible lying there and allowed the words of the passage she'd just contemplated to wash over her again. She took a deep breath and sighed. "Tomorrow you go see Dr. Robinson. Why don't we talk to him? Let him decide what's best."

"What does Dr. Robinson know about a man like me, Katie?" Ben asked, pacing now. "What does he really know about a man in my position?"

"Ben," Katie said, keeping her voice low and easy. "You're getting worked up again. I'm going to ask you to try to stay calm."

He swung around then, pointed a finger at her, and said, "I'm not one of your employees. Do not forget who the real president is." He then pointed to the Bible. "Isn't there something in that Book about that? About serving your husband?"

"That's not what it says. What you are referring to—"

"Never mind what I'm referring to." He took a deep breath, then exhaled and began to laugh. A chuckle at first, then more heartily. "Katie," he said. "Katie." He took a step toward her, opening his arms. "Come here, sweetheart."

Katie took a tentative step toward him. "Ben, I don't understand these mood swings. This anger you have inside. You were never like this before, and I don't know how to deal with it."

He coaxed her with his fingers to come closer. "I know, sweetheart. I know. Come here."

She stepped fully into his embrace then and allowed him to kiss her the way he had before all the madness of two years ago had begun. Allowed herself to believe that none of it had even happened, that they were the same people they'd been before Bucky Caballero and Andi Daniels had changed everything for them. As the kiss deepened, she felt herself turn to melted wax, and she leaned back into his arms. It was a moment of trust. And hope. "Ben," she whispered, when they finally broke for air. She reached up and stroked his face. "I do love you, you know."

He reached down and nibbled at her bottom lip, then kissed the tip of her nose. "You're pretty, did you know that?"

She smiled at the compliment, though it wasn't the line she'd hoped to hear. "So you've said a few times before."

"You are." Then he shook his head. "I think the better word is beautiful."

She teased back, "What's wrong with stunning?"

He thought for a moment, then nodded. "Stunning works for me."

"Then do me a favor?"

"Anything."

"Kiss me one more time like you just did. And then carry me on that sleigh ride you promised."

"Dinner first?" he asked, his lips moving closer to hers.

"Who needs dinner?" she asked, then laughed as he wiggled his eyebrows at her before pressing his lips against hers for a final kiss.

Andi Daniels had just placed her hand on the doorknob of the suite when the telephone rang. She turned sharply, staring at it, wondering if it might be Silver calling to cancel. She made purposeful steps toward the small table where it sat, shrilling at her, begging to be answered. "I'm coming, I'm coming," she said, then jerked the handpiece up. "Hello."

She was met by momentary silence.

"Hello?" The message in her voice was crystal clear: *I don't have time for this.*

"Hello, puppet."

She felt the air being knocked out of her. Her eyes widened as she scanned the room, as if the man on the other end of the line were right there with her. "Bucky," she finally said.

He chuckled, the way he'd always done when he'd caught her off guard and he knew it. "Oh, good. You haven't forgotten me."

She didn't answer.

"I take it that's a no."

"No," she whispered.

"Good. Glad to hear it."

"Where are you?" she dared to ask.

He chuckled again. "You'd like to know that, wouldn't you, puppet?"

"Don't— Don't call me that, Bucky. I'm not your puppet anymore. I'm—"

"No arguing with me, now. You're exactly what I say you are." He paused. "Puppet."

Andi looked down at her feet. *Tiny feet,* she thought almost hilariously, like her mother's.

"Good," he said again. "I now have your attention. Though obviously not your devotion."

"What is it that you want with me?"

"I think you know that we need to talk."

"I don't want to see you, Bucky." She swallowed. Hard. "We're through. I'm done with you." The last words were added for clarification. . .on the off chance he didn't understand what she was saying.

She heard a roar of laughter from the other end of the line. "Oh, but you see, puppet, *I* want to see *you*. And I'm *not* done with you."

Andi sighed, thinking that it was all over now. Her life. Her hopes. Her dreams and ambitions. "I suppose you intend to kill me. Well, go ahead. I don't care. I don't have a life anyway, so what's killing me going to prove?"

He tisked her. "Now, pet. No drama. I have enough of that from Mattie. You remember Mattie, don't you?"

"Yes. Of course I remember Mattie."

"I have no such intentions. . .no such murderous motivations. But I do want to see you. To. . .*apologize*, actually."

"What?" She placed a hand on her narrow hip.

"I have come to realize that I put you in a terrible place, my love."

"Don't call me that either. I'm not your love. I never was." She spotted the remains of her drink—one swallow, at best—sitting forgotten on the nearby coffee table. She stretched to reach for it as she spoke, then as she paused, took the final sip before continuing, "Though I could have been." She felt the warmth of the golden liquid spread down her esophagus, past her heart, and into her belly. "I could have loved you like you'd never been loved in your whole life. But I wasn't good enough for you, I suppose."

"How much have you had to drink?" he asked, interrupting her.

"What makes you think I've been drinking?"

"I know you. You've never had the backbone to hold your own in a conversation with me before; ergo, you've been drinking."

"So what you're saying is that no woman talks to you like this unless she's been drinking? Is that what you think, Bucky?"

He was quiet before answering. "I do believe that I like this new Andi."

She sighed. "Bucky—"

"What are you doing right now?"

She raised her chin. "I'm about to have dinner with Phil Silver. What do you think about that?"

"I think you'd better behave yourself, puppet. He's a married man, you know."

She laughed a single, sarcastic laugh. "Since when do you care what a person's marital status is?"

"Perhaps I've changed, too. Hmm? Ever think about that? Two years away. . .to think about all this. . .about what I lost. . . about you?"

"Bucky." Andi looked down at her watch. "I have to go."

"Listen to me," he commanded. "You keep this conversation between the two of us, and I'll make you a very happy. . .very wealthy woman. Love and money, Andi. You still desire love and money above all else, don't you, puppet?"

Andi didn't answer.

"That's what I thought. I'll call you later tonight. I'm assuming you'll be back later tonight."

"Yes."

"Good. Until then, be sweet. *Ti amo.*"

CHAPTER THIRTY-SIX

When Andi finally arrived in the lobby of THP-New York, Phil Silver had already been waiting on her a good ten minutes. As she approached him from the centrally located elevators, she spotted him, then slowed her steps, wondering if she should apologize for being late or let him stew for awhile. A glance over her right shoulder to an antique baroque wall mirror reflected a woman who seemed flushed and anxious. *Perhaps,* she surmised, *I should make something up.* . .anything less and he might assume something had been going on with her. . .something he might want to know about. . .something like Bucky Caballero calling her.

She reached him apologizing. "I'm so sorry," she began. "I was on the phone with my father and didn't realize the time."

She thought she saw Phil's features soften, and she mentally congratulated herself for her choice of lies. Phil Silver was probably a father, she decided, and maybe even the father of a daughter. "That's okay," he said. "We're in no particular hurry." He placed his hand on the small of her back, gently leading her toward the outer doors toward the street and the blustery outside. "I'd put that coat on if I were you," he said, removing his hand and slipping into the overcoat he'd had draped over one arm. "It's unbelievable out there."

Andi pushed her arms into the parka she'd brought with

her. "You should try France in the wintertime sometime," she commented.

Phil smiled down at her just as they reached the revolving doors. "I have," he said.

Andi didn't respond to the comment.

"So where are you taking me?" she asked when they'd descended the few steps to the sidewalk.

"Turn right. There's a small café just down the street. We can walk this one." He moved to her left and began to walk beside her.

Andi buried her hands into the pockets of her jacket and burrowed her chin into the downy warmth of the upturned collar. "When you say casual, you mean casual," she said with a chuckle.

He laughed with her. "I like this place. Kind of a greasy spoon, but the hamburgers will take your breath away, they're so good."

"Take my breath away? How about raise my cholesterol?"

"That, too." They stopped at the crosswalk with dozens of other pedestrians, then headed across the street when the light changed.

Andi gazed around her. "This place is somewhat different since I was here before."

"Nine-eleven changed everything."

Andi looked up at him. "I went down to the site the other day. Amazing. It's almost. . .I don't know. . ."

"Sacred?"

"Yeah."

They came to the next intersection, moving forward with the flow of human traffic. "We'll take a left at the next street over."

Andi nodded, looking down for a moment, catching the rhythm of her feet.

"How did you find out about it?" Phil asked then.

"What? The trade towers?"

"Mmm."

"We were at work. It was midafternoon where we were.

Someone came in and told us. For once I was glad we didn't have a television there or at home."

"Why's that?"

"It kept William from seeing too much. I wasn't sure what he could handle. Wasn't sure what he might see that would trigger a memory he wasn't ready for." She was aware that Phil had stopped walking. She, too, came to a stop and looked back the two or three steps where she'd left him. "What? What's wrong?"

He narrowed his eyes at her, shook his head as though shaking a distant thought away from the cobwebs, then moved toward her. "Nothing," he said. "Turn here."

They stepped to the left side of the curb, Phil now moving automatically to her right. They remained silent as they waited for traffic to come to a stop, then moved forward once again. "It's just three or four doors down," Phil said, pointing with a hand he'd brought out from his overcoat.

"Dimitri and Fano's?" she asked.

"Greek brothers," Phil answered. "Been here since. . .well, who knows how long. Trust me on this one."

"At least it's not Bonaparte's."

As they reached the door of the establishment, Phil shifted behind her, opening the door with a stretch of his arm. "After you," he said.

"Thank you." She looked around the fifties-style diner.

"Mr. Phil!" A balding, olive-skinned man approached them. "Look, Dimitri!" he called back where a soda fountain dominated the left side of the room. "It's our friend, Phil Silver."

Phil raised his hand as nearly two dozen patrons glanced up from their burgers and fries to see who had walked in. "Hello, guys," he called back jovially enough.

Andi giggled in spite of herself.

"We'll see ourselves to your back booth there," Phil said to the man Andi assumed was Fano.

"What can I get you to drink?" Fano asked.

Phil looked at Andi, who was coming out of her jacket. "Ah. . ."

"Their hot cocoa is to die for."

"Hot cocoa then," she answered.

Phil held up two fingers on his right hand. "Two hot cocoas, Fano," he said, then nodded toward the back. "This way," he said.

"Yeah, I got it," Andi shot back.

When they'd sat opposite each other, pushing their coat and jacket into the space between the wall and their bodies, Andi asked, "So what was that all about out there? What did I say that caused you to look at me the way you did?"

Before Phil could answer, the hot cocoa arrived, topped with whipped cream and chocolate shavings. Andi looked up and said "thank you," noting how happy Fano seemed to be that "Mr. Phil" had arrived.

"Fano," Phil said, "this is Miss Andrea Daniels. You remember my friend William Webster, of course."

"Naturally," he said. "And I read all about his return, too." He looked from Phil to Andi. "Are you the little woman who took care of him while he was away?"

"I am." Andi neither smiled nor frowned at the thought.

"Then you are a good woman." He clapped his hands together. "Now, then. What can I get for you?"

"Two cheeseburger specials," Phil answered for them.

Andi raised a brow.

"Is that okay?"

"Mr. Phil," she mocked. "This is your call." She kept her attention away from Fano, dipping her head a bit to take a sip of cocoa. As soon as she swallowed, she licked the cream from her upper lip, her eyes shooting up to Fano. "Wow. This really is good."

Fano's frown turned right side up. "Thank you, Miss Daniels. I'll be right back with your food."

When he was gone, Phil leaned back a bit, looping his finger into the steaming mug before him. "Told you."

"So you did," she said, swallowing another gulp. She returned her mug to the table. "Now, then. The look?"

Phil's lips thinned. "I guess it just suddenly dawned on me that you really cared for William. I mean, cared in your heart. Not cared like a nurse. You looked after him in the full sense of the term."

Andi raised her chin. "I did my best. And I think perhaps Katie has misunderstood my motives. I never meant for them to be. . ." She took up her mug again. "He was no more than a friend in trouble," she spoke into the cocoa. Phil remained silent until she looked back up at him. "What now?"

His answer was gentle but sure. "I'd think that spending that much time with a man like William would lead to feelings deeper than friendship."

Andi felt herself blush. "Nothing happened."

"I'm not saying it did."

"Then drop it." She returned the mug to the table a little too firmly.

"Okay." He smiled then. "Just don't break the china."

Andi closed her eyes as a momentary chuckle escaped her. "China," she repeated sarcastically.

They ate with little conversation. When Andi had finished half her food, she wiped her mouth with a paper napkin from the napkin dispenser and said, "What does your wife think about your bringing me out for this gourmet meal?"

"She understands. She was also a friend to William and knows how important this is to me."

Andi lowered her eyelids as though studying him. "Why is this so important to you? What, Mr. Silver, are you fishing for?"

He laughed at her, leaning against the table with his forearms. "Tell me, Miss Daniels. . ."

"Oh, it's Miss Daniels now," she toyed.

"I'm talking business now. Humor me."

She blinked at him. "Okay."

"If your main objective in France was to keep William safe, you certainly would continue to feel the same way now that you're back in the States."

Under the table, Andi crossed her legs and began to lightly tap the foot of the top one. "Why wouldn't I?"

"I suppose my concern is whether or not you've heard from Caballero." He studied her for a moment before continuing. "Have you?"

Andi licked her lower lip. "Honestly? No."

She watched Phil raise his chin a notch, then lower it in a nod. "You'd let me know if you did, of course."

"Of course," she answered with a jerk of her brow.

Fano returned to the table. "Apple pie?" he asked.

Phil looked from Fano to Andi and back to Fano again. "Tell you what, Fano. Let's have a large slice of your homemade cheesecake and two forks."

"Raspberry sauce?"

Andi watched a slow smile etch itself across Phil's handsome features. "But of course."

CHAPTER THIRTY-SEVEN

Katie begged Sabrina and Dylan to remain at the house with Maggie while she and Ben took another trip into East Hampton, but they were hearing nothing of it.

"The interviews have been done, and the news is out," Sabrina told her. "I'd lose my job if Caballero was lurking in the shadows somewhere out there and cornered the two of you."

The two women stood just inside the doorway of the downstairs library, the door only partially closed. Katie turned, peered out into the hallway, then closed the door gently behind her after drawing her head back into the room. She rested against the paneled door, still gripping the brass door handle in one hand behind her back. "Sabrina." She smiled weakly. "Sabrina. We really need this time alone. We don't need the two of you lagging behind and. . ."

Sabrina held up one hand. "I appreciate that. I do. But this is my job, Katie. We fully expect Caballero to come out of the woodwork at any time, given his usual manner of narcissistic attitude."

"Meaning?"

"Meaning: William is Caballero's nemesis. As far as he's concerned, whatever he's lost, it's William's fault. William's and—" Sabrina grew quiet, crossing her arms and looking toward the window over her right shoulder.

"Ben's and mine? Is that what you were going to say?"

Sabrina nodded. "He's been playing games with you all along, Katie. I don't trust the man further than. . .well, you know. Further than I can throw him. Trust me on this one."

Katie sighed in defeat. "I suppose you're right. The man is probably two steps behind us." She looked down at her feet. "It would be so nice." She took a deep breath and exhaled again, then felt the light touch of Sabrina's hand on her arm. She looked up. "Sometimes I wish we could just all go back."

"Mmm. And what would you do different?"

Katie shook her head. "I would have told Ben the truth from the beginning. The whole truth about me. . .and David Franscella."

Sabrina raised her eyes fully to meet Katie's. "Excuse me?"

Katie shook her head again. "It doesn't matter now. It really doesn't. Water under the bridge, as they say."

Sabrina didn't answer.

"I'll meet you outside, then," Katie concluded, reaching behind her to open the door. Turning to leave the room, she glanced over her shoulder at the federal agent. "I only hope you enjoy the view as much as we do," she teased.

Sabrina patted her on the shoulder. "Good girl."

"What's first?" Katie asked Ben as they drove the darkened highway toward East Hampton. "Sleigh ride or food?"

Ben looked over at her. "I thought we agreed we didn't need food."

Katie patted her flat stomach and cut her eyes at him. "You weren't serious, were you? I'm starving."

"Really? Starving?"

Katie returned her attention to the highway. Flecks of snow began to dance around the windshield. The road ahead took on the look of a scene in a snow globe. "Oh, Ben. Look."

"Perfect," he said. "Snow for our sleigh ride."

Katie grinned over at him. "I can wait for food."

He laughed. "That's my girl."

Katie's heartbeat quickened. "Yes, I am." She kept her words low and sensual.

Ben looked back at her. "What do you think Sabrina and Dylan would do if we pulled over again?"

Katie pursed her lips. "Seems like every time we go to East Hampton we end up on the side of the road necking."

"Necking," Ben repeated. "Now there's a term you don't hear every day of the year."

"Well, maybe you should. I mean, what's wrong with the old-fashioned things of life?"

Ben raised a finger and placed it against his temple. "Oh, I remember. You love the classics. Old movies, old songs, old furniture."

"I do."

"Favorite old movie is. . .let me think for a minute on this one. . ."

Katie hummed an old tune.

"Ah, that's it. *Rebecca*."

"Joan Fontaine and Lawrence Olivier. It just doesn't get any better than that."

Ben chuckled. "How many times did you make me watch that movie with you?"

"Only a few dozen."

"A few dozen. Then why do I feel as though I could recite it word for word?"

Katie slowed the car, looking over at him. "Could you? Really?"

He gave her a "don't dare me" look, then began, " 'Last night I dreamt I went to Manderly again. It seemed to me I stood by the iron gate leading to the drive, and for awhile I could not enter, for the way was barred to me.' "

Katie had parked the car on the side of the road and turned

her attention fully to her husband. "Bravo. British accent and all. But do you recall why it's my favorite movie?"

Ben thought for a moment. "No. Not really."

Katie's eyes darted about. "Maybe I never told you." She laughed. "I suppose it's one thing to expect you to remember what you've already been told but quite another to expect you to remember what you haven't been told."

"So tell me now." His eyes grew dark as he traced the line of her face with a fingertip.

Katie tipped her head a bit before answering. "I was spending the day at an old relative's house. . .I can't even remember who now. But the house was old, you know? One of those gothic monsters built back in the 1800s with secret rooms and musty closets and wide hallways." Her tongue darted out to moisten her lower lip. "I remember there was an old, unpainted wrought-iron fence around the perimeter of the property, which was shaded by giant oaks that dripped Spanish moss like giant gollops of molasses." She paused again. "Anyway," she continued, raising her eyes to his, "there was an old black-and-white television in this room near the back of the house. While the adults sat around on the front porch talking, I meandered back there and turned on the television just as *Rebecca* was starting. Of course, it's a Hitchcock, so it's dark in its own right, but as the movie continued, the sun went down and the room grew dark. I was too afraid to get up and turn on a lamp. I just sat there on the floor, in the middle of the TV's glow, spellbound by the movie." She bit her lower lip as she smiled. "I had never been so terrified. It's the first time I can remember being truly afraid, but somehow it made me feel alive."

Ben's hand now rested on her shoulder, and he squeezed it. "Your language changes when you speak of your old home; did you know that?"

"What do you mean?"

"You speak of Spanish moss dripping like molasses and—what was that word? *Gollops?*"

For good measure, she stuck her tongue out at him.

He pinched her nose. "What you're saying to me is that the movie scared the dickens out of you. How do you feel whenever you think about it now?"

Katie nodded. "Like I said, alive. Something inside me just stirs. But the real question is: How does it make *you* feel whenever you think about that movie?"

He seemed to think about it for a long time before he added, "Nostalgic."

"And?"

"Anxious."

"For?"

Ben laughed heartily then. "The movie to end!"

She threw herself into his arms. "Oh, Ben. That's good, don't you see? You're beginning to place feelings with memories."

He nuzzled her neck. "What a thing to begin with."

Katie kissed her husband's face several times as she said, "I don't care. . .I don't care. . .I don't care. It's a memory and an emotion. Thank You, Lord."

Ben drew back.

"What?" Katie asked, her arms still locked around his neck.

He kept his eyes steadily on hers before answering. "Nothing. We'd better get going. Sabrina and Dylan will think we're up here. . .necking." He kissed her lips lightly before detangling himself from her. "Hurry, before it stops snowing."

Katie adjusted herself behind the steering wheel. "Onward, sweet prince," she said as she pressed the accelerator, coaxing the car forward toward their destination.

The sleigh ride was as much fun as Katie remembered them to be. Under the warmth of a blanket of faux fur, she snuggled with her husband, their arms linked together. Her temple rested against the hardness of his shoulder. They remained silent for the majority of the ride, allowing the gentle fall of snow to whip about their rosy faces.

Katie was glad she'd thought ahead and brought a pair of ear-muffs. Periodically, as they passed storefronts and landmarks, she would hear the low rumble of Ben's voice, and she'd pull one side of the earmuffs away from her ear.

"What's that?"

He would merely smile and say, "Nothing."

One time she smiled back at him, then turned her head between them to see a second sleigh behind them. Unlike the one she and Ben were in, the couple were sitting apart, acutely aware of their surroundings. Katie turned back to Ben. "Poor things back there. Shame they aren't lovers."

Ben pulled the muff away from her nearest ear, leaned down, and spoke. "Shame we aren't either." He replaced the muff as she playfully slapped at his chest, and he laughed.

She raised her eyes to his. "In love with me yet?"

He leaned down to kiss her. "Getting close."

"Honesty," she said with a pout. "It's had its better moments."

He chuckled, pulling her closer to himself. "Don't worry, sweetheart. We'll get through this. I know we will."

Unbeknownst to Ben and Katie, behind them Sabrina was answering her cell phone on its third ring. "Agent Richards."

"Sabrina. Phil."

"What's up?" She pulled the scarf she'd wrapped around her chapped lips and nose over her mouth for easier conversation.

"What's up with you?"

"Agent O'Neal and I are following William and Katie in a sleigh ride."

She heard him laugh from the other end of the line. "Beats

most stakeouts, though, wouldn't you say?"

"You know, I have to tell you: For two people who sleep in separate bedrooms, they sure do cuddle a lot."

There wasn't an immediate response. "Well, ah. Here's the deal. I had dinner with Andi Daniels this evening."

"Do tell."

"Something interesting I think you should know about."

Sabrina looked down at her feet and wiggled her toes, wondering if they were still attached to her body or if they'd broken off a few miles past. "What's that?"

"When I asked her if she'd heard from Caballero, she said, 'Honestly? No.'"

"Really?" Sabrina looked from her where her toes were supposed to be to the agent sitting next to her, seemingly unperturbed by the bitter cold. He looked back at her. "She used the word *honestly?*"

"She did."

"That's a dead giveaway. Can you get the phone records from THP?"

"Sure. But they will show only about a hundred calls coming into the hotel. They won't specify what room."

"Where are you now?"

"Still in the hotel lobby. I just saw Andi to the elevator. She seemed a bit anxious as our evening came to a close, so I fully expect her to receive another call tonight."

"Phil, what are you planning?"

"I'm getting ready to go to the hotel's switchboard. If Andi gets another call, I'll be there to intercept it."

Sabrina took a deep breath and sighed. "Phil. This really isn't your case anymore."

Again, he remained silent.

"Phil?"

"I know. But try and stop me."

Sabrina heard a click on the line. "Phil? Phil?"

"What is it?" Dylan asked from beside her. He hadn't bothered to move his scarf, and the words were muffled at best.

"Phil Silver. Our little Andi Daniels has heard from Caballero."

"You're kidding me, right?"

"I wish I were. What bothers me is that Phil is going to interfere where he doesn't belong."

Sabrina thought she heard a laugh from behind the wool of the scarf. "Tell Katie that. From what I see, she trusts him more than she trusts us."

Sabrina pulled the sleeve of her coat up and glared at her watch. "I wonder how much longer this ride lasts?"

Dylan nodded forward. "If they have their way? All night long."

CHAPTER THIRTY-EIGHT

As soon as Andi arrived back in her hotel suite, she slipped out of the black jeans and the sweater she'd chosen for her "date" with Phil and into warm flannel pajamas she'd purchased at Victoria's Secret. She finished the change with a pair of woolly socks and curled up on the bed, pulling the comforter over her. She'd brought the *Vogue* magazine to bed with her, along with an after-dinner drink, which she set next to the phone on the nightstand.

She didn't release the glass right away, however. She took several shallow breaths, allowing her gaze to linger on the telephone, wondering if it would really ring again that night and if Bucky would truly be on the other end of the line.

Andi shuddered, but she knew it wasn't from the cold. She brought the glass back to her lips, took a swallow, and allowed the hot liquid to warm her. . .to strengthen her for what might lie ahead this night.

She tried to be stronger than she had been nearly two years ago when she'd left him and his lies and corruption and. . .deceit. Still, one note of his voice had changed her stamina. All through dinner she'd managed to focus on what Phil Silver was saying to her, but now. . .alone in her room with only a glossy fashion magazine and a quarter glass of alcohol to keep her satisfied. . .she wondered.

And imagined.

What was it he had said to her? *I'll make you a very happy. . . very wealthy woman.*

What had he meant by that? There was only one way she'd be happy by him. . .only one. . .but he'd never allow her to love him. He'd kissed her, sometimes even passionately, but had never taken the relationship further. . .never permitted her to—

A knock on the suite's main door startled her, and she jumped, causing the drink to slosh in the glass. She steadied it, slipping out from under the bedcovers and heading for the living area. Reaching the door, she peered out through the peephole, where she spied one of the hotel concierge employees standing on the other side of the door, looking first one way down the hallway, then the other.

"May I help you?" she asked.

His young face jerked back to attention, looking directly to the peephole, which had distorted his features. "I have a package for you, Miss Daniels."

"Just a moment," she said, turning to go back into the master bedroom, where she yanked a robe from the closet and, jerking it onto her small frame, returned to the door.

When she opened it, she noticed a small brown bag, its opening folded into tiny accordion-style pleats, which the young man extended toward her. "Miss Daniels?"

"Yes."

"This was just delivered for you." He pushed it farther toward her.

She reached out for it, noting the trembling of her fingers as they grasped the top of the bag. "Ah. . .hold on," she said, turning back into the room, carrying the bag with her. "Let me get a tip for you."

"Tip was taken care of, ma'am."

Andi spun back around. "What?"

He smiled at her. "Yes, ma'am."

She looked from the bag to the messenger. "Who is this from, please?"

"Can't say."

She dipped her chin. "Can't or won't?"

"Either or. An employee at Radio Shack delivered it. That's all I know."

"Radio Shack?"

He grinned, showing slightly bucked, narrow teeth. "That's right. The guy who delivered it said the person who sent it included his tip and mine. So." He held his hands out by his sides and shrugged his shoulders. "That's that."

Andi pressed her lips together. This could only mean one thing. "Thank you." She stepped back toward the door. "Good night."

"Good night, Miss Daniels." He held up a finger. "Oh, and the guy said to tell you it's fully charged."

"What?" Andi asked, but the hotel employee was already walking away.

She took the bag back to bed with her, setting it before her, atop the opened pages of the magazine. She stared at it for several minutes, not wanting to open it. She turned back to the bedside table, grabbed her glass, downed the drink in one deep swallow, then turned back to the mystery package. She took a deep breath before tearing into the bag, finding a cell phone, neatly packed into its purchase box. Removing it from the Styrofoam, she hunched her shoulders, drawing her face closer to it.

It was turned off.

She switched it on, then set it down and began to go through the remainder of the bag's contents, in search of a note. . .or instructions. . . .

The cell phone rang in a tone she'd heard in nearly every store and on every sidewalk Andi had found herself at or on since she'd returned to the States. She frowned, picked up the phone, and pressed the answer button with her thumb. She knew, of course, who would be on the opposite end of the line, and she took a deep breath as she brought the phone up to her ear. "Andi Daniels," she said, trying to sound as professional and assured as possible.

"Hello, puppet."

"Bucky. What is this?" She extended her hand across the bed before her, where it appeared the package had regurgitated over the comforter.

"Ah, my love. Don't you yet know how very, very smart I am?"

"Meaning?"

"Meaning when you told me you were having dinner with Silver, my guess was that he'd manage to weasel our conversation out of you."

Andi sighed. "You'd be wrong. For once. He did no such thing."

He chuckled. "That's neither here nor there. I want a way to contact you immediately if necessary. So, listen to me. You will keep this with you and on at all times."

"No, Bucky. *You* listen to me. I'm not up for your games anymore—"

"Andrea!"

She jumped so hard she felt a muscle in her back pull. She winced momentarily, then allowed her face to fall forward as her hand cupped her mouth. If she didn't do so, she knew she'd scream.

"This is no game," he continued, his voice lower and in control.

Andi felt tears stinging the corners of her eyes, and she pinched her nose with her thumb and index finger.

"I can ascertain from your silence that I now have your full attention. Now, if I only had your devotion."

She raised her eyes and set her jaw in a firm line. "You do." Her voice was barely a whisper.

"I don't think so. At least, not yet." He paused. "But I will."

She allowed herself the wisdom of silence.

"Andi," he purred from the other end.

"Yes."

"Oh, Andi. Sweet Andi. You know, you really must allow me to apologize properly."

"Bucky—"

"No, no. By tomorrow evening you will know how I feel. How I truly feel. I'm telling you, puppet. I've changed. Please allow me to show you how much."

Andi released a breath she hadn't been aware she'd been holding in.

"Sit tight," he continued. "And learn to trust me again. I'll talk to you soon."

She licked her lips.

"Are you there, my love?"

"Yes."

"I love you, Andi."

Andi closed her eyes, wishing it to be true. She swallowed hard before she answered him. "I love you, too, Bucky."

She pulled the phone away from her ear, pressed the off button, then fell face forward across the contents of the box, the phone, the magazine, and the satiny finish of the comforter, where she cried harder than she had for nearly two years.

Bucky Caballero returned the phone to its cradle, taking a few moments to study it, as though it might have comments to make of its own. He massaged his jawline, then rested his chin in the palm of his hand, casting his dark eyes across the room to where his sister, still dressed in her dinner clothes, sat in an occasional chair. She held a glass of Merlot in one hand and a cigarette in the other.

Bucky hated it when she smoked.

"Well?" she asked, bringing the slender cigarette to her painted lips.

Bucky watched as she took a long draw from it, and then—almost in slow motion—brought her hand back down and allowed her elbow to rest on the arm of the chair. She blew a trail of white-gray smoke upward as she waited for his answer.

"We'll leave first thing tomorrow afternoon."

"Home again. . .home again. . ." Her voice was as cold as her heart had always been, though if Bucky thought about it long enough, he could remember a time when she laughed easy and often. "And are you, dear brother, prepared to do what you must do to win Andi over?"

"Don't worry about Andi." He looked beyond her, toward the back windows where the Canadian cityscape mocked him.

"I'm not worried about Andi, darling. I'm worried about you."

He shot her a cold glance, then returned his gaze to the window. "No need. The tide has turned, my dear, sweet Mattie. The tide has indeed turned. Like you said, home again. Home again."

She smiled like a cat. "Jiggidy jig."

CHAPTER THIRTY-NINE

Katie was tired when they arrived back home, and she said so.

"I take it that means you're ready to go upstairs," Ben said, watching her take the first step of the foyer staircase.

Katie turned a bit, looked over her shoulder, and watched the hush of moonlight as it cast shadows across his face. It seemed to her that he winced, and she watched him raise a hand to massage his forehead. "Are you all right?" she asked.

"Just one of these headaches I get."

Katie descended the one step she'd taken. She placed her fingertips atop his and allowed them to move back and forth in the rubbing motion. "You'll see Dr. Robinson tomorrow. I want you to remember to tell him about this."

Ben dropped his hand, removing Katie's at the same time. "I don't need you to tell me what you want me to do when I see my own doctor."

Katie's breath caught in her throat. "What?"

He turned, heading toward the living room.

"Ben?"

When the darkness had enveloped him, she decided to follow him into the room, standing at the doorway until he'd switched a small table lamp on. He stood over it, hunched at the shoulders, gazing down almost as though he might be studying it.

"Ben?" She crossed her arms over her abdomen.

He gazed over at her. "Let me ask you a question."

"Okay."

"Where do you see this going?" He turned fully then, crossing his arms as well.

Katie thought before answering; she nearly smiled at what they must look like, but instead she dropped her arms and began walking toward the sofa. "Can you be a little more specific?" she asked, taking a seat near the end as she pulled a throw pillow from behind her and wrapped it in her arms.

He took the necessary steps to join her, sitting on the opposite end, resting his elbows on his knees. "More specific. Okay. Where do you see yourself as far as THP is concerned a year from now?"

Katie's shoulders fell. "Oh."

"Oh. Yeah. THP." His voice was mocking.

"Where did *that* come from?"

"Don't answer a question with a question."

Her shoulders squared. "I have to answer a question with a question. I need to understand where all this is coming from. All I did was suggest that you tell Dr. Robinson about the headaches."

"No. That's not what you did. What you did was *tell me* what you wanted me to do. 'I *want you* to tell him. . .' Like I'm one of your employees, who, by the way, are *my* employees. Which is why I asked where you see yourself in a year."

Katie took a breath and shook her head. "I don't know how to answer this."

Ben leaned against the back of the sofa, slouching a bit in the process. Katie saw him wince again.

"Let me get you something for your headache," she said, standing.

"No, no." He closed his eyes against the pain.

Katie continued toward the door. "That wasn't a suggestion," she said, leaving the room. When she returned a few minutes later, Ben had stretched himself out on the sofa. Being nearly six and a half feet tall, he had to leave one foot on the floor, with the other bent and crossed over the first. Katie paused at the doorway, observing him until he opened his eyes and rose up on one elbow. "There you are."

"I didn't know if you were sleeping or not." She sat near his hip, handing him the water and pain reliever she'd brought back from the kitchen.

He took it dutifully, thanking her in the process, then laid his head back against the pillow behind his head.

Katie slipped the glass from his fingers and set it on the coffee table next to her. "Close your eyes," she whispered, then smiled when he complied. She stroked his forehead with her fingertips.

"Feels like butterfly wings," he said after a few moments.

"Let it relax you then. You're still tense."

He took a deep breath, then exhaled.

She waited before saying anything else. Then, "I don't know."

He opened his eyes, though they were hooded and appeared almost weak. "Don't know what?"

Katie pulled her hands into her lap and studied them. "I don't know where I'll be in a year. I suppose that's up to you, isn't it? After all, you *are* the president. Not me. My role was to fill in until your return. I just didn't think it would be such a long-term thing."

"What I want to know is how you came to be the president in the first place."

Katie smiled, cutting her eyes upward to his. "Pretty amazing, huh?"

He wrapped an arm around her hip, allowing it to rest there. "If I remember correctly—and I admit the chances are that I don't—but if I do, you weren't the take-charge kind of girl who would have done something like that."

Katie's hand slipped up his arm and, finding a place of rest, fingered the material of his shirtsleeve. "May I ask you a question now?"

"Sure."

"How *do* you remember me?"

He turned his head a bit, his hair making a rustling sound against the fabric of the pillow. "I remember a woman who was afraid of her own shadow. I remember a woman who guarded her past to the point of being unwilling to draw any attention to herself whatsoever. I remember a woman who trusted my judgment completely. . .who listened when I spoke and pretty much went along with whatever I suggested."

"I'd have to say that's accurate."

"So what happened?"

She paused for a moment before answering. "Do you remember sending me to Georgia?"

He nodded.

"You said that I should face the shadows of my past."

"And did you?"

"Yes, I did. Difficult as it was, I did. Of course, I didn't know that you already knew about my early years in the city, but once I was able to come to grips with my mother, I figured I could then come back and tell you everything there was to tell about it all."

"The dancing."

She nodded.

"I've talked with Maggie. She told me more about you and Franscella. And about the night he broke in here."

Katie nodded again, attempting to swallow the knot that constricted her throat. "David and I had known one another before."

"I know."

"I'm sorry, Ben. I'm sorry I came to you with my past, with all its secrets, with—"

He hushed her. "Don't go there. You're dwelling in the past, and I want to talk about the future. Although I suppose to do so, we need to talk about the days immediately following your return to the city."

"I suppose you could say I obtained a strength in Georgia."

"How so?"

"I not only returned to the people of my youth; I also returned to the God of my youth. The Bible says, 'You will know the truth, and the truth will set you free.' When I came to grips with the truth, I was set free from my own paralyzing nature. I became a different woman. A new creation. After David was killed and I realized you weren't coming right back, I went to your cousin Cynthia."

"I see."

"I told her I didn't want to see you lose your position, but I didn't know how to keep it from happening. I made the suggestion of sitting in, thinking it would be very short-lived. We brought Vickey in, asking if she would be willing to help me with the details." Katie smiled. "I had absolutely no idea as to what you did all day."

"And Vickey said yes."

"Mmm-hmm." She felt him pat her hip.

"Impressive."

"Well, I made it sound easy, didn't I? It wasn't."

"I imagine not."

"James Harrington nearly raised the roof."

"Harrington has no voice when it comes to the corporation."

Katie laughed lightly. "Try telling him that."

Ben chuckled, too.

"Your headache better?"

"A little."

"I didn't mean to sound like I was barking an order to you earlier. I suppose I am accustomed now to saying what I want done and seeing it done." Katie cupped her husband's face with the palm of her hand. "A lot like someone we both know and love."

"Do you, Katie?"

"What? Love you? Oh, yeah. I never fell out of love with you, Ben. I never dishonored you or even dated, for that matter." She had a fleeting mental picture of sitting in Harrison Bynum's kitchen, eating dinner with his son and dogs. She blinked it away.

"And you're content to wait on me to fall back in love with you?"

She swallowed. "Yes, I am."

He closed his eyes again. "You know, you still haven't answered my question."

"Where do I see myself?"

"Yes." His eyes remained closed.

"I really haven't thought that far. But I have to be honest. I don't see myself merely attending French classes or art sessions at the university at your insistence. I don't see myself being your shadow, gliding into a room on your arm, with no identity of my own, other than that of William Webster's wife."

"William Webster's *beautiful* wife," he reiterated, still keeping his eyes closed.

She didn't respond.

"I don't see you that way either," he finally said.

"How *do* you see me?"

Katie remained silent, waiting patiently for an answer that wouldn't come. When her husband's breathing became even and the muscles in his face relaxed, she realized he'd fallen asleep. She inched away from him, bringing his arm away from her hip and laying it next to his own. She stood, blew a kiss to his sleeping form, then tiptoed toward the foyer.

She turned at the doorway, noticed the lamp still glowing nearby, and chose to leave it burning. "Sleep well," she whispered. "Tomorrow is another day."

CHAPTER FORTY

Simon drove Katie, Ben, and Maggie back to the city. Sabrina and Dylan followed close behind.

Katie sat in silence for the better part of the journey, gazing out the window to watch the landscape whiz by, listening to her husband and housekeeper make small talk about events that had occurred in his youth. Periodically she smiled, imagining Ben as a toddler, or boy of twelve, or young man getting ready for his first date. But for the most part, she thought over the items she wanted to discuss with Dr. Robinson when she met with him privately and the details that needed her attention at THP.

When the view through the window changed from landscape to cityscape, she turned to her husband and said, "I was thinking you and I could stop by the office after your appointment and go over a few things." She swallowed, tilting her head a bit, and added, "Together."

He nodded. "Sounds good."

"Maggie, would you like to go straight to the hotel or would you care to go to the hospital with us?"

"Oh, little lambs," Maggie answered looking first to Katie and then to Ben. "I'm a bit tired again today. Would you mind taking me home first?"

Ben patted the elderly woman's hand and said, "Not at all, Maggie. You don't need to be out in the cold anyway."

Maggie looked up to his eyes, all the love in the world shining in her own. "You're a dear."

Ben smiled, then looked over at Katie. "Hear that, Katie? I'm a dear."

Katie returned the smile. "I could have told you that."

"Ah," Maggie interjected. "It's good to see you two in love again."

Katie turned her head then, bringing her attention back to the city's buildings, which now loomed overhead like monsters of glass and steel.

"How are you feeling, Mr. Webster?" Dr. Robinson asked Ben, who sat across from him, in a chair directly in front of a white lacquer desk.

"Pretty good." Ben rested one leg over the other.

"How is the recall going?"

"I've pretty much got the house down. I remember buying some of the things I see in it. I remember being there over the years. We went into East Hampton, and the journey came fairly easy. I remembered stores, their layout, even what store would come after the one we were in."

"Any problems there?"

"Only one."

Dr. Robinson, poised over Ben's file with a ballpoint pen, came to a stop in his note taking. He looked up at his patient without moving his head. "And that was?"

"We—Katie and I—went out to dinner. I got a little upset when I realized that I didn't have any money on me. . .that I basically had no money at all."

"Did you lose your temper?" Dr. Robinson dropped the pen

and rested his chin on the ball of his hand.

Ben nodded.

"How did Katie handle it?"

"Well. She handled it well."

Dr. Robinson stared at his patient for a moment before picking up the pen and returning to his note taking. When he'd written several lines, he brought his interest back to Ben. "How are you two getting along otherwise?"

Ben opened his mouth to answer, then closed it just as quickly, shaking his head and looking over his right shoulder toward a small window.

"What's the problem?"

Ben looked back at the doctor. "I've always been a private man when it came to affairs of the heart, Dr. Robinson, so you'll have to forgive me. This is difficult, at best, to discuss with my wife. I trust you as my doctor, but you are a stranger in that respect. I hope you understand what I'm saying."

Dr. Robinson nodded. "I do. Let's do this then: Let's say you'll discuss those items with me as you see fit."

"I can live with that."

"Do you feel like talking a little more about how you're adjusting to your wife's new role at the hotel?"

"I still feel the same this week as I did last time I was here. It's somewhat unnerving, but in my observation, she seems to be doing a good job. I just hope she can let go when the time comes."

"And how will you feel if she can't. . .let go. . .so easily?"

Ben looked at him for several moments before answering with a firm, "She'll just have to get used to it."

Dr. Robinson closed the file and leaned back in his office swivel chair. "I see. That's a little blunt, don't you think?"

"Not really. Katie always trusted me before. She's had to learn to trust herself these past two years. Now she'll learn to trust me again."

Dr. Robinson paused. "I hope you're right."

Ben smiled. "I may not remember what it feels like to be in love with her, but I certainly remember what it's like to have her trust me. She did it before. I believe she'll do so again. This whole thing will just take time. Everything. Everything will take time."

"I couldn't agree with you more. However, you've changed. She's changed. All I'm asking is that you keep an open mind to her changes, just as she is keeping an open mind to yours. Now then, are you ready to talk a little more about the accident?"

Ben's face darkened. "Not really, but I suppose we must."

Dr. Robinson laughed easily. "I'm afraid so."

Ben nodded. "Let's begin then."

With Dylan standing guard over Dr. Robinson's office door and Sabrina "running an errand," Katie found a quiet waiting area where she could call Phil, using the complimentary phone that sat on a low table.

"Silver," he answered on the second ring to his office number.

"Hi, Phil. It's me."

"Hey. Where are you? I just now tried to call the house."

"Hospital. It's Ben's scheduled appointment."

"How is he?"

"Good." Katie sighed as she took two steps to a window and peered out at the city below.

"I've got news. Which is why I was calling."

"Oh?" She turned, resting her backside against the window ledge. It was cold, and she knew she wouldn't perch there for long.

"I took Andi out last night, and I suspect she's heard from Caballero."

"Really?"

"Yeah. Bad news is I truly thought she'd hear back from him after I returned her to the hotel, but my post at the switchboard left me empty-handed. She didn't receive a single call after we arrived back."

"What made you think she'd hear from him again?"

"Hunch."

"So, if she heard from him before, it's only a matter of time—"

"Before he shows up. Now listen, Katie. This means you need to stay in some kind of contact with Andi. She's an emotional bowl of spaghetti, so don't get *too* close. . . ."

"No problem there."

"But you've got to stay close enough."

"I'll see what I can do." Katie pushed off from the ledge and made her way to the corner chair next to the telephone table. "Hey," she added softly, "I'm about to call your favorite girl."

"Now, Katie—"

Katie chuckled. "I promise not to tell her too much. I'll be good this time, okay?"

She heard him growl from the other end. "Talk later?" he asked?

"Yeah." She disconnected the line, then placed a call to Marcy, using a calling card she extracted from the wallet inside her purse.

"Hi, Marce," she greeted, replacing the card and the wallet, then securing the purse next to her hip.

"Hey, girl. What's going on up there?"

Katie laughed. "How much time do you have?"

"That bad, huh?"

Katie laid her head against the wall behind her, turning slightly to the right and away from the door where the room opened to a wide hallway. "Not too bad, actually. I'm just a little worn out."

"Hey, I got those magazines you told me about. Good articles. I'm just wondering how long it will take before Caballero comes out of the woodwork."

"I'm banking on it not being too far in the future."

"Ben know what you're up to?"

"Not really, no."

"I see." There was a moment of silence before she added, "Is he still unsure as to whether or not he's in love with you?"

Katie laughed. "Why do I suddenly feel like I'm in high school again? Remember that time I had a crush on. . .what was his name. . .Toby something or another?"

"I remember."

"And you insisted that I give him a note telling him of my undying devotion and eternal love?"

"Yeah."

"And what happened? He called me that night and told me he liked me—really, he did, he said—but only as a friend. And maybe we could go out sometime, and he could decide after that if he loved me or not. Like I didn't know what *that* meant."

Marcy laughed heartily. "What a catch."

"His family left when we were in the tenth grade. Wonder what ever happened to him?"

"I dunno. He probably became a gynecologist."

Katie's mouth fell open. "Marcy!"

"Well!" There was another short stretch of silence. Katie listened to her friend's soft breathing, in contrast to the overhead sound system that played various classical pieces interrupted by the occasional "Dr. Stiles, third floor STAT. Dr. Stiles, third floor STAT."

"I guess you know by the noise that I'm at the hospital with Ben," Katie finally said.

"I figured. How's he doing, really?"

"I think we're on track. He's having some headaches, but for the most part his memory seems intact."

"Memories but no emotion."

"Sometimes I think I see a glimpse of emotion. Anger. There's an emotion he's apparently doing very well with."

"What do you mean? He hasn't hit you or anything, has he?"

Katie rolled her head a bit. "Oh, goodness, no."

"Don't make me have to come up there."

"No, no," Katie countered, hearing both seriousness and jest in her friend's voice.

"I've done some reading. Apparently it can happen, these mood swings."

"It's true. They can. Change of subject. How are my favorite little people?"

"Mark got an A on a test the other day. His first in forever."

"Really? Good for Mark. Tell him I'll send him a little something in celebration."

"Melissa is. . .Melissa."

Katie's chuckle was reflective. "Ah, yes."

"But she's a good kid. Just dying to stretch her wings."

"How well I remember. Tell her Aunt Katie said not to stretch too far. Those wings could get clipped."

"I'll tell her."

"And Michael?"

"We're a bit concerned down here about Michael."

Katie sat up straight, crossing one leg over the other. "What do you mean?"

"Of course his French grades are above average, but he's struggling in a necessary math class. He needs to make the grade if he's going to get the scholarships for school."

"Have you thought about a tutor?"

"We just hired one."

"Would you mind if I talked with him?" Katie looked down at her watch, noting the time. Ben would be coming out of his session any minute, then it would be her turn.

"Why? You were never very good at math."

"Ha, ha."

"If you want my personal opinion, Michael would do just fine if it weren't for all the time he spends on the Internet with his little e-pal, FiFi."

"FiFi?"

"That's what Mark calls her. Some girl he met on-line. Lives in Paris."

"Ah—" Katie sensed movement coming from the hallway. She looked over her shoulder to see Ben walking toward her. His face was dark and serious, but when his eyes met hers, he smiled. "Gotta go, Marce. Ben just came out and is walking toward me."

"Call me later. And do call Michael if you want."

Katie stood. "Thanks. I will. Love you all."

"We love you, too."

Katie hung up the phone just as Ben ambled into the alcove. "Talking to your boyfriend?" he asked.

"You've found me out," Katie answered with a smile. She reached out and touched the sleeve of his sweater. "My turn?"

"Your turn," he said, nodding.

She took a step toward the hallway. "I won't be long."

"I'll wait here," he said, already beginning to sit.

Katie paused for a moment, watching him before turning and making her way toward the doctor's office.

Katie returned within a half hour to find her husband reading a magazine. She was startled at first; fearful he'd read one of the interviews she'd given in the past few weeks. "Hi," she said from the doorway, her voice elevated. "What do you have there?"

Ben flipped to the front of the periodical. "An ancient *Time* magazine." He stood, tossing the magazine over to a nearby end table. "You may be surprised to know that man just may walk on the moon someday."

Katie laughed. "Oh, Ben. The magazine's not that old."

He walked up next to her, placing his hand on her shoulder and guiding her away from the room and toward the elevators. "Nearly." They began their walk. "How'd your visit go?"

"Oh, fine. He agrees that you're ready to go to the office and possibly look over a few records from the past two years. What do you think? Do you feel ready?"

They arrived at the elevators. Ben pushed the down button, then crossed his arms. "I told him I thought I was, and he agreed."

"Let's go directly to the office. I'll grab some files I need, and we'll also pull together a few things for you to go over. Then lunch. Sound good?"

The elevator doors opened and they stepped in. "Sounds great."

Katie stared straight ahead as the elevator doors closed, pressed her lips together, and fought tears of frustration she didn't wish her husband to see. Yes, she'd agreed with Dr. Robinson that Ben was ready to begin again. But Ben's moving forward meant her moving backward. Or so it seemed. *Dear God,* she prayed, *how am I supposed to do this? Please tell me how.*

She felt Ben's arm slip protectively around her shoulders. She looked up at him and smiled, then turned back to face forward.

To raise her chin one more time and to try not to fall apart.

CHAPTER FORTY-ONE

Andi Daniels didn't think she could take another minute of waiting.

Then again, it's what she did best when it came to Bucky Caballero.

Waiting for him to kiss her, which he'd hardly ever done.

Waiting for him to fall in love with her, which he never did.

Waiting for him to make her his mistress, which he also never did.

Waiting for him to make her his wife, which—she knew—he never would.

She'd hardly slept the night before. In fact, once her crying spell was over, she'd taken a shower and developed a plan all her own. She knew Bucky had one; she may as well have one, too. After all, nearly two years of playing it straight certainly hadn't worked.

She'd learned from the best when it came to diabolical ideas and preparations. Even now she smiled, thinking of how Bucky would be somewhere between taken aback and impressed if he knew what she had up her sleeve.

First things first, however. First thing on the list was to listen to what Bucky had to say to her. . .should he ever call again.

And she was sure he would. She was as sure of it as she had been about her decision to turn his records from the escort service over to William twenty months ago. There were just some things that had to be done first. Steps. One step leading to another, and then another, and eventually she would be standing at the top of a grand staircase.

She stared out one of the living room windows of her hotel suite, pushing the sheers to one side with the back of her hand. Life had come to full swing below. Everyone rushing off to this place or that, while she was relegated to this room. . .in this hotel, of all places. She turned away from the scene, casting her glance over to the coffee table where her new cell phone lay in wait for the one phone call that was due to come.

Whenever.

She swung away from the window, marching into the bedroom and over to the closet where she jerked her coat from a wooden hanger and then onto her thin form. "This is for the birds," she said to no one. "And I ain't no bird."

Phil returned the handpiece of the telephone and twisted his chair to face the desktop computer. With his hand over the mouse, he clicked onto the Internet and opened his business E-mail account.

He had about seven or eight E-mails from his students, a few he knew needed immediate attention. Still, while he began answering them, his mind was more on Katie and William than his students, and even more on his concerns over Andi Daniels. He'd been so sure Caballero would call her again the night before. Why hadn't he? What had he missed? Had he misread Andi completely?

He shook his head. No, he didn't think so.

He heard a rap on his office door, and he turned his head toward it. "Come in," he called out, hoping it wasn't a student. He just didn't have it to give right now.

When the door opened, however, it was Sabrina Richards who walked across the threshold.

"So this is what you do all day, now that you've left the agency," she said with a grin, pushing the door closed behind her.

He leaned back in his chair. "Yep. This is it. I peruse the Internet and answer E-mail."

She pulled a dark purple scarf from around her neck. It perfectly matched a double-breasted coat that hung a little too large on her petite frame. Unbuttoning the coat with one hand and stuffing the scarf into a deep pocket with the other, she nodded toward the chair in front of Phil's desk. "May I?"

Phil stood then. "Oh, sure. Forgive my manners. I guess I'm a little taken aback."

Sabrina sat, crossing one leg over the other. "By?"

Phil returned to his seat, as well. "You. Here. This is a first, I believe."

She smiled again. "I thought it was time I saw what my old partner left me for." She looked around. "Not bad."

Phil leaned over his desk, bracing his forearms against the paper-and-file-littered top. "Uh-huh. I don't think so, Richards. What's going on here?"

Sabrina smiled but with only one side of her mouth. Pointing to him with her index finger, she said, "See, this is what happens when agents spend too much time with one another. They get to where they can read the other's mind."

"Uh-huh. And do you want me to try my hand at my psychic ability now?"

She spread her hands wide. "Please. Go ahead. I'm game."

"You're here to tell me to back off the Webster case."

She tilted her head in affirmation. "So far you're batting a thousand."

"And you want to know more about what I found out last night when I was with Andi Daniels."

"I'm impressed." Her blue eyes grew large against the paleness of her complexion.

"And finally, you want to know what happened after I escorted Miss Daniels to the hotel."

"A regular Miss Cleo, you are. And you aren't even faking it." Phil laughed, reaching for a pack of gum lying nearby. "Gum?"

Sabrina leaned over, took the extended pack, and popped a small square from the seal. "I see you've moved away from Wrigley's stick gum."

"I'm moving on up in the world. The new job and the new gum is just the tip of the iceberg."

She popped the gum into her mouth and began to chew. "Mmm. Good. And what is the rest of the iceberg, Phil?"

Phil placed his own piece of gum near his molars and bit down. "Let's see," he said, swallowing. "Point one: Back off the Webster case." He shook his head. "Nothing doing."

Sabrina leaned over a bit, resting her elbows on the chrome arms of the chair. "Look, Phil. I can't stop you. . .legally. You've got your rights as a P. I. But you know the sensitivity of this case."

"I also know that William Webster has been my friend since we were kids. And I let him down two years ago—"

"Is that what this is about? You letting him down?"

"In part."

"Phil, two years ago when William Webster concocted a plan to blow up his car and fly off to Paris as. . .what was the name he used?"

"Jean Luc Louisnard."

"Yes. Well. You were on another case, Phil. Which, in case you have forgotten, was your job. Who knew how the dominoes were going to fall? You can't hold yourself responsible for that."

Phil leaned closer to his old partner. "I know that." He tapped his temple with a forefinger. "In here." He moved his finger to his chest. "But not in here. So. On to item number two:

I told you everything there was to tell last night when I called. I'm not above keeping you informed, Sabrina. Especially when it comes to what I think you should know, but—"

"But you aren't going to back off."

"Nope." Phil relaxed in his chair.

Sabrina stood and prepared to step back into the cold of the outside. "And will you tell me everything you find out?"

Phil stood. "Probably."

"Probably?" she asked, raising her thin, arched eyebrows. She wrapped the scarf around her neck, slinging the end of it to the back. "That also means probably not."

Phil smiled at her, walking around the desk to escort her out. "You know," he said, placing his hand on the small of her back and turning her to the door, "you'd make an excellent detective."

Sabrina stepped back. "Phil. Please listen to me. You can't do everything by yourself. You have your job here. . . ."

"And you have your job in the Hamptons. You can't be in two places at one time, and neither can I. Oh, by the way, Miss Daniels did *not* receive a call last night. So apparently I was off in my assessments."

"Uh-huh," Sabrina returned mockingly. "I'm calling head-quarters anyway. We need to have someone follow her. If you're right, Caballero is just a hair away from where we want him to be."

Phil reached over and opened the door. "Caballero is too smart to meet her in the open."

"He's also a master of disguises, if his little visit to our fair city last year is any indication."

"I'll keep that in mind." He gave her a gentle push. "You'd better get back to work, Sabrina."

Sabrina took a tentative step, looking over her shoulder. "You win, Silver. For now." Then she pointed to him. "But God's going to get you back for this, you know," she said with a cynical smile.

Phil leaned a shoulder against the door facing. "How's that?"

Sabrina raised her brow in a mocking fashion. "I believe Mrs. Webster spends a lot of time with Marcy Waters on the telephone." She poked him in the chest. "If you're not careful, she'll be up here doing the same to you as what you're doing to me." She smiled again, nodding her head in a victorious salute. "*Ciao* for now."

CHAPTER FORTY-TWO

"William," Vickey said, standing from her office chair and walking around her desk to embrace the man who had long been both her employer and her friend.

Ben returned the hug. "Vickey," he said. "Good to see you again."

She stepped back, beaming as she looked over at Katie. "Hi, Katie."

"Well, hello to you, too. I guess I don't rate a hug," she teased.

"Of course, you do," Vickey said. "We've missed you around here."

Katie moved past the two of them and toward her office door. "I call you every day. How can you possibly miss me?"

She felt more than saw Vickey glance from her to Ben and back again. "Oh. Well, it's not the same."

Katie opened the door, then turned to look at Vickey. "Any messages I need to be aware of?"

"They're on your—" She pointed from Katie and then to Ben. "Your desk." She took a deep breath and exhaled. "Oh, dear."

Ben laughed then and Katie jumped, though perceivable only to herself. It wasn't what she'd expected, and she smiled in the relief of the laughter. "We're going to do some work, Vickey, and I'd—we'd—appreciate it if you didn't let on that we're here, okay?"

"You've got it."

"Ben?" Katie asked. "Ready?"

Ben nodded and after a brief, "Thank you, Vickey," shoved his hands in his pockets and walked into the inner office that at one time had been his alone.

Katie was already halfway to the desk when he closed the door behind him. "So where do we begin?" he asked.

Katie made her way to the opposite side of the desk, picked up the message slips, and began to flip through them, leaving him standing there, caught somewhere between the desk and the door. "Hmm?"

He took a step. "Katie, I'm not going to just sit here and watch you work." His tone was firmer with her now than it had been with Vickey just a moment before.

She raised her head. "I'm sorry. Of course not." She dropped the messages, then sat in what had been his chair, opened a bottom drawer, and brought out a short stack of files. Standing, she said, "These are the general monthly reports from each of the hotels worldwide. Would you like to begin by looking at them while I tend to what's pressing and urgent for now?"

She observed as his face changed to stone, though his words remained emotionless. "That seems like the best place to begin," he said, taking the files from her.

"I need to call Byron Spooner."

"The new comptroller?" He walked over to the sofas to take a seat.

"Yes," she answered, watching him choose the farthest sofa from her. This was, she knew instinctively, so that he could watch her as she worked from the desk. She smiled. "I'd like for him to come up. To meet you formally. I'm sure you'd like to talk with him."

He nodded. "Sounds good." He paused, then added, "And call for James Harrington, as well. After looking over these reports for THP-New York, I should be able to talk with him further about the progression of things in my absence."

Katie opened her mouth to comment but, knowing her words might sound sarcastic, only nodded and reached for the phone. "Vickey, could you ask Byron Spooner to come to my—our—office, please? Also, James Harrington. Thank you."

Ben opened a file, spreading it out over the leg he'd crossed over the other, the ankle resting on his knee. "You don't have to do that, you know," he said without looking at her.

"Do what?"

"The my/our thing. I understand."

Katie sat again. "Do you?"

He looked up then. "Of course, I do. I'm not a monster, Katie, and I remember what it's like to run this place." He looked at her for a moment. "I just don't ever remember seeing you sitting behind that desk."

Katie just stared at him, not answering. When he finally looked down, she went back to the messages before her until Vickey buzzed her from the outer office. "Yes, Vickey. . .okay. Thank you." She replaced the phone. "That was Vickey. Byron is out right now but should be back shortly, according to his secretary. She'll send him up as soon as he arrives. Oh, and while you're here, I'd like you to meet Ashley and Brittany. You remember me telling you about them, right?"

Ben nodded, never taking his eyes off the file before him. "This is interesting," he said.

Katie stood, walking over to where he sat and cocking her head just enough that she could glimpse what he was looking at. "What's that?"

He looked up at her then, patting the seat beside him. "I'm looking at the figures for December of last year."

"Ah. My Christmas tea had a lot to do with that." Katie slid back on the leather of the sofa.

"Your what?" He turned slightly to be able to see her better.

"My Christmas tea. It was a mother-daughter event. When the idea came to me, I didn't have a lot of time for planning, so I intend to go overboard this year. The banquet room I was able to obtain was filled to capacity. Oh, Ben," she said, touching his sleeve. "It was truly magnificent." She bobbed her head from the left to the right and back again. "And my having been in the news just before it didn't hurt any." She smiled. "I think some people were just here to see if I'd really survived the incident earlier in the month."

"The one you told me about. With the McKenzie twins."

Katie answered with a nod, and her husband touched the tip of her nose with his finger. "What is it with you and brother-and-sister duos?" he asked lightly. "First the Caballeros and next the McKenzies."

"Ha, ha. But if you don't mind I'd prefer not to think about that right now."

Ben looked back at the folder. "Okay, then let's talk about this. I am impressed." He began flipping through the remainder of the papers, stopping only when Katie leaned over and kissed him on the cheek. "Thank you, Ben," she whispered. "You have no idea how much that means to me."

He cut a glance over at her, closing the file and setting it on top of the ones he'd placed on the coffee table. Turning back to her, he cupped her chin with his fingers and drew her to him for a deep kiss. She closed her eyes, falling back against the sofa. "Oh, Ben," she whispered.

"You are driving me crazy, lady," he spoke against her lips.

She opened her eyes; the blue of them shimmered beneath her tears. "Then we're heading toward the asylum together."

He chuckled just as there was a knock at the door. Ben turned fully to the opposite side of the room as Katie stood. "Come in," she said.

James Harrington entered the room. Ben stood, the two men shook hands, and then Ben asked James to join them on the sofas. When they had sat, Katie clasped her hands together and pressed her knuckles into the upper part of her thighs.

"I'm assuming you've resumed your role, William," James said, keeping his focus on his former employer and away from Katie.

Ben shook his head. "Not right away. This will take time, but time is something we now have."

Katie watched Harrington raise his chin. "I see."

"Is there a problem, Mr. Harrington?" Katie asked.

James gave her a cursory glance. "Of course not." He turned back to Ben. "As I told you the night the two of you came by, your wife has done an excellent job." He swallowed. "I realize there were times when she thought I was not in full support of her, but my loyalty lies more with the hotel than with a person." He gave a catlike smile. "I'm sure you understand that, sir."

Katie blinked slowly, hearing her husband say, "Of course I do." He tapped the files on top of the coffee table. "From the looks of things—and mind you, I've only given these a superficial review—the two of you have worked well together."

Katie pressed her lips together, then ducked her chin, waiting for the GM to express the things she had gotten wrong in the beginning, the stumbles and bumbles along the way. Most especially, his disdain at her work with Brittany, Ashley, and Misty.

"I think we did just fine, sir," she heard Harrington comment. *One of these days,* she thought, *I just may understand this man.*

Ben stood then, and she and James followed. The two men shook hands. "I'll let you get back to your work," Ben said to him.

James extended a hand to Katie—a first since she had taken over the presidency—and she responded appropriately. *Best to play his game,* she thought, *than to stir a hornet's nest.* After all, she reasoned, it was James and Julia who had offered the house in Vermont, where she had even found a few days of retreat.

James had been gone for nearly a half hour when Byron Spooner ducked his head around the opening door. "You called for me?" he asked.

"Yes," Katie said. "Please come in, Mr. Spooner. I'd like to formally introduce my husband to you." The two men shook hands.

"Have a seat, Mr. Spooner," Ben said, extending a hand toward the sofas.

"Thank you, sir," he replied, sitting opposite them. This time it was Spooner who clasped his hands. Katie gave him a sympathetic smile. *He's meeting the great William Webster,* she thought, *and he's a bit nervous.* It had been different meeting her. *Perhaps,* she thought, *he views me as a pussycat next to the lion king now sitting across from him.*

Byron smiled back at her, though Katie thought it resembled more a wince, and she chuckled silently.

"We haven't had an opportunity to meet, and I'm afraid I don't know much about you," Ben began. "Can you tell me something about yourself?"

Again Byron looked at Katie before returning his attention to Ben. "There's not a lot to tell, sir."

"Married?"

"No, sir."

Katie interjected, "We'll have to work on that."

Byron reddened. "One day. There's an awful lot on my plate right now, and I prefer to concentrate on my work." He returned his eyes to Ben. "My work here is very important, Mr. Webster, and I've done my best to be a good asset to your wife and your hotel. I pride myself in doing a job well and being a man of high integrity. I appreciate Mrs. Webster's trust and faith in my abilities with numbers and business. Like I said, I've done my best to help her in any way and all ways."

Ben nodded. "I'm sure she appreciates your loyalty."

"Loyalty. Absolutely. You can ask anyone. . .I've been loyal. And I will continue to be so."

Again Ben nodded. "Well, then," he said, standing. Byron stood as well, but this time Katie remained seated. "I won't take up any more of your time. Mrs. Webster felt it important that we meet, and now we have."

Byron extended his hand for a shake, then moved toward the door. "Good day, then."

"Good day, Mr. Spooner," Katie said from her seat, smiling warmly up at him. He returned the smile.

When he'd left the room and closed the door behind him, Ben looked down at Katie and asked, "Wonder what he was so nervous about?"

Katie stood, slipping her arms along her husband's shoulders. "Are you kidding me? You're the great William Webster. Fear and trembling is an only fitting set of emotions from young men like Mr. Spooner."

Ben drew his wife close. "And what about you? Are you afraid?"

She brushed the tip of her nose along his. "No," she said in a near whisper. "But I am trembling."

Andi Daniels returned to the hotel a few hours after she'd left, arms hanging at her sides, pulled downward with shopping bags heavily loaded with packages. Packages, she felt certain, that she'd be returning within twenty-four hours. She truly couldn't afford to spend money the way she had on this particular shopping excursion, but it had felt wonderful—the doing of it.

She'd been smart enough not to buy more than one thing in any given store, thereby making the returns all the more simple. No one would judge her. They would take her at her word. "Too small." "Too large." "Not the right color."

As she approached THP's door, she spied Miguel standing

within the doorman's Plexiglas booth. Spying her, he stepped to attention, coming out of it and reaching for the doorway.

"Good afternoon, Miguel," she said.

"Miss Daniels," he greeted her. "I see you've been out today, helping the economy of the city."

She'd always liked Miguel. Her departure hadn't changed that, nor had what she'd done seemed to change his opinion of her. With a smile she said, "I've done my best."

"New York thanks you," he said as she stepped into the hotel lobby.

She looked over her shoulder at him, gave him a wink, watched him smile, then walked on, past the front desk and Concierge, where employees she didn't recognize waited on several hotel patrons. She frowned; a fleeting thought of Juan Ramierez—the young man who'd been with Concierge when she'd managed Jacqueline's—crossing her mind. The young man who'd worked, as she had, for Bucky Caballero, making certain all the international bigwigs came to the boutique for their escort needs.

Andi had managed not to go into Jacqueline's since her arrival or even past it for that matter. She was eternally grateful the hotel's central elevators were located closer to the front door than the boutique; she had absolutely no desire to enter through its doors. The memories were just too painful.

"May I help you?" a voice behind her asked.

She turned, noticing a young blonde woman, who wore what she knew was an expensive business suit graced by the obligatory hotel ID tags clipped to a collar. The name read: ASHLEY.

"Pardon me?"

The woman smiled at her, showing perfect teeth. "Do you need help with the elevator button?"

Andi looked around, caught completely off guard.

The peaches and cream complexion of the young woman pinked with uncertainty. "You were just standing here," Ashley went on. "I thought you might need some help."

"Was I?" Andi shook her head. She'd been unaware of it. "I'm sorry. No. I don't need any help." She extended her index finger and, raising her arm, pushed the Up button.

Ashley nodded. "Have a nice day, ma'am," she said, taking a few steps toward the back of the hotel.

"Yeah, you, too," Andi replied after her, frowning as the elevator doors opened for her. Stepping into them, she pushed her floor button and watched the doors close in front of her just as she heard someone from the hallway say, "Oh, Ashley. Did you know Katie and Mr. Webster are here?"

Andi tried to look out of the doors quickly enough to determine who was speaking to the woman named Ashley, but she was unable to do so before they closed. Defeated, she took a step back, pausing in her thoughts. William and Katie were here. Bucky would surely be interested to hear this. When she spoke with him again, she'd be sure to let it out somehow.

She'd left her cell phone lying on the coffee table and she knew—with absolute certainty—that Bucky would have tried to call her by now. He'd be furious, knowing that she hadn't waited for him. Perhaps, she realized now, this is why she'd stalled in the lobby. Perhaps she dreaded the confrontation she was sure to have with him. . .had to have with him.

To avoid him would be a sure way to get killed.

It would also keep her from doing what she'd planned to do.

The elevator doors opened at her floor, having not stopped along the way, for which she was grateful. She turned right, heading down the richly decorated corridor toward her room. After turning another corner, she was at her door. Juggling her packages, she slipped the key card into its slot, waited for the green light, then pushed the door open. It bumped against something, jarring her. She stuck her head around the door to see a large box, sitting just inside the small foyer of her suite.

"Bucky," she whispered.

She kicked the package farther into the room, then walked in, closed the door, setting her packages down on either side of her, all the while looking at the wrapping of the box in front of her, searching for some indication as to where it was from. There was none. It was wrapped in glossy white paper, tied with string.

Andi walked immediately over to the coffee table to peer down at the cell phone. According to its screen, she'd missed five calls. All of them, she knew, from Bucky.

She turned then, returned to the foyer where she picked up her packages, then took them into the master bedroom, returning to the living room wet bar for a drink. She poured it a little too hastily, drank it a little too quickly, then turned and braced herself against the bar, licking her lips and waiting for the phone to ring again.

She didn't have to wait long.

"Andi Daniels."

"Mind telling me where you've been?"

Andi squared her shoulders. "Shopping."

"I thought I'd made myself clear. You were to wait for my call."

She thought the anger in his voice traveled well. "I had other plans," she returned. *Boy, do I,* she thought.

"What other plans?"

"I told you. I went shopping."

There was a pregnant pause from the other end. "Andi. Don't make me angry, puppet."

"Don't call me that, Bucky. I'm not your puppet. Doesn't the fact that I didn't wait on you this morning prove that much, at least?"

She heard him swallow. . . take in air through his nose and then exhale the same way.

"Bucky."

"Yes."

"Did you send this package?"

"Then you received it?"

She turned to look at the neglected box near the front door of the suite. "Yes."

"And have you opened it?"

"No." She sat in a nearby chair.

"And why is that, exactly?"

She stood again, turning toward the bar for another drink. "I just now walked in. Which leads me to a point: How did you manage to get this into my room?"

"Never mind, puppet. This is Bucky you're talking to. . . . I have my ways."

Andi rolled her eyes. "Like I need to be told that."

"I want you to open the box, Andi."

"I will," she said, pouring the amber gold liquid into the glass.

"Now."

She swallowed her drink, turning the phone away from her lips. "Give me a minute, Bucky." He didn't answer as she set the glass down and walked over to the box. "What is it? A bomb?" She heard him chuckle. "Is that it? Are you planning to blow up the hotel when you know you've got your three worst enemies under the same roof?" She pressed her back against the wall near the door, sliding down it as she crossed her legs Indian style.

"What are you babbling about, Andi?"

"Don't tell me you are unaware that Katie and William are here." She grinned in spite of her resolve not to. Again, there was no comment. "Bucky?"

"I'm here. Open the package."

"No comment from the peanut gallery?" she toyed, pulling at the wrapping string.

"Andi, you are about to cross a very serious line with me."

The string and the paper fell away from the box. "What is this?" she asked, opening it fully to reveal an auburn wig, body suit, a pair of slacks, an oversized shirt and sweater set, and a large pair of dark sunglasses.

"Do not be foolish, puppet. They'll be watching you now. You must not look like your beautiful self when you leave the hotel to see me."

"So I'm going to see you?" she asked, pulling the wig from the box.

"Very, very soon."

"And I'm going to wear this getup? What's this body thing, anyway?" She set the wig down and removed the body suit.

"It will make you look larger than you really are. But not too large, of course."

She dropped the heavy item to the floor and removed the sunglasses. She put them on, all the while saying, "You've lost your mind, Caballero." Then she laughed. "But I have to admit this is going to be fun."

"You have no idea just how much fun it's going to be."

"When and where?" She pulled the glasses off as she stood, then dropped them back into the box.

"I'll let you know something very soon."

"Stay with the phone."

"Stay with the phone, yes," he repeated. "And in doing so, my love, stay with me."

CHAPTER FORTY-THREE

Andi stepped into Vickey McWhorter's office. "Hello, Vickey," she said, her voice cool and indifferent.

"Miss Daniels."

Andi leaned her back against the doorframe, perching really, never taking her eyes off the blonde powerhouse on the other side of the desk. "I understand William and Katie are here."

Vickey cocked an eyebrow. "They don't wish to be disturbed. Anyway, how did you hear this?"

Andi smirked, pushing herself from the door to walk toward the inner office. "You can't keep good news from the masses, I'm afraid," she said.

Vickey was faster than she. Standing between Andi and the door, she said, "You can't go in there."

"I need to speak to William."

"I'm sorry. No."

Andi crossed her arms in defiance, laughing sardonically. "Excuse me?" She allowed her voice to rise, knowing William would hear her.

"Don't play games with me, Miss Daniels," Vickey shot back, just as the door behind her opened. She jerked around to see William standing there, a firm frown on his face.

"What's going on out—Andi! Hello," he said, reaching for her.

Andi stepped into his embrace, patted him a few times on the back, then pushed herself away, giving Vickey a curt nod in the process. "I've missed you," she said.

"I've missed you, too. Come in." He stepped aside, allowing Andi to walk past him. She heard his apologies to Vickey but was more focused on seeing Katie sitting ramrod straight behind the massive desk before her.

"Katie," she said.

Katie didn't stand. She seemed to be attempting to focus on who had just walked into the room as well as why, then said, "Hello, Andi."

"Don't get up," Andi instructed, like a cat who knew the mouse would remain secure in its hole.

"I wasn't planning on it."

William closed the door behind them, saying, "Now, girls. No catfights please."

Andi turned and looked up at him. "You've been gaining weight. You look good," she said, lightly touching his chest with her fingertips.

He rested his hands on his hips. "Maggie's cooking." He walked toward the sofas; one was strewn with files. "Would you like to have a seat? Something to drink?"

Out of the corner of her eye, Andi saw Katie stand. "I'll have Vickey bring some coffee in for us along with something to nibble on." She picked up the phone, and Andi listened as she placed the order.

Andi forced a smile. "That's kind of you."

Katie licked her bottom lip. "The least I can do." She took a deep breath, exhaled, and then moved away from the desk and toward where Andi was heading. "We've got a bit of a mess here," Katie was saying behind her. "Ben is readjusting himself to the corporate world."

Andi's mouth twitched. "I see." She looked at the files. "The doctor thinks you're ready then?"

William stood smiling in front of her. "Yes. And I have to tell you," he said, sitting and slapping his hands on his knees, "it seems to be coming back to me. I'm having very few problems connecting the dots, so to speak."

"I'm happy for you, William." She looked up at Katie, who had positioned herself at the end of William's sofa. "For both of you."

Katie nodded. "Thank you, Andi." She lowered herself to the arm of the sofa. "Do you need anything? I've tried to see to it that all your needs are met."

Andi shook her head as the door opened and Vickey entered pushing a cart loaded with a silver coffee service and tea cake server. Andi kept her eyes on William, exchanging an unspoken tenderness with him as Katie dealt with her assistant. It was only when Katie extended a cup of coffee to her that she looked away from him. "Thank you," she said. "I could use this about now."

"Do you?" William asked, as Katie handed a cup and saucer to him. "Do you need anything, I mean?"

Andi took a sip of the steaming brew. "I'm toying with the idea of going to the West Coast to see my family. I'll need to think about what I'm going to do from here. I can't live in that suite upstairs the rest of my life, though it would surely be nice."

"Take all the time you need," he said.

Andi watched Katie's chin rise a bit, as she returned to the curved arm of the sofa and crossed one long leg over the other. "Absolutely," she said in compliance with her husband's words.

Andi set her cup and saucer on the coffee table. "I appreciate that. William, you know me fairly well, I'd have to say. I'm sure you'll understand what I mean when I say that I need direction. And while I can't go into any details at this time, I think I'm finding it."

"It's time we both did, don't you think?"

"Oh, yes." She stood. "I must be going, really. I'm expecting a phone call."

Both Katie and Ben stood. "A phone call?" Katie said. "Have you been meeting up with old friends since you've been here?"

Andi could read Katie's face clearly. "You'd stink at poker, Katie," she said, stepping away from her and toward the cart. "But don't worry. All's well." She plucked a tea cake from the tray. "I'll just take this to go, if you don't mind." Then, to Ben: "Please. Don't be a stranger when you're here. It wouldn't be right, you know?"

He stepped past his wife to walk her to the door. "I won't. I promise. We'll talk soon."

She smiled up at him. "I'm counting on it."

Bucky had taken a short walk before making his next phone call. He wanted to make sure he was calm, or at the very least that he sounded calm. In control. As always.

He settled into his favorite chair, cell phone in one hand and a cigarette and a gold, engraved lighter in the other. He placed the call, and when the recipient answered, Bucky got right to the point. "I understand the Websters are in the hotel this afternoon."

"How did you hear that?"

"Amazing how news travels, wouldn't you say?" He allowed his fingers to slide down the slender shaft of the cigarette, flipping it and repeating the action.

"Amazing is hardly the word."

"I gave you detailed instructions—"

"All taken care of, sir."

Bucky chuckled. "Yes, I know. Then again, I pretty much know everything. Or do you know that about me already?" He twirled the cigarette until it settled between his fingers.

There was a pause. "Yes, I believe I do."

Bucky lit the cigarette he'd been playing with. "Good," he said, blowing smoke from between his lips. "Very good. Well then, you'll hear from me again soon."

"Thank you. I look forward to it."

Bucky disconnected the line, laughing out loud. "I just bet you do," he said. "For what I'm paying you." He then placed a second call, this time to his broker.

"This is Bucky," he said when the man answered.

"Yes, Bucky."

"Have you begun the process?"

"Yes. Things are moving along quite nicely."

Bucky smiled, drew on his cigarette again, and said, "Perfect. Perfect."

"I take it you'll be here soon."

"We're leaving as soon as Mattie returns from the hairdresser."

"Wants to look her best, does she?"

"You know Mattie."

"Yes, I know Mattie."

"The apartment is ready for us, I take it."

"Completely. As per your instructions, I used your alias."

"I am indebted."

"Don't be silly. Call me when you get in, then."

"Indeed."

CHAPTER FORTY-FOUR

It was precisely nine o'clock when Andi's cell phone rang. She'd eaten dinner in her room that evening, too afraid to take the phone with her and too afraid to leave it.

She'd also had more to drink than she should have, but she really didn't care about that right now. She'd need the strength, and she didn't know where else to get it. She resented every hold Bucky had on her, but her voice was steady when she answered.

"Hello, pet."

"Bucky."

"Tell me how happy you are."

Andi moved to the window of her bedroom. She had yet to close the draperies, but the sheers were drawn. Without pushing them aside, she stared out at the city beyond, watching it shimmer and flicker in its nightlife. "About what?" she asked.

"I have arrived in town, my love."

Andi swallowed. "There are no words to tell you how happy I am."

"I don't want to wait another day to see you."

"Where are you?"

"A friend has arranged an apartment for Mattie and me."

Andi turned from the window. "Mattie's with you?"

She heard Bucky laugh. "Don't fret, love. She won't bite you. Nor will I. Now, I want you to put on the things I sent earlier. I'll have a car pick you up in exactly one hour. Understand?"

"Yes."

"Until then, be sweet. *Ciao.*"

Andi switched the phone off and threw it on the bed, then stared at it as though it were a snake. She looked over at the digital bedside clock. It was 9:05. That gave her fifty-five minutes, which she was certain she'd need.

She walked hurriedly into the bathroom, jerked the shower curtain back, and turned the water on as hot as she could stand it. She slipped out of her clothes, then into the shower, where she spent nearly ten minutes washing her hair, shaving her legs, and bathing with a scented gelée. She stepped out of the shower, wrapped herself in a towel, then walked back into the bedroom where she dressed in the slinky lingerie she'd purchased just that day.

First she had to clip the tags. . .and she did so precisely, all the while deciding that Bucky would pay for her purchases made earlier that day. She then stepped over to a chair where the box of things Bucky had sent—save the wig—were kept. She strapped on the body suit, juggling herself a bit to adapt to its weight. Five minutes later, she was dressed and standing in front of the bathroom mirror, slipping the auburn wig onto her head.

She spent the next several minutes putting on her makeup, changing her look entirely. It would look suspicious if she wore sunglasses, so makeup would have to do the trick for tonight.

When she was done, she stepped away from the mirror, then turned away from it, swinging back around to look at herself, to determine if she might recognize her face were she to see it out in public. The effect was alarming. Not only did she *not* look like herself, she found that she was completely unrecognizable.

She walked out of the bathroom and back into the bedroom,

once again glancing at the clock. It was five 'til ten. She had no time to spare.

She grabbed the cell phone off the bed and dropped it into her brand-new Prada handbag; along with some cosmetic items she thought she might need for touch-up later in the evening. . . if things went her way. Seconds later, she was cloaked in her winter coat and at the front door, but before opening it she paused, turned back to the wet bar, contemplating just one for the road. Deciding against it, she exited the room, making certain the door was shut and locked behind her.

When the elevator door opened onto the lobby floor, she found it to be nearly as busy now as it was during the rush of the day. Her years at Jacqueline's had taught her that this hotel seldom slowed down. She was counting on it; the more people in the lobby, the more she could fade in. Walking toward the front door, Andi made a quick visual sweep of the elegant room. Well-dressed men and women sat in the scattered seating arrangements of the room and near the grand piano where a pianist expertly played a show tune. Casual conversation blended with the tinkling of laughter. For a Midtown hotel lobby, nothing seemed unusual. More importantly, no one seemed to be looking at her. . .and this was good.

She kept her face pointed straight ahead, as though she knew exactly where she was going and why. Nearing the door, she shoved her hands into the pockets of the coat, drawing it together in anticipation of the blast of cold that would meet her upon exiting the door.

She was unaware of Dylan O'Neal, who had been sent to watch for her, sitting in a low chair near the piano, nor had she noticed Phil Silver pretending to read a book near the front window.

As it turned out, neither man had noticed her either.

In the living room of their Hamptons' home, where a fire had nearly burned out and shadows—cast from the moon and lamps—danced around the room, Katie looked from the fashion catalog she was skimming to her husband, who sat on the sofa, continuing to study files he'd brought back from the office. He looked up at her, as though subconsciously aware of her gaze. She smiled at him, but he didn't smile back, and she forced her eyes back to the catalog.

A shuffling at the door caused them to both look up. Maggie had entered the room, wearing the slippers and thick robe Katie had given to her the Christmas before. "Ah, lambs," she greeted them, walking steadily toward her "son." "Time for me to get some shut-eye."

"You're pretty tired, aren't you, Maggs?" Katie asked from her chair.

The elderly woman sat on the edge of the sofa, near Ben, scooting back only enough to keep from falling onto the floor. "That I am. It's been a long day. A good day, but nonetheless a long one."

Ben patted her back. "You deserve the rest, Maggie. Dinner tonight was wonderful."

"All your favorites, Master William. I hoped you'd notice."

He beamed at her. "I noticed," he replied softly. "And I love you for it."

Katie felt tears spring to her eyes, knowing how much she and Ben meant to Maggie. She dabbed at them, trying not to call attention to her emotional self.

"You know, Master William," Maggie went on, "I prayed to the Lord every day that you were gone. I prayed that you would come home, and you did."

Ben nodded. "Yes, I did."

Maggie raised a hand, as though to indicate that she had more to say. "The good Lord hears our prayers, son. He loves us and forgives us and makes us His own."

From across the room, Katie watched Ben wince a bit, though

she knew Maggie was unaware of it because Maggie had glanced at her. "I have prayed for you every day of your precious life, and when you brought Miss Katie home, I began to pray for her, too."

"Thank you, Maggie," Katie said. "Your prayers worked."

Maggie stood then. "That they did, my darling. That they did." She leaned over and kissed "her William" on the cheek. "And they will tug at your heart, too, lamb," she said, then turned toward Katie and began to shuffle toward her. "Because it won't be long— as we all know—before I will be with the Lord in His kingdom." Katie reached for Maggie, and the two women embraced, kissing one another on the cheek.

"Don't talk like that, Maggs," Katie said.

Maggie tittered. "Can't be helped, dear. I'm an old woman now. It's my reward for a life well lived, and I'll embrace it when it comes." She pointed a stern finger at them both. "Don't you two cry for me, you hear? If anything, you cry for yourselves because you will still have a ways to go." She began walking toward the door, continuing to speak. "The good Lord willing." And then she giggled. "G'night, lambs."

When they could no longer hear her footsteps, Katie turned to Ben. "What a sweetheart."

He crossed his arms. "All my life she's talked about God as though He were more than just something to go hear about one day a week or twice a year on Easter and Christmas." He shook his head. "I remember going to services with her on Sundays when I was a child."

"Your parents didn't go even then?"

"No. My father said it just wasn't necessary."

Katie nodded. "I see."

"What about your family?"

"Oh, yes. Every week whether we wanted to or not." She smiled. "First United Methodist in Brooksboro." Katie folded the catalog in her lap and crossed a leg. "You have to understand that in the South, especially in those days, church was a social event."

"Ah."

Katie narrowed her eyes. "Don't 'ah' me, young man," she said in her best "Maggie" accent.

Ben chuckled, pointing a finger at her. "That was pretty good."

Katie grew pensive. "But when I went back to Georgia, Mama insisted I go to church with her." She was quiet for several moments, then nodded. "It was good to be back."

Ben leaned forward. "Is this where this faith thing came in for you?"

She shook her head no. "It came around the kitchen table with Mama. I'd told her everything there was to tell about my past. . . ." She looked down at her hands, then back to her husband. "And then Mama asked me where I stood with God, and I told her that I didn't think God could love me after everything I'd done. Mama said, 'That's not true. God loves His children no matter what.' "

Ben rose, sighing heavily. "That's all very well—"

Katie stood, too. "What is it, Ben? Why do you brush away any talk of God?"

He placed his hands on his hips. "I do no such thing."

"Yes, you do. Would you like me to be specific with you?" Katie crossed her arms as Ben turned for the door. "Ben?"

"What?" he asked, turning back to her. "You want me to believe you're a devout Christian, and then what? You want the same from me, too?"

"What do you mean by that remark? You don't think I'm a Christian?"

Ben stepped over to the back of a chair and gripped it with his hands. "I'd think a real Christian would have been a bit nicer to Andi today, for example."

Katie opened her mouth in protest, but just as quickly closed it.

"Nothing to say?"

She cocked a hip. "Oh, I have plenty to say, but I don't know that you'd understand."

Ben returned to his seat. "I'm game."

Katie, too, returned to the chair where she'd previously been. "I waited for two years, or almost two years, nearly out of my mind with worry about you, Ben. Forgive me, but I can't understand why she couldn't pick up the phone and call me. . .to put me out of my torment. And it *was* torment."

"How do you think it was for her? Stuck in that chalet with a man who could hardly tie his shoes in the beginning. Having to pretend to be someone she wasn't. Constantly having to make sure my needs were met before hers, that we were safe from Caballero."

Katie's voice was monotone as she blinked. "She could have called me, Ben."

"You don't know what you're talking about—"

"I think it's the other way around. I most certainly do know what I'm talking about. I'm a woman, aren't I? If there's one thing a woman knows, it's another woman's motives. And if you think her motives were pure. . .well, sir. . . ."

Before Katie could blink, Ben leapt from the sofa. Standing immediately over her, he grit his teeth and, leaning over, said, "Don't you *ever* talk about her that way again!"

Katie's eyes grew wild as she pressed against the back of the chair, her hands gripping the arms. Before she could say anything, however, he whirled around and headed for the door, turning just inside the foyer. "I hope I've made myself clear."

Still unable to speak, Katie cut her eyes at him.

"Good," he said, then turned and disappeared into the shadows of the foyer.

CHAPTER FORTY-FIVE

Once inside the master suite, Ben closed the door, walked over to the settee in the seating area, picked up a throw pillow, and launched it across the room. It landed against the bedside table, toppling the wrought-iron lamp that—he was certain—Maggie had switched on before retiring as she'd always done. He watched it rock as though in slow motion, finally slipping between the table and the bed. The shade angled to one side and the light went out.

"That's just great," he said. Waiting for his eyes to adjust to the room's dimness, he took in a deep breath and exhaled, trying to regulate the beat of his heart. He placed his hands on his hips, looked down to his feet, and swore under his breath. His return home had become anything but what he'd thought it would be.

He swore again, raising his eyes, then walked over to the place where he knew a light switch graced the wall. He flipped it on and went to retrieve the lamp and set it back on the table.

"Why did I have to do that?" he asked, sitting on the edge of the bed and running his fingers through his hair. He paused, allowing the question to wash over him. . .to leave him wondering if he'd asked the question about the way he'd treated his wife or the way he'd thrown the pillow.

In his heart he knew it was more the former than the latter.

He stood and walked into the master bath, to the vanity on his side of the room, and, leaning over just a bit, stared at his reflection in the mirror. Flecks of gray were beginning to show against the black of his hair. He pushed at the hair growing from his temple, turning first to the left and then to the right, then looking straight ahead again.

Right now, he decided, he very nearly hated himself.

Where is this anger coming from? he wondered. Why weren't things simply falling into place for him like they always had?

He returned to the bedroom, where he sat in a chair and, leaning over, removed first one shoe and then the other. He placed them side by side to the right of the chair and sat for a moment, elbows resting on his knees, studying his hands.

Most particularly, he considered his left hand and the third finger of it, remembering that when he'd awoken in the hospital in France, he'd not been wearing his wedding ring. It wasn't until he'd begun to ask about "a woman named Katie" that Andi had returned it to him.

Ben pondered that now. *Why* hadn't she? To keep him from asking questions? To keep him from moving too fast in his recovery?

Or, as Katie might think, to keep him from knowing he was married at all.

He looked from the ring to the bed. He missed her—his wife. He missed her more than he was willing to admit even to himself. And, happily, he was falling in love with her. He was almost there. . .he could feel it in the very depths of his heart, but he wasn't quite there and, for Katie, it was important that he was.

Ben stood and walked over to the chest of drawers where he kept some of his clothes. Sliding one of the drawers open, he caught a glimpse of the silver-framed wedding photo, which was sitting on top of the chest. He pushed the drawer to, reached for the photo, and brought it closer to him, touching the image of his wife's face with his fingertips.

"Have I lost you?" he asked, a sudden realization settling on him of what it must have been like to be in her shoes. He imagined her hearing the news of the car bombing, coming back to this house, finding the clues and the files against Caballero almost completely by herself, mourning him, and then rising upward to take over the presidency so that it would be there for him upon his return.

From the looks of the files he'd been studying earlier, she'd done a very good job.

He would have never thought she had it in her. At least, he now reasoned, not the girl he'd sent to Georgia. The woman she had become while she was there—the woman she had become since—was a stranger to him. She'd been easier to understand then than she was now, but she certainly didn't deserve the behavior he'd shown earlier.

Ben replaced the photo, turned quickly, and headed back to the door. He jerked it open, headed down the hallway, past Katie's darkened room, and toward the stairs. In his stocking feet, he was forced to take the stairs one at a time, holding onto the banister. As soon as he hit the foyer, he called out, "Katie."

There was no answer.

The living room was empty and dark, save the glow cast from a small table lamp she'd obviously left burning when she'd left the room. Ben turned and looked past the doors, through the foyer, and up the staircase. He knew she wasn't upstairs. She could be anywhere downstairs, of course, but in his heart he knew where he could find her.

Ben stepped to the French doors overlooking the terrace and rear grounds and looked toward the carriage house. There he spied amber light illuminating the front room window. Hands on his hips, he nodded in defeat. She had gone to her safe place, and he must be content to allow her to do so.

But tomorrow. Tomorrow he would do better. He would tell her he was sorry.

And that he loved her. That he loved her very much.

CHAPTER FORTY-SIX

Andi watched from the back window of the taxi as the view of Midtown changed to that of the Upper West Side.

So this is where Bucky is holed up, she mused.

She hummed an old tune in her head, changing the words just enough to fit her thoughts. *Where have all the wealthy gone?*

The cab came to a stop in front of an old four-story brown-stone that appeared to have been converted into apartments. She peered up, then back to the cabbie.

"Building 402, the man said to tell ya. Number 4-D."

"Ah—"

"Fare's taken care of," he barked at her, as though she should have known already.

Andi jerked the door handle, stepping out of the taxi and onto the sidewalk, uncomfortably aware of the extra weight she was laden with. She slammed the door with intensity, hoping her message to the driver was loud and clear.

Apparently so, because he tore off into traffic as soon as the door closed.

"Jerk," she said to no one.

She looked up at the building before her, then tugged a bit at the wig atop her head. It was hot, and she wondered how women could wear them regularly, then shook the thought away. She had bigger problems than a hot head. What she had was a real hot-head no more than a matter of steps and a staircase away from her.

And that was just Mattie. Bucky was another issue.

But she had her plan, and she intended to carry it out.

She approached the steps leading to the beveled glass front door. She took each one slowly, for in doing so she remained in control. After all, if she knew Bucky—and she did—he was very much aware of the fact that she'd already been delivered to his doorstep.

Andi took a long breath before pushing the buzzer to the right of the door.

"Yes?" she heard Bucky's voice through the speaker.

"It's me."

The lock on the door buzzed, and she turned to open it, allowing it to close securely after she'd stepped inside. She craned her neck upward, thinking of the effort it would take to drag the extra thirty pounds up the stairs. Another deep breath and she began taking them, again one at a time, slowly. . .deliberately.

When she reached the fourth floor, she was out of breath and her heart was pounding, though she didn't truly believe the latter was due to the stair climbing she'd just endured.

Apartment 4-A was directly before her, a window overlooking another apartment building to the right of her, and a narrow hallway to the left that appeared to cut to the left once again. She walked just far enough to stand between A and B, took out a compact from her purse, and assessed herself in the mirror. For a fat redhead she didn't look bad, she decided. Not that she would want to look like this all the time, but she could certainly get away with it, especially with the makeup job she'd given herself.

The compact clicked closed, and she took the necessary steps to 4-D. Standing before it, she rapped on the door with the knuckle of her index finger, then stood back and waited, though not for long. Within seconds, the door swung open. As the musical lilt of "The Sands of Time" wafted from a CD player, she found herself face-to-face with a man she thought she'd never see again as long as she lived.

If she lived.

"Don't you look fetching," he said.

"The beard's a nice touch for you," she returned.

He stroked his chin, then stood back. "Please, come in."

Andi stepped inside the room, which was a small, sunken living room with sparse furnishing and bare walls. To the left of the room a large window overlooked Manhattan. To the right of it a bar bordered off a tiny kitchen. In its center was a wine bucket chilling a bottle of champagne and looking socially out of place. Two doors led away from the rear wall of the living room, where, she imagined, were the bedrooms of Bucky and Mattie. It was a great step down for the Caballero siblings.

As the door shut behind her—and the safety of the world with it—Andi swung around to meet her old employer and friend. The man she would have sworn complete allegiance to, had he given her any indication of hope toward a future. Feeling a moment of melancholy, she pursed her lips and attempted a smile. "You really do look fine," she said.

He held out his arms then, and she stepped into them, kissing first one cheek and then the other as he patted her middle. "Dear me, did I do that to you?" he asked.

"Yes, I'm afraid you did," she said, leaning back a bit.

"Would you like to get out of this and into something more comfortable?" he asked, just as she said, "Where's Mattie?"

"Mattie has already connected with an old friend. I tried, of course, to stop her from going out, but she could not be deterred." As he spoke, he moved toward the bar. "I see you didn't bring a bag." He turned. "Am I to assume you do not intend to stay long?"

Andi walked toward the doors. "Which one is yours?" she

asked, keeping her eyes on him the whole time.

She could have sworn the complexion behind and above his beard flushed, and she smiled at him.

"The left."

"I'll be right back," she informed him.

Andi slipped into the semidarkness of the sparsely furnished bedroom. As she'd suspected, a bath separated the two bedrooms, and she moved quickly into it, closing the door behind her and flipping on the light. She placed her purse on the vanity, opened it, and pulled out a brush as she whipped the bothersome wig from her scalp. Her dark hair fell from captivity, and she ran the brush through with several quick strokes.

That done, she removed her top and the body suit, remaining in slacks and her bra, then opened the door and, locating Bucky's closet in the next room, strolled to it and opened it, as well. She grabbed at the first of his shirts that met her eye, closed the door, and returned for a final trip to the bathroom where she slipped it over her small frame.

The shirt nearly swallowed her, causing Andi to smile at the irony of it. She watched her reflection in the mirror as she buttoned each tiny button, then flipped the monogrammed cuff at her right wrist, followed by the left.

She was ready.

When she returned to the living room, Bucky was sitting on the sofa, two glasses of champagne on the coffee table before him. His head had been resting backward; his eyes had been closed. But upon hearing her, his dark eyes opened, and his head came up as a sigh escaped his lips. "Look at you," he said, his voice low and decidedly seductive.

Andi smiled again as she took the necessary steps to reach him, content that the effect of her change of clothes had been exactly what she'd hoped. "You don't mind, I hope."

Bucky reached for a glass of champagne, handing it to her as she sat next to him. Sliding back on the sofa, she crossed one leg over the other as she kicked off her shoes. "I don't mind at all." He took up the second glass, tilting it toward her. "To old friends," he said.

Andi touched the tip of her glass to his. "And new business associates."

Bucky's pleasure at her words shone in his eyes, eyes he kept focused on hers. "And new business associates," he repeated.

CHAPTER FORTY-SEVEN

"Did he hit you?" Marcy asked from the other end of the line.

"No." Katie's voice was barely audible.

"Did you think he might?"

Katie curled herself a little tighter in her favorite chair, tucking an old hand-knitted afghan under her legs. "No. Not really, no."

Marcy didn't respond.

Katie began to cry again, something she'd been doing without ceasing for nearly a half hour.

"Oh, Katie. I'm so sorry, girl. I really am. This isn't turning out at all like you'd hoped, is it?"

Katie shook her head no, then buried her face in the crook of her arm that rested on the padded chair arm. "I called Dr. Robinson before I called you," she said.

"You sound like you're in a tunnel. What happened?"

Katie raised her head. "Nothing. I just. . .never mind."

"What did Dr. Robinson say?"

"He doesn't honestly seem to be concerned, though he did ask me the same thing you just did. Did I think he was going to hit me? And I told him I didn't. He said that if I felt I was in danger, we'd need to look at bringing Ben back to the hospital." She paused, resting her temple against the knot of her fist and her elbow on the arm of the chair. "I never really thought he'd hit me. . .it's just that he came at me so fast, it scared me."

"But that's not really why you are crying, is it?"

The tears began to flow again. "No."

"Do you care to tell me or shall I tell you?"

Katie couldn't help but smile. "You tell me."

"You're crying because your husband seems more interested in what Andi Daniels is feeling than what you are feeling. . .or have felt for these past two years."

"Yes."

The confirmation was followed by extended silence.

"I'm coming up there," Marcy finally said.

"No, Marce—"

"Don't even try to stop me. And I'm going to just tell you something here: I don't care if he is your husband. If he doesn't straighten up and fly right, I'm going to give his head a mess like he's never experienced before."

Katie burst out laughing. "What did you just say?"

"You heard me." Marcy's tone was short and sassy.

"Oh, Marce. Will you really come? You just left, you know, and I don't want you to leave your family again."

"Charlie will understand."

"But your children—"

"Not to worry, princess. I'll be there as soon as I can."

"Thank you, my friend." Katie shifted, resting her back against the corner of the chair, a wash of excitement filling her.

"Tell Maggie to start baking some of those tea cakes I like so much."

"I'll do it."

"See you soon, kiddo."

The line went dead, and Katie hugged the phone to her breast. "I love you, Marcy," she said, then disconnected the cordless phone in her hand and rested her head against the cushion of the chair.

When Katie awoke she had a kink in her back, rivaled only by the one in her neck. She moaned as she twisted herself forward, wishing she'd gone inside after her phone call with Marcy rather than allowing herself to fall asleep in the carriage house. Standing, she stretched and said, "Well, Lord. I don't know whether to say 'Good Lord, it's morning,' or 'Good morning, Lord.' Would You mind if I said both?" Then she smiled at her own humor.

The afghan that had kept her warm during the night was now pooled around her feet. She bent over and retrieved it, casting it over the seat of the chair, then headed toward the door. When she opened it, she was surprised to see a fresh blanket of snow lying on the lawn. The wind had begun to whip up, bringing the scent of the sea inland and making the early morning air bitter and cold.

In her haste, Katie had forgotten to wear her coat out the night before, so it was necessary to duck her head, hunch her shoulders, and step with determination toward the French doors of the living room. Shivering, she wondered what time it was. The grayness of the sky told her it couldn't be too late. In fact, she might be the first one up, she reasoned.

But she wasn't. As soon as she stepped into the warmth of the house and made her way into the kitchen, she found her husband sitting at the small table, sipping on black coffee, the way he preferred it. It smelled warm and cinnamony.

Katie jerked to a halt as Ben stood. "Good morning," he said.

"Good morning."

"May I get you some coffee?"

Katie started to answer in the affirmative but chose to nod instead. She moved tentatively toward the table, pulling out the chair across from his and sitting in it, all the while watching him prepare her coffee. "Creamy, with just the right amount of sugar," he said, bringing the steaming mug to her and setting it on the table before her. "Just like you like it." Katie looked up at him, wishing she'd cleaned the crud out of her eyes or had—at the very least—run a brush through her hair. "Amazing what a man can remember. . . ," he continued, then touched the mass of chestnut hair cascading past her shoulders. She remained silent, staring up at him as though in anticipation of his next move, which was to lean over and kiss her tenderly on the lips. ". . .about his wife," he finished his thought, then returned to his seat as Katie took a sip of her coffee.

"Good," she said. "Very good."

"Glad you like it. I prepared it myself."

Katie looked over at the oven in search of the digital clock. "Goodness, is it really after eight already?"

"I'm afraid it is," he answered, wrapping his hands around his coffee mug.

"From the looks of the outside, I would have thought it was much earlier."

Ben twisted, looking out a side window. "It's going to be bitter cold today." He brought the mug up to his lips and drank from it. "Should snow again, I'd think."

"Maggie's not up yet?" Katie asked, looking toward the nearby door leading to Maggie's small suite of rooms.

Ben shook his head. "Let her sleep. We need to talk, I suppose, about letting her retire."

"Letting her? Forcing her, you mean."

Ben nodded. "That it will be. What do you think? How should we handle this?"

Katie set her mug down on the table. "Do you really want my opinion?"

"Of course I do," he said, his dark eyes focused on the light color of hers.

Katie hunched a bit. "I think we have other things we need to discuss before we talk about Maggie's retirement. . .forced or otherwise."

Again Ben nodded. "Last night."

"For starters." She watched his head twitch a bit. "Ben," she continued, "I'm willing to be patient where you are concerned, in so much as your health is concerned. I understand that these fits of temper are to be expected—"

"I'm so sorry—"

"Don't," Katie said, raising her hand. "Don't apologize until you hear what I have to say here."

Ben set his jawline. "Okay."

"As I was saying, I can patiently wait for your complete healing. I understand from Dr. Robinson that the mood swings or flashes of anger are typical of the amnesiac. I also have been informed that they will continue until he can successfully take you step by step through the day of the accident—and those days immediately preceding the accident—which, he tells me, you are very close to completing."

"Yes, we are."

Katie blinked for emphasis. "Good. I can also release my interim presidency of THP over to you as you as soon as you deem you are ready." She shook her head. "I won't fight you on that, though—as I said previously—I won't. . .can't. . .return to simply being the elegant piece of fluff escorted on your arm at dinner parties and gala events."

"I never thought you were," he insisted, leaning over and sliding a hand along the top of the table.

She touched it, more as a command for him to allow her to continue than for the sake of compassion. "I'm even willing to wait for you to fall in love with me again with a somewhat clear amount of understanding as to emotion versus memory. But, I will not—*will not*—" she repeated the last two words with emphasis, "play second fiddle to Andi Daniels."

Ben drew back.

"Draw back if you want to, Ben Webster. Clench your teeth

and fire off if need be. I've learned to take it from the best of them. I've stood my ground in executive meetings held in posh boardrooms for nearly two years. I'm not about to cow down in my own home. So, you can get angry and that's fine. But know this: I won't shed another tear over it." She watched his brow furrow and knew it pained him to hear her admit to her sorrow. "I won't. I love you—more than life itself—but to allow Andi's feelings to dictate how we heal with one another would be foolish on my part." Katie stood and walked over to the coffeepot, taking her nearly untouched mug with her. Grabbing the pot's handle, she turned her head to face her husband. "If there's anything you should know about me now, it's that I'm not a fool."

"I never thought you were."

"Yes, you did," she said, retracting the pot and topping off her coffee.

Ben shifted to face her better. "When, Katie? When did I ever do that?"

"The very moment you thought what I went through was of less trauma than what Andi went through." She set the mug on the counter as she returned the pot. "Ben. Ben. Don't you understand that I vacillated between fearing my husband was dead and trying to hold on to a faith that said he was not? I had to learn to live without you, and living without you is something I never wanted to do. . .*never* want to do again. Can you possibly grasp hold of that?"

Ben stood and walked over to where she leaned against the counter. Taking the mug from her hand and setting it on the countertop, he slid his arms around her waist, encouraging her to do the same.

It didn't take much. Katie pinked, turning her head to face the floor. "Don't," she said lightly.

He nuzzled her ear. "Why not?"

"Because." She laughed. "Because I haven't brushed my teeth and—"

He kissed her lightly anyway. "I find myself in a very strange place here," he said, releasing her and returning to his coffee.

Katie picked up her mug and joined him. "In what way?"

"I never thought I'd say what I'm about to say, but here goes. Mrs. Webster, when we *both* deem me ready to take over the presidency, I'd like you to continue to work with me."

"Do you mean that?"

"I do. I noticed in some of the files yesterday that you've been setting plans in motion for a new hotel."

Katie sat straight. "A spa, really. In Montana."

"Sounds interesting. What if I were to make you the vice president of. . .I don't know. . .new ideas or something."

Katie smiled so hard she thought her face would break. "New ideas. I don't think that's the right title, but—"

Ben slid his hand across the table again, but this time when she took it, it was for a different reason than before. "We'll come up with something. Now," he concluded, leaning over, "why don't you go upstairs and take a shower—do something with your hair," he teased. "And we'll see what trouble we can get into today."

Katie stood. "Sounds like a plan. First, I need to check on Maggie. And to tell her we're going to have a visitor soon."

Ben stood, mug in hand, and headed for the sink. "A visitor?"

Katie walked toward the door of Maggie's suite. "My friend Marcy. I can't wait for you to meet her. I talked to her last night, and she said to be certain to have Maggie bake tea cakes."

Katie opened the door, stepping into the filtered light of the sitting area of Maggie's rooms. Leaving the door ajar, she flipped on a small table lamp, then headed toward the opened bedroom door. She had a clear view of Maggie, sleeping on her back, her mouth slightly open, and it made her smile. *If Maggie knew,* Katie thought, *she'd be horrified.*

At least, she concluded, *she's not snoring, though it's a small wonder.*

"Maggie," Katie called softly, padding across the carpeted room. "Maggs, are you going to sleep the day away again?" As she reached the bedside, she noticed Maggie's Bible, resting next to her. Her index finger continued to mark a page. "Maggs," Katie said again, reaching out to touch her shoulder, to shake it gently.

Maggie's body was stiff and cold.

As the realization of the moment made itself clear to her, Katie cupped her hand over her mouth. "No," she wailed, then dropping her hand, screamed, "Ben!" as she ran out of the room.

CHAPTER FORTY-EIGHT

Andi Daniels slept later than she'd hoped she would; then again, having returned from Bucky's apartment near two o'clock, she hadn't gone to bed until the wee hours of the morning.

He'd assumed she'd stay, of course. But he had assumed wrong, and it had given her great delight to tell him. "If we're going to do this kind of business together, I think it's in our best interest—both of ours—to keep this a little less than personal. Besides," she concluded, reaching for a line from the show tune that had been playing when she had entered his apartment earlier. "Princes come, princes go."

Sitting up in bed now, dialing for room service, Andi couldn't decide whether she'd seen relief or disappointment cross his handsome face. Neither one of them—in all honesty—mattered much to her.

She was in control now. Finally. So much control, she'd managed to get enough money from him to pay for the previous day's purchases.

Having placed her usual order for eggs, wheat toast, and coffee, she pulled herself out of bed and headed for the shower. She frowned at the wig, body suit, and clothes she'd left abandoned on a chair before climbing between the crisp cold of the sheets. She'd have to put them on again soon, and she knew it. Bucky would want a daily report, and—to fill his ego—he'd press her for one in person.

Andi's morning shower did her a world of good, allowing her to think about her next move. Bucky hadn't said so, but she knew he was watching her every move.

"I have a connection at THP," he had said.

A connection. Drying the rivulets of water from her body and slipping into a robe, Andi wondered who it might be, knowing it could be anyone from the janitor to a vice president. Not that it mattered, she told herself. Whomever Bucky had hired, he or she was sure to do a fine job. Bucky wouldn't have it any other way.

For now, everything she did had to appear to be on the up-and-up. Not only for the eyes and ears of Mr. Caballero, but for the eyes and ears of the Websters.

A knock at the door told her that her breakfast had arrived. She strolled into the living room and opened the door without thinking, ready to eat and more than ready to set part two of her plan into action.

Sabrina Richards sat in a chair of the Webster's guest bedroom she had been using, speaking to Dylan O'Neal, who had—just the day before—been transferred back to the city to keep a watch on Andi Daniels.

"I take it you met your replacement earlier this morning."

"Yeah," Dylan informed her. "Name's Nixon. As soon as he came on, I went to see the switchboard operator. Miss Daniels has not received any calls nor has she made any calls in the last twenty-four hours."

"What about before that?"

"Before that the phone records indicate that she received a call from a Canadian listing—"

"When?"

"Just a few days ago, but no other calls have come from that number."

"Canada—what was that?" Sabrina jerked in her chair, standing at the sound of what sounded like a shriek from the first floor.

"What?"

Sabrina turned toward the closed door. "Something's going down here, O'Neal. Stay near the phone."

Phil Silver spread his notes on his desk at John Jay before him.

Andi Daniels had received a phone call the very evening he'd taken her to dinner, and the call had come from Canada. A small amount of investigation had showed the number listed to Anthony Martino, 49 Whitecourt.

Phil's palm pilot was sitting atop the desk. Using it, he searched for the phone number of a man he'd at one time worked a case with when the investigation took him into Ottawa.

"Crawford," the man answered.

"Gene, this is Phil Silver. I don't know if you—"

"Phil, hello! What causes our paths to cross again?"

"Listen, I'm going to be honest with you here and tell you I'm no longer with the Bureau."

"Is that so?"

"I've got a private license. . .working on a case that has connections in your city."

"What can I do for you?"

"I've tracked a man to 49 Whitecourt. Goes by the name of Anthony Martino. I have reason to believe he may be a man I've been looking for."

"Hold on a sec," Gene said from the other end of the line. Phil could hear the faint sounds of his straining, as though he were reaching for something, like a pen or pencil to write with. "Say that again," he then said. "49 Whitecourt?"

Phil repeated the information. "Can you call me back with

anything you might be able to find, including any outgoing calls to the States?"

"Not a problem."

"Let me give you my numbers," Phil said, then did so and, after thanking him, disconnected the line.

He leaned back in his chair, miserable at the prospect of waiting. Before he could become too comfortable with his misery, however, his cell phone rang.

"Silver," he said answering.

"Phil."

Phil sat up straight at the sound of Katie's voice. "What's wrong?" he asked.

"It's Maggie, Phil," she said. "She's gone."

CHAPTER FORTY-NINE

Ben lay on the plush leather sofa of his Hamptons home office, his legs crossed at the ankles and the heels of his stocking feet resting atop one of the sofa's arms. His eyes were closed, but he was fully awake, thinking of the things that had transpired in the past two days since Maggie's death.

Maggie was gone. The idea of it rocked him, left him feeling unsettled and insecure. She'd always been there for him. Always taken care of him. Always been quick to offer her advice—requested or not.

The memories he'd struggled with over the past nineteen months, and most especially over the past few weeks, seemed to shoot to the forefront of his mind with a rapidness he'd never experienced before. By and large, Maggie was a part of them.

Maggie riding in the back of the limo with him when, as a five year old, he'd experienced his first day of school. Maggie and him, sitting in the quiet reverence of her church's sanctuary on Sunday mornings, followed by a trip to the bakery where she always bought him a chocolate éclair and cold glass of milk, praising him for having been "such a good lad" during what felt like—to him—an endlessly long sermon. Maggie, fretting over the bow tie of his tux as he prepared for his first boy-girl dance.

Maggie, waiting up for him in his teenage dating years. Maggie, giving him a thumbs-down when he'd formally introduced her to a former sweetheart, the snobbiest woman he'd ever dated—whom Maggie would only refer to as "that Trenton woman"—and a thumbs-up when he'd brought Katie home to meet his family.

Maggie, waving good-bye to him from the front door of this very home when he drove away, about to stage a ruse, a car bombing that would appear to take his life but would not. Maggie, firmly believing he'd return, and then fluttering over him like an old mother hen when he finally did.

Even now, lying here in the quiet of what was his favorite room of the mansion, he could hear her last words to him before she'd retired for bed two nights ago.

"The good Lord hears our prayers, son. He loves us and forgives us and makes us His own. I have prayed for you every day of your precious life, and when you brought Miss Katie home, I began to pray for her, too."

"Thank you, Maggie," Katie had said. "Your prayers worked."

Maggie had stood then. "That they did, my darling. That they did." *She then had leaned over and kissed him on the cheek. "And they will tug at your heart, too, lamb," she had said to him. "Because it won't be long—as we all know—that I will be with the Lord in His kingdom."*

Ben squeezed his eyes so tight he could see explosions of color behind his lids. His brow furrowed as he envisioned the woman who'd always been there for him. Through the pain of losing Maggie, it brought him comfort to picture her walking down streets paved with gold, her arm linked around the arm of Jesus, telling Him—

A knock at the door interrupted his thoughts, and he opened his eyes. "Come in."

The door opened, and Katie peeked around it. There was a look of poignancy about her, mixed with something he couldn't quite read. "Hi," she said.

Ben shifted his hips a bit and patted the sofa beside him. "Come here," he said, though it was more like a desperate request than an order.

Katie closed the door behind her then stepped over to the sofa, slipping her narrow hips up next to his. Her arms automatically draped over his middle, and her hand rested over his heart. "How are you doing?"

He nodded before answering as he drew her closer to him with his arm draped over her hipbone. "You know," he said. "I was just thinking about what Maggie said before she went to bed the other night."

"I think about that a lot, too. It's almost as if she knew." Katie began to play with a button on his shirt.

With his free hand, he rubbed his forehead. "Do you think that's possible?"

"Like some sort of premonition?"

"Mmm-hmm."

Katie shook her head. "I don't know. I think she certainly understood her death's imminence, but I don't know if she thought it would come within hours."

"You may find this strange—coming from me—but I was just now lying here, picturing her walking in heaven with Jesus, arm looped through His—" He watched Katie as she smiled weakly. "Telling Him she'd serve Him his tea at four o'clock and He'd better not be late if He knows what's good for Him."

Katie tilted her head and raised her brow. "A servant to the True Servant."

Ben swallowed hard, nodding. "That's my Maggie. . .*was*. . . my Maggie."

Katie dropped her temple to his chest. "She will always be your Maggie, Ben," she whispered. "And she will love you forever and ever."

Ben slid the hand nearest her hip up her spine, allowing it to rest in the tumble of her hair, wondering if she could hear what his heart was trying to reveal. "And you, Katie. And you."

Katie lifted her head, leaned over enough to reach his lips with hers, then drew back. "I'm going out to the carriage house for a bit. We have about five hours before we need to get ready for the funeral. I'm going to go have some quiet time out there."

He watched her stand. "You're not working, are you?"

"Oh, no. Who could work today?" She looked at her watch. "I imagine that the guests from the city will be arriving within the next two hours."

Ben sat up. "I talked with Mother last night at the bed-and-breakfast—"

Katie crossed her arms. "I wish she and your father would have considered staying here."

Ben stood and walked over to his desk, where he picked up a paperweight and shifted it from one hand to another. "I know. She's a stubborn girl, my mother. But she did tell me she's brought their housekeeper with them and she'll bring her over around eleven to help with the guests."

"Good. I'll be sure to thank her for that." Katie turned toward the door. When she reached it, she turned and said, "See you in a bit."

Ashley rapped on the door of the carriage house, waiting for the quiet "come in" she was sure to get.

When it came, she pushed the door open and stepped into the bright office. "Hi," she said.

Katie sat curled in an oversized old chair. Her eyes were puffy and lined in pink, and though she was well-dressed, the lack of attention to details such as accessories, hair, and makeup were a giveaway to Ashley of the true condition of her employer and mentor. "Hey, Ashley. Come on in," Katie said to her.

"Mr. Webster said you'd be out here. I just came by to see how you're doing," Ashley informed her, taking soft steps toward her.

Katie merely nodded. "The funeral can't come soon enough," she said. "And yet, it will come too soon."

Ashley crossed her arms. "I remember when my grandmother died," she said, walking over to the chair's matching sofa and taking a seat. "To me, she was everything I wanted to be when I grew old. Living her whole life on a farm, she was a bit weathered, but so kind and gentle, you know?"

Katie nodded.

"But I remember my daddy—her son—saying to me that he knew where his mama was and that was really all that mattered."

Katie looked down at her hands, playing with an imaginary piece of string she'd balled up between her fingertips. "I feel the same way about Maggie, but I'm going to miss her anyway. My sorrow is truly for those of us who loved her and not for her." She looked up at Ashley. "You know, it feels like a part of my heart is missing."

Ashley's eyes took on a faraway look. "That's the way it was with Grandma. I still miss her." She took a deep breath and exhaled. "Brittany came up with me."

"Misty?"

Ashley shook her head. "She said she didn't really know her, so she'd just stay behind."

Katie swallowed. "That's fine. Did Simon drive you up?"

Ashley pinked as she smiled. "Yes."

"When are you going to tell me about you and Simon?"

"You know?"

"Yes. I know."

"Who told you?"

Katie smiled. "You did. Every time you two are even remotely within reach of each other, you both get flustered."

Ashley tossed her long blonde hair over one shoulder. "I don't know what it is about him. . .I would have never considered his type as being my type before, but. . ."

"What is *his type?*"

Ashley pinked again. "You know. Like an overgrown teddy bear. He's so good to me, Katie. And he's got such plans for us."

"So this is pretty serious." It wasn't a question, but Katie was pleased to say it.

"Yeah. As a matter-of-fact, he told me he wants to talk to me later tonight. After the funeral. I'm—I'm going to go with him back to the city to pick up Mrs. Waters when her plane lands."

Katie nodded. "Oh, yes. She gets in rather late tonight. I told her I'd be unable to meet her, so I'm glad you'll be going, too."

Ashley stood. "Well, we'll see what Simon has up his sleeve then."

Katie stood as well. "I'll go back to the house with you. I need to finish getting ready," she said, linking her arm around Ashley's waist and steering them both toward the door. "And I'll be most anxious to hear what it is Mr. Simon wants to discuss with my favorite young associate."

CHAPTER FIFTY

Simon and Ashley arrived back in the city early enough to have a late dinner at a small but intimate restaurant near LaGuardia. Simon specifically asked for a table near the back of the room and was easily accommodated. As soon as they were seated and the server had taken their drink order—both requesting caffeinated coffee—Simon cleared his throat.

"I thought today's service was nice," he said, though Ashley could tell it was the last thing on his mind.

"Especially when Katie got up and talked about finding the Bible lying next to Maggie. . .and about the place she'd marked with her finger."

Simon hunched his shoulders a bit. "Do you remember that Scripture she read?"

Ashley nodded. "It's one of my favorites. It's from the tenth chapter of Ezekiel and talks about seeing the glory of the Lord."

"I suppose that's what Maggie is doing now."

Ashley nodded, the blonde of her hair shimmering in the glow of the orb of light emanating from the small lantern in the center of the square table.

Simon cleared his throat again. "You sure are pretty, you know that?" he said, just as their server returned with their coffee.

"Know what you want?" their server asked.

"Can we still order the special that is listed on the sidewalk chalkboard?"

"Yes, sir."

Simon held up two fingers. "Two, please." He then looked at Ashley. "That okay with you?"

Ashley nodded. "That's fine." She took a deep breath and sighed in desperate anticipation.

When the waitress walked away, Simon turned back to her, resting his arms against the edge of the table, hunching his beefy shoulders all the more. "I have something for you," he said, keeping his voice low.

Ashley pressed her lips together. "Okay." She watched him reach into the inner pocket of his suit coat and draw out an envelope. He laid it on top of the slick grain of the table, sliding it toward her.

"What's this?"

"Open it."

She raised her eyes to meet his and in doing so witnessed the anxiousness of the gift-giver. "What are you up to, Simon?"

He blushed. "Just open it."

"Okay, okay," she said, picking up the envelope and pulling back the unsealed flap. She extracted a folded piece of paper, then dropped the envelope and unfolded the paper. "It's a certificate."

"It's a stock certificate," he explained. "Remember when you told me that Mrs. Webster was taking part of the stock public in order to open the spa?"

Ashley studied his face. "Yeah. . ."

"Well, the way I see it is this: That spa is her baby, but it's your baby, too, because you're working so hard on it. . .have put your heart into it, really. And I wanted you to own a part of it."

Ashley pressed her hand against the place where her heart was about to burst from her chest. "Oh, Simon," she exclaimed breathlessly.

"You like it?"

"I love it!"

He reached over and took her hand. "I love you, you know that, right? I mean, I know that I don't say it a lot. In my family we don't always say things like that, but I do, and I want you to know it."

"I love you, too. We don't say it a lot in my family either. When you're doing all you can do to run a farm, it's kind of unspoken."

The waitress returned to the table, carrying two platters of steaming food. "Two specials," she said, holding them high over their heads.

Ashley scrambled to gather the certificate and envelope out of the way. When the plate was set before her, she noticed a small ring box nestled in its center, surrounded by her dinner. "What's—?" She looked up to the waitress, who was grinning at her.

"Tonight's special," she said as she set Simon's plate before him, sans a ring box. "Enjoy," she said with a wink, then strolled off.

Ashley pointed to the ring box. "Is this what I—?"

Simon plucked the box from the plate and, opening it, displayed a delicate diamond, encrusted with rubies, her birthstone. "Will you marry me?" he asked.

Ashley extended her left hand toward him. "Yes, I will," she answered as he slipped the ring over her finger. She brought the hand closer so as to study it, then looked back at the man she loved so very much. "Is this to get a share of my stock in the spa. . . or do you really love me?"

He smiled at her. "You found me out."

She looked back to the ring. "Oh, well," she teased. "I say let's kiss on it, and then we can eat."

CHAPTER FIFTY-ONE

Katie awoke the following morning feeling tired and heavy laden. Her joints ached, as though she'd climbed a mountain the day before. What she had done, however, was bury one of the dearest, kindest women she'd ever been so fortunate to love and be loved by.

Katie rolled to her side, ran the palm of her hand along the satiny smoothness of the pillow next to hers. She closed her eyes, said a silent prayer for her husband. . .for his strength now that Maggie was gone. . .and that he, too, would come to love God as much as Maggie and she.

And that maybe. . .just maybe. . .Ben would fall in love with her again.

She pulled herself out of the bed just as the door creaked open and Marcy stuck her head into the room. "Morning," she said.

"Marcy!" Katie ran across the room, wrapping her arms around her friend. "You made it."

Marcy shut the door behind her. "How are you, my friend?"

Katie squeezed tight, then released Marcy as she stepped back. "Better now that you're here."

"My flight was extremely late last night. I'm glad you went on to bed." She frowned. "Alone, apparently. Good thing you warned me you were sleeping in here. I might have walked in on that good-looking husband of yours in his altogether."

Katie laughed. "I can't believe you're already up and dressed."

Marcy blinked. "It's nearly eleven o'clock in the morning."

"What?" Katie looked down at her watch. "Oh, for heaven's sake. I guess Ben decided to let me sleep."

"He's downstairs talking with Sabrina."

Katie planted her hands on her hips. "You've met him?"

Marcy nodded, her eyes wide. "Good move, girl. He's a doll." She walked to the bed and plopped down on it. "Kind of has that 'Bond, James Bond' look about him. No small wonder you were so vehement about hanging in there."

Katie opened the door of the adjacent bath. "Just keep your mitts to yourself. Come keep me company while I shower?"

Marcy jumped from the bed. "Hey, remember locker room after gym?"

Katie frowned. "Don't even go there." She pointed to the vanity stool. "Sit," she ordered.

Marcy grinned and sat. She grabbed for a nail file lying forgotten on the vanity and began to work on her nails. "You've got a pile of people in this house."

Katie stepped into the oversized shower and closed the frosted glass behind her. "I know." She slipped out of her gown, reopened the door, and threw it at Marcy, who attempted to catch it but missed. Katie giggled, then closed the door again and turned on the water. "Ben's cousin, Cynthia, is staying here. Brittany, Ashley, Simon, of course—" Katie opened the door again and looked around it. "I think Simon may have proposed last night," she said with an air of confidence.

Marcy looked up from her lap where she'd folded the discarded gown. "He did."

Katie's mouth fell open. "How do you know so much?" She shut the door and continued with her shower.

"Get up earlier and you'd know more."

"Oh, please," Katie said. "I'm the one who's usually at work by eight in the morning, so don't even go there with me."

"Who else is here?" Marcy asked, ignoring the jab.

"Sabrina. . .as you know. Phil and Gail—oops!" Katie turned off the water, pulled the towel from the towel bar, and wrapped it around her. She jerked the door open and stepped out of the shower and onto the fluffy cream-colored mat in front of it.

Marcy was grinning at her. "Yeah. I know. Saw them."

Katie frowned. "I haven't had the chance to tell him you were coming."

Marcy nodded. "I know that, too."

Katie tightened the towel around her. "Marcy, try to behave."

Marcy stood. "I was a perfect angel. Though I do have to tell you that the look on his face when he saw me was priceless."

Katie marched into the bedroom and toward the closet. "I'm surprised I slept through the earthquake," she called out.

Marcy stepped out of the bath. "Me, too. Hey, I'm going to head on downstairs and see what trouble I cannot get into while you dress."

Katie turned to face her friend. "Please do so. I'll be down in about a half hour." She grew pensive. "I was just going to ask you to have Maggie make me some coffee, but—"

Marcy gave Katie a tender hug. "How about if I do the honors?"

Katie kissed the top of Marcy's head. "Thanks, friend."

Marcy headed for the door. "Not a problem."

Phil and William decided to take a walk along the shoreline before everyone left for East Hampton for lunch. The air was bitter cold, and it stung their cheeks, turning them bright red, but neither man seemed to care.

"Do you think Katie will make it down in time to leave?" Phil asked.

"Her friend says she'll be down soon enough. That she's awake now." William pulled a wool cap tighter over his scalp.

Phil dug his fists into the pockets of his coat. "Watch her, William. She's trouble."

William chuckled. "Katie told me about your run-ins with Marcy."

"Run-ins? Is that what we're calling it?"

"That's what *I'm* calling it."

A moment of silence fell between them before Phil continued. "How are you and Katie doing?"

William looked at him. "These past few days. . .she's really a strong woman, isn't she? She's really something else."

"That she is."

"Listen, Phil. . .I know this might be a little strange to talk about. . .to you of all people, but what do you think of this new faith she's developed?"

Phil cocked his head at William. "To me of all people? Why, because I'm Jewish?"

William only nodded.

"That's never really been an issue between us, now has it?"

William smiled. "If you say so."

Phil smiled back at him, then shook his head. "To answer your question, I don't think what I think has anything to do with it. Faith is a personal thing. Katie. . .I didn't know her before, so it's hard for me to compare. But Katie is one of the best people I've ever met. She attributes her goodness and strength to God. What's so bad about that?"

William looked down at his feet. "Not a thing." Several moments passed before he repeated his words, this time reflectively. "Not a thing." A seagull cawed at him, and he looked up at it, then turned his head back to Phil. "We don't have much time, and I need to ask you something else. Somewhat unrelated. I want to talk about Bucky Caballero."

Phil paused, considered his friend for a moment, then continued on with William keeping step. "That question leads me to believe you're feeling better."

William nodded. "I feel better today than I've felt in a long time. I'm much stronger than when I first returned. I can't say that I remember everything in my past, but I don't honestly feel like I'm missing anything."

"What does that mean? Exactly."

"It's like this: If I asked you to tell me what you did on. . .say. . . February 15, 1979—"

"Where'd that come from?"

"I don't know. Just seems like an 'out of the hat' kind of date."

"Oh."

"So, if I were to ask you what you were doing on that date, how would you answer?"

Phil remained deep in thought before finally answering, "I have no idea."

"That's what I mean. Just because you can't remember what you did on that exact date doesn't mean you've lost the memory of it. But if someone said, 'Phil, remember when we did so-and-so?' and you said that you did, and the date of that event just happened to be February 15, 1979—"

"Ah. Okay. I understand."

William looked down toward his feet, shod in his oldest, most comfortable leather boat shoes. He was walking closest to the water's edge, and he veered himself a little more inland. "I've been studying the files from THP that we brought back from the city. And I think I'm ready to begin with some little things in the office. I'm telling Katie today that I believe we should go back to New York tomorrow. It's time to get back to the job of living."

"And in order to do that, you need to put the issue of Caballero to rest."

"Exactly. I was talking to Sabrina this morning, but she's not releasing any information to me other than to tell me that her partner, O'Neal, was sent back to the city to follow up on another part of the case."

"O'Neal." Phil pulled a packet of gum from the inside pocket of his coat, popped a piece out and into his mouth, then offered the pack to William, who readily accepted. "What does he look like, this O'Neal?"

"Your quintessential Irishman. Reddish-blond hair. Fair complexion. Freckled face. About thirty or so."

Phil shook his fist once in the air. "Man! I thought so."

"Thought what?"

"The other night I was hanging out in the lobby of the hotel, and I noticed another man doing the same thing."

"Why were you doing that?"

Phil hunkered into his jacket. "If I tell you, I want you to promise you won't get bent out of shape."

William looked away from the driftwood-littered shoreline, toward the grassy dunes shielding the mansions and compounds of his neighbors. "You're watching Andi."

"Yes. Chances of Caballero trying to contact her are pretty good," he said, then filled William in on what he knew. When he was done, William turned and headed back toward the house. Phil did the same. "You understand, don't you? This is my job, and I'm simply moving toward the most obvious destination."

"I understand. And it does make sense. Did you see anything?"

"Nothing. She was, according to Miguel, in the hotel. If she left, she didn't do it through the front door. And she hasn't received any other calls from Canada since the one the night I took her to dinner. If I know Caballero, he's moving back into position."

"Position for what?"

Phil shook his head. "That's what we've got to figure out. And we need to figure it out before he knows we have."

The cell phone William carried in his pocket vibrated, and he extracted it. "Probably Katie," he said. "Telling me she's downstairs and ready to go." Phil nodded at him as he flipped the bottom portion of the phone and said, "Webster."

"William? It's Andi. If you're with anyone, please don't say my name."

"Okay."

"You're with someone?"

"Yes, I am."

"Can you call me back, please? When you aren't?"

"Of course." He flipped the phone off. "It was Mother," he said to Phil. "I'll call her back when we get to the house."

"Will they go to lunch with us?"

William nodded. "Yes, I'm sure they will." He sighed. "She's adamant that Katie and I hire another housekeeper soon, but. . . well, we'll see."

As soon as everyone had returned from their East Hampton lunch, Ben asked Katie to join him in his office. He closed the door behind him and asked her to take a seat on the sofa.

"Is something wrong?" she asked.

"Oh, no." He took the seat next to her, settling between the arm and the back of the sofa. "I wanted to talk to you about a few things. The first is that Mother thinks we need to hire a housekeeper as soon as possible—"

Katie looked down. "Oh, Ben. I–I don't know. So soon? Can't we just coast along for a little while?"

Ben reached over and nuzzled the back of her neck with his fingertips. "Sure. I'm putting you completely in charge of this. You've shown fairly good skills in the hiring department."

She looked up at him, a little suspicious. "Fairly?"

Ben shook the thought away with the wave of his free hand. "Let's not go there right now. The other thing I want to talk to you about is that I'm ready to go home—to the city—and back to work. I know the idea of stepping aside hasn't been easy."

"Ben, I—"

He touched her lips with a finger. "Let me finish, Katie. This isn't easy for me either."

She nodded, and he went on. "I want to do this gradually, with you by my side in the presidency until I'm ready to take over completely. But I'm not kicking you out then either, if you're willing. I'd like to see you set up an office as the. . ." He leaned over a bit. "Vice president of Research and Development."

Katie bit her bottom lip. Unable to speak, she merely nodded again.

"With Ashley as your assistant? Is that okay?"

"Yes." She took a deep breath, then exhaled. "Just give me a minute to get used to it."

He touched the tip of her nose. "We've always contracted out for this kind of thing, but under your presidency, THP has taken new and—I might add—*exciting* turns. So then, the first order of business: We'll set up an office for you near mine. Second order of business: I want a complete report on this new spa you were telling me about."

Katie grabbed his hand. "First order of business is that the president of said corporation should not flirt with the vice president of newly developed office."

Ben chuckled as he stood. "Okay, then. Pack your bags, dear woman. I have a phone call to make."

Katie stood as well, touching her husband on his shoulder as she walked past him. "I'll get us both packed later. For now, Marcy and I are going to watch a movie on television."

Ben nodded, watched her leave the room, then walked over to the desk and picked up the phone, dialing the number to THP. When the switchboard operator answered, he gave Andi's name and room number without formal introduction and waited.

She answered on the second ring.

"Hi. It's me. William."

"Thank you for calling."

He perched on the edge of the desk. "What's going on?"

"I need to talk with you. Privately."

"We're coming back to the city tomorrow."

He heard her sigh. "Come to my room tomorrow evening, then. Say, seven o'clock?"

He paused, calculating the time. "Seven works. What is this about?"

"I don't want to say. Just be here. And, William? If you know what's best for you. . .and me. . .you'll keep this meeting between us. Okay?"

Ben stood. "I would never betray you. I'll see you at seven."

CHAPTER FIFTY-TWO

Driven by Simon, the Websters and Marcy arrived in the city at a time when few would want to—rush hour—though Marcy made sure to comment that if one was going to be stuck in traffic, being stuck in a limo was the way to do it.

"You have quite the sense of humor," Ben told her. "I can see why my wife enjoys your company."

Katie reached for Marcy's hand and squeezed. "I can't believe I managed to stay away from her for so long," she said to them both. "When we first saw each other, it was as if the years simply melted away."

Marcy frowned. "Except that you originally thought I was my mother."

Katie laughed. "Isn't it funny? We know we change with the years, but we don't expect those we left behind to change. I wonder why that is?"

No one answered her question. Just as it was asked, Simon pulled up to the front of the hotel and stopped the car. "We're home," Ben said.

When they had exited the limo, Katie turned to Simon and said, "Bring our luggage up to the room as soon as you can." To which he replied, "Yes, ma'am."

As they entered their apartment, Marcy said, "I suppose I'm in my usual bedroom?"

"Yes," Katie said. "That'll be fine."

"I'm going to go lie down for just a few minutes before dinner, then," she said. Then, smiling at them both, said, "I'll see you in about—"

"Eight o'clock, ladies," Ben said. "I'm taking you both out to dinner."

Katie beamed. "How lovely. Though I suppose it's either that or my cooking," she said.

Marcy turned toward the bedrooms. "I'll see you in a couple of hours then," leaving Katie and Ben alone in the foyer.

Katie crossed her arms as she looked toward the kitchen door. "I'm going to have to think about clearing out Maggie's room," she said. Then, looking at Ben, "Tomorrow. Not today." She placed her hands on her hips. "Well, then. Here we are."

"Here we are," Ben repeated. There was a light rap on the door and he turned. "Must be Simon."

Katie started for the door, but before she could reach it, Ben reached out and took her hand. "Hey," he said softly.

"Hey," she said back.

He continued to look at her for as long as he thought he could, then asked, "Would you do something for me?"

She turned to face him fully. "Certainly. If I can."

With the crook of his finger he stroked under her chin. "Would you have Simon place your luggage in our room?"

Katie took a deep breath, just as they heard another knock. "Just a moment," she called out, though she kept her eyes on her husband. "Ben," she said, stepping toward him, "are you in love with me?"

Before she could blink, he wrapped his free arm around her. "More than you can imagine, lady. More than I could ever say."

At about ten 'til seven, Ben excused himself for a few minutes.

"I just have a short errand to run," he told Katie in the privacy of their bedroom. "I'll be back very soon."

Katie seemed apprehensive, but she didn't argue. "Okay."

Already dressed for dinner, he left the apartment quietly and walked down the narrow hallway toward the elevators. Moments later, he arrived at Andi's door. A glance at his watch before knocking told him he was right on time.

Andi answered almost immediately. "Come in," she said, then stepped aside. She stuck her head into the hallway and looked both ways before closing the door. "Hi," she said. A tone of nervousness was in her voice.

"Hi," he said, leaning over to kiss both her cheeks.

She extended an arm. "Come in, William, and have a seat."

He walked into the darkened living room and took a seat on the edge of the sofa cushion. Resting his elbows on his knees, he said, "What's going on?"

Andi sat in a chair opposite him. "We need to talk."

"I assumed as much."

She took a deep breath before continuing. "What I'm about to tell you, I want your word you won't repeat."

"You have it. I'd do anything for you—after what you did for me."

"Bucky is in the city."

Andi's words sounded rehearsed. He shifted forward. "How do you know?"

"I've seen him. I've talked to him."

William could feel his jaw flexing. "Did he—?" He looked down for a moment, then back up. "Did he try to hurt you?"

"No. What he did do was make a very generous offer should I help him bring down your little empire, as he calls it."

William's eyes narrowed. "What does he want you to do?"

"For starters, keep him informed about the spa."

"The spa?"

Andi shook her head. "I don't know all the details yet. He's not about to just hand them to me on a platter. But I can tell you that he has a plan." She pressed her lips together. "Then again, so do I."

William stood, walked over to the bar, and poured himself a drink. "Can I get you anything?"

"Please."

He poured shots of Scotch into two glasses, brought one over to her, then walked over to the window where the drapes were drawn. He parted them in the middle and peered out, all the while nursing his drink, knowing the woman behind him was doing the same thing. "What kind of plan?" he asked, turning to look at the back of her head, which she shook.

"No. I don't want you to know just yet." She stood, turning to face him. "But you have to trust me. I've never lied to you, and I won't start now."

William took another swallow of his drink. "What I don't understand is why he'd be interested in the spa. Or how he'd even know about it, for that matter."

"I'm going to do my best to get as much information out of him tonight as I can."

"Tonight? You'll see him tonight?"

"Yes."

William took several steps toward her. "Andi, we should call Phil. We can simply arrest him for—"

"For what? For running an escort service out of your hotel two years ago? Do you really believe that the state of New York has time for this? What with the war on terrorism occupying everyone's mind right now?"

William returned to the bar and set his glass atop it. He started to swear, then stopped himself.

"Go ahead," Andi said. "You can say whatever is on your mind with me."

He shook his head no.

"William, listen to me. The oldest profession in the world—whether enjoyed by dignitaries or not—is a drop in the bucket in this town. Believe me, if anyone knows, I do. If you want Bucky put away, you'd better have more than just the old records from two years ago that point fingers to a bunch of dignitaries."

"Why do you say that?"

"Do you remember when you and I first went to the chalet after you were released from the hospital? Remember your head-aches, day in and day out?"

"I can never forget them."

"But after awhile, the pain became less severe because you had learned to live with it, remember?"

He nodded.

"This country has survived a major scandal of impropriety within its own White House. So what if a few congressmen and foreign dignitaries get their jollies at an escort service? The people are practically numb to it now. When we were in France, as soon as someone learned I was from the States, they asked me what the big deal was anyway. So the old records aren't enough anymore. We need more."

"What are you thinking?"

Andi smiled as she moved toward the bar where she stood next to him. "Bucky says he's been keeping himself in the black by buying and selling art. If I know Bucky—and I do—there's some shades of gray in that story. Bucky doesn't go far without his records, so somewhere in that apartment he's holing up in is a gold mine of illegal activity."

"And if there's not?"

She cocked her head. "If there's not, I've always got Plan B."

"Which is?"

Andi pushed herself away from the bar and began walking

toward the door. "Time for you to go, Mr. Webster. Back to your wife, I imagine. And to some dinner by candlelight from the looks of you." She turned. "I'll contact you tomorrow. Until then, be good."

CHAPTER FIFTY-THREE

Dressed in disguise, Andi slipped out of THP a little before ten o'clock that evening and arrived at Bucky's within a half hour. As before, the cab driver had already been paid.

She took the steps quickly this time, rang upstairs, and when the door buzzed, opened it and hurried up the stairs.

Mattie answered her knock. A forced catlike smile crossed her face and was then gone. "Come in," she said, releasing the door and walking back into the apartment.

"Where's Bucky?" Andi asked, closing the door behind her.

"He's on a phone call," she answered, looking toward the closed bedroom door, and then back to Andi. Her eyes raked up and down her torso. "Don't you look. . .fat?"

Andi pulled the wig from her head and tossed her hair. "Funny, Mattie. Then again, you always were a barrel of laughs."

The bedroom door opened then, and Bucky stepped out, carrying a manila file. Andi managed to catch a glimpse of the room beyond him. A drawer in the highboy was opened, and a few files were scattered on the floor. "Andi, you're early," he said, closing the door and crossing over to her.

When he'd kissed her cheek, she said, "I'm on time, Bucky. Check your watch."

He looked down. "Where'd the time go?" he asked.

Mattie moved across the room. "I don't know where the time went, but I can tell you where I'm going. To bed. Andi, as always, it was a pleasure to see you." She gave a curt smile. "Darling brother, I'll see you in the morning." Without another word, she left the room, closing her bedroom door behind her.

Bucky held up the folder in his hand. "Let me finish up a few things. I imagine you want to get out of that garb as soon as possible, but we'll need to give Mattie a few moments in the bath."

Andi sat in a nearby chair. "Not a problem." She watched as Bucky left the room and closed the bedroom door behind him. *At least,* she thought, *I now know where he keeps his important papers.* Though she couldn't do anything about it tonight, she at least had that much.

She kicked off her shoes and stretched her feet as she peered around the room. For a man who bought and sold art, he hadn't put much effort into decorating his apartment. There was not one single item of worth within the apartment. No pictures on the walls, no statues perched on tables.

The bedroom door reopened and Bucky stepped out. "Drink?" he asked.

"No," she said. "No, thank you."

Bucky stopped short. "My, my. No drink with me?"

She shook her head. "I'm not in the mood."

He held up his hands in surrender. "All right then. Mattie is most probably out of the bath now. Would you like to go in and—?"

Andi crossed one leg over the other. "I don't have a lot of time tonight, Bucky. I'm tired, really, and ready to get some sleep. So let's just keep this to business, shall we?"

Bucky walked over to the sofa and sat. "You are all business now, I suppose."

Andi sighed. "Let me ask you a question."

"By all means."

"Will you ever fall in love with me, Bucky? In your wildest dreams could you see me as your wife? The mother of your children?" As she spoke, she kept her eyes directly on his, watched them change from dark to darker still. "Honestly."

He shook his head. "No." Then he laughed. "You have become a very smart woman in the past two years."

"I know what I really want now. That's the only difference."

"And what do you want?" he asked, ducking his chin.

"I want to make enough money from whatever you've got up your sleeve so that I can start over."

"Starting over. Yes, I seem to hear the theme a lot from the women in my life."

"Mattie, too?"

"Mattie, too."

Andi swallowed. "So then, tell me what it is you want me to do so we can get on with it."

Bucky held up a finger. "Hold on. I'll be right back." He stood, returned to the bedroom where he opened the same drawer as she'd seen open before, removed a folder, and returned to stand before her. Extending it, he said, "Take it."

She did. Opening it, she found a short magazine article about the construction of THP's spa as well as a stack of other papers. She looked up at Bucky. "What is this?"

Bucky returned to his seat. "Mrs. Webster is building a spa. A spa of outlandish proportions, from what I gather, considering the amount of money needed to build it."

"You told me that the other night."

Bucky narrowed his eyes. "But what I didn't tell you is that I own a sizeable portion of the stock."

"What?" Andi looked back down and to the papers behind the article. They were stock certificates. "How did you manage—?"

"It's amazing what a man can do when he's determined, isn't it?"

Andi closed the folder. "So where do I stand in all this?"

"Twenty percent of the stock is out there, of which I own about 17 percent."

"Who owns the rest?"

"Doesn't really matter to me. Whoever it is, I'm sure they'll be trading it soon, and I'll purchase it as well. The main thing to focus on is getting Katie to release more of the stock. That's where you come in."

"Me?"

"I'm about to tell you what to do. If you follow my instructions exactly, I will soon own 51 percent of Katie Webster's stock and will therefore be 'in bed,' as they say, with her husband."

Andi pursed her lips and leaned forward. "I'm listening."

Bucky chuckled. "That's my girl."

The following morning, as Katie and Ben enjoyed a breakfast cooked by Marcy, the front doorbell rang.

"I'll get it," Marcy said. "You two just sit back and enjoy."

Ben looked down at his plate of waffles and fresh fruit as Marcy left the room. "This is pretty amazing. Do you think she'd consider leaving her family and moving in with us?"

Katie cupped her hand over his. "I don't think so."

Ben leaned over and kissed his wife. "Have I told you this morning that I love you?"

"About a hundred times," she answered, her voice low and throaty.

Voices entering the kitchen caused the two to sit up straight. When Marcy returned, Sabrina Richards followed her close behind.

"Good morning," Katie said as Ben stood. "What brings you here so early?"

Sabrina pointed to a chair. "May I?"

"Please," Ben said, pulling the chair out for her.

"Coffee? Waffles and fresh fruit?" Marcy asked.

Sabrina's eyes swept over the plates on the table. "Sounds good."

Marcy busied herself as Sabrina placed her arms against the tabletop and leaned forward. "What brings me here so early. . . well, I'm not sure how to say this. . .but O'Neal and I will no longer be watching over you."

Katie sat back. "Do you think Bucky won't return to the States, then?"

Sabrina shook her head back and forth just as Marcy set a cup of coffee before her. "Thank you," she said, looking up, then back to Katie and Ben. "Oh, he'll be back. But until we have a nibble that he's threatened you in some way, we'll be working other factors of the case."

"What other factors?" Marcy asked, now setting a plate covered with two waffles before Sabrina.

Katie noticed the sharp glance Ben gave her friend. "Marce," she said. Marcy sat in the single unoccupied chair.

Sabrina bit her bottom lip as she began the process of buttering and pouring syrup over her food. "I suppose you've probably already figured out that this is more than just a matter of the escort service operated out of the hotel."

As though in answer, Ben took a sip of coffee, keeping his eyes on Sabrina.

"We're looking at much more. There's been a link between Caballero and the buying and selling of stolen art, forgeries of legitimate works, and importation of artifacts." Sabrina cut a piece of waffle and slipped it between her lips.

"What kind of artifacts?" Ben asked.

"Works from the Middle East, pre-Columbian art from Latin America, South America. You may or may not be aware, but the U. S. of A. has some pretty strict guidelines concerning this, as well as their adherence to international treaties. Canada has some of the same laws, but getting art and artifacts across the border into the US from there is easier, especially with the right contacts."

"I see."

"There's one other thing. Do you two remember the galas he used to throw?"

Katie and Ben looked at one another. "It was at one of his gala events—for AIDS research, if I remember correctly—that we discovered the truth about his running the escort operation out of the hotel," Ben said. "Why do you ask?"

Sabrina chased the waffle with a swig of coffee. "We're also looking into just how much he was skimming off the top of the money he'd raise. Naturally, he'll say it takes a certain amount to throw one of these benefits, but he's not a nonprofit, so legally he shouldn't be able to make any money off it."

Marcy sat up a little straighter. "There are people out there who would actually make money giving AIDS research benefits?"

Sabrina nodded. "Sure, if that's what they do for a living. It's aboveboard. But not in the case of Caballero. His profit is getting people into his real estate office—or was, I should say—not in fund-raising."

Ben cleared his throat. "So what you are saying is that there is more than one reason for wanting Caballero."

Again Sabrina nodded as she set down her fork. Picking up her coffee mug, she rested her elbows on the table and brought the rim to her lips. "Much more. Phil Silver can tell you. There's always been a notion that Bucky Caballero was involved in much more organized criminal activity than we ever knew."

"You think he's with the Mafia?" Katie asked.

"Not *the* Mafia. Bucky is his own mafia, as Silver used to say."

Ben crossed one leg over the other, shoving away slightly from the table. "Question: Just how dangerous is Bucky Caballero?"

"You mean would he kill if he had to?"

"Yes." Ben raised his chin just a bit.

"Absolutely." Sabrina speared a strawberry and popped it into her mouth. "Why do you ask?"

CHAPTER FIFTY-FOUR

Phil Silver's cell phone rang as he drove to work that morning.

"Silver," he answered.

"Phil, it's Gene."

"Gene. Good to hear from you. Have you been able to get any information for me?" Phil lifted the cup of coffee he'd purchased just minutes earlier to his mouth.

"I have. The address you gave me—now vacant—was recently occupied by Antonio Martino—who goes by the name of Tony—and his wife, Ana. Spelled A–N–A. I did a little snooping with the neighbors, and they tell me that as far as they know, Mr. Martino was an art dealer."

"What made them think so?" he asked, turning his car onto Tenth Avenue and heading toward his office.

"One neighbor said that he witnessed shipments of art coming in and going out of the apartment."

"Anything else?"

"Yeah, one or two things, actually. One neighbor, a Mrs. Lucent, said Mr. Martino walked to a newsstand every day for his paper. Said a few times he's picked up a paper for her when the weather was too bad to get out and that he always came back with a stack of U. S. newspapers."

"Do you know which newsstand?"

"Not only do I know it, I've been there. Here's the part where you're really going to love me."

"I'm waiting." Phil drove his car into the parking garage.

"The newsstand is operated by a man named Thad Finch. Thad seems very impressed with himself that he even knows Mr. Martino. Apparently, one afternoon when Martino was purchasing his papers, a street photographer happened by unbeknownst to Martino. He took a photo of Finch making the sell, and then sold the 8 x 10 black-and-white glossy to Finch. Finch allowed me to take the photo and make a copy, which I can fax to you along with the phone records, which, by the way, are extensive."

"The photo. Is it a good shot?"

"Not really. It's a side view, but you may be able to make something out of it."

"Do you have my fax number at the office?"

"Yeah. You gave it to me the other day. I'm at home now but will be in my office within the hour. I can fax them to you then. I'll also mail the originals to your office address. You said you were at John Jay?"

"Yeah. Thanks, Gene," he said, pulling his car into his parking space. "I owe you."

Bucky handled the ancient artifact before him with trembling fingers. Anyone who knew anything about South Indian treasure would be sure to bid high for the Chola Bronze, which he would—of course—insist was an excellent price. Little by little, with the help of those he used and abused, he would make his way back into New York's social elite.

"What is that awful thing?" Mattie asked from across the room.

He turned to look at his sister, who was dressed in one of the most fetching peignoir sets he'd ever seen. Her dark hair had been brushed to a sheen, but other than that she was devoid of personal attention. "Her highness awakes," he said by way of a "good morning." "Coffee, pet?"

"Please," she said, making her way across the room to where her brother rose from the small dining table. "What is this thing?"

"Ancient art, my love. Just came in this morning," he said, bringing a cup of coffee from the kitchen. He set it before her on the table. "As you like it, black and strong."

"What is it doing here, this ancient art that looks perfectly evil, in my opinion? Is it dancing or merely hiking its leg?"

Bucky sat. "Evil or not, it's worth a fortune. Not only a monetary fortune, but this beautiful bronze item will place us very favorably with the city's elite."

Mattie pursed her lips. "I'm already there, darling. I keep telling you that all you have to do is see just the right people."

Bucky stood, walked over to an end table, and picked up a manila folder. "Perhaps you can see just the right people, but I'm as wanted as they come. I trust very few in this town, pet. I suggest you do the same." He returned to the table with the folder.

Mattie took a sip of her coffee. "Does that include Andi Daniels?"

Bucky opened the folder, pausing for a moment before answering. "I believe it does." He could feel his sister's eyes shift from her coffee cup to him.

"Stupid man."

"Mattie," he warned.

She touched the sleeve of his shirt with her slender fingers. "Sorry, darling. I just don't happen to trust her."

"Then you'll just have to trust me." He closed the file, stood again, then leaned over and kissed his sister on the cheek. "Have I ever let you down?"

At about ten o'clock Ben excused himself from Katie's presence in the office they were now sharing.

"Where are you going?" she asked him from her place behind the desk.

He was standing near the door. Walking over and placing a kiss on the top of her head, he said, "Not to worry, sweetheart."

She looked up. "We have an appointment with Dr. Robinson in an hour. We'll need to leave within thirty minutes."

He smiled down at her. "I know. I'll be back in about twenty minutes. Be ready to go."

He could feel her watching him as he left the room.

"I'll be back shortly," he said to Vickey, who was oblivious to much more than her computer screen.

Opening the door, he nearly bumped into Ashley, clutching a folder to her breast. "Oh!" she said. "Hello, Mr. Webster."

"Good morning, Ashley," he returned, stepping to one side to allow her entrance.

He closed the door behind him, then made his way toward the elevators.

There was one very important thing he remembered about being the president of THP; he'd never before had to account for where he was going or what he was doing. He wasn't about to start now.

When he exited the elevator on Andi's floor, he was grateful no one he knew had taken the ride with him. When he knocked on her door, she answered almost as if she'd expected him.

"Come in," she said. "I have something for you."

William strolled in, turning toward her when she'd closed the door. "And I have something to tell you," he said.

Andi stopped short. "What is it?"

He crossed his arms. "I had a talk with one of the agents from the FBI assigned to this case."

"When?"

"This morning. Bottom line, because I don't have a lot of time:

Bucky Caballero is considered very dangerous, Andi. I don't want you playing games with him."

Andi stared at him for what felt like eons. Then she sighed, a choked laugh escaping her throat. "Do you think I don't know how dangerous he is?"

"I don't want you to get hurt. You mean too much to me."

"Oh, William," she said, stepping toward him and then stopping herself. She cocked her head to one side as she said, "I would hug you for that, but something tells me you're really a married man again."

William merely nodded. "I don't want you to do this, Andi. I want to tell Sabrina Richards what I know. What you know."

Andi shook her head no. She walked toward the window and peered out. "Another frigid day in the city. I can't wait to get to California."

"Go now, then," he said, walking up behind her.

She turned. "No. I'm going to finish this, William." She patted his upper arm. "I know you're used to having things your own way, but you don't own me, and I won't allow you to control this issue. I need control here, William. Please understand that. I *need* control."

He stared down at her.

"Please."

With a heavy sigh, he relented. "I swear, if I suspect for one second that you're in over your head. . ."

Andi gave him a half-smile. "I was in over my head the night I first went out with Bucky and agreed to work for him." She closed her eyes. "Oh, so many years ago." Opening them, she then asked, "Would you like to know what I found out last night? Why the spa is so important to our Mr. Caballero?" She crossed her arms over her middle.

"Go ahead."

"Unbeknownst to you, sweet William, you're in business with the great man himself."

William's brow furrowed. "What are you talking about?"

"Stocks. Katie allowed 20 percent of her personal stock to go public in order to raise the money for the lavish spa she intends to build. Wanna take a guess at who owns the majority of that 20 percent?"

CHAPTER FIFTY-FIVE

When Ashley entered Katie's office, she found her employer and friend standing in the middle of the room, arms crossed. A perplexed look etched itself across her face, and she frowned.

"Katie?" Ashley said. "Sorry to barge in, but I wanted to talk to you for a minute."

Katie jumped a bit. "What?"

"I wanted to talk to you," Ashley repeated herself, closing the door behind her.

"Oh. Sure."

"Are you all right?" Ashley asked, walking toward Katie.

Katie uncrossed her arms. "Yes. I'm fine. Let's take a seat on the sofa," she said, turning that way.

When the two women were seated, Ashley said, "Are you sure you're okay? I can come back later."

"I'm fine. I just—I'm fine." She waved her hand, as though she were shooing away a pesky thought. "I'm glad you came by. I want to talk to you about the new office we're going to occupy."

Ashley gave a look of stunned pleasure. "You're kidding."

"No, I'm very serious. Mr. Webster and I are looking into it now. There's a vacant office—as luck would have it—near the end of this hallway. You and I will work out of there. I will be the VP of Research and Development, and you will be my trusty assistant."

Ashley pressed her palm against her chest. "This is so exciting!" She giggled a few times, then took a deep breath and sobered. "The assistant to the VP of Research and Development must at all times behave as a professional."

Katie patted Ashley's left hand, aware now of the sharp piece of jewelry that now adorned it. She took Ashley's fingertips in hers and brought the ring closer. "It's so pretty. Have you set a date?"

Ashley shook her head. "Not yet. We'll decide on it later."

"Have you called your family?"

"Oh, of course. The very next day. Mama's nearly beside herself with happiness, and Daddy's beside himself with grief. 'I guess this means you won't be moving back home,'" she quoted.

Katie patted her hand again. "I know."

"Especially since the tragedy of 9-11. Daddy wants me home pretty badly. But, you know, I think Mama really understands. It's nice to have this new relationship with her."

"I know about that, too. Now then, what did you want to talk to me about?"

Ashley pulled several glossy items from the folder she was carrying. "Here are the high points of the spas you asked me to look into. Poolside manicures and pedicures. Fresh fruit baskets in the guest rooms, changed out daily. Gourmet boxed lunches for departure."

Katie flipped through the sheets. "Marvelous. We'll take the best ideas from spas all over the world and make this place the do-all, be-all of resorts. There will be nothing like it on the entire planet."

Ashley shifted a bit. "There's one other thing."

"What's that?" Katie asked, looking from the glossies to the young woman.

"For an engagement gift, Simon purchased a small amount

of the stock for me that you took public."

Katie smiled. "Really? That's wonderful! Now we're really business partners."

Ashley pulled another stack of sheets from the folder. "I'm perplexed about one thing, though." She put the papers in Katie's lap. "Simon says that the rest of the stock was purchased by five companies in large quantities."

Katie looked up sharply. "What?" She looked back to the papers. "I'm surprised Mr. Spooner didn't keep me posted on this."

Ashley pointed to a date on page one. "They were bought almost immediately by the first three companies. Then, as you can see here, Simon purchased the minute amount we can afford, and then the other two companies finished the purchase." Ashley's shoulders shrugged a bit. "What I don't understand is this: Typically—Simon says—when a company buys this amount of stock, they'll begin a process of buying and selling."

"Right."

"But none of these five companies have done that."

The door of the office swung open and Ben stormed in. "We need to talk," he said forcefully.

Both women stood and turned to face him. "Ben, I—"

"We need to talk," he repeated, closing the door. "Now."

Ashley looked from Katie to Ben and back again. "I'll leave," she said. "We can talk later, Katie." Leaving the folder with Katie, she slipped around the two Websters and left the room.

"What is the meaning of this?" Katie asked.

Ben was at her within a flash. "I can't believe you did this."

"What?" she asked. "And keep your voice down."

"I'll scream out the window if I want," he said, moving toward it.

"Ben!" Katie hissed. "What is going on?"

He turned from the window. "Did you take part of our stock public?"

Katie looked down at the papers still clutched in her fist. "How did you—?"

"Never mind." Ben rubbed his forehead. "I'm getting another one of my headaches. Get me something for it," he barked.

Katie moved quickly to the desk and called Vickey. "Can you bring something for a headache?" she asked. She replaced the phone, then walked over to the bar and poured a glass of water while Ben returned to one of the sofas and lay down. When Vickey entered, Katie watched the look on her face change from professionalism to concern. "Are you okay?" she asked Katie.

Katie took the painkiller from Vickey as she said, "Yes. Call Dr. Robinson. Tell him we'll have to reschedule."

"Sure," she said, turning with hesitation toward the door. "I'll let you know what his receptionist says." Vickey closed the door behind her. Katie walked over to the sofa, sat next to her husband, and handed him the aspirin and glass.

"Here," she said as gently as she knew how.

Ben took both from her, swallowed the aspirin down, then handed the glass back to her. "Why did you do it?" he asked, this time more quietly.

"I took 20 percent of my stock public when the board wouldn't approve the building of the spa. It's my stock, Ben. If anyone loses, it's me."

He closed his eyes, flexed his jaw, and said, "The family has always owned THP stock. Only family." As though the light of day was blinding him, he crossed an arm over his eyes. "What were you thinking?"

Katie didn't answer for a moment. "Do you know how hard it's been for me to prove myself around here?" she asked. "First with the board, with the employees, then with the rest of corporate New York, and with the board again?"

Ben jerked himself up. "I'm so sick of hearing about how hard you had it." He pressed a fist to his forehead and groaned.

Katie jumped up and returned to the desk. "We need to get you to the hospital."

"I don't need a hospital!" he screamed at her.

Katie jumped just as the office door opened, and Vickey ran in. "Is everything—"

"Vickey, call Dr. Robinson's office again. We're on our way," Katie ordered.

Ben went to stand, staggered a bit, then fell back against the sofa.

"Ben!"

"William!" Vickey called out. She turned back to her office. "I'm calling now."

Katie reached her husband and wrapped her arms around him. "It's okay. It's okay." She felt him press his head against her breast, and she clasped him tighter still. "Take a deep breath, Ben. Breathe. Breathe."

CHAPTER FIFTY-SIX

Inside the single bath of Bucky and Mattie's apartment, Andi slipped out of the wig and weight garb. She reached into the small bag she'd brought with her, pulling out a silk shirt, which she slid over her arms and began to button down the front. She then retrieved the matching skirt, stepped into it almost methodically, and buttoned it in the back. A quick fluff of her hair and she was ready to walk out to the living room.

Today was the day. And there was a lot to accomplish.

Mattie and Bucky were sitting opposite one another—Bucky on the sofa and Mattie in a matching chair—sipping on cups of tea. An empty china cup rested on the coffee table, indicating to Andi that she was to sit there. "Is it already teatime?" she asked, cutting a sharp eye to Mattie.

Mattie returned the glare. "Do you have anything to tell us today, or are you just here to entertain us with your presence?"

Andi sat on the sofa, and Bucky began the process of pouring her tea from the silver tea service nearby. "What is it, Mattie? What are you so angry at me about?" Andi asked.

"Two years ago you willingly gave our records away to Webster. Let's just say I'm not as forgiving as my brother."

Andi slid closer to Bucky, who offered her the cup of tea,

which she readily accepted. "Thank you," she purred toward him.

He turned to her with a smile. "For what, puppet? The tea or the forgiveness."

She smiled a slow smile. "Both."

He chuckled in his throat. "Very good."

Andi took a sip of her tea. "As a matter of fact, I do have something to report to you today." She watched Mattie sit straighter in her chair. "I know for certain that William Webster is completely unaware of the public stock at THP for the sake of the spa."

"You don't say?" Bucky replied.

Andi stretched her arm along the back of the sofa and began to twirl the hair at the nape of his neck. "I *do* say. . . ."

"Trouble in paradise?" Mattie asked.

"A lot of trouble. I also have reason to believe that the money made from the stocks isn't enough for what Katie needs."

"So, she'll most likely sell more soon," Bucky surmised.

"Right."

Bucky leaned over and kissed Andi's cheek. "Excellent news, my pet. Excellent news indeed."

Mattie rose from her place across the room, set her cup and saucer on the coffee table, and said, "Well, darlings, I must be off."

"So soon?" Andi purred.

Bucky stood. "You are out too much for my happiness."

Mattie kissed his cheek. "I don't know how long we'll be in the city. I intend to enjoy every minute of it." She turned to Andi. "*Ciao*, darling."

CHAPTER FIFTY-SEVEN

On the return trip from the hospital, with Ben resting in the limo next to her, Katie decided that so far the course of the day had not been the best and that it couldn't possibly get worse.

She was wrong.

After they slipped in the back way of the hotel, Marcy met them at the front door of their apartment. "I turned back the covers on your bed when you called and said you were on your way," she said softly, as though Ben were sleeping in Katie's arms.

Ben glared at her. "I appreciate that," he said, though to Katie it didn't sound like it. She wove her arm around his waist, which he shrugged off. "Where'd the flowers come from?"

Katie looked to the foyer table where a vase filled with yellow roses and baby's breath had pushed the centerpiece out of the way, then forced her arm around Ben again. "Let's get you to the bedroom so you can sleep off the medication."

They walked together toward the bedroom. "I'm not finished discussing the stock issue with you," he said.

"Yes, I know," she told him. "But let's wait until you feel better and I can deal with it."

Katie pulled the draperies as Ben slipped under the sheets

and comforter of the bed, then stepped lightly to the door. "I'll check on you in an hour," she said.

"Hour's good," he mumbled.

She closed the door behind her and returned to the foyer where Marcy remained near the roses.

"Who *are* these from?" she asked.

"I haven't looked at the card, but they are for you. However, I can tell you I had a moment of déjà vu when they arrived."

"Thinking about the flowers I received from the McKenzie twins a couple of months ago?" Katie pulled the card from its holder.

"You know it."

Katie turned the card's envelope toward her. "It's from the hotel's flower shop."

Marcy shoved her hands into the back pockets of her jeans. "I noticed that, too. Just like the last time."

Katie pulled the card from the envelope, flipping it over to read it. "Oh, no."

Marcy craned her neck to look. "Oh-no-what-oh-no?"

Katie handed her the card. "These are from Harrison Bynum."

Marcy took the card. "You've got to be kidding me. Oh, wonderful. He's here in the hotel." Her mouth dropped. "He's *here* in the hotel."

"Yes, I see that. Room 759."

Marcy handed the card back to Katie. "Now what are you going to do, Rapunzel?"

"I suppose I should call him. Have him meet me—oh, dear. I can't have him meet me in Bonaparte's. Everyone there knows me. Then again," she began to pace, "he could be anybody. He could be a relative or something. Someone I'm interviewing."

"You sound like a girl in trouble."

Katie stopped and placed her hands on her hips. "I *am* a girl in trouble. How am I going to explain this to Ben?"

"He's asleep. Why don't you go take care of this now?" Marcy looked down at her watch. "I'm going to head up the street here. I saw a store with clothes I think my daughter would just go wild over, so I'll do a little shopping for her. That should keep the apartment nice and quiet for your husband."

Katie placed the card on the table next to the vase. "Okay. I should only be gone a few minutes." She grabbed Marcy by the shoulders and squeezed. "Pray for me."

"So, what's next?" Andi asked Bucky when he returned to the sofa after seeing his sister to the door.

He took a deep breath and sighed as he sat, then slapped his thighs with the palms of his hands. "Good question."

Andi ducked her chin in thought. "Don't tell me you don't know what your next move is?"

Bucky smiled at her. "Oh, I know what I'm doing next. I just don't know what you're doing next."

Andi felt her shoulders straighten. "What do you mean by that?"

He stared at her for a long moment. "I don't mean anything by that, pet. I simply mean we'll have to wait and see what transpires within the Webster household. For now I want you to find a reason—any reason—to go to their home and spend time with them. I want to know just how stormy the *Isola del Paradise* truly is."

Andi looked down, then back up. "If that makes you happy, Bucky."

Katie tapped on the door of room 759. Waiting the brief millisecond before the door opened, she glanced down at herself. She was still wearing the suit she'd put on this morning for work. Her hair was still pulled back, although she suspected a few strands of hair had managed to get loose. She wondered if her makeup could have used a little freshening. She then flattened her left hand over the palm of her right and looked down. She wore her wedding ring and the matching bangle, symbols of her undying devotion to her husband.

Her shoulders sank just as the door opened.

Straightening, she brought her eyes up to see the smiling face of the man who'd come to her rescue on more than one occasion while she'd been in Vermont. "Hi," she said.

"Katie," he said. "I didn't expect you to come here. I was sort of hanging out, waiting for you to call." He turned to face the room beyond, then looked back to her again. "Do you want to go downstairs? I understand you have a five-star restaurant; we could get something to eat."

"Bonaparte's, yes. Ah. . .no." She indicated the room behind him. "May I come in?"

He seemed uneasy. "Sure," he said, stepping aside. Closing the door, he continued, "You received the roses?"

Katie walked to the center of the room and turned. "Yes. Yellow roses, a representation of friendship. Thank you."

Harrison smiled at her. "I thought we were friends," he said. "But I'm just not sure what happened. One day you're there, and the next you're gone." He chuckled shyly. "It's taken me this long to get up the nerve to come here. I had to practically bribe Kristy to give me the name of your hotel." He held up a hand. "I confess I forgot the name of it."

"I forgive you. How is Matthew?"

"Matt's great. Still asks about the tall lady."

Katie laughed. "I'm sorry, Harrison. I should have called you by now, but. . .with so much going on. . ."

Harrison indicated the chairs behind her. "Would you like to sit down?"

Katie turned to look at the chairs, then gave her attention back to Harrison. "No, I'd better not. I just wanted to come down and explain that my husband came back while I was in Vermont."

Disappointment didn't take long to register on Harrison's face. "Oh."

Katie clasped her hands together. "I'm sorry. I really owe you an apology."

Harrison leaned against the nearby dresser, crossing his arms over his middle. "In what way?"

"I used you, I suppose. I was lonely. You were there. You were kind and. . .well, I used you. I'm sorry."

"Lonely. Now there's a concept I have no trouble relating to."

"But you have Matt—"

"Children don't make up for a wife, Katie." He cocked his head to one side. "Or a special friend."

Katie bit her bottom lip. "I understand." She sighed deeply. "I really shouldn't stay."

Harrison nodded in agreement.

"Before I go, however, allow me to say a couple of things? Like an old friend?"

His brow furrowed. "Sure."

"First thing is this: Your room is compliments of the establishment. I'll call down and make the necessary arrangements, so don't worry."

Harrison straightened. "You don't—"

"It's the least I can do. Also, might I suggest one of our fine Broadway plays for this evening?"

He shook his head no. "Nah. I'm going to just chill out in this room and then head out in the morning. But thank you."

"Lastly: Something struck me as being rather odd while I was in Vermont."

"What's that?"

"While there I met two wonderful people—one male, one female—who both happen to be single parents and both happen to be lonely." She shrugged. "And I'm wondering why those two haven't found each other."

Harrison's eyes narrowed in thought. "You're talking about Kristy Hallman?"

Katie merely nodded, then started for the door, patting him on the arm as she passed him. "You think about that." By the time she reached the door, he was right behind her, reaching around to open the door. "Thank you," she said, turning to look at him. She smiled. "I can see I planted a seed of thought that had never occurred to you before. It's funny sometimes; what we pray for has already been given to us."

He rested his hand and forearm against the opened door. "I have to say you're correct, though I can't come up with a single reason as to why I haven't realized this."

Katie smiled as she stepped into the hallway. "Now you have." She pointed a finger at him. "I'll expect to hear all the details. Thank you, again, for the friendship—and the roses." She turned and headed back up the hallway, to the elevators, and back to her apartment's floor. She opened the front door quietly, turned and closed it behind her only to be caught off guard when the voice of her husband said, "Would you mind telling me who Harrison Bynum is?"

CHAPTER FIFTY-EIGHT

"Ben!" Katie pressed her palm against her breast. "You nearly scared me to death!"

He stared at her for a moment, then waved the card from the floral arrangement in her face. "*Who* is Harrison Bynum?"

Katie moved around him, moving purposefully toward the privacy of the living room. "Come in here, please," she said.

"Katie, I demand an answer," he said from behind her.

Katie spun around. "You demand?" She could feel her eyes narrow. "You demand?"

"That's right. I demand. I'm your husband. Did you go see this man when you thought I was resting? Is that it? Have you been in his room?" Again, he waved the card, which she promptly snatched from his hand.

"Yes. Yes, I went down there. . .but to explain things to him." She fingered the card in her hands, looking at it.

He moved closer to her. "What kind of things?" It wasn't a question; it was an accusation.

Katie stepped away from him. "That my husband was home. And to apologize to him."

"For what?"

"Harrison is a gentleman—and allow me to stress the word

'gentleman'—whom I met in Vermont. Who, by the way, took care of me when Andi Daniels dragged me down the street while I was holding on to her SUV. Or did you even know about that?"

He pointed a finger at her. "I told you to keep her out of it."

Katie stomped her foot in frustration. "I won't take this, Ben. I can't! First one way, then another."

"Just tell me this," he asked, beginning to pace. "Did you. . . were you. . . ?"

When he didn't finish, she looked at him puzzled and said, "Did I what?" When he still didn't answer, she spoke softly. "You want to know if I was unfaithful to you?"

Ben rubbed his forehead with the fingertips of his right hand. "Yes."

Her shoulders slumped. "Oh, Ben. Never." Katie could feel the tears well up in her eyes and begin to spill down her cheeks. "It goes against everything I believe in. You must know that." She shook her head. "I was lonely. Not knowing whether you were dead. . .I had all the grief of a widow with no idea if I was or not. I was single, but *not*. You had Andi, and I had *no one*. Don't you understand how I felt after nineteen months of *not knowing?* I was *lonely*." Katie stopped and took a deep breath. "And Harrison was a kind man, and I admit it was tempting. But I was *not* unfaithful to you."

"You told me before you never even dated."

Katie clenched her teeth. "It wasn't a date."

"What wasn't a date? Did you or did you not go out on a date with him?"

She held up a hand. "I promise you. I have not been unfaithful to you. I had dinner with him, yes. But that was it. He was just being kind. . .and I. . .I was just. . ." She exhaled slowly, audibly. "Lonely."

She watched the color of his eyes become more vibrant. "I'm

sorry." He moved toward her, but she stopped him by raising her hand.

"No, don't." Katie set her jaw. "While we're in this frame of mind, we need to talk about the stocks."

Ben moved from where he'd been standing to the sofa. Sitting, he said, "This hotel has been family owned from the beginning. I wouldn't have wanted to take the stock public. It was a stupid thing to do."

"Stupid?" Katie raised a brow.

He raised a firm eye to her. "Bucky Caballero now owns the majority of the stock you put on the market."

Her face fell and she sat in a nearby chair. "Oh, no. How did you—?"

"Andi told me."

"Andi?" Her shoulders squared again. "Is that who you went to see the other night?"

"Yes." Again he pointed to her. "And I want you to listen to what I have to say before you begin judging her—" he started.

"Judging her?"

Ben stood, planting his hands on his hips. "Judging, Katie. You know, that thing you Christians are not supposed to do."

Katie threw her hands up in the air as she, too, stood. "Oh, here we go again. 'You Christians?' Excuse me for sounding cliché, Ben, but we aren't perfect. We're forgiven."

He stared at her for a few moments before lowering his voice to say, "Then forgive her. For whatever it is you think she did that was so horrible, forgive her."

Katie's lips parted to speak, but she couldn't. Her husband had sent an arrow through her heart, and it had pierced the exact emotion she'd tried to keep at bay, the one thing she didn't want to face. She had to forgive Andi Daniels.

Ben reached for her hand then, guiding her back to sit with him on the sofa. "Look, Katie. I love you. You know I love you."

"I know," she said, moistening her lips.

"And while I may not understand your new faith or some of your choices over the past two years, you've certainly done everything within your power to understand mine."

Katie turned fully to him. "But you couldn't help—"

"That's not the point," he said, shaking his head. "And I want you to know something, sweetheart. I think you've done a fine job as interim president."

Katie felt her shoulders fall again. "Oh, Ben. When you say things like that, I—"

"Except," he interrupted her, placing a finger on her lips, "this one thing. The stocks. I wouldn't have wanted you do a thing like this."

She shook her head. "If you'd been here, this wouldn't have happened. If or when you suggest things like a spa, they happen."

"That's not true. Believe it or not, some of what I considered to be my best ideas have been shot down by the board."

"Really?"

"Really." He crisscrossed his index finger over his chest. "Cross my heart."

Katie slipped her arms around his neck. "Just don't hope to die," she whispered into his ear.

He turned his face to hers. "We'll fix this thing with Caballero," he said against her lips.

"Okay," she mouthed, ready for her husband's kiss.

The doorbell rang.

Bucky stood from the sofa where he and Andi sat.

"It makes me happy. Having you on my side again makes me extremely happy. You have no idea how sad. . .how distressed. . .I have been over the past two years."

Andi couldn't keep the smile from spreading across her face. "Bucky. Don't be such a thespian. For a man who hates drama so. . ."

He turned to face her, a smile also across his face. Andi couldn't help but notice that as a man in his mid-fifties, he was remarkably distinguished. It was no wonder that women half his age still found him desirable. "What are you thinking, puppet?"

She leaned back on the sofa. "That you are a very handsome man."

He gave a mock bow. "Thank you. And may I add that these two years have made you only more ravishing."

Andi stood, laughing lightly. "Oh, Bucky. If you only meant it." She patted her middle. "Time for me to go put on the garb so I can head back to the hotel and do my dirty work." She pointed to the bedroom. "I'll be just a minute."

She could feel him watching her as she stepped into the bedroom—kept dark by the blinds and thick draperies in front of the windows—closing the door behind her. She rested her back against it, taking deep breaths before moving into the bathroom and, in record time, slipping out of her clothes and into the body suit. She twirled her long hair, pulling it to the top of her head, and donned the wig on top of it. She topped it with the sunglasses, as if the shades were a headband, then stuffed the removed clothes into an oversized, black leather bag, which she hung over one shoulder. She then stepped into short Italian boots she'd bought on her most recent shopping spree. As she turned to go out the bathroom, she heard the phone ring.

Stepping lightly to the bedroom door and pressing her ear against it, she heard Bucky answer. "Yes?" Andi took a deep breath and held it, waiting for his next line. "I have the piece with me and can meet you at the warehouse for the exchange." Andi exhaled slowly. "An exquisite piece," Bucky continued. "Yes, I have the particulars. . . ." Andi turned to face the highboy from where Bucky had removed the manila folder. Without hesitation, she walked over to it, sliding open the one drawer she'd seen open the evening before.

She sighed heavily. There were so many files, and the room was so dark, it would be difficult to tell one from the other. She grabbed the top few, walked over to the nearby window, and held on to its edge, pushing back the curtains enough to expose a fraction of light. The writing in the tab of the top file was small and printed in Bucky's handwriting. It read: THP Stocks.

Opening it, she flipped through the small stack of papers and certificates, frowning. The pages indicated that Bucky had formed a number of dummy corporations, obviously with the help of his broker, and one had been named Brandon's World. Brandon—Bucky's given name. "That pompous, arrogant man," she whispered, then closed the file and stuffed it into her bag. The other files, upon inspection, appeared to be information on works of art, their purchases and sells. Andi couldn't make it all out, but Bucky appeared to be bringing valuable antiquities into the country, as well as a few forgeries.

She heard Bucky saying, *"Ciao,"* on the phone and knew her time for snooping was at an end. She forced the files into her bag, wedging them behind the THP folder. She then moved back to the highboy to push the drawer shut.

At just that moment, Bucky Caballero opened the bedroom door.

"We need to talk," Phil said, walking into the Webster's foyer.

Ben, who had answered the door, closed it and turned to see Katie exiting the sitting room. Phil paused, looked from husband to wife and back to husband. "What's going on?"

Katie rubbed her hands together. "Come in, Phil," she said, returning to the sitting room.

Phil was right behind her. "Did I interrupt something?"

Ben pulled up the rear. "Nothing we can't begin again," he said.

Katie sat on the far end of the sofa with Phil sitting nearby. Ben sat in an occasional chair. "Can I offer you anything, Phil?"

Katie asked.

Phil gave her a soft look. "No. I'm fine."

"What is it, then?" Ben asked. "What do you need to talk to us about?"

Phil unbuttoned his coat and began to peel it away, pulling the phone records from his suit coat pocket. "It's this," he said, starting to hand the papers to Katie, then pausing and handing them to Ben. As Ben began to flip through them, they heard the front door open and click shut. Katie looked to Phil. "That will be Marcy."

Sure enough, within seconds, Marcy stepped into the sitting room. "What's going on—oh. Hi-ho Silver."

Phil rubbed his eyes. "I would ask you to leave, but it would be pointless."

Marcy walked over to the end of the sofa where Katie was and perched on the arm. "What's going on?"

"Where do these calls come from?" Ben asked, looking up at Phil.

"The phone records are from 49 Whitecourt in Ottawa, Canada. The phone is listed to a man named Antonio Martino." He pulled another piece of paper—folded—from the same pocket. "This is a faxed photo of Mr. Martino." Again, he handed the photo to Ben.

"That's Caballero," Ben said.

Both Katie and Marcy moved forward for a better look.

"Ben—" Katie said.

Ben looked at his wife, shaking his head.

"Ben, tell him."

His jaw flexed. "Andi has been in contact with Caballero."

Phil leaned closer. "You knew this, and you didn't tell me?"

"She. . .this is important to her. She's bringing her relationship full circle with him. She told me she wants to help us. . .to get information for us. . .and I believe her. But she asked me not to tell anyone, and I promised." He looked from one person to the other. "She's done too much for me," he said in defense. "I owe her."

Katie looked down to her lap, then felt Marcy's hand lightly touch her back. Phil took the papers from Ben and handed them over to Katie. "There's something I think you should see. He's been calling the hotel on a regular basis."

"Andi?" Marcy asked.

"No. Before Andi and William returned." Sitting back, he began pointing to several of the recorded lines. "Look here. And here. And here. . . These calls come in regular intervals."

Marcy looked Phil in the eyes. "So, what are you saying? Someone in the hotel is in business with Caballero?"

Phil nodded. "I think so." Looking from Katie to Ben, he asked, "Is there any way to trace this?"

"Switchboard would know," Katie said.

Phil stood. "Then let's go." He pulled a card from his shirt pocket and handed it to Marcy. "Do something useful for a change, will you? Call this number. Ask for Sabrina Richards. Tell her what you know. And tell her to get over here ASAP."

Marcy took the card as Katie said, "We'll be right back."

CHAPTER FIFTY-NINE

"What are you doing?" Bucky asked from across the room.

Andi could feel her eyes growing round and large, her tears forming a glassy sheen of fear. "Bucky," she said in a whisper that caught in her throat.

He slammed the bedroom door shut and began to move toward her.

Trapped between the highboy and the bed, Andi's only option was to scale across the latter. . .to try to get into the bathroom. With a leap, she was on top of it, scurrying across its satiny comforter, the spiked heels of her boots catching in the fiber.

But Bucky was faster. He reached for her, grabbing her by the ankle, forcing her down to the bed on her belly, and dragging her across it. She worked her legs as though she were crawling across a war zone, clutching for the edge of the bed. "Bucky!" she screamed. "Bucky, no!"

He jerked her then, bringing her to the floor. The leather bag fell from her shoulder and the wig went askew. She struggled to stand as she felt the sting of the back of his hand across her face. Struggling again, she felt him pulling her up, only to slap her again. . .to call her the vilest of names.

"Bucky, let me explain. . . ."

"Explain?" he repeated, grabbing her arm and twisting it behind her back, bringing her up against him. He gripped her hair with his other hand, forcing her head against the steeliness of his chest. With her free hand she pulled the wig from over her face, dropping it to the floor. She writhed, but it did little good. She was fighting more than just an angry man. She was fighting the weight strapped to her body.

"Yes, please!"

"You lied to me," he said, wrenching her head to stare down at her. His face was so close to hers that she could feel the heat of his breath against her skin.

"No. . .no. . . ," she said, hearing the panic in her own voice.

"Yes," he hissed, jerking her, then pushing her, causing her to land on top of the bed. "Stay there!" he ordered.

Andi was too frightened to move. She watched from the corner of her eye as he opened the bedside table drawer, removed a revolver, and pointed it toward her.

"Bucky, no!" she screamed, then wrapped her arms around her head and pulled herself into a ball.

Katie led the way into the switchboard operator's office.

THP employed four operators for the daytime and evening shifts; two for the late night. The supervisor, Melvin Swank, had been with them for more than twenty years. If anyone would know anything about the records, it would be him.

Fortunately, he was still at work. He welcomed the Websters and Phil into his small but private office as he adjusted the gold-rimmed glasses he wore low on his nose. Phil showed him the records as Katie and Ben stood on the opposite side of the desk.

"By looking at these records, can you tell what office these calls went to here at the hotel?" Phil asked him.

Mr. Swank took the records in his hands, studied them for a

moment, and then shook his head. "No, sir. But I *can* tell you what floor they went to."

"Are you serious?" Katie asked.

Swank looked at her and nodded. "Yes, ma'am. Just hold on a minute." He sat in his chair, angling himself to the computer screen, and began to type in a series of dates and codes.

Ben and Katie walked around the desk for a better look, standing behind Phil, who had shifted forward.

When the computer had flickered through various screen pages, it rested on what, to the untrained eye, looked like gibberish. Swank pointed to the middle of the screen. "There you go. Third floor."

Katie turned to Ben. "Do you know who all has offices on the third floor?"

"Not to worry," Swank continued, typing along as he spoke. "Here you go," he said. "Harrington, Presley, Burrell, Spooner, Caines. . ."

Katie caught her breath. "Harrington. . ."

"No." Ben said firmly. "Spooner."

Katie's brow furrowed. "What about him?" Katie asked. "That's Byron. He's not only been an excellent employee; he's also been kind to me. While, on the other hand, for the most part Harrington's been—"

Ben moved back to the other side of the desk, then looked to his wife. "I told you I wanted to talk to you about the people you'd hired."

Katie crossed her arms.

"Don't get defensive," he said, extending a hand toward her as Swank continued typing. "There's something about him. . . something I don't like. . .something I can't put my finger on."

Swank interrupted him. "Then you may want to look at this."

"What is it?" Phil asked.

Again Swank pointed at the screen. "There's calls from Mr. Harrington to Vermont, but none to Canada. However, it looks like Mr. Spooner has made calls to the very number in Canada you're looking at."

"Bucky!" Andi screamed again, pushing herself against the headboard.

"Shut up!"

Andi listened silently as he pulled open a drawer from the highboy and watched him remove several slender neckties. He moved quickly, grasping her ankles with one hand. He lay the gun next to her legs and began to tie her feet together. "Bucky, if you will just listen."

"Be quiet, Andi. I know when I've been had." On his knees, he climbed onto the bed, straddling her as he flipped her to her stomach and pulled her arms behind her.

"No, Bucky. I was merely trying to get a piece of information that might interest Webster. . .something to bait him. . ." She felt the full weight of Bucky's hand as it clenched the nape of her neck, and she winced.

"Do not presume to treat me like a fool, Andi," he seethed, lips near her ear. "If you say one more word, I'll gag you. Now shut up and let me think," he said, slapping the side of her head before coming off the bed. Andi kept her chin on the bed, but raised her eyes to watch him remove his cell phone from his pocket. She could feel the swelling of her face and mouth where he'd hit her earlier.

When he'd pushed a few numbers, he waited, breathing heavily. "Answer," he said, cursing under his breath. Then, "Spooner! Get over here. . .I don't care if you are at work. . .I need you. . .now you listen to me, you little weasel. I've got Andi Daniels here, and she's obviously been sent as a spy. I want you here, and I want you here *now*. Make me wait five minutes too long, and I'll blow her head off and make it look like you did it, which, by the way, I can easily do. . . . That's better. Glad you see it my way."

As Phil, Katie, and Ben headed toward the third floor of the hotel, Ben turned to Katie. "Go back upstairs."

"No."

"Katie." He stopped, reaching for her hand and pulling her toward him.

Phil shifted uncomfortably. "I'll grab the elevator," he said, allowing them their privacy.

"Ben," she whispered. "I'm going. I've come this far."

"I think Andi is there. . .with Caballero. If that's so, time is of the essence. We don't know but what he's figured things out."

Katie swallowed. "No. I'm going. I know Byron. I hired him. If he's involved with this. . ." She licked her lips, looked down to her feet, then back up. "Are we going to stand here all day arguing about it, or are we going?"

Ben closed his eyes slowly, then opened them again. "Come on," he said.

Byron Spooner could feel sweat popping out over his face.

Dear God, he prayed irreverently, *what have I gotten myself into?*

The young man with the boyish features reached for the handkerchief he kept in his pants pocket and wiped his face as he pulled his suit coat from the back of his chair and looked at his watch in one swift movement. It was nearing five o'clock, so his departure wouldn't be questioned.

For that, he breathed a sigh of relief, but before he could reach the door to his office, it opened.

"Mr. Spooner, I'm Phil Silver," a man said, showing him credentials.

"Oh, man. . . ," Byron said, then looked beyond the man before him to see Katie and William Webster enter. "Katie—"

Katie's jaw was firm and set. "Bottom line, Mr. Spooner. Are you or are you not in business with Bucky Caballero?"

Byron backed up until he hit the front of his desk with his backside. "I—"

Katie raised a hand. "Mr. Spooner, I will not pretend to understand this."

Byron shook his head, though he knew it was fruitless to do so. "What are you talking about?"

Phil displayed the phone records that had been in his hand. "You've been receiving phone calls from Canada, Mr. Spooner."

Bryon jerked his head from one person to the other, then sighed. "All right. All right."

"Where is he?" Ben asked.

Byron held up his hands, palms outward. "Now wait a minute. I'll talk, but I want some kind of—" He was interrupted by the ringing of a cell phone, and he nearly jumped out of his skin.

"It's for me," Phil said, pulling his cell phone from his coat pocket. "Silver," he spoke into the phone. "Yeah. . .Byron Spooner's office. Third floor." When he discontinued the call, he looked at Ben and Katie and said, "It's Agent Richards. She'll be here in a minute." To Byron he said, "I suggest you remain quiet until she gets here. "

Byron looked at his watch, breathing heavily.

"What is it, Mr. Spooner?" Ben asked. "What's your hurry?"

Byron swallowed. "My hurry is that Mr. Caballero is expecting me. He's got—"

Sabrina walked in, followed by Marcy. "Well, well," she said. "Mr. Spooner, allow me to get to the point. I understand you know the whereabouts of Mr. Caballero."

Byron crossed his arms. "I do. I also know that he's got Miss

Daniels captive—" Byron watched expectantly as Ben moved toward him. "Hold on, now. I want some kind of guarantee. . . ."

"Just talk, Mr. Spooner," Sabrina said. "We'll work out the details later."

CHAPTER SIXTY

"You three stay here," Phil said to Ben, Katie, and Marcy as he and Sabrina got into her car in front of the hotel. She had placed the bubble light on top of it, and as she got into the driver's side, she turned it back on. Katie watched as the blue light spun around, cutting into the cold dusk of evening.

"No way," Ben said, the frost of cold air puffing around his mouth.

Phil pointed to him. "No arguments. I'll call you immediately." He slammed the door on his words, and the car peeled into traffic, siren going full blast.

Katie turned to Ben, wrapping her arms around herself against the cold. "We can't just stay here."

"You're right about that," Marcy replied. She ran up the steps of the hotel to where Miguel stood in his doorman's booth, signing out for the day. "Miguel," she called out to him.

"Yes, Mrs. Waters," he called back, stepping out.

"Call Simon. Tell him it's an emergency and to get here pronto."

Miguel tipped his hat at her. "Yes, ma'am."

Marcy jogged back down the steps. "Simon will get us there."

Katie sighed. "Do you remember the address?"

"Perfectly."

Bucky paced the shadowy room where Andi still lay silent on the bed. "Where is that idiot?" he asked. "I give him one small thing to do. . . ."

He stopped then, and Andi watched him as he picked up the wig and sunglasses that she'd pulled from her head. Sitting on the bed, he snatched her own hair back and said, "I was going to be so good to you."

She looked up at him. "Since when, Bucky? Since when did you ever really care about me?"

He hit the back of her head. "Shut up."

"No, Bucky. I was the one. I was the one who could have been so good to you."

He stood then and kicked the leather bag near his feet. Andi held her breath, thanking God the room was dark enough that he wouldn't see the files inside it. He turned, began kicking the side of the bed, then leaned over and asked, "What did you want from me, puppet? To love you? To marry you?" He yanked her by the forearm and flipped her over to her back. "To make you my mistress?"

Andi didn't say anything initially. Then, "I could have loved you like no one ever loved you."

The sound of sirens came from the distance in the city. It was not an unusual sound, but Bucky's eyes shot to the window as though he instinctively knew they were for him. "What are you going to do?" she repeated.

She watched him then, pulling open the drawer of the highboy, scooping up the remaining files. "I'd take you with me," he said. "But you'd slow me down. Know this," he continued. "I'll never be far from you. Everywhere you go, I'll be one step behind." She didn't move as he leaned over, traced the line of her face with the cold barrel of the gun, and kissed her lips like a man hungry for life, then pulled back and said, "But I'm not staying here to die, Puppet. To me, you are, and always have been, trash. And trash isn't worth dying for." A laugh came from the back of his throat, and patting her on the face, he ran from the darkness of the room and into the shadows of only God knew where.

When the limo pulled up to the Upper West Side address, Katie peered out the window, looking at the number of police cars and ambulances, lights blazing, which had cluttered the street. "Goodness," she said. "Should we sit still or get out?"

"Sit still," Marcy said. "For once I think we shouldn't get in the way."

"I agree," Ben said. He and Katie sat next to one another, and he put his arm protectively around her, pulling her closer to him. "Maybe this wasn't such a good idea."

Katie looked into his eyes.

"If anything happened to you, I'd never forgive myself."

Katie reached up and touched his cheek. "I love you."

"I love you," he said back.

"Hey, you guys," Marcy interrupted. "That all sounds very romantic, but here comes Phil and Sabrina out of the building."

The three exited the car and walked toward the investigative duo.

"I thought I—" Phil began, then looked over to Marcy. "Never mind."

"Were you able to arrest him?" Ben asked.

Sabrina touched Phil's arm and said, "I'm going to talk to these guys over here."

Phil nodded at her, watching her walk away, then turned back to Ben. "No. He'd already gone."

"Andi?" Katie was the first to ask. She felt Ben look at her.

"She's upstairs. She's been knocked around pretty badly, but she's alive."

Katie and Ben looked at one another; then Katie moved toward the door. "I'm going up. I have to," she said, making her way past a few officers who were attempting to keep the small crowd that had gathered at bay. One of the officers tried to stop her, but Phil called out, "Let her go."

She turned back to Phil and as though he could read her mind, he said, "4-D."

Katie ascended the flights of stairs until she reached the fourth floor landing, along the way passing an officer who was descending the stairs and speaking into his mobile unit. "Copy that," he was saying. "Mattie Franscella spotted at Palm Court. 10-4. Sending a unit over." Katie paused, lips parted, watching the man turn toward the next landing, then she continued upward. On the fourth floor, she turned left and followed the sound of squelching police mobiles. When she stepped into the door of the apartment and saw Andi lying on the sofa with a paramedic in attendance, her heart nearly stopped.

"Ma'am," an officer from the dining area called out to her.

She turned to him, holding out a hand. "I have permission. Sabrina Richards," she said, invoking the name of the senior in charge. Katie walked over to the sofa. "Can you give us a minute or is this critical?" she asked the paramedic.

The young man looked up at her. "No, ma'am. We're set here," he said, then walked away, carrying his medical bag with him.

Katie sat beside the woman who, in a time that seemed so long ago, had been her dear friend. "Are you okay?" It was a stupid question, but it was the only thing she could think to say.

Andi nodded as she attempted to moisten her swollen lips with her tongue. Katie reached up and stroked her cheekbone, which was badly bruised and appeared to be broken. "Did they get him?" Andi asked her in a voice that cracked as she whispered.

Katie shook her head no.

Andi closed her eyes; a tear escaped, tracing a line to her ear. "I'm sorry. I tried."

Katie felt tears slipping down her cheeks as well. "What were you thinking, Andi? Putting yourself in that kind of danger?"

Andi's eyes opened, and she attempted a laugh. "Do you know how much I've hated you these past two years?"

"Probably about as much as I've hated you since your return." Katie tried to sound lighthearted about it, even though in her heart she knew it was true.

"And then. . .I don't know. . ." Andi attempted to shift a bit on the sofa, cringed in pain, then settled. "You and William. . .so kind to me, really." She managed to shake her head. "And I really loved him, Katie, though not like you've loved him. I don't know if I'm even capable of that kind of love."

"Mercy," Katie whispered in answer.

"What?"

Katie raised her voice but only a little. "I said 'mercy.'" She shook her head. "I don't want to sound like I'm preaching to you, Andi. . .but on my way up the staircase, I was thinking about the concept of mercy. . .and love. . .and friendship. Did you know the Bible says that there is no greater love than that of a man who would lay down his life for his friends?"

"The Bible. . ." She laughed lightly, then winced again. "I don't know about that. And I don't know a whole lot about mercy, unless you want to count the fact that I'm still alive right now to even have this conversation."

"I do. I count it very much so."

Andi nodded a bit. "The way I saw it, I owed you that much." She swallowed hard. "You were right, you know. I shouldn't have kept him over there. . .but I. . ."

Katie waited. When the rest of the sentence didn't come, she said, "You what?"

Andi closed her eyes again. "It's not important," she whispered, another tear slipping down her cheek. She opened her eyes then. "You and William together again. That's what's important." Her eyes rose a bit, and she looked beyond Katie to the front door.

Katie turned, and saw that Ben, Marcy, Phil, and Sabrina had walked back into the room. "Speak of the devil."

Katie smiled at her husband as he joined her.

When he had squatted on his haunches beside them, Andi cut her eyes over and said, "I'm sorry we didn't get him."

"Don't worry about it," Ben told her. He cupped the top of her head with the palm of his hand. "They'll get him later. He can't run forever."

"When I was a little girl," Andi said, after moistening her bottom lip with a swollen tongue, "there was a bad dog that lived next to us." She closed her eyes, then reopened them. "My family and I had a great dog. Then the bad dog moved in next door. Named Lady, if you can imagine. Everyone knows the kind—a cat-chasing, trash-digging, car-chasing, prowling, street dog. Always barking. Bark, bark, bark." Andi winced as she attempted a smile. "Anyway, my dog had never chased cars in his life, but Lady got him to doing it. Lady was savvy enough that she never got hit, but my dog did. After we buried him, my dad told me a bad dog was like a bad penny. They just keep turning up. Bad dogs, he said, are almost impossible to catch. He said, you can poison them, but they won't die. And they are always getting the good dogs into trouble, because the good dogs don't know what they're getting into."

Andi looked from Katie and Ben to the rest of the group. "The moral of the story is that maybe there's some evil you just can't kill," Andi said as she looked at Ben. "That you simply have to learn to live with it." Again her tongue darted out and tipped the middle of her bleeding upper lip.

Marcy stepped up, leaning over to stroke Andi's hair. "Bucky will have to answer for what he's done, eventually. We just may never see it."

Andi nodded, then looked back at Katie who cast her eyes over Andi's face. She could see the evidence of all the years that Andi had been involved with Bucky etched there, a sketch of what she would have looked like had she been held emotionally and spiritually captive by the likes of her old associates. People like Leo, the possessive manager of the first club she'd danced in. People like the faceless, nameless men who'd leered and groped at her near-naked body. People like the girls working the streets in the filth of the old avenues, the ones she passed as she made her way to work every night.

Katie found it strange somehow. Strange that now, in this apartment with her husband close by and the woman she'd blamed for keeping him from her, she was feeling something akin to compassion. Perhaps, she reasoned, God was allowing her this visual lesson as she gazed at Andi's sorrow and regret, and it rang familiar. It was the look Katie had seen in her own mirrored reflection before she'd gone home to Georgia two years earlier. . .home to her mother and her broken past. . .home to her friends. . .

. . .and home to her God.

EPILOGUE
Christmas Day 2002

The early morning light filtered into the master bedroom of the Webster's Hamptons' home in a smoky gray. Outside, the snow blanketed the lawns as the wind whipped around the sides of the house. Katie burrowed herself under the heavy comforter of the bed, drawing herself into as tight a ball as possible. She reminded herself that this was Christmas Day, and with it came the promise of new life. *I'm ready to put the old behind me,* she thought. This had been an interesting couple of years to say the least; especially this past year. They had endured two trials, one for the McKenzies and the other for Mattie Caballero Franscella. Thanks to the justice system, Katie and Ben wouldn't have to worry about them for a long time.

Byron Spooner turned state's evidence, served a light sentence, and found employment as a day trader in Marietta, Georgia.

Andi returned to France, where she married a politician.

Bucky remained, as Phil put it, at large, and the loss of Katie's stock was still an open issue.

But Katie's spa was nearly complete, and she and the newly married Ashley were working hand in hand on the finishing touches.

Katie sighed in contentment. With one foot, she reached behind her, to touch her husband and find the comfort of knowing he was there. When she felt nothing but cold sheets, she turned to see his side of the bed empty.

She smiled, knowing exactly where he was.

Without reluctance she pushed the covers away, reached for the thick robe draped at the base of the bed, then slid her feet into the slippers lying next to the bed stool. For a moment she thought of Maggie, who'd always kept her slippers in the hidden compartment—and who had always been there to say, "There's a good girl, now. Must keep your feet warm, or you'll catch your death. . . ."

Lord, how I miss her.

Katie tied the sash of her robe as she walked to the bedroom door, which was ajar. Stepping into the hallway, her eyes automatically went to the place where, a few feet away, a puddle of light slipped from under the closed doorway. She crossed her arms in the chill of the house as she moved toward it, then stopped and pressed her ear against the door.

From within, she could hear the sound of her husband's voice. Warmth radiated within her. Like a church mouse, she inched her hand toward the door handle, turning it ever so slowly, then pushing the door open just enough that she could peek in.

As she'd expected, Ben sat in the white nursery rocker, dressed in his pajamas and robe, holding the bundle of joy they'd recently adopted, their daughter Hannah.

The bright-eyed six month old was staring up at her father in total trust and expectancy as he read to her from a small book. When he heard Katie, he turned slightly and smiled. "Letting Claudia sleep?" she asked.

Ben nodded. "No need to wake her when Hannah's father is just a door away."

"Keep reading," she said, walking to the rocker and kneeling beside them. She reached up and took her baby's hand in hers, brought it to her lips, and kissed it. "Daddy reading to you, princess?"

"Da—" Hannah said in answer.

Katie swallowed hard, then laid her head against Ben's knee. "Keep reading," she said again.

She felt his hand rest against the back of her head. " 'So they hurried off and found Mary and Joseph, and the baby, who was lying in the manger. When they had seen him, they spread the word concerning what had been told them about this child, and all who heard it were amazed at what the shepherds said to them.' "

Katie felt her husband's hand cup her chin, bringing her face around to look at him before he continued. When their eyes met fully, he quoted the final line of the story.

" 'But Mary treasured up all these things and pondered them in her heart.' "

"Amen," Katie said. They smiled at each other, then looked over to their daughter, whose eyes were now closed and whose breathing was deep and even.

"Amen, indeed," Hannah's father said.

FROM THE AUTHOR

Since the first book in the "Shadow Series," *Shadow of Dreams,* was released I have been asked more times than I can count if Katie's story is my own.

No.

And yes.

No, in that her story is completely from the depths of my imagination.

Yes, in that—like Katie—God has redeemed my life, turning it into something useful and good.

You may already have a personal relationship with my God. But you may not. Would you allow me a moment to speak to you?

When Katie arrived in New York City, she thought she was unredeemable. . .that she had to "clean up" to go home. It took a long time, but she eventually discovered that wasn't so and that her mother would have loved her no matter what and would have welcomed her with an undying forgiveness.

This story, of course, is a parable (if you will) representing our lives apart from God. Without Him we feel (as Katie said) like "the scum of the earth." But Jesus said that, with Him, we would be the "salt of the earth" (Matthew 5). It doesn't matter where we've gone, what we've done, or where we are. God loves us and stands before us with open arms, coaxing us to "come home" to where the Light always shines. His love is unconditional; His forgiveness knows no bounds.

If you feel as Katie did before she returned "home to her mother and her broken past. . .home to her friends. . .and home to her God," I encourage you to take a moment to ask Him into your life, to forgive your past, to redeem your future, and to begin using you right now. I would also encourage you to find a good, Spirit-centered church, home group, etc. And I would also love to hear from you. I can be e-mailed through my website www.evamarieeverson.com or by mail at Barbour Publishing, P. O. Box 719, Uhrichsville, OH 44683.

Eva Marie Everson

ACKNOWLEDGMENTS

The final page in Katie's life has now been written. . .or at least as we know it. I began the Shadow Series in 1997 with my dear friend, G. W. Francis Chadwick, so let me begin by thanking him for his undying belief in my talent and his encouragement along the way (even when he said it was time for me to fly solo!). I would also like to thank my husband who said, "You really ought to do something with this talent." I want to thank everyone I interviewed for the first two books (you know who you are) and the ones who helped with this book.

Specifically my NYC connections: Mr. Robert Marino and Ms. Kaye Noble; my Vermont connections: Mrs. Jane Weiss, Mrs. Lila Walbridge, Mr. John Taylor, and the sweet town of Williamstown, Vermont, for being a role model.

Thank you, David Lipscomb, "Ron-Jon" Robinson, Glenn Hansen, and Craig, for your technical help.

Thank you, Becalin Adams, for your proofreading. Good luck in your own career!

What would a girl writer be without those who have helped along the way? Jerry "Chip" MacGregor (A+ Agent and #1 Braves Fan; I'm so glad I repented!), Ramona Richards (Content Editor; you not only know my heart but Katie's as well), and Shannon Hill (Barbour's Editor-at-Large; thank you for believing we should do this).

A special thanks to Sharon Durling (because you deserve a thank-you) and Deb Haggerty (for pointing out something very important that I hadn't thought of and for investing so much into my career).

Finally, but most importantly, thank You, heavenly Father, sweet Yeshua, and Holy Spirit of God for equipping me, loving me, and empowering me to go beyond what I ever thought I could. This is all about You. . .all for You. . .thank You for redeeming my life and making it into something worthwhile. You have truly shone a great light into a very dark shadow. Quite frankly, You blow me away.

EVA MARIE EVERSON

ABOUT THE AUTHOR

Eva Marie Everson is an author, nationally recognized speaker, and Bible teacher. Awarded the AWSA (Advanced Writers & Speakers Association) Member of the Year in 2002, she is also the president of one of Florida's largest writers' groups, a member of Florida Writers' Association, and a board member of Right to the Heart Ministries. Eva Marie's acclaimed series for Crosswalk.com, *Falling into the Bible*, led to a permanent author-to-author column, *The Cross & the Pen*. Married to husband Dennis, they are the parents of four and grandparents of three. In her spare time, Eva Marie is a seminary student.

Now Available from Barbour Publishing, Inc.

The Dandelion Killer
ISBN 1-58660-753-7
A mentally handicapped man is suspected of murder while his longtime friend is threatened by the real killer. Is she ready to face eternity?

Body Politic
ISBN 1-58660-600-X
Medical science and political drama collide in this "Grishamesque" thriller that centers on fetal stem cell research.

Operation Firebrand: Crusade
ISBN 1-58660-676-X
When Muslim raiders destroy a village in the south of Sudan, the Firebrand team of Christian commandos is sent into the breach.

The Crystal Cavern
ISBN 1-58660-767-7
Danger surrounds the icy Ozark hills when Dr. Sable Chamberlin and Paul Murphy go searching for a murderer's motive—and discover that their names might be next to appear in the obituaries.